I Found My Heart
in San Francisco

this Book Belongs
to

theresa ann
<u>hanna</u>

í founo my heart
ín
san francísco

By: s x meagher

SLÁINTE

SX Meagher

I Found My Heart in San Francisco

S.X. Meagher

Fortitude Press, Inc.
Austin • Texas

Published by Fortitude Press, Inc., Austin, Texas. For further information about this or other titles, please contact Fortitude Press, Inc., P.O. Box 41, Melbourne, FL 32902, or visit our website at www.fortitudepress.com.

ISBN: 0-9718150-3-8

First Edition, April 2002
Printed in the United States of America

Edited by Anne Brisk
Technical edits by Medora MacDougall
Book and cover design by Ryan Daly
Web design by Mya Smith

Acknowledgements

My thanks to **Francine Love** for possessing the creative spirit mixed with the indefatigability needed to successfully launch and manage Fortitude Press.

My editor, **Anne Brisk,** has miraculously managed to turn me from a grammarphobe to a grammarphile. Not only has she managed this without resorting to violence in the process, her charm, wit and unflagging good humor have made me a Briskphile as well. If the paragraphs I labor over ever sound as smooth and effortless as the e-mails she blithely dashes off, I'll be a happy woman.

For **Carrie**, my partner in life

⌘ CHAPTER ONE

STRIDING ACROSS THE FLOOR OF THE SECOND-HAND CLOTHING store, a remarkably tall, remarkably attractive woman paused mid-step as a garment caught her eye. Spending less than a second to contemplate the vintage Hawaiian shirt, she took it from the hanger and slipped it on over the khaki green tank top she wore.

The small blonde woman who owned the shop had been watching her only customer ever since she had entered the place, idly musing that the long-limbed woman looked as though she was on a quest to spend as little time shopping as possible.

As the tall beauty tugged the shirt into place, the owner decided to see if she could engage her customer in a little conversation. Approaching her with a warm smile on her fine-boned face, the blonde asked, "Can I help you?"

Without benefit of a mirror, the woman had already made her decision, but the shop owner's warm smile and slightly-twinkling green eyes were sending off a signal that she chose not to ignore. "I'm thinking of buying this shirt," she said, as she performed a quick turn to show it off. "How does it look?"

"Hmm …" the owner tapped at her lips with a pencil and said, "I'm trying to think of what I have in here that you wouldn't look good in." Her eyes brightened even more as she spoke, and a delightful crinkle formed on the bridge of her nose.

"That's the nicest compliment I've had all day," the dark-haired woman drawled as a smile twitched her lips.

"It's only eleven o'clock," the shop owner playfully responded. "I'll bet that you'll have more than you can handle by nightfall."

Well, well, well. This wasn't how I was expecting to spend my day, but now's as good a time as any to jump back into the pool. A wolfish grin formed on the full, pink lips, and the woman's eyes settled on the shop owner, frank interest showing in the blue depths. "Are you offering to help me fend off the compliment overflow?"

"I would," the shop owner stated hesitantly as she darted a glance around the store, "but I don't have any other help today, and I'm open until 9:00 tonight."

"Hmm, that is late," the dark-haired woman agreed with a regretful shake of her head. Her perfectly shaped eyebrows knit together for a moment, and then her features broke into a sly grin. "How do you stop for lunch or a break?"

"When business is slow, I can just lock up for a little while." She paled as the implications of this thought — and the knowing grin of her pursuer — hit her simultaneously.

"I haven't seen another soul come in since I've been here," the dark woman said with a gaze that locked on green eyes.

"I'm not sure I would have noticed if someone had," she replied, feeling just a little weak in the knees. As the words tumbled from her mouth, she gaped in astonishment at her open flirting with this woman. She had never flirted this shamelessly, but something about this woman made her unable to control the responses coming from her mouth or her body.

"If you were to take a little break to nibble on something, where would you go?" Blue eyes darkened with open desire, and the blonde had to grasp one of the clothing racks for support.

Her dry mouth squeaked out, "I have a little office with a couch in the back of the store," and she felt her hand point weakly at a door in the rear of the shop.

"I'll be right back," soothed the stranger as she made her way with confident strides to the entrance. She glanced at the door and spotted a sign that mimicked a clock; it read "Will Return In" and had hands that could be pointed to any hour. She moved them to noon, turned the sign around and slapped the bolt in place, returning to the small woman's side before the shop owner could take a step in either direction. A warm, soft hand grasped her trembling one as the dark woman confidently guided her to the office.

In less than the beat of a heart, the blonde found herself sprawled against the worn, dark leather of her couch, responding with ferocity to the caresses of her beautiful customer. The suddenness of the encounter, the intensity of the knowing touch and the powerful aura that radiated from this woman were truly overwhelming, leaving her completely powerless to slow the pace or collect her scattered thoughts.

The leather of the coach groaned as the women moved against each other urgently. The cool air hit her suddenly bare back as she felt her clothing being gently removed — first her deep red, French-cut T-shirt, then her short, black skirt. Both were tossed casually to the floor. She shivered a little at the shock of the cold leather on her skin as she was gently lowered to the surface.

The strong hands moved over her body, teasing her breasts through the lace of her bra. Then they slowly glided over her grinding hips to caress the curves there through silky panties. The practiced hands then removed even these insubstantial barriers to fierce eyes and warm, wet lips.

Soft lips descended the small woman with a burning fire that ratcheted her desire into a range she didn't know she possessed. Craving more contact, she wrapped her fingers in the onyx tresses and ground the woman's mouth to her breasts, arching into the sensation. Reluctantly, she released her grasp when she felt the head sliding down her abdomen. She raised her legs and slid them around the powerful shoulders that paused above her for just a moment. As she gazed beseechingly at the woman, she uttered the only word that would tumble from her lips, "Please." She was met with a wide smile and a look of quiet pleasure from those beautiful orbs. The dark head dipped and tasted her passion, which flowed from her like lava, burning in its intensity. She gasped and tried to vocalize her pleasure, but was unable to utter more than a low growl. That tortured sound was met by an even lower rumble that sprang from the dark woman's lips, sounding like the contented murmurings of a panther over its kill.

She thrust her hips at the mouth that covered her, watching with half-closed eyes as the dark head moved slowly between her legs. Long, blissful moments passed as she allowed herself to be completely consumed. After far too short a time, she felt herself go rigid for a split second as she teetered on the edge of climax. One firm, wet kiss and she plummeted over, unable to hold back any longer. She grunted out her pleasure as she grabbed the dark head and pressed it against herself firmly. Finally she felt the mouth slowly still. As she relaxed limply against the couch, she felt delicate kisses begin to tenderly remove the traces of the passion from her still-shaking thighs. Her legs relaxed, and she was finally able to speak. "That was wonderful," she languidly enthused. The dark head tilted up, and bright eyes appeared as the woman rested her chin on the still-quivering belly.

"You did seem to enjoy it."

"Let me return the favor," the small woman huskily responded as she reached up to unbutton the new shirt.

The full lips formed a regretful pout. "I wish we had time, but it's almost noon, and you probably have customers lined up outside your door. Remember, I promised to only keep you for a little nibble."

"There are plenty of other clothing stores on Telegraph Avenue," the golden-haired woman responded lazily from her still-blissful languor.

"Yes, but none of the others has the great customer service that you offer," the dark woman teased. She was rising from the floor and straightening her clothing as she responded.

"Are you really leaving?" the small woman said with genuine surprise. "But ... don't you ... I want to please you, too," she insisted.

"You already did," said the smiling, blue eyes. "I'm glad I decided to buy this shirt, however," she indicated the rumpled garment with the wet marks gracing the placket. "The ah ... design might not appeal to all of your customers." A quirky grin lit up her face as she spoke. "But I can tell it will become one of my favorites." Her right hand went to her back pocket to find her wallet. "That reminds me; what do I owe you?"

"I should pay *you* for that little lunch break," she said sheepishly. "Please consider it a small thank you gift."

"Okay, but next time I'll try not to damage the merchandise before I've paid for it," she said with another warm smile.

"Will there be a next time?" the honey-haired woman asked tentatively, searching the stranger's eyes for an honest answer.

She was met with a confident leer. "Count on it." Then the tall woman turned and started to leave, giving her one last dazzling grin as she paused at the office door and was gone.

The small woman dressed and made herself as presentable as possible, floating dreamily out of the office to walk behind the counter. Resting neatly on the glass surface were two $20 bills and a note that read, "Thanks for the nibble. You made my day."

⌘

Maybe this wasn't such a good idea. I mean, it's one thing to have an academic interest in the subject, but I really don't want to stick out like a sore thumb. I want to fit in, but of course I don't want to fit in too much ... She was pulled from her idle musings by a particularly pleasurable sensation, and she focused her attention on her lover, who was tenaciously trying to drive her arousal to meet his own. "Oh, that feels really good, sweetheart," Jamie murmured into Jack's ear. But as soon as the words left her mouth, the feeling left her — and the pleasure evaporated. *Damn,* she groused to herself. *I was so close!*

She tried to shift her body to have him hit the right spot, but she was thinking too much now — and once her head got into it — she knew it was futile. Since she recognized the inevitable, she stopped worrying about it and fell back into her reverie. *I can always drop the damn class if I feel too uncomfortable. It's really no big deal.*

Jack was close now, and she whispered words of love into his ear to hasten his climax. She loved his ears — they were perfectly shaped and had just a light covering of downy blond hair on them. When he was excited, they glowed with an attractive flush that Jamie found irresistible.

He threw his head back as his eyes became glassy and unfocused, and a soft grunt left his lips as he collapsed onto her body. After a moment his breathing slowed, and he looked at her with concern in his deep blue eyes. "You didn't finish, did you?"

Shrugging off his concern, she lightly said, "That's okay, you can get me twice tomorrow. You look so tired, love, put your head down here." She patted her chest in an inviting fashion, and even though he looked like he wanted to argue, she was gently tracing patterns on his back, and he quickly lost his will to insist. He rested his sandy blond head on her breast and was asleep in moments.

She regarded his attractive, tanned face with loving eyes. *I am so lucky to have him,* she thought. *He tries so hard to please me. Not many men would be so concerned with my pleasure. I just wish I knew how to explain how I like to be touched without offending him.* She lightly ran her fingers through the damp hair covering his forehead. *I love him; I'm sure of that. And I'm just as sure that he loves me!* She was deeply frustrated, knowing that something was wrong, but not knowing how to make it right. *It's so hard to figure out how to get this right.* She shook her head, musing, *I really thought it was best to wait to have sex with the man I wanted to spend my life with — but I feel so incompetent sometimes. I guess I just need to relax about the whole thing. I'm only twenty years old, and they say most women don't hit their sexual peak until they're in their forties.* Jack shifted a bit and nestled his head into her neck, flexing his large hand against her breast and sending a wave of sensation through her partially-aroused body. *Well, that's really reassuring,* she groused at the thought of twenty more years of unsatisfying encounters.

As she watched him sleep in her arms, she felt a wave of emotion build up. *I'll try to be what you need, Jack, but I need you to be patient with me while I figure some things out for myself.*

⌘

Sunday morning dawned bright and clear. Jamie was up early, as was her custom. When Jack made his way into the small kitchen, she was sitting at the counter drinking a large latte and reading the *New York Times.*

"Hi, sleepyhead," she teased as their eyes met.

"Wow, I didn't realize how tired I was," he said sheepishly. "It's past 8:00! I never sleep that late." As he shuffled over to her, she opened her

5

arms and enveloped him in a big hug. "Maybe Dr. Jamie's sleeping potion was too strong for you," she murmured.

He grinned down at her, replying, "That reminds me, I need to give you a double dose of that potion today."

"Okay, Doc, but at the moment I would like to get you into clothes, not out of them. Remember, you promised we could go to church today."

"Oh, right. Let me take a quick shower, and we can get going. Did you want to hit the nine or the eleven o'clock service?"

"I thought nine o'clock, and then maybe we can play a round of golf with Daddy, if he's available," she said.

"Sounds good, sweetie," he said over his shoulder. "Why don't you give him a buzz?"

Jamie's father gladly agreed to play golf, and since her mother had just returned from a month-long vacation to visit her family in Rhode Island, she wanted to come along and have brunch beforehand. *Gosh, I can't believe I completely forgot that she was back this week,* Jamie thought. *I really should have called her to welcome her home.* She shrugged as she got up to get ready and thought, *No big deal. I doubt that she noticed one way or the other.*

⌘

As the procession filed into the small Episcopal church on the outskirts of Nob Hill, Jamie made eye contact with the gray-haired, elegant-looking priest. She wrinkled her nose at him, and he winked back, adding a tiny wave. "He looks good," Jack whispered. "His month-long vacation must have really relaxed him."

"It's not a vacation," Jamie quietly reminded him. "He was in Israel, studying."

"Well, it's a priest's version of a vacation," Jack decided, earning a pinch.

Looking carefully at her grandfather, Jamie fully agreed with Jack's assessment. He looked tanned and rested and very content — not that he was usually very far from that state in the most hectic of times. When he strode to the pulpit to deliver his sermon, Jamie smiled, realizing how much she had missed them over the last month. She was pleased to hear that his topic that day was love — one of his favorite themes. He spoke of love's being God's greatest gift to man and the most visible sign of His presence among us. Through love for another, humans acknowledged this gift of love from God and expressed it in concrete form. In no other way could we feel His love for us as completely. This manifestation was a gift to be cherished — never taken for granted or squandered. Through the loving pairing of two people God dwelt within them.

Jamie was thoughtful through the rest of the service. *Is that how I feel? Do my feelings for Jack reflect that peak experience? Is this the height of my expression of God's love?*

As they filed out of the church, hand in hand, Jack turned to Jamie and said, "Wasn't that a great sermon?"

"Yes," she said quietly, "it really gave me something to think about."

"Your grandfather just expressed exactly how I feel about you, Jamie," he said with a beautiful smile on his face.

She pasted a similar smile on her own face and said, "I'm very happy that you told me that, Jack." She stretched on her tiptoes and reached up with tears in her eyes to give him a chaste kiss.

He beamed down at her and remarked, "We are two lucky people, Jamie."

"We are that, Jack," she agreed. *I just wish I was as sure of my feelings for you as you seem to be about yours for me.*

⌘

The Olympic Club had been the setting for the majority of Jamie's Sundays since she'd been a small child. As she and Jack sat with her parents at their table overlooking the eighteenth green, Jamie regarded them all with an appraising eye. *This is exactly where I will be in twenty years,* she thought. *Jack and I will be with our children at a table just like this one. We will be eating the same food from the same china. Some of the waiters will still be here. We will be having the same topical conversation with the other club members about our golf games and our families and our busy lives. He and I will love each other, but we won't share much other than the children. His real love will be his career. Is this what I want? If not, what do I want?*

She was jolted from her musings by the crisply uniformed waiter saying, "Miss Jamie, what would you like to drink?"

"Oh, I'm sorry, Harold; lemonade would be great, thank you."

"Jamie, you seem a thousand miles away this morning," said Jack. "Is anything wrong?" He reached over and covered her hand with his, gazing deeply into her eyes.

"No, of course not," she replied lightly. "I'm just thinking about school starting tomorrow. I guess I'm preoccupied."

"Do you have your pencils sharpened and a new *Star Wars* lunchbox?" he teased.

"I was partial to Malibu Barbie myself," she retorted.

"I'm sure this will be a great year for you," he reassured her as he squeezed her hand. "And for us," he added with a confident grin.

⌘

At the conclusion of the weekend, Jamie made her way back to the home she shared with her roommates. She plodded along 101 in her pale yellow Porsche Boxster, fighting the heavy traffic. *Why does every living soul have to leave the city for the weekend?* she groused, tapping her fingertips against the wheel in an irritated gesture. *I hope that Mia's home tonight,* she mused, considering her good friend from high school and now one of her two roommates. *Maybe she'll be able to help me out of this funk. Of course, it's gonna be tough for her to help, since I have no earthly idea of what's wrong.*

She didn't really have a name for the feeling that had been stealing into her subconscious for months now. She just felt so — restless. When she considered the feeling — naming it — she had to admit that she'd been restless for years, rather than months. She really thought that her engagement to Jack would settle her feelings — wrap this element of her life up so that she could have a little peace. But to her complete dismay, her engagement did not make her feel more secure. If anything, it had made her feelings of disaffection grow. But no matter how much thought she devoted to the problem, she did not know how to rectify it. There was nothing wrong with Jack, of that she was sure. *Nine tenths of the women in America would give their right arm to be with a man like him,* she thought. The problem seemed to be with her. There was just something missing. There was a feeling of peace that she craved, but could not conjure up when they were together. And if she was honest with herself, the peaceful feeling was not something that she experienced very often with Jack or alone. *Oh, well, my friends don't seem much more settled than I do. Maybe this is just what twenty-year-olds are supposed to feel like,* she thought as she drove on through the night.

⌘

"Hey, Mia, are you here?" Jamie called out.

"Yeah, I'm upstairs."

"You want anything from the kitchen?" Jamie shouted back up the stairs.

"Yeah, bring me a diet anything."

After making her brief stop in the kitchen, Jamie lugged her overnight bag and two diet Sprites up the wide oak staircase. Mia was lying on her bed, her room a total mess as usual. Jamie stood in the doorway and watched her friend for a moment, looking at the usually sunny, slightly cherubic face that was now twisted into a bored grimace as she inattentively watched television with a CD playing in the background. "Couldn't decide?" Jamie asked, pointing at the TV and the CD player in sequence.

"I'm bored," Mia moaned, shaking her curly, mid-length, medium-brown hair. "I'm so glad you're home early, James," she said as her dark brown eyes looked up at her friend. Jamie smiled at the nickname that Mia had bestowed on her during high school, liking the fact that she was the only one who used it. Mia stretched languidly, pulling her five foot four inch frame to its full length. Her friend's body resembled her own in both size and weight, though Jamie was a bit taller. Both women were quite thin, almost painfully so at times, but there was a sturdy athleticism lurking within both that had never really been tapped.

"I'm glad I'm back, too. I missed you, buddy."

"You did? Why?" Mia asked suspiciously. "Did the perfect couple have a fight?"

"No, of course not. You know we don't fight. I just wanted to spend some time with you and get some girl talk in," Jamie said.

"What's going on, James? You look down."

"Damned if I know," she sighed. "I feel down, but there sure isn't anything specific I can pin it on."

"Are things any better between the sheets with old Jack?" Mia asked, not even trying to hide her devilish grin.

"Mia, don't tease me," Jamie said with more than a hint of irritation in her voice. She knew she should not be irritable with Mia, but she was too unhappy with her sex life to take teasing well.

Mia gave her a puzzled look, then reached out to touch her shoulder lightly. "I didn't mean to piss you off, James. We don't have to talk about this."

The blonde shook her head and said, "Sorry for snapping at you, but things aren't any better, and I'm getting frustrated."

Mia sighed and leaned back against the headboard, considering her thoughts. "You know, I didn't start really enjoying sex for three years after I started. And it's only been since Jason that I really love it."

"Really?" Jamie asked, her expression reflecting her surprise. "For someone who didn't really enjoy it, you sure spent enough time doing it!"

"Well," she admitted as she tossed her curls, "there were parts that I always liked, but I didn't really like intercourse until Jason."

Jamie shook her head and made a face. "I really thought that waiting until I was sure about Jack would make sex better," she grumbled. "Before we actually had sex it was great — really great. We would kiss and touch each other for hours, Mia," she moaned dramatically. "I felt so close to him and wanted him so badly. I would go home some nights and just feel like I was on fire. But since we started to, well, you know," she mumbled, "it feels so mechanical."

"James, I hate to break this to you, but you are experiencing what nearly every woman goes through when she goes from teasing a guy to really doing it."

"Huh?" Jamie asked blankly.

"Look, guys and girls are really different. Most guys want to get in and get off. You've really got to train them to want to take their time and please you. Have you done that with Jack?"

"Well, no," Jamie fumbled, "but he tries hard, Mia. That's just the problem, actually — he tries too hard! It really bothers him if I don't come. He attacks my body like it's a legal brief. He believes if he works harder and smarter, it'll be great — but that's obviously not true." She flopped down onto the bed, her frustration evident.

"Have you asked him to just relax and let you guide him?" Mia suggested.

"Yes — God knows I've tried to get him to relax. I've even considered faking an orgasm, but he watches me so closely, I know he would know I was faking, and that would really hurt him."

"Have you tried to, ah, lend a hand, so to speak?" Mia asked in a playful tone.

"Yes," Jamie quietly admitted as she looked down at the bed. "But he seems to regard that as a failure on his part, even though he'd never admit that. I've tried to tell him that I'm just helping a little, but it's hardly worth it when I see the hurt look on his face."

Mia shook her head, unable to think of another suggestion. "I feel for you, hon. I've engaged in more bad sex acts than I can count, but it must be doubly disappointing when it's with a man you love."

Slapping the bed in frustration, Jamie moaned, "That's what really scares me, Mia. I'm going to spend the rest of my life with Jack. If we don't enjoy sex now, I have no reason to believe it will be better in the future. Honestly, at times I just hope he comes to bed and doesn't want to do it," she said, shaking her head in disgust. "I mean, shouldn't we just be tearing each others clothes off this early in our relationship?"

"Well, I would think so, judging from my limited experience in doing it with guys I love," she agreed. "But don't worry so much, James. You have a great relationship, and Jack is a fantastic guy. Maybe he's right, and more hard work will help everything to work out," she said hopefully.

"Yeah, you're probably right," agreed Jamie. "I mean, we have only been doing it for three months. Maybe we just have to get used to each other a little bit more." She rolled over and got to her feet, reaching over to give Mia's leg a squeeze. "Thanks for the talk. You're the only one I trust enough to talk with about this."

"You're welcome, sweetie. I hope you know you can tell me anything."

As Jamie got ready for bed, she thought over what Mia had said. *Well, I've got the rest of my life to work on this; I guess I don't have to be in that much of a hurry. Mia's right. There's no reason to think this will not all work out in the end. Lord knows we've got time to work on it — till death do us part is a very, very long time.*

⌘

As the students in her first period class settled noisily into their seats, Professor Linda Levy scanned their faces. *Not bad,* she thought, *at least I've got a few men.*

"May I have your attention, please?" Twenty mildly expectant faces gazed at her. "Welcome to Psychology 197 — The Psychology of the Lesbian Experience. My name is Linda Levy. I'd like to get some housekeeping matters out of the way, and then I'll give you an overview of the class."

Jamie closely regarded the professor, trying to decide if she would like her based solely on her appearance. After careful study, she decided that the pleasant-looking, energetic woman would probably prove just fine to spend her early morning with.

Linda walked from row to row, handing out three by five cards. "I would like you to give me a little personal information on these cards," she stated. A number of giggles hit some of the women. "It's not necessary to give me *that* information, unless you think it's relevant," she replied with a laugh of her own. "I suppose we should tackle that little issue right away," she said as she returned to the front of the room and perched on the end of the large wooden desk.

"I am now, and I have always been, a practicing lesbian," she said with a grin. "However, lesbianism is not a pre-req for this course. I'm sure that will relieve you guys," she said as she pointed at the three men sitting near one another. "This class deals with the psychological issues that may be encountered by a group of people who have in many ways been marginalized by society. We will be undertaking this survey with the eyes of scholars — not participants. This is not a 'How to be a lesbian' course.

11

You do not need to declare your sexual orientation to the rest of the class. Now, even though the class usually does turn out to be predominantly lesbian, I not only welcome heterosexuals, I really encourage straight people to take the class. It is the people who are not part of the peer group who can have the biggest impact on changing societal perceptions," she stated with conviction.

Jamie was relieved by this little explanation. *I think I'm going to like this.*

Linda continued, "On the cards I would like you to give me your names, phone numbers and a general idea of when you're available to do outside projects. I want to pair up class members based on their time availability to make it easier for everyone."

The class worked on their cards for a few minutes as Linda watched. *Well, they look a little less nervous now. This looks like it might be a good group.*

Jamie worked on her card — neatly writing her relevant information on the white rectangle. She indicated her home number, and, just to be thorough, she included Jack's number with the words "fiancé's home number." *Well, it doesn't hurt to get that out of the way right from the start,* she thought.

Linda looked quickly at the cards as they were turned in. *Oh, that's cute,* she said to herself as she saw Jamie's card. *It always amazes me how people get those little tidbits of information in.* She tried to match people's availability and was pleased that she was able to do so fairly easily. "Okay, people, I'm going to write down partner names on the board. After we do our introductions, you'll be able to find each other."

She strode to the board and began to list the ten pairs. Jamie saw her name go up on the board next to that of Ryan O'Flaherty. *Oh, great,* she moaned to herself, *I take a class in lesbianism, and I get paired up with a guy. Well, at least he won't assume he can hit on me,* she grumbled. A thought hit her, and her eyes widened as she considered, *Unless he's the type who thinks lesbians are hot!* She shook her head forcefully, trying to order her thoughts. *God, Jamie, get a grip! Yesterday you were afraid of the women, and today you're disappointed that you're with a man!*

Linda returned to her perch on the front corner of the desk. "Okay, let's get to work." She launched into a rather lengthy speech on how the course was developed, how long she had been teaching it and how it fit into the curriculum for psych majors. After covering all of the points that she felt were critical, Linda looked at her watch and noted with surprise that the seventy minutes were just about up. "I apologize for going on so long," she said. "If you don't mind, you can try to find each other after class to meet your partner. I'll see you all on Wednesday morning, and we can discuss some of the class projects."

Well, at least I have it easy, thought Jamie — *there are only three guys.* She approached the first and tentatively asked, "Are you Ryan?"

"Nope," he replied, "I'm Todd." The other two men were Demitrius and Mike. Now she was at a loss. As people began to drift away, Jamie noticed one lone figure sitting quietly. The woman was idly twirling a pen on the surface of her desk and did not seem to be in any hurry to find her partner.

Jamie approached her from the back and asked, "Are you Ryan?" with a hint of exasperation in her voice.

The dark head turned, and Jamie was nonplussed to see the most dazzling, white smile she thought she had ever encountered. "Well, if I wasn't before, I am now," the beautiful woman answered with a little tease in her voice as a devastatingly sexy grin lit up her face.

Jamie blushed all the way to the roots of her blonde hair. The woman unfolded herself from a desk that was obviously too small for her long frame and extended her hand, which Jamie mindlessly parroted. "I'm Ryan O'Flaherty," she said, flashing that smile again. Jamie knew that it was her turn to speak, but for some strange reason, she felt unable to as she stared blankly at the increasingly-amused woman. "And you are ..." Ryan cast a quick look over at the chalkboard, "Jamie Evans?"

Suddenly verbal, Jamie heard her voice automatically respond, "Oh, right! I mean, yes, I'm Jamie Evans."

"It's good to meet you, Jamie Evans," Ryan stated rather gravely, her smiling eyes belying her tone.

Jamie knew that she must stop staring, but she was unable to control herself. In a very unconventional way, Ryan was probably the most beautiful woman she had even seen. She had to stand over six feet tall, with a sturdy, but lean, build. There was something very feminine about her body that the layers of muscle paradoxically seemed to accentuate. Jamie guessed her jet-black hair was quite long, even though it was pulled back in a ponytail and partially hidden under a black, knit driving cap, worn backwards. She wore a tight, blindingly white, thick cotton T-shirt that hugged each of her ample curves, and over that a black and maroon paisley vest. This topped a pair of well-faded jeans that looked like they were created specifically for her long legs. A pair of shiny, cordovan penny loafers, worn without socks, completed her ensemble, and even though the outfit was a little quirky, it somehow looked perfect on the long-limbed beauty.

Jamie realized that she was still gripping Ryan's hand, and as that realization hit her brain, she immediately dropped it as though it were burning her. Ryan just continued to smile at her, a gentle, patient look in her bright eyes. Jamie actually found the gaze to be so penetrating that it was very difficult to meet, and when she finally forced herself to do so, she was again shocked to discover the most dazzling pair of ice blue eyes that one could imagine. *Jesus*, she thought as she tore herself away from that intense gaze, *how does one woman get this many perfect parts?*

When it became obvious that the rest of the day could pass without Jamie's breaking the silence, Ryan finally stooped down a bit, moving her head this way and that as she tried to capture the darting green eyes. "Uhm, Jamie, did you want to exchange phone numbers or arrange to meet or something?"

"Oh! Phone numbers ... good." Jamie began to curse herself for her inarticulate ramblings. *I'm an English major!* she shouted at herself in exasperation.

With Ryan providing most of the leadership they finally exchanged their personal info. Ryan took down Jamie's number in a neat, black organizer that held a very busy schedule, meticulously filled out. "When is the best time for you to get together?" Ryan asked.

"Well, I don't have a job, and my bo ..." Jamie caught herself and decided that she did not want this woman to know about Jack — for now at least. "My time is pretty open," she finally stated without elaboration.

"Great. I'm pretty swamped, but weekday afternoons and weekend mornings are my best times," Ryan said. "My schedule is really kind of unpredictable, but I'm sure we'll be able to get together." She smiled that impossibly dazzling smile again, and Jamie felt her brain once again begin to freeze.

"Where do you live?" Ryan asked with a small chuckle, as she unsuccessfully tried to hide a knowing grin, this particular brand of tongue-tied behavior rather commonplace for her and something she generally shrugged off. Ryan graciously took pity on her and removed her piercing gaze, allowing Jamie to catch her breath. The dark head tilted, and she looked down at her organizer and tried again, hoping to finish before her next class. "Do you live in Berkeley?"

"Yeah," Jamie breathed out in relief. "Really close to campus."

"Oh, that's good," Ryan said. "I live over in Noe Valley, but I'm sure we could meet here. You don't have a car do you?"

"Car?" Jamie said as though this was the first time she had ever heard the strange word.

"Yeah, you know, a big metal object with wheels — let's you go places that your feet can't take you," Ryan said, as she mimicked holding a steering wheel.

"Oh, yes, I do! I do have a car!" Jamie was outrageously pleased with herself for being able to get a complete sentence out without stuttering. She decided against all reason that she liked being teased by Ryan and felt herself begin to loosen up a little bit.

"That's great," Ryan said. "I've got a bike, but some people don't like riding on them," she added. Jamie dully wondered where on Ryan's bicycle she would ride, but banished that thought as Ryan once again extended her hand.

"I guess I'll see you on Wednesday then, okay?" Jamie felt her hand being engulfed by the much larger one and gently shaken, then felt her head bob a bit in response. Ryan dipped her head to make eye contact and winked playfully as her lips curled into the most adorable combination pout/grin that Jamie had ever seen in her life. As she released the limp hand, Ryan turned gracefully to stride from the room, her confident bearing turning the remaining heads of their fellow classmates.

Jamie felt herself slide limply into a desk. She dropped her head to the cool wooden surface and sat in puzzled confusion for a moment. Finally she lifted her head and asked herself in a befuddled haze, *What in the hell was that all about?!*

⌘

That night after a quickly-prepared dinner of salads and soup, Jamie and Mia sat cross-legged on Jamie's king-sized bed. The room was spotless, as always — a fact that befuddled Mia, even though she did find it nice that she could easily find the things she wished to borrow.

"Just back up a minute there, honeybunch," Mia commanded.

"What?" Jamie asked, trying to get past this part of the discussion quickly. "You, of all people, are taking a class called the Psychology of the Lesbian Experience? Uhm, Jamie, is there something you want to tell me?" Mia asked with a somber, yet accepting look on her face.

"Mia, you don't have to be a lesbian to take the stupid class," Jamie said with a bit of exasperation as she slapped at her thigh.

With a face full of sweet innocence, Mia said, "That's an odd reaction. I just wondered if you were switching to psychology as a major. Why would you jump to the conclusion that I think you're a lesbian? Odd — very odd," she teased, finding her own joke hilarious.

Rolling her eyes in exasperation, Jamie smirked, "Very funny, Mia. You really should consider a career in comedy. You're wasting your talents in college."

Her wicked smile showed that her innocence was, as usual, feigned. "No, really, James. Why would you take that class? I've never known you to be overly interested in our more androgynous sisters."

"I'm not interested, per se, Mia. I needed an easy three-hour class. I haven't taken any other soft science so far, and this one meets early in the morning, which is my favorite time of day." Warming to her subject, and pulling a few more reasons from her carefully prepared list, she added, "There is no final, just a bunch of special projects that I have to do with a partner. I only have to write two short papers, and I can use all the easy classes I can get this fall."

"Just how special are these projects?" Mia asked with a leer.

Having had about all she was going to take, Jamie removed any hint of humor from her face and said, "Well, one is to participate in a bondage scene at a lesbian S and M club, and the other is to make a multi-media collage about the joys of cunnilingus." Her tease was rudely interrupted by Mia spitting a mouthful of Diet Coke all over her sleep shirt.

"Mia!" she shouted as she jumped from the bed, trying to hold the Coke onto her shirt to keep it from dripping onto the spotless carpet. Glaring at her friend, Jamie scampered into the bathroom and emerged moments later to retrieve another oversized T-shirt from her dresser.

"Serves you right, Jamie," Mia chided. "Don't make me laugh when I've got a mouthful of Coke. You know I have very little control over my reflexes."

"Well, it was worth it to get you like that," Jamie admitted. "Normally, I'm the brunt of jokes around here."

"Hey, did you say you have to do these projects with a partner?" Mia asked as Jamie resettled herself on the bed.

"Yeah, we got assigned partners today," Jamie replied, trying to keep the tremor from her voice when she even thought of the tall, dark beauty she had been paired with.

"Ooo … a partner. Did she bring her big rig to campus or leave it idling out at one of the truck stops?" It was obvious that this class, and all of the participants, would be a semester-long joke, and Jamie was determined to stop the teasing as soon as possible.

"Why do you assume it's a woman, Mia? There are men in the class," she said smugly.

"Not so fast on that one, buddy. I think you'd better order up some chromosome tests before you state that with such conviction."

Jamie glared at her friend as she shook her head. "You know, Mia, as the professor said today, it's people like you and me who can make the biggest impact on getting rid of stereotypes about gay people."

With a puzzled gaze, Mia defended herself. "Aw, Jamie, you know I'm just kidding. And you, more than anyone, know that I have gay friends."

"Gay friends," Jamie nodded. "Not lesbian friends. I've never known you to bring a gay woman home."

Mia blinked and gave her an impish grin. "Whatever are you suggesting?"

Jamie grabbed her pillow and plopped it onto Mia's head. "My life is just fodder for your comedy routine, isn't it?"

"Well, yeah. Actually, I'm pretty excited about this class — I'll finally have something interesting to make fun of." She wrinkled her nose up at Jamie, and the blonde couldn't help but smile at her. "Now, tell me about this partner," she urged. "I've heard that only dyed-in-the-wool dykes take the class." She blinked and added, "Except for you of course. You're just some modern-day Margaret Mead, observing the natives in their natural environment."

Rolling her eyes once again, Jamie said, "For your information, my partner is a woman named Ryan. We talked for a few minutes after class."

"Hmm ... she's got a guy's name," she said thoughtfully. "Suspicious." Twitching an eyebrow, Mia asked, "Do you think she's gay?"

"Yeah, I'm sure she is," answered Jamie wryly.

"Oh, scoop, scoop, why are you so sure?" Mia smelled some dirt, and Jamie knew she would never let go now.

"Well, to be honest, I think she flirted with me," Jamie finally admitted, cursing under her breath when she felt her flush start to redden her cheeks.

"Jeez, James, what do you expect? You're probably the hottest woman in that class, and they can all smell fresh meat. They were probably drawing straws to see who got you!"

Something about her tone got to Jamie, and she snapped, "Mia, you are being ridiculous! If anyone would be lusted after, it would be Ryan. Trust me!"

"A hottie, huh?"

"Calling Ryan merely good-looking would be an insult," Jamie stated with finality.

"Gee, Jamie," she drawled, "maybe it was you who was flirting with her."

With her eyebrows drawing together in a frown, Jamie said, "That's not funny, Mia. It really kind of made me uncomfortable." Of course, she wasn't going to tell Mia just how uncomfortable she had been, but she wanted to get some feedback on how another straight woman would have reacted in her situation.

"Maybe she wasn't really flirting; maybe she's just friendly," Mia supplied helpfully.

"No," Jamie snorted. "I've been flirted with enough to know the difference, Mia. It was just like talking to a really good-looking guy. You know the type. The guy who is just oozing with self-confidence and has a really easy time dropping a line on you."

"I doubt that she meant anything by it, pal. And if she did, you've got three class meetings to drop it if you really don't like the vibes you're getting."

Jamie stretched and nodded. "I know. I'm pretty sure that she'll knock it off when I tell her that I'm straight — and engaged."

"What? You didn't tell her that you're straight?" Mia exclaimed.

"No, it didn't come up, but I'm sure it will when we meet on Wednesday. Don't worry, I'll make it clear that I have a really big boyfriend right down the freeway who I *think* could beat her up."

"Well, I'm sure that will be very reassuring to Jack," Mia said with a grin. "By the way, what does he think about your taking this class? I know Jason would want me to bring a cute one home for him to play with."

"Uhm, we haven't really discussed my class schedule. You know how busy he is this year, Mia, what with law review and everything."

"Mm-hmm, I see," said Mia, nodding her head agreeably, accompanied by a suspicious glance.

"Knock it off, will you? I'm sure we will discuss my schedule, and then I'll tell him," she stated flatly. "It's really no big deal." *Is it?*

⌘

Splash! "Not yet … wait … wait … okay, fetch!" Ryan watched the curly-haired, black dog gambol through the surf, boldly ducking his strong head under the water as a small wave hit the shore. She observed him closely as he paddled his way out to the large stick that she had thrown and grabbed it with his soft mouth.

He made his way back through the waves and galloped up next to her, waiting until he was right next to her, of course, before he violently shook his coat. "Lucky for you, I could use a little cooling off, Duffy boy," she laughed. They had been running on the beach since just after dawn, Ryan's favorite time of the day. She loved the smell of the ocean, loved to hear the gulls crying overhead and especially loved spending time with Duffy in his true element.

Throwing the stick again, Ryan mentally went through her schedule for the day. *Psych class first thing,* she reminded herself. *At least that class should be fun. It's nice to take a class where you get to interact with humans. Living humans,* she added as an afterthought as she considered her anatomy class. *I wonder how much we'll interact with our partners? That Jamie was sure a cutie,* she recalled. *I really loved that little blush she got when I teased her. But, God,* she thought with a laugh, *she sure did seem nervous around me. I wonder what that was all about?* Turning to the recently returned Duffy she asked, "What do you think, boy? Is she really interested or really nervous?"

Duffy wasn't sure, and he expressed his uncertainty by shaking his entire body violently.

"Yeah, I'm not sure either, pal. I guess there's only one way to find out, huh?"

⌘

Later that morning Jamie arrived at class about five minutes early, secretly hoping that Ryan would be there early, too, so that they could chat for a few minutes. *Relax, Jamie,* she reminded herself when her heart started to pick up as she entered the room, *it's a long semester.* Initially she was pleased to spot the woman, but her pleasure turned quickly to pique when she got a good look at Ryan. Her long, lithe body was casually slumped in a small desk as she looked up at another student — female of course — leaning over her. The look on her face was one of passive, relaxed amusement. The woman flirting with her was pretty cute, too, Jamie thought, assessing her critically. About five foot six inches, dark skin, with coal-black hair pulled back into a braid. Ryan watched the woman with polite interest, her dark head cocked slightly. After a few more moments, Professor Levy made her way into the room. Jamie saw Ryan take her felt-tipped pen and write a phone number right on the palm of the woman's hand. The recipient of this little gift looked extremely pleased and a bit smug as she made her way back to her desk. Ryan slowly turned her gaze to the left and unexpectedly made eye contact with Jamie. Her face broke into that damned grin again, and Jamie could not help but smile back with the same intensity, completely forgetting her pique.

As Ryan turned back to look at the professor, Jamie studied her intently. Today her outfit was quite a bit more casual than Monday's ensemble had been. Faded denim overalls covered a form-fitting, red tank top, along with red, high-top basketball sneakers and a red Nike cap, once again worn backwards. Ryan's black hair was pulled back, this time held in a neat braid that peeked out of the bottom of the bill of her cap. Jamie looked at her own clothes with a mental smirk. A mint green, sleeveless sweater — covered by a matching, long-sleeved cardigan — topped tight, stretch Capri chinos, and a new pair of delicate, black leather sandals graced her feet. *We certainly don't look like we're going to the same event,* Jamie thought wryly.

As Professor Levy continued to speak, Jamie found her ire with Ryan rising again — even though she realized it was completely irrational. *I hope she's not going to spend every day flirting with the other students. We'll need that time to get to work on these class projects.* Unable to fool herself with that ridiculous complaint, Jamie reminded herself, *It's the second class meeting, and you don't even know what the projects are. It couldn't be less urgent.*

As if she read her mind, Linda spent a few minutes outlining the activities that she had designed for the students to choose from. Each pair needed to do three activities from the list of six, and Jamie made careful notes of the details. She shook her head, letting out a nervous laugh when Linda said, "I know this won't be anything out of the ordinary for some of you, but if you've never been to a lesbian bar, this might be a good time for your first visit." Jamie's stomach fluttered nervously as she considered the possibility — relieved beyond measure when Linda added, "Of course, that only holds if you're twenty-one." More thankful than she had ever been for her tender age, Jamie sat back and listened to the remaining choices.

They could spend a day exploring the Castro, the predominantly gay and lesbian neighborhood in San Francisco; visit a lesbian coffeehouse or bookstore; attend a film during the gay and lesbian film festival; "play" gay for a day if one of the partners was straight; or volunteer in a lesbian community organization for a day.

After an activity each partner was required to write a short paper exploring her feelings about the event and what she had discovered about lesbian life from the experience. *Not bad,* Jamie thought. *Not bad at all. If I can't pull an A in this class, I'll be amazed.*

At the end of the hour, Jamie watched Ryan pull her long form from the small desk. She stood at her full height and gracefully began to stretch her back out, tugging her body into a variety of amazing contortions. Jamie approached her from the side and gave her a small, hesitant smile.

"Were these desks made for a grade school or what?" Ryan asked as she bent over from the waist and let her fingers tickle the linoleum.

"I don't know, they seem just right to me," Jamie said as she stood at her full height and gave Ryan a quick once over.

Ryan looked her over from top to bottom, appraising her as if for the first time. "Well, you're about the size I was in grade school, so I've made my point," she said with a laugh.

"Hey, don't make fun of the height impaired," Jamie said with a scowl as she crossed her arms and tried to look intimidating.

"I wouldn't dream of making fun of you, Jamie." The serious, almost somber, look in the blue eyes brought the smaller woman up short.

"Right," Jamie said, her mouth suddenly a little dry. "So, which of these projects do you think we should tackle?"

"Well," Ryan drawled, "I don't have a strong preference. Do any of them particularly interest you?"

"Uhm, I guess I could do any of them," Jamie replied. "But since you said you have a busy schedule, maybe you should decide."

"We live on different sides of the bay, so it might be easier to do the things that would keep us in the East Bay most of the time. We could go to a women's bookstore in Oakland, and I know of a good lesbian community organization right here in Berkeley. You're not twenty-one yet, are you?" she asked a little hesitantly.

"Is it that obvious?" Jamie sulked mildly.

"Well, it is a little, but I looked you up in the student directory and saw that you were a junior. That made me think there was a pretty good chance that you were about twenty."

"Well, aren't you the amateur detective?" She tilted her head and narrowed her eyes. "Judging from purely physical signs, I'd guess that you're past the age of majority."

"Quite," Ryan admitted. She was not forthcoming with any more information, but Jamie let it pass, deciding she could grill her later.

"So, that eliminates going to a bar. What about the film festival?" Jamie asked.

"I might be able to squeeze some films in," Ryan said hesitantly. "But as I recall, most of them are at night. I usually work at night, so that might be kind of tough."

"That's okay," said Jamie. "There are still three other activities that we can do. And lucky for you, I'm obviously straight, so we can do the 'play gay for a day' thing," she said, trying to lay her cards on the table.

"Do you think it's ... obvious?" asked Ryan as she cocked her head a little and looked at Jamie very dubiously.

"Uhm ... er ... ah ... well, yeah," stammered Jamie in alarm. "Don't you?"

"Yeah, it is," Ryan admitted as she leaned her head back and laughed heartily.

"You're teasing me again, Ryan," she said while tapping her foot and narrowing her eyes.

"Well, it is kind of fun, Jamie, but I'll stop if it bothers you," she replied sincerely.

"No, I'm used to being the butt of jokes. My roommates do it constantly."

"How about I make it up to you by buying you some coffee later," Ryan offered. "Actually, if you're free, we could go to the bookstore I mentioned and get one of our activities out of the way today."

"All right, that would be fun," Jamie agreed. Actually, she had planned on going shopping with her roommate, Cassie, but she was sure she could put that off until later in the week.

"I've got a lab until 2:00," Ryan said. "Could you meet at 2:30?"

"Yeah, I can go get my car and pick you up. Where do you want to meet?"

"How about right in front of the little salad place on Telegraph and Durant? I could dash in and get a salad, since I won't have time for lunch."

"Okay," Jamie agreed. "See you then."

⌘

After a long, tedious morning of classes, Jamie walked home, thinking about her psych class in general — and her partner in particular. *Granted, I hardly know her, but she seems really sweet. Funny, too, in a different way than I'm used to. I hope we can become friends,* she mused. *Although that will not be easy unless Jack likes her, too. Hmm … I wonder what Jack will think of her? I wonder what Jack will think of this class? I know I should have told him, but he didn't directly ask me what I was taking this term.* With a self-righteous scowl she grumbled, *I don't have to tell him everything about my life, do I? He's my fiancé, not my owner!*

Jamie knew that she was trying to convince herself of something, but she wasn't sure of what. She was really uncertain what Jack's reaction would be to the class. Actually, she had no idea what he thought of gay people in general, since it was not a topic they had ever discussed. *It's not like there has been a reason to discuss gay people. We don't know any as a couple. All of the gay people I know are hairdressers or decorators, so that's kind of expected. Of course, I would never have guessed that some of those women in the class were gay. I honestly would never guess that Ryan was either … if she weren't such a flirt that is! I can't believe she was already hitting on someone from class. Although … it looked like that woman was doing most of the hitting.* She reassured herself with the thought, *Ryan was probably just being polite. I'll bet she's really one of those "all talk, no action" types.*

Punctual, as always, at 2:15 Jamie hopped into her car and took off to meet Ryan. She had dropped the top, and her short, blonde hair blew in the light breeze. She gazed at herself in the rearview mirror appraisingly, wondering why Ryan had been so quick to label her as straight. Her hair was cut in a relatively short style, about three inches long on top, tapering to about an inch at the base of her neck. *My hair looks more lesbian than hers does*, she thought defensively, imagining Ryan's long, silky strands, very unconventional for a Bay Area lesbian. Jamie had cut her long hair when she was a freshman, and she recalled that Jack was none too happy about the event. With a shudder, she remembered that his first comment was that she looked "kinda butch" with the new style. *Lord! If he thinks I look butch because of a haircut, what on earth would he think of Ryan in those overalls and that baseball cap!*

As she maneuvered through the crowded streets of Berkeley, she hoped to herself that Ryan would be on time. *Nothing worse than having to circle around the block in this mess*, she thought. Traffic was really snarled in front of her. She could see the sign for the restaurant about one and a half blocks ahead, but her progress was glacial. As she inched closer, she thought she could make out Ryan's cap-bedecked head. *Yeah, that's her. Wait a minute* — Ryan was sitting on a short concrete post that protected the sidewalk diners from errant cars. Her legs were spread wide, and between them stood one of their classmates. Her arms were around the taller woman's neck, and Ryan's hands loosely encircled her waist. The woman, who Jamie recalled was named Chitra, was bent over slightly with her mouth firmly attached to Ryan's. Her head moved slowly as she thoroughly kissed the tanned face. *My God!* Jamie thought. *They look like they just got out of bed! I hope she's not planning on going with us*, she thought angrily. *I only have room for two people!*

As she got closer, she saw one blue eye open and catch sight of her. Ryan gently tried to remove Chitra from her death grip on her mouth, but she was obviously having a difficult time of it. Jamie could see the muscles of her arms tense as she firmly pushed Chitra away, giving her another little kiss as a reward. The beaming smile that she gave her was an added bonus that Chitra seemed to relish. The dazed-looking woman gave Jamie a little wave, which she returned after forcing a smile onto her face. Ryan waved to her friend as she opened the passenger-side door and settled herself comfortably. Turning, she met Jamie's somewhat shocked gaze and gave her a little shoulder shrug along with a delightfully crooked grin.

"Ah, we were just having lunch," she explained helpfully, twitching her head towards the departing woman.

"You looked like you *were* lunch," Jamie replied in a mock scolding tone.

Ryan actually looked disconcerted at that comment, and Jamie instantly felt a stab of regret at the sharp tone she had used. But Ryan didn't seem to mind, recovering quickly. She lobbed back, "I like to make friends in class. You never know when you might need to copy someone's notes."

"Were her notes written on her tongue?" Jamie drawled as she cast a wry glance at her project partner.

The grin was still firmly affixed to her handsome face, but Ryan's voice showed her hesitancy. "Uhm, Jamie, that didn't bother you, did it?"

"Why would that bother me? You're my partner, not my girlfriend," she replied logically.

Ryan looked at her profile and said, "I know that, but I don't know how comfortable you are with the whole lesbian thing. I'm certain that would have bothered some women."

"This is Berkeley, Ryan, you can't walk two feet without tripping over a lesbian!" she said good-naturedly.

"Good, I'm glad you're comfortable. Now, have you ever been to a lesbian coffeehouse?"

"No, can't say that I have. But there is a first time for everything," Jamie opined.

They drove the short distance to the small store in Oakland just chatting about things. Ryan was very impressed with the Boxster. She seemed to know a lot about cars and asked scads of questions about its engine and handling capabilities. Knowing very little about her own vehicle, Jamie finally gave Ryan a little shake of her head and pulled over with Ryan looking at her with a puzzled expression.

"Come on, Ms. NASCAR, you drive it and answer your own questions," she said as she walked around to the passenger door and opened it. Ryan gave her a dazzling grin, protesting weakly while grabbing the windshield and the back of the driver's seat, hoisting herself gracefully into it.

Jamie began to latch the seat belt over her shoulder as Ryan carefully adjusted the rearview mirror. She dropped the belt and leaned over Ryan to point out the somewhat hidden switch by her left thigh, which adjusted the side-view mirrors. As she did so she felt her arm brush against the taller woman's breast, and a little jolt of electricity shot up her arm as the contact occurred. *Yipes!* she shouted to herself. *Where did that come from? Next time, you'd better just tell her where things are, Jamie,* she scolded herself.

Ryan settled herself comfortably and pulled smoothly away from the curve. "Oh, wow!" she nearly moaned in delight. "I have never in my life been behind the wheel of anything this delicious." She closed her eyes slightly in pleasure. Finally, she turned her head a bit to lock eyes with Jamie. "I can't tell you how pleasurable this is for me," she sighed.

Jamie was struck dumb for a moment, but finally got out, "I have never seen anyone enjoy anything quite so thoroughly, Ryan."

"I really love cars as you can tell," she admitted. "But I think I love this car more than any other," she said dreamily. "Do you know what it reminds me of?" she asked with a wiggling eyebrow.

"Uhm, no, I can't guess what a car would remind you of," Jamie admitted.

Ryan closed her eyes slightly as she gave Jamie a very satisfied smile. "A woman," she said simply.

"My car looks like a woman?" the blonde asked in amazement.

"Yep. This car not only has beautiful breasts," Ryan purred, "it has absolutely luscious hips."

Well, she is most definitely a lesbian, Jamie thought as she tried to get some moisture back into her mouth. *I've never met a straight woman who looked so sexy when she talked about breasts and hips!* "I'm not sure I see that," she replied as casually as she could manage, hoping for a lengthy explanation.

"Really?" Ryan asked, incredulous. "Just look at the front fenders! Don't you see that graceful curve? It looks just like a firm, young breast. See it?"

She had to admit that the fender did have a nice curve, and, yes, it could look like a perky, young breast. "Okay, I think I see what you mean. Now show me the hips."

Ryan had to quickly pull over for that part of the demonstration. "Okay, turn around," she instructed. "See the rear fenders? They remind me of the nice, cushy hips of women in the paintings of the Renaissance. See how they curve so smoothly around to the tail lights?"

Once again, Jamie had to admit that Ryan had a point. "Gee, I had no idea I was driving such a woman-centered car," she said with a laugh. "My father bought it for me; do you think that's what attracted him? "

"Subconsciously, I'm sure of it," Ryan smirked.

When they started up again, Jamie looked over at Ryan and saw how much she was enjoying the experience of driving the car. "I don't have the heart to deprive you of this much happiness," Jamie teased. "Why don't we just go for a drive up in the hills? What time do you have to be at work, anyway?"

"Uhm, four o'clock, but I work over in the city. To get there on BART, I need to leave here by 3:00," she said, while giving the dashboard clock a regretful pout.

"Tell ya what," Jamie offered, "I owe my grandfather a visit." She didn't mention that she'd seen him three days ago. "He's right off Nob Hill. Where do you have to go?"

"I work near Castro, and that's not very close to Nob Hill," she said, her dejection growing.

"It's close enough for me. This car eats real estate faster than you can imagine," she teased.

"I really don't want to inconvenience you," Ryan said, somewhat convincingly. But Jamie could see the hopeful look in her eyes and knew that she would not mind walking to Castro in order to satisfy it.

"It's really no bother, Ryan. I would love to have dinner with my grandfather. I don't see him nearly enough." While she spoke she pulled her tiny cell phone from the glove box and dialed the number she knew by heart, making the arrangements when he answered.

They drove through the Oakland hills, chatting about nothing in particular, until Ryan began guiding them down to the highway that would take them to the city. She was a good driver, but she drove as fast as she could, given the conditions. Jamie noticed how she was able to move the car effortlessly through the growing traffic, and after a bit, she found herself sliding sideways in her seat so that she could watch Ryan as she drove, mesmerized by the look of pure pleasure on the handsome face. *It is really cute how gleefully she accepted this small gesture,* Jamie mused. *She doesn't seem afraid to really let herself go — even with a stranger. Well, after that demonstration on the street today, it's clear she doesn't mind letting herself go with strangers,* she reflected with a slight tinge of disapproval. *I wish I could be that free and unconcerned about things, though. Hard to believe that she was kissing a woman like that right in the middle of a busy street. I wouldn't kiss Jack like that on the street. Actually, I don't kiss Jack like that at home anymore,* she thought with a touch of envy.

As they crossed the Bay Bridge leading to San Francisco, Jamie let herself relax in her seat and just take in the beautiful view of the city. *I feel so peaceful and happy,* she thought idly. She turned to look at Ryan again and was met with another charming smile that caused a chill to roll down her whole body. *Jeez, Jamie will you please get a grip!* she chastised herself.

Since it was only 3:40, Ryan took Market all the way to Castro. Jamie could tell that she chose the slow route to prolong her test drive. *I think she has gotten more pleasure from this car in an hour than I have in two years. It's kind of nice to see things through such appreciative eyes.*

Ryan again offered to go directly to Jamie's grandfather's place and take Muni to her job, but Jamie insisted that she go directly to work. Ryan did not offer any details on her job, and Jamie was in too relaxed a mood to do her usual cross-examination, so she just relaxed and enjoyed the next few minutes.

"So, are you still up for a visit to the coffeehouse this week?" Ryan asked as they neared the Castro.

"Absolutely," Jamie replied lazily, forcing herself from her near torpor.

As they pulled up to a rare empty meter, Ryan tugged her organizer out of her black, nylon book bag and began to peruse her schedule.

Jamie noticed that they were parked in front of a Blockbuster video store. "Is this where you work?" she asked tentatively.

"Huh? Oh, no," Ryan replied absently. She pointed vaguely down the street as she continued to check her availability. "I work a little down the street. Okay," she finally said. "I'm free from 10:00 to noon and from 6:00 to 9:00 tomorrow. On Friday my schedule is about the same as today. Are any of those times good for you?"

Jamie thought for just a moment before she chose a Thursday slot. "Do you want to get dinner before we go, or do they serve food there?" she inquired.

"Well, dinner would be great. I have to work afterward, so that will be the only time I have to eat. I don't think they serve anything substantial enough for me at the coffeehouse, so we should probably go somewhere else for dinner. Do you have any suggestions?"

"You start work after 9:00 p.m.?" Jamie asked in surprise.

"Yep. Open all night," Ryan grinned.

"How much time do you think we need to spend at the coffeehouse?" Jamie inquired, momentarily too fragmented to inquire about Ryan's job.

"Well, since we have to write a paper, we should probably hang out for a bit — you know, look at the books, revel in the flora and fauna."

"Why don't you come to my house, and I'll cook dinner for us? That'll save time," Jamie offered.

"Are you always this nice, Jamie, or do you just take pity on starving lesbians?" Ryan asked, her eyes settling on Jamie's face with a relaxed, open gaze.

"Well, I'm generally pretty nice. And you certainly don't look like you're starving," she added as she passed a look at Ryan's solid form.

"You've got me there," she agreed. "I don't miss many meals. Now, let me get your address so I can get to work. My clients hate to be kept waiting."

Ryan hopped out of the Boxster and was halfway up the street, while Jamie's mind was still gnawing on her last comment. *Clients ... working late at night ... what in the hell does she do?*

CHAPTER TWO

JAMIE PULLED INTO HER DRIVEWAY, ROLLING HER EYES IN DISMAY when she noticed her fiancé's car parked in front of the house. Balancing bags of groceries in her arms, she pushed the door of her car shut with a healthy hip bump, venting a little frustration with the move. Her heart started to beat faster as she considered how to proceed. *Ryan gave me her pager number. I could probably reach her before she got here and tell her that I have to cancel. That would be incredibly rude — but it would keep her away from Jack. Shit!* she groused morosely. *I don't want to cancel!* She was nearly pouting as she reached the side door, determined to figure out a way to spend the evening with her new classmate, without too much collateral damage to her relationship. *How bad could it be?* she asked herself rhetorically. *It's not like she has "I'm a lesbian" written on her forehead, and if I want to be friends with her, he's got to meet her sooner or later.* She mentally rolled her eyes, adding, *I'd just rather he didn't find out about my class and meet Ryan at the same time.*

Her internal dialogue was continuing at a frantic pace, and the news only got worse when she poked her head in the back door and saw Jack sitting in the kitchen with Cassie; the world's cattiest roommate. Jamie managed a genuine-looking smile and greeted them both as she put her bags down on the marble counter.

"To what do I owe the honor?" she asked as she crossed the kitchen and kissed Jack gently.

He rose and enveloped her in a hug, holding on a bit longer than was his norm. "I had to drop off some research at the office, and I figured this would be a good place to ride out rush hour." He released her and walked to the counter, commenting, "I thought we could have dinner before I have to head back. Ooo, this looks good," he said, poking into the bags and pulling out the fresh pasta and marinara sauce.

"Oh, honey, I would love to, but I have a classmate coming for dinner. We're working on a special project together, and we need the time to discuss it," she said with more regret than she really felt.

Cassie piped up with an unwelcome contribution, as she narrowed her eyes and scoffed, "What kind of a group project can you have for an English class?"

Jamie was unreasonably annoyed at both of them and moved to Jack's side to remove the items from his hands as soon as he pulled them from the bags. "It's a research project, Cassie. I really don't have time to go into it right now, since my partner will be here any minute. I hate to do this, Jack, but ..." She looked at the ingredients of her planned dinner, then back at him and shrugged her shoulders helplessly.

He gave her his little puppy dog look as he said, "I thought you'd want to see me. You always say I never do anything spontaneous."

"I do want to see you," she insisted. "It's just that I've made plans ..."

Cassie, to Jamie's surprise, actually made herself useful. "Jack, why don't you let me take you out to dinner? You and I don't get to see much of each other, what with Jamie monopolizing all of your time."

Jamie was completely grateful to her roommate for this unexpectedly thoughtful offer. Jack looked like he wanted to refuse, but when Jamie just looked at him with a blank expression he shrugged his broad shoulders and said, "Okay, Cassie. That would be great. Can we wait until Jamie's guest gets here, so the two of us can have a few minutes together?"

Say no, say no, say no, Jamie pled silently, *leave right this minute!* Regrettably, Cassie was not prescient, and she said, "Sure. I'll go upstairs and get ready. Call me when you want to leave."

As soon as Cassie left the room, Jack came up behind Jamie and wrapped his long arms around her waist, placing quick, light kisses on her neck as she tried to wash some lettuce for a salad. The softness of his kisses contrasted starkly with the slightly rough feel of the stubble on his face, and she giggled when he reached her sensitive ears. Turning in his loose embrace, she smiled up at him as he bent and captured her lips, turning up the intensity of his kisses. *Un-unh, Jack*, she thought wryly. *I'm not going to change my mind no matter how turned on you try to make me.* She began to release him when the door to the living room opened, and her second roommate, Mia, escorted her classmate in. Jamie jumped in surprise, nearly hitting Jack's chin with the top of her head as she did so.

"Knock it off, lovebirds, your company is here," Mia commented, stating the obvious.

Jamie stared at Ryan, completely nonplussed. Slightly tousled jet-black hair hung loosely around her broad shoulders. A black, leather, baseball-style jacket covered the tight, black T-shirt that molded to full, rounded breasts. Black jeans topped a pair of sleek, black, low-heeled leather boots, and her right hand clutched a shiny, black motorcycle helmet. *Oh, my God. She looks like the centerfold for "Leather Dyke Magazine"!*

"Hi, Jamie," the black-clad vision uttered, her low, honey-toned voice making Jamie's knees weaker than Jack's kisses had managed to do. Her brain nearly cramped as she tried to process the messages that flooded it. *Get her out of here before Jack starts asking questions! Sit down before your knees give out!* And finally, *Good Lord, if the cow that gave its life for that jacket saw how she looked in it, it would have volunteered for the slaughterhouse!*

Time seemed to stand still — but only for Jamie. Jack fully realized that an uncomfortable amount of time had passed without a word being spoken. He cleared his throat as he stepped back out of Jamie's loose embrace, waiting to be introduced, but when it became obvious to him that wasn't going to happen, he extended his hand and said, "I'm Jack Townsend, Jamie's fiancé." As he spoke he tucked his arm around Jamie's waist, pulling her in tight against his body. They had only been engaged for three months, and in that time, Jack had never introduced himself with that title. The still-stunned woman cast a quick glance up at him and saw that he projected an attitude that could only be described as proprietary.

If Ryan noticed the attitude, her eyes certainly didn't reflect it. She extended her hand and gripped Jack's lightly, then quickly increased the pressure to match his. "Ryan O'Flaherty," she said, again tweaking Jamie's curiosity when she detected just a hint of an accent as she pronounced her surname.

Cassie entered the room at that minute and stopped dead in her tracks, looking at Ryan with undisguised fascination. Her eyes darted from Ryan to Jack then landed on Mia, and Jamie noticed that the two women shared a significant, knowing look. *Oh, shit! Mia must have told Cassie that my psych class is about lesbians! She'll tell Jack for sure!* Once again she thought about telling Ryan that her plans had changed. *If I send her away now, Jack will be thrilled that I chose him over school — and Ryan probably won't be too upset.* But even as the thought flitted through her mind, she knew that she wouldn't act on it. She wanted to get to know this woman — no matter the cost. She wasn't sure why it was important, but it was — vitally so — and she immediately decided that she was willing to suffer the consequences of her decision.

"So, what is this project you two are working on?" Jack asked Ryan, his arm still wrapped firmly around Jamie's waist.

Ryan gave Jamie a quick glance and almost imperceptibly raised an eyebrow, silently asking if she should answer. Jamie jumped in after flashing her a smile of thanks. "It's just a little project for our psych class. I'll tell you all about it later, sweetheart. We've got to hurry up and eat, and you two need to get going," she said to Cassie and Jack. "I'm sure you've got a ton of work to do tonight."

"Actually, I don't," he said, holding on tight. "That's why I dropped by. Sure you don't need another pair of eyes or ears for whatever this mysterious project is?"

"No, we're fine," she said, sliding out from under his arm, inexplicably feeling trapped by his usually welcome touch. "I'm sure it's nothing that would interest you anyway, Jack. You know how boring you find psychology."

"Psychology, huh?" he said thoughtfully. "Are you a psych major, Ryan?"

"No," she said, giving him a smile and nothing more. Ryan wasn't sure what was going on in the suddenly tension-filled room, but she knew she didn't want to be caught in the middle of it.

"Well," he said after a short silence, "I guess we'd better get going, Cassie. It's obvious that the two scholars have some top secret work to get to."

Jamie tried to lighten the mood, saying, "We're not doing anything top secret, Jack. It's just a silly psych class that we have to write a couple of papers for. It's not even worth discussing."

"Okay," he said, his smile looking forced. "I'll see you later, sweetheart." He bent and gave her a kiss that bordered on inappropriate, and Jamie felt her cheeks begin to flush with embarrassment. "Have fun," he added as he and Cassie exited through the back door.

The remaining threesome watched them depart. Mia obviously found the tension-filled kitchen too interesting to leave, making no move to do so. "What's for dinner?" she asked as she peeked at the assembled ingredients.

Jamie came up behind her and physically removed her from her position. "Ryan and I are having pasta. You are having whatever you make for yourself after we leave," she stated with authority.

"Okay, okay," Mia laughed as she retreated. "Can I at least get a soda? And maybe a little of that bread?" she asked hopefully.

"Yes, Mia, you may have some bread," Jamie responded. "Then scram."

"You run a pretty tight ship around here, Jamie," Ryan commented after Mia scampered out with her snack.

"Those three would have eaten every bite," she said lightly with a shake of her blonde head.

"Well, I don't blame them, especially if they're as hungry as I am ," Ryan said. "I didn't get a proper lunch today."

"I forgot to ask you if there were any things you don't eat. I figured pasta was on almost everyone's list."

"I don't eat anything that's currently breathing," Ryan stated. "Other than that, I'll eat it."

Ryan proved herself true to her word. Jamie had made the entire two pounds of fresh pasta in order to have leftovers for lunch the next day, but Ryan acted as though her two massive helpings of pasta were the bare minimum required to keep her going. Jamie mused that she had never seen a woman eat quite so much, but her thoughts were interrupted by Ryan's beginning to eye the salad bowl. Jamie pushed it over to her, and Ryan bent her dark head and ate every bite, finishing off the loaf of bread along with it.

"Do you have room for some gelato?" Jamie asked warily, knowing that her guest had to be full to bursting.

"What flavor?" Ryan asked, a slight frown settling between her dark brows.

"Chocolate."

Her eyes lit up, and a wide grin split Ryan's face. "I've always got room for chocolate."

"You looked pretty hesitant there," Jamie observed. "What flavor would you have refused?"

"I can't think of one, but you can't be too sure," Ryan replied prudently.

Jamie had only bought one pint of the freshly-made gelato, and as Ryan finished her second bowl she regretted her decision. "Uhm … have you had enough?" she asked, as Ryan leaned back in her chair with a satisfied smile on her lovely face.

"Why, is there more?" she asked as she looked around the kitchen hopefully.

"Are you teasing me again, Ryan?" Jamie asked with a tolerant smile.

"Just a little," her new friend replied. "I think that delicious dinner has managed to actually fill me up for a change. Not an easy task, I concede."

"You do have a healthy appetite," Jamie observed tactfully. *Healthy for a defensive end!*

"Hey, I'm a growing girl."

"Don't grow too much, or I'll need a stepladder to talk to you," Jamie said with a smile.

"That's not the direction I would grow if all of my meals were that delicious," Ryan replied with one of her dazzling smiles.

After they quickly cleaned the kitchen, they made their way to the front door. "Would you like me to drive?" Ryan asked.

"Sure," Jamie replied as she handed her the keys to her car.

"No, I mean, would you like to ride on my bike? It's the perfect ride for a visit to a lesbian bookstore," she grinned.

"I've never been on a motorcycle before," Jamie admitted with a nervous laugh. "But I've always thought they were cool …"

"My motto is 'Always give in to temptation,'" Ryan said with a sexy leer that made Jamie's heart race.

"But … I don't … uhm … have a helmet; wouldn't I need one?"

"That's why I brought this one in," Ryan reassured her. "I thought we could adjust it where the light was better."

"Isn't this yours?" Jamie asked as she narrowed her eyes in concern.

"No, mine is on the bike. This is my extra one."

"Okay, I'm game." She forced her voice to sound significantly more confident than she felt.

⌘

"Wow, that is a good-looking bike!" Jamie enthused when they had stepped outside. She regarded the aqua and cream-colored Harley with a critical eye. She knew absolutely nothing about motorcycles, but it was clear that this one was well loved. The leather was supple and immaculate, the chrome gleamed, and the paint was perfect.

"Yeah, I really love this one. I've had a Yamaha, a Honda and an Indian. But this one really sounds like a bike. You feel it all the way through your spine," she said proudly as she trailed her hand lovingly over the saddle.

Jamie was unsure of what that really meant, but she figured she would find out soon enough. Ryan threw her long leg over the saddle and pushed the bike off the kickstand. "Come on," she said as she held out a hand.

Jamie took her left hand and placed her right on Ryan's shoulder as she swung her leg over the seat. It was a stretch, but she accomplished the feat with a little hop on the planted foot. She settled down comfortably, feeling a little exposed as she nestled her thighs behind Ryan's.

"Hang on tight," Ryan instructed. "Feel free to put your arms around my waist. All you have to do is hold on and lean into the turns like I do. And don't worry, you'll have fun," she said as she patted Jamie lightly on the thigh.

Jamie privately admitted that she was already having fun. She loved sitting on the big bike, snuggled up so close to Ryan, and she filled her lungs with the delightful scent of her leather jacket. As the bike roared to life, she understood what Ryan meant about the sound. She definitely heard it, but she realized that she felt it with her body more than heard it with her ears. *Now **this** is intense.* The intensity grew as the bike began to glide smoothly down the street. Involuntarily, she threw her arms around

Ryan as the bike moved through its gears, unconsciously holding on tighter as the bike gathered speed.

As she become accustomed to the sensation, Jamie realized that this was truly a glorious feeling. She had never realized how insulated she was while in a car, even a small convertible like her own. This, however, was a feeling of complete freedom. She almost felt as if she were flying, and the sweet scent of flowers and damp grass made her grin. *Wow, why would you ever ride in a car if you had one of these?*

The trip was over much too soon, and as they pulled up in front of the bookstore, Jamie regretted having to get off.

"I take it you enjoyed your first time?" Ryan asked knowingly as she saw the luminous grin that lit Jamie's face.

"That was awesome, Ryan!" she gushed, her enthusiasm bubbling up. "I had no idea it would be so cool! Why would you ever ride in a car?" she asked with a puzzled look on her flushed face.

"Well, when it's under fifty degrees and raining, cars start to look pretty good," Ryan said with a wide smile as she slid her arm around Jamie's shoulders to lead her inside.

As they entered, Jamie was very aware of how Ryan unconsciously touched her, now guiding her with a hand at the small of her back. *She treats me kind of like a guy would if we were on a first date,* she mused. *But it doesn't feel like she's coming on to me today. It feels like that's just part of her personality. She's obviously used to being in charge.* At the thought of Ryan's natural dominance, Jamie's imagination began to roam. *I wonder if lesbians really have roles when they're together? If so, Ryan's definitely the guy — but a guy with an absolutely drop-dead gorgeous body!*

As they acclimated to the bright light of the bookstore, Ryan caught her wandering gaze and quietly asked, "Would you like to sit and have a coffee, or would you rather look in the bookstore for a bit?"

"Since it's not too crowded, let's look around first, then maybe we can sit down for a while." She noticed a chalkboard that announced a singer performing that evening. "Oh, do they have music?"

"Yeah, in about an hour," Ryan replied as she checked her enormous watch. Jamie grasped her hand and took a look at the timepiece.

"God, Ryan, what does that monster do?"

"Well, I have to time my clients so they don't overstay their hour," she replied reasonably. "And sometimes I'm doing two people at once, so I need two timers." She indicated the two timers with her index finger. "And I use it for running and swimming. See, it has two lap counters," she indicated them both. "I also use it as my alarm in the morning, and every once in a while, I can get a little nap in at work," she said with a conspiratorial wink.

What in the hell does she do for a living? Just as Jamie's lips were forming the question, a short, pleasant-looking, middle-aged woman appeared from behind the bar. She was heading right for them, and Jamie noticed Ryan's face light up in a smile.

"Ryan O'Flaherty, as I live and breathe!" the woman gushed in a broad, theatrical, Irish accent.

"Hi, Babs. It's good to see you again," Ryan said as she gave the small woman a big, friendly hug. "This is my friend, Jamie. Jamie, this is Babs Jablonski; she owns this den of ill repute," Ryan teased.

Babs elbowed Ryan sharply in the ribs as she grasped Jamie's hand in a firm shake. "Any friend of Ryan's is still welcome here," she joked in her normal voice.

After a few more minutes of banter, Ryan showed Jamie around the bookstore. The blonde was surprised to find the store sectioned off into categories just like at a regular bookstore, although why that surprised her, she didn't know. Even though the store looked like a normal one, the categories were a bit different than she was used to. "Coming Out," "Lesbian Sexuality" and "Lesbian Parenting" caught Jamie's eye as she glanced around the small space. She also noticed that there was a section where CD's and tapes were sold. She strolled over to that area and realized that none of the artists were familiar to her.

"Are these … uhm … 'lesbian specific' singers?" she asked tentatively while holding up a CD for Ryan's inspection.

"That's a cute way to put it," Ryan said. "I would say for the most part, these artists are lesbians, but there is a good bit of generic women's music also, along with some self-help and spirituality tapes," she added.

"How do you know so much about this place, and how do you know Babs?" Jamie found the courage to ask, hoping that she wasn't prying too much.

"This was a nice place to hang out when I was a kid. I became such a pest that Babs took pity on me and let me help out on the weekends and earn a few bucks."

"So you've known you were gay for a long time?" Jamie asked with interest.

"I'll tell you the whole sordid story," Ryan promised, "but let's finish up in here first."

Jamie spent quite a few more minutes looking carefully at the titles that lined the lilac-painted, wooden shelves. "I must admit, this is all a bit surprising to me," she said with a touch of wonder. "I guess I just never thought that there would be a whole industry catering to lesbians. Do you think it's necessary, Ryan?"

Ryan seemed to consider her question for a moment. She gazed at her carefully as she replied, "Yes, I really do. When you think about it, gay people are among the few minorities who don't share their minority status with their parents. When people come out, many of them are overwhelmed by the experience. Even if their parents are supportive, they don't know how to help. Places like this can be a lifesaver for people who are really struggling. I know it was for me," she admitted quietly.

"I can see that it would really help someone who was sure of her preferences," Jamie stated after a moment. "But what about girls who are just confused? Don't you think this could push them into a place that they don't really belong?"

With a tiny scowl on her face, Ryan said, "I know you don't know all of the lingo, but most gay people really prefer to have their sexuality be considered an orientation, rather than a preference, Jamie."

"I'm sorry," she said quickly, reaching out to touch Ryan's forearm. "What did I say?"

"You referred to someone's being sure of her preferences," Ryan explained. "It's not a real big deal, but it's not a preference for me."

"Okay," she said slowly, drawing the word out while she considered this. "I don't really see the difference."

"Well," Ryan said, "I assume you consider yourself heterosexual, right?"

"Well, yeah," she laughed mildly. "So does Jack," she added with a grin.

"But if you broke up, would you accept a date from a woman?"

"Uhm …" Jamie found herself absolutely dumbstruck at this question. She seemed to have lost her ability to speak, so Ryan replied for her.

"I take it that's a no," she said helpfully. "I think sexuality is like that for many people. You focus on one gender for your sexual attraction. You don't look at the whole human race and decide which one you slightly prefer, Jamie. Your orientation leads you to only look at men as sexual partners, right?"

"Uh … right!" she finally said, as a deep blush covered her face and neck. "Right!" she reiterated again for emphasis.

"Please don't be embarrassed, Jamie," Ryan said gently. "You're not offending me at all." She smiled sweetly and maintained eye contact as she continued. "That's how it is for me, too," Ryan advised. "I don't 'prefer' women. The thought of being with a man sexually has as much appeal for me as being with my dog. And that's not a put down of dogs or men," she added with a laugh. "It's just something so outside of my orientation that both of those options seem equally far-fetched to me."

"Okay," Jamie said slowly. "I think I get your point. And I can see why having it called a preference could be offensive."

"Sorry if that seemed like a lecture," Ryan said. "But I figure that you want to understand this stuff or you wouldn't have taken the class."

"Absolutely!" she agreed. "Now do you remember the rest of my question?"

"Verbatim," Ryan said with a grin. "I don't think a place like this can push someone into a life that isn't right for them, Jamie. The purpose of this place is not to recruit. It's to help people figure out their true orientation and learn to be comfortable with it."

"But," Jamie interrupted, "what about all the girls and women who are just dabbling in lesbianism? It sure is popular now to have 'done it' with a woman."

"I doubt that those women will eventually consider themselves lesbians," Ryan replied. "I think for many of them it's a rite of passage — kind of like getting a tattoo or a piercing. In the long run, though, that might be a good thing — it might remove some of the stigma from being gay if more people have some experience with the act."

"I guess you could be right, but how do you think it will affect those women who are just playing around in the long run?" Jamie persisted.

"You're kind of making it sound like *The Scarlet Letter*," Ryan said with a tiny frown. "For many women having sex is just that — sex. It's no big deal for most women, if they're just playing around. They know they're just experimenting. I think the women who have a harder time are the true lesbians. For many of them, having sex with a woman finally confirms their feelings. Then they have to deal with all of the fallout from that realization — and that's where this place comes in."

"I guess I see your point, but this is a lot to absorb. It's kind of like visiting another culture. It takes time to get acclimated," she reasoned.

"Maybe some coffee would help," Ryan suggested with a smile. "Let me buy you one."

As she settled down into a burgundy velour sofa, Jamie accepted two large mugs of latte from Ryan. She waited until her friend was seated at a polite distance and handed one mug back to her.

"Ooo, this is good. I like the little sprinkle of chocolate on the top," she said as she licked a white foam mustache from her upper lip. "Do you have time to tell me the story of your sordid lesbian past?" she chuckled, reminding Ryan of her earlier promise.

"I've only got an hour," the dark woman replied as she looked at her watch. "That should get us through a year or two if I gloss over the scary parts."

Once again reaching for Ryan's arm, Jamie gave it a squeeze and asked, "Was it really hard for you, Ryan? You seem very happy now."

"Yeah, I am perfectly content with who I am now — sexually at least," she said with a smile. "But it was really hard for me. I mean, I knew from a very early age that I was somehow different from the other girls. I didn't understand how I was different — I just knew there was something."

"Did you have boyfriends when you were younger?" Jamie inquired gently.

"Nope — never had one. No dates, no crushes, nothing. And I don't think I ever will at this point," she added with a small smile.

Jamie shot a look up and down her rather voluptuous, but still sleek, form. "I don't mean to embarrass you, but how did you avoid having boys hound you? You're pretty gorgeous, you know."

"Thanks," Ryan grinned, looking away shyly. "I was lucky because I went to an all-girls high school, so that took some of the pressure off — there weren't any guys around to make it obvious that I wasn't interested. I was really into sports, and the girls I hung out with weren't very boy crazy either. Plus, I was almost five foot ten by the end of eighth grade. I was a head taller than the boys my age until I was sixteen or so."

"So, you really had no interest in going out with guys?"

"Zip," she said decisively. "I liked boys, but I thought of them as friends. I just couldn't imagine kissing one of them. I really didn't understand what was going on with me. I mean, most of my friends talked about guys they liked, and by high school, guys were the main topic of conversation for nearly all of my classmates. But it wasn't until the end of my junior year that it all fell into place for me."

Jamie waited expectantly for Ryan to continue, but her face had clouded, and she stared into her mug with a very sad look on her face.

"We don't have to talk about this, Ryan," she said softly as she once again gently touched her.

Ryan looked up at her with such pain in her eyes that Jamie had to resist the urge to reach out and wrap her in a hug. "It's okay, Jamie," she replied with a little catch in her voice. "I knew I was gay because I finally realized that I was madly in love with my best friend." She pursed her lips as she added, "Let's just say that she did not share my feelings."

Jamie slid her hand down and grasped Ryan's hand. She gave it a little squeeze as she caught and held her gaze. "I'm sorry," she said simply.

Ryan's lips slowly curled up into a shy smile. "I don't know why, but I'm kind of embarrassed by this," she admitted as a look of shame passed across her face. "I know it was a long time ago, but it still hurts me to think about it. Those early wounds don't ever seem to go away. When I think of that time, I feel just as devastated today as I did then."

"Well, I think it's her loss to refuse a prize like you," Jamie said before she could censor the words falling out of her mouth.

Ryan looked at her with a large measure of surprise on her face, but she recovered to give Jamie a huge, crooked grin. "Easy for you to say now, but I was kind of a mess back then."

"I rather doubt you were ever a mess, Ryan," she replied confidently.

They passed the next few minutes in idle chatter. Ryan stood after a bit and shrugged out of her leather jacket, folding it neatly and placing it over the arm of the sofa. Jamie had a hard time controlling her desire to stare at Ryan's sculpted body, starkly outlined by the skintight, French-cut T-shirt that covered her. To her relief, Babs approached again. "Hey, Irish, are you gonna ride again this year?" she asked as she nodded her head towards a large poster proclaiming the "Sixth Annual California AIDS Ride."

"Yep, I'm doing it again," Ryan replied. "Don't worry, Babs, I'll be hitting you up for a sponsorship sooner than you wish."

Jamie's eyes grew wide as she said, "Oh, Ryan, that is so cool! Every year I watch the news coverage of the ride. But I've never known anyone who did it."

"Well, now you do," Ryan said, sounding pleased. "And don't think I won't try to wheedle money out of you, too," she added as she pinched Jamie's cheek.

"No problem. I would be honored to support you. You know, I don't know anyone who has had AIDS," Jamie said as she wracked her brain and came up empty.

"You're lucky," Ryan said as a flash of pain clouded her face. "You're really lucky."

⌘

At 8:30 sharp, Ryan stood and stretched and gracefully slid her jacket back on. She held a smooth hand out to Jamie and said, "I can't be late for work, so I've got to run."

They rode the short distance in silence, which was fine with Jamie since she needed all of her concentration to focus on the sensations of the ride. She had to admit that she enjoyed the experience even more on the return trip now that she felt more comfortable being with Ryan. *God, she's so easy to talk to,* she thought. *It was just so easy to open up to her.*

As the bike pulled up in front of her house, Jamie struggled to get off with a little assist from her new friend. The engine was still running as Ryan retrieved Jamie's helmet and secured it. "I had a nice time. Thanks for going with me," Ryan said, raising her voice to compete with the engine.

"I really enjoyed it, Ryan. Thanks for being such a good tour guide and for giving me my maiden motorcycle ride," she added with a grin.

Ryan reached out and gave her shoulder a little squeeze. "Always happy to initiate a new convert," she grinned. "See you tomorrow," she called out as she roared away.

Jamie was so occupied in watching her ride away that she did not see Jack glaring at her from the front door.

⌘

With a satisfied sigh, Jamie filled her lungs with the heavy night air, momentarily mulling over whether to sit on the porch to hold on to some the magic of the evening. Approaching the steps, she noted with alarm that Jack's Accord was still parked in the driveway. *Uh-oh, this is probably not good.* When she hit the first step of the wraparound porch, the front door opened.

"Hi," Jack said quietly with an unreadable expression on his face.

"Hi yourself," Jamie replied, trying for a casual tone. She made sure that she was smiling and did her best to adopt a neutral expression. "This is a nice surprise," she said. Standing on her tiptoes to wrap her arms around his neck, she noted with alarm that he did not respond to the kiss she offered — that, in fact, he seemed to pull away from her touch. She stepped back slightly and placed her hands upon his broad chest as she looked up into his eyes with concern. "What's wrong, honey?"

"Where were you tonight, Jamie?" His cold blue eyes stared directly into hers.

"I had to work on a class project with Ryan, like I told you," she answered with more than a touch of defensiveness in her voice. "Why?"

Turning away from her, he began to climb the staircase apparently to go to the bedroom. She noticed that he looked very tired, and his posture did not show its usual confident attitude.

Jamie began to follow him up the stairs, grabbing at his hand as she caught up with him to pull him to a stop. "Jack, what's wrong?" she demanded with growing alarm.

"In private," he responded wearily and continued his plodding gait.

Once in the room, he faced her, his confused, blue eyes revealing a depth of sadness that she had never seen before. "You lied to me, Jamie."

"Lied to you? I've never lied to you, Jack." She approached him gingerly and tried to grasp his hands, but he shook her off roughly.

"Why didn't you tell me about this class, or about this ... woman?" he demanded as his eyes bore into her.

"What? *What?* What on earth are you talking about?" She was becoming angry now, both at his attitude and his obvious disapproval. "I'm taking a stupid psych class. Since when are you so interested in my schedule?"

"Jamie, this is not a class that a normal girl should ... or would want ... to take," he explained as if talking to a slow child. "I do not understand why you want to spend your time learning about the lesbian experience."

With a jolt, a light went on in Jamie's head. She took a deep breath and asked slowly, "How did you know the name of the class?"

Now it was his turn to look defensive. "Jesus, Jamie, you're out late, on a motorcycle no less, with some big dyke — and you've told no one where you're going. Cassie didn't know, Mia didn't know. I was worried about you!" he shouted.

Making sure that her gaze reflected both her outrage and her hurt, she said, "Oh, I see. You were worried about me because I was out until," she checked her watch, looking at it dramatically, "almost nine o'clock, right? So you did what — looked through my book bag and my organizer?"

"Yes, Jamie, I was worried about you, and I did look through your stuff. But only to find out where you were. Cassie had to be the one to tell me that," he pursed his lips, obviously trying to control his anger, "that *woman* was hitting on you. What if you had needed my help?"

Jamie was flabbergasted — both by his behavior and by his assumptions. "You have got to be kidding! Do you think I would willingly spend the evening with someone who frightened me?" She began to pace in a tight circle, her hands balled into fists. "What did you think would happen? Did you think she would throw me across her bike and kidnap me? Or do you think lesbians have to rape straight women to get any action?" She was really heating up now as she stood in front of him, feet spread slightly as she leaned in. "I am furious that you looked through my things. I never want you to do that again. Do you hear me?" This last was said at full volume as she glared at him.

"Yes, Jamie, all of Berkeley heard you," he said bitterly. "It's obvious that you are in no place to discuss this rationally. I'll call you tomorrow."

He turned and started to make his way to the door, but Jamie was on him like a panther, grabbing his arm and abruptly whirling him around.

"How dare you start this and then try to leave!" she shouted in frustration.

He reached over to her small hand which was wrapped around his bicep and gently began to remove her fingers one by one. "I'm not trying," he enunciated carefully. "I'm leaving." With that he strode from the room, his confidence having returned.

Jamie stood in the center of the room, panting from the flood of emotions that raced through her body. She felt a stomach-churning mixture of anger, sadness, hurt, betrayal and fear that combined to make her feel like she would explode. Hurling herself to the bed, she began to cry, remaining in the exact same position until exhaustion overtook her. She fell asleep still fully dressed, visions of a dark woman astride a powerful motorcycle filling her vivid dreams.

⌘

Running into class with less than a minute to spare, Jamie took her seat just as Linda began to speak. "Hello, people," she greeted them in her usual cheerful manner. "Today we're going to discuss social attitudes towards lesbian identity." She launched them into a fascinating discussion of the subject. Jamie paid rapt attention, even while running her mind on two tracks. Although she was very focused on Linda's words, she was concurrently applying those words to Jack's behavior the previous evening. The hour passed much too quickly, and she was still so filled with unanswered questions that she just could not turn off her brain at the end of class. As she sat at her desk, deep in thought, she sensed, and then saw, Ryan squat down next to her so they were at eye level.

"Hey, you look a little down today," Ryan said carefully, her voice filled with concern. "Are you all right?"

Jamie took a deep breath and tried to answer, but she just couldn't find the words to express how she was feeling. Her head was still tilted down, causing a shock of blonde hair to hang over her eyes. With an achingly tender gesture, Ryan reached up and gently brushed her bangs back to reveal her troubled eyes. "Yeah, sure," Jamie lied weakly, "I'm fine." Then, almost as an afterthought, she asked, "Do you have a few minutes to talk?"

Ryan glanced at her watch. "I have nearly an hour at my disposal." With a warm grin she held out a hand and pulled the troubled woman to her feet. "Let's spend it together."

Jamie gave her a hesitant smile, nodded and followed her out of the room. When they reached the sidewalk she said, "Something happened last night that is really bothering me."

"Was it something I did?" Ryan asked with concern clouding her face.

"Oh, no, not at all. I had a great time with you," Jamie admitted with a shy grin. "It was after you dropped me off that the shit hit the fan."

Ryan took a deep breath and let it out slowly. "Let's get something to drink. I always think better if I have some juice."

Jamie suggested a spot close to campus, and when they reached the restaurant Ryan reached for her wallet. "I'll buy — what'll you have?"

"Uhm, some kind of soda, doesn't really matter," Jamie replied absently.

Ryan nodded and started to walk away, but she spent another moment looking at Jamie's face. *She really doesn't seem like herself today. I think I'll get her some juice. She could use some energy instead of empty calories.*

"You look like you could use a little energy," Ryan said when she returned, placing four bottles of juice on the table.

Jamie was charmed by this thoughtful gesture and without stopping to censor herself, she reached out and patted Ryan's hand while giving her a sincere smile. "Thanks for caring," she stated simply.

Ryan looked a little embarrassed at this gesture, but she gamely returned the smile. "So, what's up?" she asked, as she began opening bottles.

"I was just thinking about our discussion of this morning," Jamie said thoughtfully. "You know, about homophobia and heterosexism?" At Ryan's nod, she continued. "I think I got a first hand example of both last night."

"What happened?" Ryan asked, genuinely interested, but also a little worried that she was involved in whatever was bothering her new friend.

"It seems that my roommates are overly interested in the fact that I'm taking this class," she finally answered. Jamie didn't want to hurt Ryan's feelings, so obviously she would not tell her that Jack called her a big dyke, and she also did not want to reveal issues that she felt belonged to her and Jack alone. She tried to tiptoe around the issue as carefully as she could, while still telling enough to be able to get some advice. "One of my roommates apparently told my boyfriend about the class, and he flipped out because I hadn't told him about it. What really has me confused is why he had such an emotional reaction to the mere fact that I was taking a psych class."

"Was he also upset that you were with me?" Ryan asked softly, lowering her eyes to the table.

Jamie did not really want to go there, but she didn't feel comfortable lying to Ryan either. "Uhm, I guess that was part of it," she finally admitted. "But I think the bigger problem is that my roommate stirred up some suspicion in his mind. I guess it just surprised me that they would all be so weird about it. You know — the class and the topic and, well, you." Jamie was also staring at the table by this time, chagrined at having to admit that her fiancé and her friends were so small-minded. She jumped a little when she felt Ryan's reassuring hand gently grip her folded ones.

"That is exactly what Linda was talking about today," Ryan acknowledged, her eyes locking on Jamie's. "Many people have an almost physical reaction to gay people and gay issues. I can't say I totally understand it, but I see it often in my life," she admitted. "Those reactions have caused me a lot of pain through the years, Jamie. I'm very sorry that you had to experience it, too. I just hope that it won't affect our friendship. I really like you," she said shyly as her eyes once again darted away.

"Oh, no, Ryan. I like you, too," she agreed forcefully. "This is an issue that they're going to have to learn to deal with. I just want to understand it better so I can help them get through it."

Ryan looked at her carefully as she pursed her lips in thought. "Can I ask you a personal question?" she finally inquired.

Jamie fidgeted in her seat as she tried to guess what her new friend wanted to know, but she replied, "Sure, what is it?"

"Why *didn't* you tell your boyfriend you were taking the class?"

An excess of excuses readily popped into Jamie's head, but as she gazed into Ryan's eyes, she felt compelled to be completely honest with her. As she opened her heart, she realized that she had not been honest with herself, either. She was surprised to hear her own answer, "I didn't think he'd like it, and I was afraid that he would either talk me out of it or somehow make me feel bad about it."

Ryan didn't say a word in response. She just slowly nodded her head as if she had expected that answer. Jamie wondered what was going on behind those guarded eyes, but Ryan wasn't giving up her secrets today. She patted Jamie's shoulder and said, "I've read some really good books on homophobia and heterosexism. Call me at home this afternoon, and I'll give you the titles." She scribbled her home number on a piece of paper and stood, chugging the remaining cranberry juice. Ryan eyed Jamie's untouched apple juice as she hefted her enormous book bag onto her shoulder.

"Go ahead," the smaller woman smirked. "You are a bit of a bottomless pit, aren't you?"

"My father always says I have two hollow legs," she happily agreed.

"You get going — I'll call you later." Jamie gave her a smile that was much more relaxed than the one she had offered after class. Satisfied that her friend was feeling better, Ryan returned the smile and took off for her next class at a surprisingly fast clip.

⌘

After spending the better part of the late afternoon in her favorite Palo Alto bookstore, Jamie checked her watch and saw that it was already 7:00. Extracting her cell phone, she dialed Jack's apartment and braced herself for another fight. "Hi," she said as neutrally as possible.

"Jamie," he said, a clear tone of relief in his voice. "I just called your house, but no one knew where you were."

"I'm right down the street, honey," she replied, trying to pump up the warmth in her voice. "If you want to see me, I can be there in five minutes."

"Of course I want to see you," he said fervently. "I couldn't stop thinking about you all day."

"Okay, I'll be right there," she agreed, with relief flooding her voice.

By the time she had put her purchased books in her bag and began to exit the shop, she could see Jack's long form jogging down the street. *That's better than an apology*, she thought as she smiled widely and met his eyes.

She walked just a step or two before he was upon her. He lifted her effortlessly off her feet as his arms fully encircled her small waist. He squeezed nearly all of the air out of her lungs as he nestled his head between her shoulder and neck. She leaned back a bit to regard him as he murmured, "I am so sorry, Jamie. I acted like a total asshole, and I hope you can forgive me."

She responded with a tender kiss to his soft lips. That kiss was followed by another — slightly less tender, but with even more emotion. As he lowered her softly to her feet, he grasped her cheeks with his large hands. He pulled her close for a dizzying series of kisses that left her panting. "Let's go," she rasped out as she grabbed his hand and began to lead him down the street.

⌘

The pent up emotion of the past twenty-four hours began to pulse in her veins as they covered the short distance. As they entered the apartment, she grabbed him by the shirt and roughly pushed him against the wall. He gasped a bit in surprise at this totally unexpected display of aggression from his normally demure lover. She pounced upon his mouth and kissed him thoroughly until she felt his knees begin to buckle. They began to slide down the wall in tandem as she fought frantically to undo his belt. He wrenched his T-shirt over his head as she bent to focus intently on her task. Finally, she had loosened his belt and unzipped him. She grabbed his jeans and shorts and yanked them as far down his legs as their bodies would allow.

He was sitting with his back against the wall, pants around his shins as Jamie straddled his thighs. He grabbed her golf shirt by the hem and pulled it over her compliantly outstretched arms. As she threw her arms around his neck for another bout of heated kisses, he expertly unhooked her bra. The only barrier now was her jeans, and Jack could not tolerate this encumbrance to her skin for another second. He grasped her around her waist and tumbled them both onto their sides. His nimble hands slid her zipper down with agonizing slowness. They could hear the click, click, click as the metal gave way, both gasping at the sound and at the promise of what lay ahead. Then Jamie pushed her jeans and panties down and out of the way.

She took the opportunity the momentary distraction provided and rolled him onto his back on the hardwood floor, needing to be in control for a change. Straddling him again, she grabbed his hands and placed them firmly on her breasts, then covered his hands with her own to urge him to squeeze them firmly. After a moment or two, she began to grind his large hands against her aroused breasts with a brazenness that Jack had never before seen her display.

Dropping her head to his, she again began the assault on his lips. Her warm, wet tongue entered his mouth as she let out a fierce, animalistic groan. His eyes were tightly closed, but his large hands never stopped grasping and squeezing her now-tender breasts.

With a stunningly sexy voice she rasped out, "Watch me." Jamie slid back on his legs and grasped him gently, amazed at the rock-hard firmness that she held in her hand. She wrapped her fist around him and teasingly rubbed her thumb over the head, making him moan. Her eyes had never left his, and with a look that could melt steel, she angled him slightly and impaled herself on his aching member. Her entire body stilled, and she grabbed onto his shoulder, her nails digging into his flesh. The room was utterly silent — neither of them making a sound for several seconds as she felt her flesh relax to accommodate him. With a tortured groan, she pumped her hips, and he slid all the way in, her hands nearly bruising his shoulders with her iron grip. After a short pause to catch her breath, she started to move, riding him for a few short moments before she howled out her release. He followed her seconds later as she collapsed onto his chest.

Their sweat-drenched bodies lay tangled together — arms, legs, jeans, all entwined.

"Does that mean I'm forgiven?" he finally asked with a sated smile.

⌘

They passed the rest of the weekend in their familiar pattern. Jamie was pleased to see that their relationship seemed back to normal. They didn't discuss the fight at all, and that was fine with her. She had quickly come to realize that neither of them was particularly good at having a rational discussion when they were angry, and once they weren't angry she didn't want to rock the boat again. She truly thought that the blow up was a one-time-only occurrence, and neither of them saw the need to rehash it.

Even though the fight had been painful, and had actually frightened her, Jamie had to admit that she had never felt as much lust for Jack as she had during their make-up sex. *Maybe a blow up is a good idea every once in a while.*

After dinner Jamie watched a movie that she had rented earlier in the day. She watched wearing headphones as Jack was diligently working away. They sat on the couch together, him sitting up, her lying on her side with her head on a pillow at the other end of the couch and her legs resting on his lap. His textbook was resting on his thighs, but propped up by her legs.

Around midnight, Jack gently stroked her arm to wake her. "C'mon, sleeping beauty, time for bed." He helped her to sit up, but she only lasted in that position for a moment before she collapsed onto his chest.

"Too tired," she grumbled sleepily.

He turned a bit and reached under her knees with one arm, while the other cradled her back. He rose with her in his arms as she nestled down into his embrace.

"My hero," she crooned softly.

They reached the bedroom, and Jack efficiently undressed her then tugged off his T-shirt and slipped it over her head. She purred sensually when the still-warm shirt caressed her body, then rolled over and curled up, falling asleep before he could slip under the covers. Jack had never met anyone who fell asleep so soundly or completely. It was a trait that he found undeniably cute, even on a night like this, when it prevented him from making love to her. He pulled her into an embrace, kissing her face and head, and then settled her against his side as they both fell into a deep sleep.

⌘

Jamie began to wake just as the dawn was beginning to break. Her first sensation was of a tender, languid touch roaming up and down her bare legs. Hands slowly moved to the front and began a slow, teasing dance on her twitching thighs. Slowly she began to gain some semblance of consciousness and began to respond to the touch by gently sliding into it. It was clear that she was not fully awake, but also clear that she was not asleep.

The touch moved up her body to tenderly rub her stomach, sides, breasts and arms. Her T-shirt disappeared, and the touch now encompassed her whole, bare body. Jack was still lying on his side behind her, and she began to move her hips in time with his touch. As she arched her back into him sensually, he turned her so they lay face to face. He began to slowly, teasingly kiss every part of her that he could reach. After a seeming eternity, she was softly moaning and grinding her hips, needing his immediate attention. He responded quickly at this point, slipping into her as she let out a small gasp. They moved together smoothly, and she was happily surprised to find herself once more groaning out her release minutes later.

Jack cuddled her and spoke nonsense words of love into her ear for a few tender moments. The feeling of warmth and contentment overtook her again, and she fell back into a sated sleep.

At 10:00 Jamie pried her eyes open and forced herself to look at the bedside clock. *Wow, I had the strangest dream,* she thought. After a quick physical inspection however, she realized that she had not been dreaming. *God, two times in two days! What's gotten into him? For that matter, what's gotten into me?*

She stretched like a cat, working the kinks out of her body and letting the warm sun caress her skin. All at once a stab of worry hit her. *What's gotten into me is right! We didn't use a condom ... again!* She rolled her eyes at her forgetfulness, then shook her head. *It's too late to worry about it now. Just put it out of your mind,* she instructed herself firmly. *It's highly unlikely that anything will come of it.*

⌘

Late Sunday night, Jamie knocked lightly on Mia's door, smiling when she opened it to find her friend awkwardly giving herself a pedicure. Making a dismissive gesture with her hand, Jamie said, "Relax. I'll take over."

Mia looked at her warily, having a pretty good idea that she was in hot water. "I screwed up, Jamie," she said, getting the matter onto the table immediately. "I don't know why I did it, but I told Cassie about your class. I'm really sorry," she insisted, her warm brown eyes searching Jamie's for signs of forgiveness.

Waving the emery board at her, Jamie's brow knit as she said, "I should still be angry, but the weekend turned out surprisingly well, so you're off the hook."

"It turned out well?" Mia gaped. "I could hear you yelling at Jack all the way in my room. How did you pull a good weekend out of that?"

"I still don't know," she admitted, shaking her head. "All I know is that we had really good sex — twice no less! It must have been from letting out some of the stress that's been building."

"I don't know how you did it, babe, but I'm glad to hear it," Mia grinned. "Just let me know the next time you want me to piss Jack off."

"I'll be in touch," Jamie jibed, adding a sharp poke to Mia's tender ribs.

⌘

By Monday morning, Jamie was still in high spirits, and she received a good bit of teasing from Ryan after the class was over. "May I assume that things got resolved between you and your boyfriend?" she asked, a smile curling the corners of her mouth.

Jamie gave her a smirk and replied, "We definitely made up. I'm not sure that we resolved anything, though. That behavior was so out of character for Jack that I'm just going to assume that he was momentarily possessed."

"Hey, I've got my usual hour free; can I interest you in another bottle of juice or three?"

"Yeah," Jamie replied, "that would be nice." As they walked through the campus, Ryan was pleased to notice that Jamie chattered away non-stop in her usual style. Jamie was first to reach into her book bag and offer to pay for the drinks, so Ryan agreed and picked out a table, watching Jamie struggle to carry the four bottles back.

"I'm not even going to pretend that two of these are for me," she teased.

"Actually, I could drink all four, so you'd better be careful," Ryan replied.

"How do you consume all of the calories you do and stay so thin?" Jamie inquired as she shook her head.

"Well," Ryan said thoughtfully, "I am really active, and then with all of the sweating I do at my job, I find I can eat whatever I want."

"What in the hell do you *do* for a living?" Jamie finally blurted out.

Ryan looked slightly confused as she answered, "I'm a personal trainer.

I told you that." Jamie began to laugh so hard that tears began to roll down her face. She clutched at her sides as she began to rock back and forth in her chair.

"Gee, Jamie, I've had a lot of reactions, but never that," Ryan said confusedly.

"No, Ryan, I'm not laughing at your job," she explained. "You haven't told me what you do for a living, and I let my fertile imagination run wild. I imagined you as some high-priced, lesbian prostitute."

At this unexpected revelation, Ryan threw back her head and roared. But after a few moments she wiped the tears from her eyes and gave Jamie a little half-scowl. "Hey, it just dawned on me that might have been an insult," she said slowly. "Are you saying I look like a prostitute?"

"No! Of course not!" Jamie cried. "But I couldn't figure out why else you would have to time your clients for an hour, potentially have two at a time and be able to take naps in between. And, let's be honest, Ryan, you are great-looking, and I could see women paying for the pleasure of your company."

"Hmm," she said as if contemplating switching jobs. "I wonder how many women share that view? Nah, I'd hate to mix business with pleasure," she finally decided with a good-natured grin.

⌘

The classmates fell into a routine of spending an hour chatting after class before Ryan's biology lab. Within a few weeks, the habit was so ingrained that they didn't even ask each other before they automatically began the short walk to Bancroft Hall.

Every Monday Ryan regaled her friend with tales of her weekend bike rides, always cracking her up with stories of neophyte riders getting helplessly lost on the hilly streets of San Francisco. "I swear, Jamie, sometimes it's like herding cats," she chuckled.

"Why do you do it, Ryan? I mean, surely you could get your training in more efficiently if you rode alone."

"True," the dark woman agreed. "But helping people to experience the ride is more rewarding for me than any increase in my own fitness. It's … I don't know," she said, giving Jamie a shy glance through the shock of black hair that had fallen in her eyes. "It means a lot to me."

"I can tell," Jamie said softly, gripping her friend's hand as their eyes met and held for a moment.

⌘

After having endured weeks of pointed, in-depth questions about the AIDS Ride, and how one prepared oneself for such an undertaking, Ryan looked at her friend one morning in October and finally asked the question. "I can't help thinking that your interest in the Ride has turned from the academic to the practical. I think you want to do it," she said in challenge, knowing that Jamie had a hard time refusing a dare.

"Ryan, I don't even own a bike! I haven't ridden at all since high school, and I wasn't very serious about it even then. The most energetic thing I do is play golf, and as I always say, if you can smoke while doing it, it isn't a sport."

Crossing her toned arms over her equally toned stomach, Ryan just cocked her head and drawled, "Doesn't matter."

"What do you mean it doesn't matter?" Jamie was nonplussed by her friend's casual treatment of such vital issues.

"Doesn't matter. All you have to do is make the commitment — I'll do the rest."

Giving her a seriously suspicious look, Jamie narrowed her eyes and said, "You'll do the rest?"

"Yep. You make the commitment — I guarantee that you can accomplish your goal. Believe me," she said with a rakish grin, "I've worked with less." Her eyes slid up and down Jamie's trim body, openly assessing her. "Yep. A whole lot less."

The thought of spending her weekends in Ryan's company was proving to be a powerful lure, but Jamie couldn't help toss off a comment, "You act like this is the equivalent of a walk in the park."

Suddenly, Ryan's sunny face sobered, and she gazed at Jamie with a look so intent that she froze in place. "I'm not saying it's easy. It's not. But for me, it's one of the most rewarding things I do." She cleared her throat and fidgeted just a bit. Obviously making some sort of decision, she nodded her head briefly and continued. "I lost my dear cousin, Michael, ten years ago to AIDS. He was …" She took a deep breath and struggled to continue. "He was only twenty-seven when he died, Jamie, and I don't have words for the impact of his loss on my family. Any small thing that I can do to stop anyone from going through that pain is worth any amount of sacrifice to me," she said, still fighting to regain her composure.

Jamie sat in respectful silence for a few moments, watching the emotions flicker across the vivid eyes. "When do we start?"

⌘

The pair made their way through the clutter of bicycles in every state of assembly — some just frames, a few fully outfitted and some obviously in need of repair. "Remember, you don't have to spend too much to get a serviceable bike," Ryan intoned.

"Stop worrying about me," Jamie said quietly, shushing her.

Their salesman, an old friend of Ryan's, came back and asked, "Well, which way are you leaning?"

"I want the lightest, fastest thing you can put wheels on," Jamie said decisively. "I also wouldn't mind if you slipped an inconspicuous engine onto it," she added playfully.

"Looks like this is your lucky day, Bill," Ryan said, shrugging her shoulders. "Show us some frames."

"Cute ones," Jamie demanded with a little pout.

"Cute ones," Ryan somberly agreed.

⌘

They left the bike shop a little before noon. "I'm famished," groaned Ryan, theatrically clutching at her stomach. "I've never seen anyone take longer to make a decision about anything."

"I wanted to make sure I got what I wanted," Jamie defended herself. "You're the one who convinced me to have Bill make the bike rather than buy a stock model."

"I would have taken you to a swap meet if I'd known it was going to take so long," she said with a teasing grin.

"Okay, you big baby, I'll buy you lunch. And I know just the place," she said with a wink as they climbed into the Porsche and drove a short distance to her favorite deli.

"Oh, wow," Ryan enthused. "I did not know there was one of these in the East Bay. I go to the main store in the Marina all the time. I absolutely love this place." Her eyes lit up as she licked her lips in anticipation of her meal.

"You really are easy to please," Jamie marveled. While they waited in line at the counter, she reflected that one of Ryan's most appealing qualities was the joy she experienced at the little things life offered. She had an unguarded, childlike exuberance that was truly infectious, and Jamie marveled that she never felt more alive than when she was with her new friend. As she watched Ryan carefully peruse the menu she had to laugh at her. Ryan read every word and changed her mind at least six times while they waited to order. "It's almost our turn, Ryan. Are you able to stick with your decision?"

"You are referring to the highlight of my day, Jamie," she explained patiently. "Lunch is my favorite meal. And since eating is my favorite activity, lunch is no laughing matter."

As Ryan spoke, Jamie began looking through her wallet. "I've only got $47 on me. Do you think that will cover it?" she asked innocently, batting her eyes.

"I'll go easy on you since you're new at this," Ryan drawled, "but next time, don't be so unprepared. A trip to the ATM is always a good idea before you offer to buy me lunch."

After ordering their food, they found a little table outside. The weather was starting to turn, but the table was in the bright noonday sun, so they were quite comfortable even without jackets.

"So," Ryan said after they got settled. "That was some exhibition of buying power. I don't think I've ever seen Bill look so happy. He hasn't made that much from me in seven years."

Jamie twitched in her chair, uncomfortable with having the spotlight on her financial status. "It just made sense to buy the best bike for a ride like this," she explained.

Ryan gazed at her for a moment as if deciding whether to ask a question. Finally, she curled the corners of her mouth up in a small grin and asked, "I don't mean to ask an indelicate question, but are you loaded?"

"Gee, I'm glad that wasn't indelicate," Jamie retorted as she playfully slapped her arm.

Ryan quickly backpedaled when it looked as if her friend was offended. "I'm sorry if I'm prying," she said quickly. "You really don't have to answer that question."

"It's not that, Ryan. I don't mind talking about private things with you, but I get kind of embarrassed by it. I mean, oh, it's hard to explain," she fumbled.

"So 'loaded' is not a strong enough word?" Ryan offered helpfully.

"Not really," Jamie said with a tinge of embarrassment. "More like filthy rich."

"How filthy?" Ryan asked with a leer.

"Obscenely," Jamie flatly stated.

"Wow! I've never been friends with anyone obscenely rich. That's really kind of cool," she admitted with a pleased smile. "Will you pay me to like you? For the right price, I could even be your *best* friend," she teased.

"Very, very funny."

"I feel like I can tease you because you *so* do not seem like a rich kid. If it weren't for your car, and the bike, you'd seem just like me," Ryan observed. "But if you're really sensitive about it, I promise I'll never tease you about it again."

Jamie considered the issue for a moment. Ryan was looking at her with that open, guileless expression that just made Jamie feel like she could trust her with any of her secrets, and she immediately made her decision. "It's okay when you tease me, Ryan. I don't know why, but your teasing never seems to bother me."

"I'm glad you told me, Jamie," she said sincerely as she fixed her with a mesmerizing stare. "It means a lot to me that you trust me to know about your financial status."

"I do trust you, Ryan. I can't imagine that you'll let this get in the way of our friendship."

"No way," she said emphatically. "After all, you haven't let my lesbianism get in the way of our relationship," she reminded her with a dazzling grin.

"I think I'm going to consider your offer to be my best friend," Jamie said thoughtfully after a moment. "How much will it cost me?"

Ryan's eyes grew wide as a server delivered their heaping plates. "Consider yourself paid in full!" she said with a happy grin.

⌘

After plowing through her sizeable lunch, and picking over the remnants of Jamie's, Ryan said, "Now, we need to work out how we will train you for this ride."

"What are our options?"

"Saddle time is critical. There isn't much you can do to duplicate the feeling of actually riding. So, we're going to have to log a lot of miles. But to get the most out of your riding, you have to be in pretty good shape. I don't mean to be rude, but I don't see a lot of muscle lurking under your skin," she said as she reached for an absent bicep.

"Just 'cause I'm not rock hard like you doesn't mean I don't have any muscle," Jamie replied defensively, as she snatched her arm away before Ryan could get a good grip.

"I *am* just teasing, you know," she said with a warm smile. "But the more muscle you have, the more you can demand of your body. So we need to increase your cardiovascular capacity, tone your muscles and ride like crazy. The easiest way to do the first two tasks is at a gym. Do you belong to a club?"

"No, I was going to join one, but I never got around to it," Jamie sighed.

"Well, now's a good time to join. My club has a decent branch in Oakland. Why don't you check it out and see if you like it?"

"I'll stop by on my way home," Jamie smiled. "It took a while to make up my mind to do this, but now that I have — there's no stopping me."

"You're my kinda woman," Ryan grinned back.

Smacking her suddenly dry lips together, Jamie's face grew serious as she said, "Now comes the hard part. Obviously, I'm going to pay you for your time, Ryan. How can we work that out?"

Ryan's eyes grew wide as she shook her head firmly. "I can't charge you, Jamie. I want to do this because you're my friend. It'll be fun for me."

"Ryan, I appreciate that, and I would agree except for one thing. I know how busy you are. I've seen that little black book of yours, you know," she said fondly. "This is how you make your living. If you weren't working with me, you'd be working with a regular client. That is a very significant fact."

"Look," Ryan said, obviously searching for a way to avoid having Jamie pay her. "I don't have any clients here in Oakland. I'm already on this side of the bay, and I can't rush back to the city to work with anyone in the middle of the day. Let me spend an hour with you — as your friend."

Jamie's mind was made up, and — as Ryan was discovering — it was virtually impossible to sway her once she had settled on a decision. "No, I can't do that. Either you train me and accept payment — or I find someone who can. I'm sure there are many trainers who wouldn't mind taking my money."

Knowing that Jamie had her over a barrel, Ryan sighed and acquiesced. "I want to make sure you're trained properly, so … you win."

The blonde head tilted back as Jamie let out a long, loud laugh. "Boy, you're easy!"

Ryan's eyes crinkled up in a matching smile. "That's my claim to fame," she admitted with a lecherous-looking leer.

⌘ CHAPTER THREE

AS PROMISED, JAMIE CHECKED OUT THE EAST BAY BRANCH OF CASTRO Fitness and found that it was perfectly acceptable. It was a fairly serious workout spot with very few amenities, but it was very close to her house — doing away with the need for showers and luxurious locker rooms.

Ryan and Jamie agreed to have their first workout on Friday afternoon. Jamie picked her friend up at their normal meeting place, and they slogged through Friday afternoon Berkeley traffic to reach the gym. They had previously arranged for Ryan to take BART to campus that morning — that way Jamie could drop her off at work before she went to Jack's. As they poked along, a thought occurred to Jamie. "Have you eaten today?" she inquired suspiciously.

"Uhm, not really", Ryan sheepishly admitted. "I did have breakfast, but I haven't had any other breaks today. Why? Is my stomach grumbling?"

"Why didn't you say something?" Jamie asked with an exasperated tone.

"I know you wanted to get moving, and I didn't want to slow you down. I can get something before work. It's really no big deal."

"Oh, please!" Jamie smirked. "The way you eat, missing a meal must be catastrophic to your system! Your poor stomach must be leading a revolt right at this minute."

"It's not that bad," Ryan said as she looked at the site of the possible rebellion. "Although," she patted her stomach as she leaned her head down to listen, "I do hear the faint signs of discord."

Jamie glanced at her watch and shot Ryan an amiable grin. "It's only 2:35 now. If you're due at work by 6:00, we don't have to leave the East Bay until 5:00. We can easily spare an hour for you to eat."

"Gosh, it all sounds so easy when you say it like that," Ryan admitted as she closed her eyes. "I do so love lunch," she purred with pleasure.

As Ryan completed her statement, Jamie looked at the sensual smile on her face and realized with a bit of surprise that Ryan no longer flirted with her. *That's kinda weird. She was so flirty when we met, and now she's just like any of my other friends. I wonder what changed? Maybe she really got the message that I was straight. I guess I should be thankful — it's a lot more comfortable to be with her now. But still ...*

56

"Hey, anybody home in there?" Ryan asked.

"Oh, sorry. What were you saying?"

"I just wondered where you wanted to stop. Now that you brought it up, I have to feed the beast or there will be trouble," she again patted her stomach as she grinned.

"What are you in the mood for? We can get you almost anything around here." Jamie waved her hand at the plethora of restaurants on the surrounding streets.

"Hmm," Ryan's eyes closed in concentration. One eye popped open momentarily as she asked warily, "I can have anything I want?"

"Yep. Anything."

Jamie glanced at the look of intense concentration on Ryan's face and had to smother a laugh, almost able to see the panoply of international dishes floating through her imagination.

Finally, Ryan's eyes opened fully, and she said with barely contained glee, "Chinese."

"Chinese it is," Jamie replied. "And I know just the place."

⌘

Ryan sat with a steaming bowl of hot and sour soup in front of her and a blissful look on her face. "This is divine, Jamie. How do you know so many good restaurants?"

"I like to eat, too, Ryan. Not as much as you do, but I can hold my own. You should get me down to the Peninsula or the South Bay. I think I have been to every restaurant within twenty miles of Hillsborough." She was playing with the salt and pepper shakers, idly moving them around on the Formica tabletop. "My dad was never home for dinner, and my mother loves to try new places, so we cut a swath through the whole area. A place can't be open for more than a week before my mother hits it."

"That could not be more different from my experience. My family doesn't go to a restaurant more than once or twice a year, and that is only under duress," she added.

"You know, Ryan, I really don't know much about your family. Who's at home with you?"

"Well, there's my father, Martin, my oldest brother, Brendan, who doesn't officially live with us, but he's always there for meals, my brothers, Conor and Rory, and me; I'm the baby. Oops, I almost forgot my dog, Duffy. I guess he's really the baby."

"What about your mother?" Jamie asked tentatively.

"My mother is dead," Ryan stated without explanation as she bent her head to concentrate on her soup.

"I'm sorry to hear that," Jamie stated sincerely. She wasn't sure if Ryan wanted to discuss it, but she asked, "Has she been dead long?"

"Yeah." Jamie continued to look at the top of Ryan's head. When her face lifted, Ryan realized that the question was still open, so she elaborated. "Sixteen years in December."

"My God, Ryan, you were just a baby!" Jamie cried with alarm.

Her previously emotionless face eased into a small smile as she demurred, "Well, not quite a baby, but I had just turned seven."

"Oh, Ryan, that must have been devastating for you," she said with sympathy.

Ryan paused for a moment, as if considering the idea. "I don't think devastating covers it, to tell you the truth. Losing your mother changes everything. I don't know if I would be a better or worse person, but I know I would be different if she were still alive," she said thoughtfully.

"How did it happen?" Jamie asked softly.

"She had breast cancer," she replied. After a moment she looked contemplative and continued, "You know, it's funny. She was only thirty years old when she was diagnosed. She had no family history, she was thin, she ate a healthy diet, she had children when she was young and she had good medical care. And she was dead in four years." Her eyes shifted and gazed at Jamie for just a moment, and the smaller woman sucked in a startled breath when she saw the hopelessly lost look that had settled in them.

Jamie wasn't able to say a word. She just reached over and tightly gripped Ryan's hand, looking into her eyes with complete empathy. They sat like that for a few minutes, sharing their feelings with their eyes alone. Ryan had never looked smaller, younger or more vulnerable. Jamie thought her heart would break at the feelings she could plainly see in her friend's eyes. A solitary tear slid down Jamie's cheek, and Ryan reached over somewhat tentatively to wipe it away with a finger.

Ryan sighed as she leaned back in her chair. "Her birthday's coming up soon. That's always a difficult time for me."

"Do you remember her well?" Jamie asked, not wanting to let go of this intimate moment.

"Yeah, I do," Ryan said with a small smile. "She was basically sick from the time I can remember, but she tried so hard to be there for me. I still don't know how she did it." She smiled sadly as she shook her head. "I'm really lucky in that my family talks about her a lot. Although, sometimes I don't know if I really have all these memories or if I remember her through their eyes. I guess it doesn't matter in the end, though," she decided.

"Your father never remarried?" Jamie inquired.

"Remarried!" Ryan laughed. "He's never had a date that I know of. I guess he wasn't much of a catch when we were young. Who wants a man with four wild kids who's away from home for three days at a time?"

"You were left alone that much?" Jamie asked with alarm.

"Well, my dad's a fireman. That's the schedule." She shrugged and said, "It's not as bad as it sounds, though. We have a gaggle of aunts and cousins who all live within walking distance. While my mother was sick, and for the first few years after her death, someone stayed with us when my father was at work. After a while, Brendan was old enough to be in charge. I'm sure it was hard on him, but he never complained," she said reflectively.

"How old are your brothers?"

"Rory's twenty-five, Conor's twenty-seven and Brendan's twenty-nine."

"Are you okay talking about all of this?" Jamie asked gently.

"Yeah, I am with you," she replied with a shy smile as she looked up at Jamie through her hooded eyes. "I don't talk about her much with people outside of the family, but it feels good to talk about it with someone who isn't as invested as we all are."

Jamie smiled at this admission and realized that she was still holding Ryan's hand. She dropped it immediately, only to have Ryan turn her hand and capture Jamie's, reflectively trailing her thumb along the pulse point. "Thanks for caring," she said as they locked eyes.

Their server interrupted the moment as he appeared, carrying plates of pan-fried noodles, Szechwan green beans and stir-fried broccoli with mushrooms.

Ryan smiled and rubbed her hands together as she waited for the plates to land. By the time the server had departed, her chopsticks were ready for action. She dug in enthusiastically as Jamie watched in amazement. She noted that Ryan didn't eat particularly quickly. But once she started, she did not slow down for a moment. She kept up a steady cadence that was not interrupted by unnecessary speech. She paid attention to Jamie, but mostly nodded and shook her head as required. Jamie understood that Ryan needed her mouth to eat rather than talk, so she kept up a running monologue mostly about school and her classes.

After Ryan had finished every bite, she leaned back in her chair in a pleasant, post-prandial haze. Jamie regarded her with a smirk. "Do your brothers eat as much as you do?" she asked.

"More, much more. Dinner time at our house is not for the faint hearted," she admitted gravely.

"I would love to witness that," Jamie laughed.

"That can certainly be arranged," Ryan replied.

⌘

"This place is just fine," Ryan decided. "No frills, no posers."

"I really like it, too," Jamie agreed. "Shall we get to work?" Jamie was wearing an emerald and navy blue sports bra over matching, thigh-length nylon shorts, exposing her completely to Ryan's considered gaze. The brunette's eyes wandered up and down her lithe form for another minute or two. She began to shift nervously, and she finally said, "I feel like a deer in the headlights, Ryan."

"Oh, sorry," Ryan said with a grin. "I was just trying to get an impression of your current musculature."

"It's that bad?" Jamie asked tentatively.

"No, of course not," Ryan assured her. "In fact, you really have a great body. But you could definitely use some more muscle here," she ran her long, cool fingers across both of Jamie's shoulders and down her arms, stopping at her elbows. "And here," another pair of gentle tracings down the front of her thighs. "Now, we haven't talked about this much, but have you thought about whether you really want to change your body?"

"What do you mean?" Jamie inquired warily.

"Nothing bad," Ryan giggled a little at her expression. "It's just that some women don't think it's womanly to show muscle. And some men don't like it, either. I just wondered how your fiancé felt about your looking buff."

Jamie realized that this was the first time they had ever discussed Jack and his proprietary interest in her body. But she was quite sure she did not like the implication. "He doesn't get a vote," she replied firmly. "My body — my choice. Besides, I think women look great with muscles. I think they enhance femininity, as long as they're natural looking." Jamie had a sudden interest in seeing Ryan exposed much as she was. It occurred to her that she had never really seen her muscles, and she briefly wondered what was hiding under her warm ups. *You'd better not go there, Jamie. What was that about being glad she doesn't flirt with you any more?*

"That's great. I'm glad you're comfortable with this. But is there anything you would like to change? I mean, if we can," Ryan added.

"I'm not sure what you mean. Are you saying I get to choose how I change?"

"To some extent, yes," Ryan agreed. "There are certain areas on any body that respond more quickly to weight training. But there is some genetic predisposition that affects the final outcome," she added knowledgeably.

"So, are you saying that you can guess where those areas would be on me?" Jamie quizzed.

"Kind of," Ryan said. "Do you mind my staring at you again?"

"Be my guest," she replied as a warm flush crawled up her cheeks and she tried to adopt a casual pose.

Ryan stood back a step or two and crossed her arms. Once again she stared at Jamie's body, starting at the shoulders and working her way down. "Because of your height, I would guess that large leg muscles would not really look great," she observed. "And I would also guess that your legs and butt tend to get big easily." She gently squeezed the muscles at the middle of Jamie's thighs and nodded her head. "I think your quads could really get big if you liked that look. But if you didn't want that, we would want to work on elongating your muscles there, rather than just making them big."

Next she placed her hands on Jamie's shoulders. "You have a nice deltoid just waiting to come out here." She placed her fingertips loosely on the tops of Jamie's shoulders again and slowly traced her thumbs over the muscles just above her breasts, "And you could develop really nice pecs. If I'm not mistaken," she said as she ran the flat of her hand slowly down Jamie's bare abdomen, starting just under her bra and stopping just above her pubic bone, "you could have killer abs." This she said with a real gleam in her eyes.

"How can you tell that?" Jamie asked thinly as she struggled to replace the saliva in her mouth.

"You hardly have any adipose tissue there. Those muscles are just dying to pop out. Me, on the other hand," she lifted her jacket and her white nylon shirt to expose her tanned abdomen, "I've got a pretty thick layer of fat here. No matter how much I work on my abs, they can't pop out like yours will." As she spoke she grasped Jamie's hand and placed it on the warm body part in question. "Here, feel the difference." Now she placed the hand on Jamie's stomach. "See what I mean?"

Jamie was now fully involved in the exercise. "I do, I really do. Mine feels like just skin covering muscle, but yours is softer." She gave Ryan's stomach a little pat. "But there's some pretty hard muscle right under that — what do you call that tissue again?"

"Adipose tissue. That's trainer talk for fat." she whispered this last word right into Jamie's ear.

This received a chortle from Jamie. "I think your fat is in all the right places, Ryan."

She received a smile and a small laugh in return. "Part of the occupational requirements. Can't have an out of shape trainer."

⌘

They decided to concentrate on Jamie's legs. Ryan spent a good deal of time explaining each exercise, showing her how to use a machine, if one was needed, and guiding her slowly and patiently through each exercise. She kept a little notebook and took careful notes about the weight, number of repetitions and machine settings as they moved along. After an hour, Ryan suggested they stop so that Jamie was not overwhelmed with information. Jamie agreed and shook her tired legs out. "Let me help with that," Ryan offered.

"Okay," Jamie agreed, a bit tentatively.

Ryan grabbed a floor mat and instructed her to lie down on her tummy. She then proceeded to knead each of the muscles with strong, knowing hands. Jamie closed her eyes in pleasure as Ryan's hands worked deeply into her tired muscles.

"Do you do this to everybody?" she asked as she slowly lifted her torso up and rested her weight on her forearms.

"Yeah, pretty much," Ryan replied.

"Then you don't charge nearly enough," she said weakly as she felt herself collapse into a boneless heap on the mat.

Ryan laughed as she offered a hand down to her. "C'mon, jellyfish. They frown on sleeping on the floor." When Jamie regained her feet, Ryan said, "The only bad thing about this place is that there are no showers." She looked at Jamie's sweat-drenched head and clothing. "You really should not drive all the way to Palo Alto in those clothes. I'm afraid you'll stiffen up."

"It's only 4:30. We could go by my house so I could take a quick shower," she suggested.

"I think you should do that," Ryan agreed. "I could just take BART home if you don't want me to come with you," she offered hesitantly.

"Why would I ..." Then Jamie realized what Ryan was getting at. "Are you worried about my roommates?"

"No, I'm not *worried* about them. I just don't want them to hassle you about hanging out with me," Ryan stated quietly.

"Ryan, I am honored to be your friend. Anyone who doesn't like you is not worth my time," she said firmly.

The tanned face broke into an adorable grin. "Thanks, Jamie. That means a lot to me."

"You and your talented hands," she teased, "mean a lot to me."

⌘

Despite her protestations, Ryan was relieved when they entered the house and found it empty. "I'll just sit down here and read, if that's okay," she said.

"Sure. Make yourself at home; I'll only be a minute." Jamie started to walk up the stairs when she winced a little bit. "I think you were right about these babies tightening up," she agreed.

"C'mere for a second," Ryan said. "I can loosen them up again. It's just because you let them get cold too quickly." She directed Jamie to the area rug in the middle of the parlor where Jamie removed her sweats and lay down on the rug. Ryan once again began her strong massage. "After I get these loose, you should stay in a hot shower for a few minutes. Then they should be fine." As Ryan continued to work on her legs, the front door opened and Cassie stared at them in surprise. Ryan dropped the leg she held as if it had burned her and immediately adopted a guilty look. Jamie looked from Ryan's face to Cassie's shocked expression and rolled her eyes.

"Hi, Cassie," she said as casually as the atmosphere allowed.

"Uhm, hi, Jamie. What's going on?" she asked tentatively.

"Ryan and I were at the gym, and my legs stiffened up. She was just loosening them up for me."

"You were at the gym?" she asked with a healthy dose of skepticism.

"Yes, I was at the gym. Ryan is a personal trainer, and she's helping me get in shape for a bike ride," Jamie replied.

"You need a trainer to ride a bike?" Cassie said uncertainly.

Jamie shot a quick glance at Ryan who seemed to have recovered her cool. "This is not just any bike ride, Cassie. Ryan and I are going to do the AIDS Ride together. It's from here to L.A."

Cassie laughed hard at the mere thought. "Jamie, you have got to be kidding. You don't even have a bike."

"I will as of Monday," Jamie replied firmly. "And I'm not kidding. I think it will be a great learning experience for me. Plus, it will give me a chance to really get in shape."

"Why on earth do you need to get in shape? You're very thin as it is," Cassie dismissed.

"I'm not trying to lose weight, Cassie. I'm trying to get fit. There is a difference, you know."

"Okay, why do you need to get fit?" she patiently inquired.

"Well, so I can do this ride," she fumbled, realizing that sounded a little lame.

"Doesn't that logic seem just a teeny bit circular to you, Jamie?"

"No, it doesn't. I really want to do the ride. And I want to be in better shape," she said a bit defensively.

"Whatever," Cassie finally said with a shake of her long, blonde hair. As she began to ascend the stairs she turned and asked, "Aren't you going to see Jack this weekend?"

"Yes, I am," Jamie relied evenly. "As soon as I take a shower, we're leaving."

"Oh, is your friend going?" she inquired sweetly. "I'm sure the three of you will have fun. Or is Jack bringing a … girl friend so you can double-date?"

Jamie laughed a little as Ryan casually picked up her leg and placed it once again on her chest, continuing the massage as if Cassie did not exist, "No, sadly not," she replied just as sweetly.

Without further comment, Cassie turned and quietly took the stairs two at a time. When she was out of earshot, Jamie mumbled, "I wish I lived alone."

⌘

When the massage was finished, Jamie suggested that Ryan wait in the library, so she would be well out of Cassie's way. Ryan followed her into the redwood-paneled, bookcase-lined room, eyes wide with surprise. "I didn't know this room existed," she commented. "I just thought it was a closet or something."

"No, I use this room to study, and I usually keep the door closed. It's nice, isn't it?"

"It is indeed," Ryan murmured, already walking towards the shelves chock-full of books. "Did these come with the house?"

"No," Jamie chuckled. "They're mine."

Ryan whirled to face her. "All of these books are yours?"

"Yep. I have a phobia about throwing a book away. I think one of the reasons my parents wanted me to have a house was so that I'd take my books with me."

"Damn, Jamie, I feel like the village idiot looking at these titles." She pulled one down and hefted it in her hand. "I read the Cliff notes for this one. Something about a whale, right?" she teased.

"Yep. That's the important part," Jamie playfully agreed.

Continuing her slow perusal, Ryan commented, "You have them grouped by author, right?" She shook her head and said, "I don't know crap about literature, but I'm thinking that this must be everything that Fitzgerald ever wrote."

"Yeah," the blonde nodded. "From the time I learned to read, if a book really caught my interest, I couldn't stop until I'd read the author's entire output. It's a habit I've continued." Chuckling, she added, "That's why I've never read a murder mystery. If I read one of Sue Grafton's novels, I'd have to read all twenty-six!"

"Wow," Ryan mused. "My Granny would love you. One of her greatest disappointments has been that not one of us has an interest in Irish literature."

"You've never read Oscar Wilde or James Joyce?"

"Nope. If it wasn't assigned in class, I haven't read it," she admitted, shrugging her shoulders.

"As soon as this term's over, I'm gonna hook you up with some of Wilde's short stories," the blonde decided. "You'd love him."

Ryan took another look at the neatly organized shelves. "This means a lot to you, doesn't it?"

Reflectively, Jamie nodded. "Books were my best friends when I was growing up."

Cocking her head in question, Ryan looked at her friend curiously.

Jamie either didn't see the curiosity in her look, or chose to ignore it. "I'm gonna go jump in the shower. Feel free to read," she teased as she walked out of the room.

⌘

When they were back in the car, Jamie summoned the courage to finally ask, "Why did you act so funny around Cassie?"

"What do you mean 'funny'?" Ryan inquired with just a touch of nervousness.

"I don't know, kind of like you were caught doing something wrong."

After a few minutes of silence, Jamie thought that Ryan was just going to ignore the question. She was almost startled when her deep voice responded, "Do you remember our class discussion on homophobia?"

Jamie wondered how this was the answer to her question, but she knew that Ryan's scientific mind sometimes worked in strange ways. "Yes, I do," she answered.

"We didn't talk about this, but homophobia is not always about straight people being afraid of gay people. There is something called internalized homophobia that you just saw a demonstration of."

"What do you mean, Ryan?"

"I know that Cassie doesn't like me. I assume it is primarily, or exclusively, because I'm gay, right?"

"Uhm, yeah, I guess so," Jamie admitted, "since that's the only thing she knows about you."

"So, I internalized her dislike of me, and when she came in, I felt guilty about being gay. I was holding your leg and rubbing it in a way that probably looked awfully friendly, and I felt like I was caught doing something I shouldn't have been doing."

Jamie somehow found the courage to ask the next question. "Do you have sexual feelings for me, Ryan? Please be honest," she begged.

"No, I don't, Jamie," she said forcefully. "I don't think of you in that way. Although, if you want me to be perfectly honest, I'll admit that I did when we first met." Her eyes shifted to the floor, and she looked profoundly embarrassed to admit to her earlier feelings. "I think of you as a friend. And I don't tend to feel sexual desire towards my friends."

"I'm really glad you admitted to that, Ryan. I'm glad to know my instincts work with women as well as men."

"Oh, no — could you really tell?"

"Uhm, yeah, at first I could," Jamie admitted.

"And that didn't bother you?" she asked, her interest overtaking her embarrassment.

"No. It didn't seem aggressive or anything. Just like you were kind of interested."

"Oh, I was, but when I started to get to know you, I just liked you too much to put you in the potential dating category," Ryan admitted.

"You don't date people you like?" Jamie asked, quite confused.

"It's ahh … complicated," Ryan sighed. "I'll tell you all about my scarred psyche someday, but not today."

"It's a deal," Jamie grinned in agreement. "I'll make a note of it."

As they crossed the Bay Bridge, Jamie asked thoughtfully, "Do you like working at your current gym?"

"Not really, no."

"Why do it then?" she inquired.

"I'd prefer to just work with my individual clients. During my evenings at the gym I only get $15 an hour. Of course, if I train someone, I get my normal $40. But much of the time, I'm just standing around answering questions. Problem is, I really need the money, and I don't have time to try to build my client base right now. So, I'm kind of stuck," she said with regret. "When I was working as a trainer full time, I had a really good client list, but when I started school again, I just couldn't make the time to be available, and I had to give up some of my best clients."

"Would it work better for you to train people in the East Bay?" Jamie asked slyly, hatching a plan in her fertile mind.

"Yeah, I guess it would. I've got some pretty good breaks between classes, and I don't mind starting to work at 5:00 or 6:00 a.m. Maybe I should talk to the manager over there and see what I can scare up," she agreed. "I really hate losing all of my evenings."

"Maybe something will turn up," Jamie said confidently.

⌘

Since she was chronically early, Ryan was usually sitting in her seat when Jamie arrived at class. However, one day Jamie was standing in the back of the room chatting with a young woman named Yvonne when Ryan entered. She made eye contact with Jamie as soon as she came in the door, flashing those incredibly white teeth in a warm grin. Jamie observed her slowly make her way to the front of the room as Yvonne kept up the conversation. She noted that Ryan looked particularly good that day. Her hair was shining, and it bounced against the middle of her back as she walked. She wore an electric blue, crew neck sweater of a very soft-looking wool that clung to all of her generous curves. The sweater covered a white turtleneck that contrasted sharply with her black hair. Well-worn button-fly jeans and shiny, black leather loafers finished her outfit. Her cheeks were rosy from the chill in the air, and she radiated good health and confidence.

Jamie watched as heads turned to regard Ryan. It was obvious from the longing glances that some of the women openly desired her. It was equally obvious that some of them had fulfilled that desire. Ryan stopped for a moment to chat with three women who looked to be in the latter category. She spoke to each of them in a casual, familiar way. She would grace them with a gentle touch or a small pat on the shoulder, giving the impression that she was very much interested in talking with each of them, but that pressing business was calling her away. Jamie watched in fascination as each of the women looked pleased that they had received even this small token of her affection. *God, is she going to plow through the whole class? There are only nine lesbians besides her. If she has gone through three already, that only leaves six. Since this is the fifth week of class, she has to make the other six last for eleven weeks. She might have to have a repeat ... or I suppose she could also date the women who don't like to label themselves lesbians ...*

Jamie was startled from her reverie by Yvonne gently poking her in the ribs. "Oh, no, not you, too!" she laughed.

"What?" Jamie inquired, truly puzzled.

"You don't have O'Flaherty Fever, too, do you?"

"What? Oh, no, no, *no!*" Jamie finally got out. "Ryan and I are friends — just friends. I've just never seen her walk into class. Does that happen every day?"

"Yep," Yvonne replied. "That's why I sit in the back. It's the most entertainment I get all day," she laughed. "She really is a player," she said with admiration in her voice.

"Yeah, I guess she is," Jamie replied with a good bit of disapproval. As she spoke, she turned towards Ryan and saw one of the women who had declared that she didn't like to be labeled as lesbian or bisexual approach cautiously. She saw Ryan's eyes light up and watched her whole body language change. Ryan drew the woman in by leaning back against the desk. She was obviously speaking softly, because the woman had to move in closer and closer to hear her. Once she had her where she wanted her, she sat on the edge of her desk and leaned dangerously close to the woman. Her smile turned a bit feral as she then leaned back again and regarded her prey. She smiled broadly and removed a business card from her back pocket. *Wasn't that handy! She must have them printed by the thousands.* She scribbled something on the back — *Probably her pager number* — and handed it to the beaming woman as she gave her hand a gentle squeeze.

Is no woman safe? Jamie screamed in frustration to herself.

⌘

After class, they made their way to Bancroft Hall, as was their habit. Ryan noticed that Jamie was not her usual talkative self, but she passed it off as a bad mood. After Ryan purchased a few bottles of juice, she returned to the table to find Jamie looking at her with an expression that could only be described as a glare. "What'd I do?" she asked with a plaintive tone.

"Oh, I'm sorry, Ryan," she said quickly, while shaking her head. "You didn't do anything. I'm sorry if I look as though you did," she apologized.

"Are you sure there's nothing wrong?" Ryan asked, genuinely concerned. She searched Jamie's eyes and found that her friend was having a hard time meeting hers. "C'mon, Jamie, you can tell me," she urged.

"No. It's really stupid, and I feel like an idiot," she sulked.

"I've never seen you do anything stupid or idiotic," Ryan said seriously. "If something is bothering you, I really would like to help if I can."

"Okay, okay, you win," Jamie finally gave her a small smile. "Last week you told me that you didn't date people you liked. Why?" she asked plainly.

"That's certainly not where I thought we were going," Ryan admitted. She paused for a moment as she looked at Jamie carefully. Finally she tilted her head and locked her gaze onto Jamie's eyes. "If that's your question, why do you look angry with me?"

Jamie hated the way Ryan's mind worked. She could always see through ancillary issues and hone right in on the crux of the matter. "All right, I'll confess," she finally admitted with a large measure of frustration in her voice. "It bothered me to watch you come into class today." Ryan looked at her blankly, clearly at a loss. "You were talking to some of the women and flirting with others. Well, you were flirting with all of them. It made me think about what you said the other day, and it just pissed me off. I think you're really depriving yourself of something by dating so many people." Even to her own ears this sounded incredibly lame.

"So, you're angry with me because I don't have a steady girlfriend?" Ryan asked slowly, clearly trying to understand but not having an easy time of it.

"I told you it was stupid," Jamie said, clearly flustered. "I don't know why it bothered me, but it really did. I'm sorry, Ryan. I know it's none of my business. You seem perfectly happy, and it's stupid for me to want something for you that you don't seem to want."

"Would you like me to explain why I don't have a girlfriend?" Ryan asked quietly, her eyes never leaving Jamie's.

"If you want to," Jamie said with just a hint of a pout showing.

"I'm happy to, Jamie. It's like this. I have been focused on earning money and going to school for over four years now. My time is very valuable to me, and I don't like giving too much of it to anyone. I have to work really hard to get all of my schoolwork in during my limited free time. I can't afford the distraction that a relationship would cause. Plus, since I live at home, I can't comfortably bring women home. And I get a ton of shit from my brothers when I stay out all night," she smiled a bit at this. "Sometimes it's like living with three maiden aunts."

"But is it fair to the women that you date?" Jamie asked as she got to the question that was really bothering her.

Ryan leaned back in her chair and considered the question for a moment. Jamie detected a momentary flash of hurt pass across her face. She pursed her lips together and blew out a breath as she softly replied, "I get it now. You think I lead them on, don't you?"

She truly did not want to hurt her friend's feelings, but she was in too deep to stop now. "Ryan, you should have seen their faces. They all looked so hopeful," she finally blurted out.

"Jamie, I swear, I have never led anyone on. I always, and I do mean always, tell women that I am not in the market for a relationship. I'm obnoxiously up front with them."

"Maybe so," Jamie said thoughtfully. "But they all looked like they hoped they would be the one to change your mind. Like the woman who was talking to you at your desk," she added as she looked down at the floor.

Ryan waited until Jamie raised her eyes and met hers again. While she waited, she wondered, *Why does this bother her? I could see that she'd want me to be happy, and I can understand that she doesn't want me to use people. But why be angry about it?* "Today was a perfect example. Blair came over and asked me if I wanted to have lunch. I know she hangs out with Lisa and Amy, so I knew she would know quite a bit about me."

"Who are Lisa and Amy? And why would that tell her anything about you?"

"They're in our class," she explained patiently.

"Do you know everyone's name?"

"Well, yeah," she admitted, looking mildly embarrassed. "I make it a habit to observe people and learn their names. Then I figure out who knows who. It makes things easier for me."

"Okay," Jamie replied as she took a breath. "I assume you've *dated* Lisa or Amy?" She pronounced dated about the same way she would have said molested.

Ryan shot her a look that was far from happy. Her voice took on an edge as she replied, "I tried to *date* Amy. We went out for coffee during the first week of class. I told her that I would love to take her out, but that I didn't have room in my life for a girlfriend. She asked me a few questions to make sure I was serious, and when she was satisfied that I was, she didn't want to go out with me. I did not have sex with her, Jamie. I didn't touch her," she added with a bit of a scowl.

Realizing that she had offended her friend, Jamie reached across the table and placed a hand on Ryan's arm. "I'm sorry," she said quietly. "I shouldn't be prying into your personal life."

Ryan's dark head shook, and she gazed at Jamie for a moment, obviously trying to order her thoughts. "It's okay," she said. "I'm just a little sensitive about my dating habits."

"Hey, I don't want to make you uncomfortable," Jamie insisted. "Let's just drop it."

"No, I don't want to," Ryan said, her eyes locked on Jamie's. "The bottom line is that I try my best to make sure the women I date know that I'm not in the market for a relationship. The problem is that sometimes doing that makes me sound like I'm really full of myself."

"And you're not?" Jamie asked teasingly.

Ryan's face twitched into a wide grin. "Well, maybe just a little."

Giving her another little pat, Jamie said, "Seriously, I'm really impressed with how honest you've been with women. I admire that about you."

A small smile finally graced Ryan's features. "You know, even if I wasn't honest, word does travel fast in the community. And there is not one woman in the Bay Area who can honestly say that she was my girlfriend."

"Not one?" Jamie was shocked at this revelation.

"Nope. Not one."

"I find that nearly impossible to believe!" Jamie struggled with this information. "Have you never met anyone that you would like to build something with? Are you that picky?" she asked incredulously.

"I guess I am incredibly picky," Ryan admitted a little sheepishly. "But I do occasionally find someone that I really like. When that happens, I try to make her into a friend."

"Like me?" Jamie asked tentatively.

"Exactly," Ryan agreed.

"So, you just have what … one night stands?" she asked hesitantly.

"No, Jamie," she smiled. "I sometimes even have a meal or go to a movie with a woman. I like the companionship of women even when they're vertical. I'm a homophile as well as a homosexual," she said pointedly.

"Homophile?"

"Yes. That's a person whose primary attraction is to persons of her same sex. The attraction is distinct from the sexual aspect."

"So, you do see the same person more than once?"

"Sure," she said with a little shake of her head. "I'll continue to see someone until I think she's getting too serious. Then I back off."

"Have you ever met anyone that you liked who didn't want to get serious?"

"Yeah, I have a few, uhm … buddies," she said, staring at the table.

Jamie noticed her discomfort and decided she had to find out what was behind it. "What do you mean by 'buddies'?" she asked with a sly grin.

"Uhm, there's kind of a term for people who just sleep together."

"What's the term?" Jamie persisted.

"Ah … fuck buddies?" Ryan finally revealed.

"Fuck buddies, huh? I must admit I've never heard that one. Do you have a fuck buddy, Ryan?" she asked with a gleam in her eyes.

"Yep, I have a couple of people that I see occasionally for, uhm …"

"Sex?" Jamie helpfully supplied.

"More or less," she admitted.

"So, these are women who feel like you do about relationships?"

"Exactly. They want the same thing that I do — occasional sex and nothing more."

"Do you see these people very often?"

"It depends. I guess I usually see each of them three or four times a year. But I see my friend, Ally, more than that. We might see each other three or four times in a two-week period, then we might not see each other for three or four months. I really like her, and we get along great in bed, but it's clear we'll never be together permanently. I think we're too much alike," she admitted.

"But you're missing so much by never letting anyone get close, Ryan," she continued to argue.

"Like what?" Ryan replied, sounding truly curious.

"Like intimacy and caring and a depth of feeling that you can't get from casual dating." Jamie was beginning to get frustrated again.

"There's nothing casual about the way I date," Ryan said with a little leer.

"Do you really not understand what I'm getting at?" Jamie moaned as she dropped her head into her hands.

"No, I think I do, Jamie," she reassured her. "I want all those things, too. Just not now. And given that I don't feel that I can commit to one woman, what would you have me do?"

"I don't know, Ryan. It just seems unfair to the women who want more of you and to yourself."

"On one level, you may be right, " she replied thoughtfully. "But I don't feel that I'm going to be ready for another couple of years. Are you really suggesting that I should be celibate for that long?"

"How long have you gone?" Jamie asked, raising an eyebrow.

"Does it count when I had broken ribs?" she asked hopefully.

"No. I want the able-bodied record."

"Hmm, I guess about two weeks or so during finals," she finally replied.

"Two weeks! Do you mean to tell me you have not gone without female companionship for more than two weeks in your adult life?" Jamie was truly floored.

"I love women, Jamie. I *really* love women. I love meeting them. I love talking to them. I love the chase. I love it when they want to play the game as much as I do. I love pleasing them. I love having someone new all the time. I am never, ever bored," she confessed. "How many women can say that?" she asked in a plaintive challenge.

"I agree that your sex life is exciting, Ryan. But who do you confide in? Who do you feel completely comfortable with? Who do you know will always be there for you?"

"Uhm, well … you, Jamie," she said with a completely open and trusting expression on her face. "I feel comfortable with you. I confide in you. I know you'll be there for me. I don't have to have sex with you to feel that, do I?" she asked guilelessly.

"Oh, Ryan, that is so sweet," she said as she threw her arms around her neck and gave her a firm hug. "You never cease to surprise me."

"I do my best," she replied with a grin as she reached out and affectionately tousled Jamie's hair.

⌘

On Monday afternoon Jamie entered the gym, rubbing her hands together as she scouted the crowd. "Ah, potential patsies," she enthused. She watched each of the women carefully from her position on a treadmill. Finally, she spotted one woman who looked both well off and clueless. Jamie hopped off the treadmill and positioned herself next to the confused woman. "Do you need help?" she asked gently.

"Oh! Well, I suppose I do," the woman agreed. "I had someone explain this machine to me last week, but now I've forgotten how to adjust it."

"I get confused, too," Jamie admitted. "That's why I've started to work with a trainer," she said conspiratorially.

"A trainer, huh? They tried to get me to sign up with one when I first came here, but I didn't really like the woman who works here at this time of day," she said.

"Why don't you try mine?" Jamie inquired casually. "I'm certain you would like her. Everyone does. She's normally down on the Peninsula, but she's devoting a few days a week to her clients in the East Bay now. She is simply fabulous." She uttered this last statement as she produced Ryan's business card, a supply of which she had stolen when Ryan wasn't looking.

"Is she really expensive? I don't want to spend a lot," she replied.

"Oh, she's terribly expensive!" Jamie moaned. "It's absolutely highway robbery! But she's so wonderful that she can get away with it." If there was one thing Jamie was sure of, it was that rich people loved to moan about how much things cost. But they also loved to overpay for everything that was trendy. "She charges me $125, but I heard that her rates are going up again! I'm going to have to hock my Porsche if she charges me much more. I see her three times a week now, and it really adds up."

"Wow, that really is a lot. Do you really think it's worth it?"

Jamie leaned in and whispered, "After I had my second child, I ballooned up like you wouldn't believe! Ryan's really whipped me into shape. I went to a benefit last week in a sleek little Dolce & Gabbana sheath. I got more attention in that dress than I knew how to handle. My entire body has changed since I started to work with Ryan. I think she's worth three times what I pay her," she confided. "But don't tell her that!" she added with a hearty laugh.

"I have my fifteen year college reunion coming up this spring. If she could get me in shape for that, I'd be eternally grateful."

"That's the attitude!" Jamie enthused. "Your classmates will think you've found the fountain of youth!"

"If you're old enough to have two kids, you must have found it, too," she mused.

"Ha! Before Ryan, people thought I was in my late thirties!"

The woman's eyes grew wide and she said, "Give me her number! Now!"

⌘

After two more visits to the club, Jamie had filled all of Ryan's afternoon time slots. Now all that was left was to tell Ryan that she could quit her other club.

After class on Friday, they sat at their usual spot and sipped their juice. "Uhm, Ryan," she started nervously, "I've been interfering in your personal life." She glanced down at the ground, seemingly in shame.

"You didn't find me a steady girlfriend, did you?" she asked with a mock scowl.

"No, nothing like that. Remember when you said you would rather work on this side of the bay?" she asked with a little smile.

"Yeah," Ryan slowly drawled.

"Did you mean that?" another little smile.

"Yeah."

"Well, then, you should call and quit your old job. 'Cause you're gonna be way too busy to get there."

"Repeat?" Ryan asked, eyes wide.

"I filled all of your available afternoon hours — with private clients," she said, swallowing nervously.

Ryan continued to look at her with a quizzical little smile on her face, so Jamie launched into her sales pitch. "I found one woman who just had a baby and is trying to get back into her old clothes; one guy who hurt his back and needs to build up his muscles so he doesn't re-injure it; a woman who's working for a big law firm and has started to get flabby from sitting too much; an older woman who's worried about getting osteoporosis; a woman who wants to look great for her high school reunion; and a mother-daughter team who want to work together. I gave them a discount — to $100 each." She looked up at Ryan, seeking approval. "Is that okay?"

Ryan's eyes went even wider, but since she didn't immediately answer, Jamie continued. "The last guy is a police officer. He wants to compete in some fittest cop thing, but he doesn't want anyone he works with to know he's working out. Only problem is that he can only do it at 6:00 a.m." Her smile brightened and she said, "But he's three days a week!"

The silence went on for quite a while as Ryan continued to stare at her with a slightly open mouth. "Well, gosh. I was working at a place I didn't like, making no money, working bad hours when I was tired, having no social life and it forced me to drive my bike through rush hour traffic every afternoon. You found me a job where I work a third of the hours for about ten times the money, during the hours I like and I get my evenings back. I guess you did okay," she stated neutrally. After a moment her eyes grew playful. She rose from her chair and stood towering over Jamie. "You know what I have to do, don't you?" she inquired sternly.

"N ... n ... no," replied Jamie, a little afraid of Ryan's reaction to her meddling.

"This," she said as she placed her large hands around Jamie's small waist and effortlessly lifted her to her feet. Ryan gazed at her in wonder, leaned close and gave her chaste kisses on each cheek, which were followed by a very large, very expressive, full-body hug. "That is the nicest thing anyone has ever done for me, Jamie," she whispered in her ear as tears formed in her own eyes. "I don't know how to thank you," she added hoarsely.

Jamie's eyes drifted shut as she relaxed completely into the tender hug.

She would have been content to stay just that way for the rest of the day, but Ryan finally released her. "I have to admit I had selfish reasons," Jamie said, a bit choked up herself. "I wanted you to be available to go on some evening bike rides with me. I actually heard about some hot ones on Mt. Tam," she winked.

"Mt. Tam?" Ryan blinked. "Where did you hear about the rides on Mt. Tam?"

"When I picked up my bike, I decided to buy a nice, used, mountain bike, so I could take it to school and not worry about it. Bill happened to mention that I should have you take me with you some Friday night."

"We'd better get to work if you want to do those, kiddo. That's where the big girls go," she declared.

"You're a big girl; can't I go with you?" Jamie inquired saucily.

"I'll take you anywhere you want to go, Jamie, anywhere at all." Ryan's face was deadly serious as she locked her eyes onto Jamie's smiling face.

⌘

The next time they worked out together, Ryan was showing Jamie some lower back exercises. "Hey, I know these," she grinned. "I had to do all of these when I was on the golf team in high school."

"You were on the golf team?" Ryan asked with interest. "That's pretty cool. You know, I have never hit a golf ball."

"Well, we're just gonna have to remedy that, missy," Jamie replied. "I'd love to do something that I can beat you at," she laughed.

At the end of their session, Jamie sat down on a bench to dry off and watched Ryan making notes in a little booklet. "Here, Jamie, I made this for you," she said as she thrust the book in Jamie's direction.

Inside the little, leather, loose-leaf book, Jamie saw each of the exercises they had covered neatly named and described. On the leg exercises, the position of the seat and the adjustment of the bars were also annotated. Under each description was a series of columns which indicated the date, time, number of reps and sets. And there was one column where Jamie was supposed to indicate how she felt when she began to exercise, on a scale of one to ten. Jamie was absolutely charmed, and her face reflected this. "Ryan, this is so thoughtful," she enthused.

"Jamie, that is the very, very least I can do for you after all you've done for me," she said sincerely.

"I like to take care of my friends, Ryan."

"Then I am very lucky to be counted in that number," Ryan replied. As she said this, she slid behind Jamie on the bench and began to knead her shoulder muscles. She worked on her for about five minutes, until Jamie was dropping her head forward in relaxed bliss.

"God, you're good at that. Those hands should be registered with the government," she sighed.

"Well, they are, kind of. I do have a license to do this," she stated.

"You are a masseuse, too?" she asked incredulously.

"Yep, these babies are trained and licensed," she held up her hands with a proud smile. "When I was taking classes to be a personal trainer, I just figured I might as well be as fully trained as possible. I'm glad I did it. I really learned a lot about relaxing people after a tough workout. And it's a skill that comes in handy in my private life, too," she grinned rakishly.

"Well, you've certainly relaxed me. I don't think I can move, much less ride my bike home," she moaned.

"I've got my bike here; let me give you a ride home," Ryan offered. "After you take a shower, we could get a bite to eat and then you could drive back to get your bike."

"That sounds mighty appealing," Jamie agreed. "But are you sure you're willing to risk the wrath of Cassie if she's at home?"

"Yeah, I am. She just caught me off guard last time. I'm ready for her now." She rubbed her hands together in a menacing fashion as she narrowed her eyes.

⌘

After Jamie showered, she came back downstairs to find Ryan sound asleep on the small loveseat. Her long legs dangled off the end, but her ungainly position didn't seem to bother her in the least. Jamie sat down in the upholstered chair next to the couch and just watched her for a few moments. Ryan was remarkably still as she slept, and Jamie was struck by the thought that she had never seen her when she wasn't in motion. Ryan was usually very active, sometimes a little hyperactive. Even when her body wasn't moving, Jamie could almost see her quick mind processing things. She again marveled at how peaceful and open her face was in repose. Ryan rarely looked severe, but she often had a cool, composed expression on her face. Watching her chest rise and fall, Jamie found herself mesmerized by the full, pink lips, slightly parted in sleep. Suddenly she felt an overwhelming urge to place a kiss on those soft-looking lips, barely resisting the urge with a violent shake of her head. *Get a grip for God's sake, Jamie! Where in the hell did that urge come from?* She sat in the chair for several more minutes mulling over the conflicting thoughts in her head. *Maybe I just feel protective of her. She has such a confident exterior, but now that I've seen her vulnerability, it just makes me feel so tender towards her. When she sleeps she just looks like the little girl who lost her mom. Yes,* she decided, *that's the part that makes me want to kiss her. She looks so sweet, just like a child,* she thought fondly. An impudent voice asked, *Yeah, and how many little girls have you ever wanted to kiss?* Finally deciding that she would not resolve this jumble of thoughts tonight, she quietly moved over to the couch. Leaning over, she gently placed her hand on Ryan's shoulder and gave her a tiny shake.

Ryan was awake immediately and amazingly seemed fully alert. Jamie was surprised at this response, and her face must have shown it. Ryan detected the startled look and asked, "What's wrong? Was I asleep too long?"

"No, no, I was just amazed at how quickly you woke up," she explained.

"Oh, that's from years of practice," she said easily. "I need about eight hours of sleep, but I only get around six on a good night. I've trained myself to sleep almost anywhere, whenever I have a few minutes down time."

"That's truly amazing," Jamie marveled.

"Not really. You can train your body to do a lot of things if you really need to."

"I'm just glad you felt comfortable enough here to be able to sleep."

"Well, I do feel very comfortable around you, but truthfully, I can sleep almost anywhere. I can even sleep pretty well sitting up in a chair. And once I got a good fifteen minute nap while leaning against a wall," she stated proudly.

"You're just full of obscure talents, aren't you?" she teased as she leaned over and ruffled her bangs.

"And you haven't seen half of 'em," Ryan grinned in response.

⌘

Over dinner Jamie asked, "So, what's on your agenda for the weekend?"

"Ooo, the weekend," Ryan said with pleasure. "I haven't had a weekend free in years. This new level of freedom is going to take some getting used to," she said with a happy expression on her face. "This is the nicest quandary I've ever had," she allowed.

"Why don't you come down and ride with me on Saturday?" Jamie offered. "You could see the Peninsula and maybe help me pick out some good rides."

"Is that really a good idea, Jamie?" she asked slowly. "I mean, wouldn't Jack mind?"

"Why would he mind?" she asked, a little confused. "He'll be studying, and he doesn't ride a bike, anyway."

"No, uhm, I mean," she stammered, "I thought he wasn't very happy about having me around ... at all."

"No, Ryan, that's not true. He was mad at me for not telling him things that he thought were important. I don't think it had anything to do with you personally," she lied.

"If you're sure," Ryan said slowly, "I would enjoy coming down. It might be nice to see a different part of the bay. And I have heard about some really great rides down there."

"Then it's settled," Jamie agreed. "Oh, but how will you get your bike down there? Should I pick it up from you on Friday?"

"No, I can get it down there. I can borrow my father's truck if I need to. When do you want to meet?" she asked as she grabbed her ever-present organizer.

CHAPTER FOUR

"CASTRO FITNESS CENTER, THIS IS ALLY SPEAKING."

"Hi, Ally, guess who." Ryan said, dropping her voice into its lowest, sexiest register.

"Hmm," she mused playfully, "is this a really hot brunette, six feet plus, legs for days?"

"Yeah," she purred.

"Huh. I don't know anybody like that. Wish I did, though. Who are you, anyway?" she asked, just barely able to keep from laughing.

"I'm just a lonely woman looking for a little companionship," Ryan said, trying to sound innocent. "Do you know anyone who might be free on Friday night?"

"Friday night? You actually want to see me on a Friday night?" she asked incredulously. "I thought you were only allowed out of the house in the afternoons."

"I've had a change of schedule," Ryan announced dramatically. "My weekends are now my own."

"Really? You haven't had a weekend off in all the time I've known you." Now Ally's voice took on a sexy timbre. "Do you have any idea how to ... fill ... a weekend?"

"That's where you come in," Ryan said, her voice nearly a growl. "You always fulfill my needs."

"Best offer I've had all day," she replied. "Wanna go out or stay in?"

"I can go out with anyone," Ryan said in a dangerously low tone. "I want to stay in with you."

"Friday night. I'll be home by 6:00. Bring dinner with you, hot stuff, 'cause you're not leaving until Saturday."

⌘

Ryan buzzed over to Castro on Friday night, thinking about Ally. They met shortly after Ryan had graduated from high school, while she was taking classes to become certified as a personal trainer. Ryan lucked into a job at Castro Fitness, where Ally had been working for a few months.

Ryan was just starting to feel comfortable with her lesbian identity, after having spent the previous year engaged in some very risky behavior. After Ryan accepted a date with one of the other trainers, Ally — whom Ryan was certain had barely noticed her — approached her and brought up a stunningly personal topic. "Listen, Ryan," she had told her, "I heard about who you're going out with this weekend, and I just have to give you a heads up. I know you're very popular, but you can't run around and be wild with everyone you meet. Some of the people you're hanging with haven't been very careful, and I'm sure that they're carrying some form of sexually transmitted disease. I know it's a drag, but if you're going to hang with that crowd, you've got to use safer sex practices every time you play."

"But the chance of contracting AIDS isn't very high for women having sex with women," Ryan had defensively replied.

"No, it's not very high, but any chance is too high. You're seventeen years old, Ryan. Don't risk cutting your life short just to get a little action. Besides, AIDS isn't the only thing to worry about. I guarantee you'll contract a venereal disease within six months if you haven't already. Herpes and condyloma are permanent, and no matter how attractive you are, your popularity will hit the skids if you have lesions or warts on your fun parts."

The slightly younger woman had blushed deeply as she admitted, "I haven't been out very long, Ally. I don't really know how to have safer sex. No one I've been with has mentioned it."

"Come over to my house tonight after 8:00, and I'll show you everything you need to know," Ally had generously offered.

Ryan laughed when she thought about how easily she had succumbed to Ally's charms. They had spent that first evening at Mission Vibes, a woman-oriented sex toy shop in the Mission district. Ally explained all of the sex toys and latex barriers that Ryan could use and explained how to keep the toys clean. Then, to make sure that her student understood everything perfectly, they had gone back to Ally's apartment and tried out every item in her little bag of tricks. By the next day, Ryan was terribly sore, but very well trained in the science of safer sex. She also had a massive crush on the older, more worldly woman.

To Ryan's regret, Ally made it clear that she was not in the market for a girlfriend. She continued to date anyone who caught her eye, and she never made an attempt to hide her lovers from Ryan. Even though her feelings were bruised, Ryan finally came to understand that Ally was never going to return her affections. With difficulty, she began to think of her as an occasional sex partner, and as long as she kept it very casual, Ally was always willing to spend a day or two with her.

Their normal pattern was to see each other quite a few times in a two or three week period. But as soon as things started to get too intense, Ally would back off. After three or four months had passed they would then start up for another round.

They sometimes went to a club or a bar, and one year they went to Gay Pride Weekend together. But they generally just got together for incredibly good sex. Ryan had never met anyone who had her number quite like Ally did. She wasn't entirely sure what the chemistry was — perhaps it was because they had slept together so many times, but there was something about Ally that just drove her wild. The intense attraction had always puzzled Ryan, since Ally was not really her type.

Ryan generally liked women who were a few inches shorter and fairly slight. She wasn't sure why, but she liked being bigger and stronger than her dates. Ally, however, was not only Ryan's equal in the size department, she was the only woman that Ryan had ever been with who could pick her up — easily. Ally did it a lot, too, sometimes just to show Ryan who was boss. It always took Ryan by surprise, since Ally was just a little bit taller, but she was incredibly strong, being a competitive body builder.

Ryan definitely found Ally attractive, but in a very androgynous fashion. She wore her dark brown hair very short, and half the time, it stuck straight up like a crew cut. Ryan loved how the bristly little hairs felt on her naked body, and Ally always managed to rub her head against some sensitive body part during their play.

Her mind wandered from one sensual memory to another, and as she waited to purchase carryouts, the counterman had to reach over and tug on her jacket to catch her attention. Forcing herself to concentrate, she parked her bike about a block from Ally's building and immediately felt her pulse begin to pick up. She didn't often get nervous when she went on a date, having learned a long time ago that a lot of great-looking women were absolute duds when you had to spend an evening with them. But she knew Ally well, and she knew what to expect — as much sex as she could handle — and just a little more.

After her first year of experimentation, Ryan had established herself as the dominant partner in nearly every liaison that she had. She liked — actually, she needed — to control the action. But she never got to do that with Ally. Even though she was only two years older, Ally had always treated Ryan like she was young and inexperienced. The larger woman controlled the entire evening, and Ryan had learned that if she wanted to keep their connection going, she had to allow her friend to be in charge.

Running up the stairs to Ally's third floor unit, Ryan buzzed the door and waited patiently when she heard her walking around inside. Ally opened the door with her portable phone in hand, blew Ryan a kiss, and indicated that she should go into the kitchen and get dinner organized.

Ryan was just finishing putting everything on plates when Ally snuck up behind her and enveloped her in a big bear hug. She snuggled her face against Ryan's neck as she held her tightly around the waist. "I've missed you, sugar," she whispered in her ear.

Ryan felt a chill start at that lucky ear and travel all the way down to her toes, while she giggled girlishly. She loved the soft, southern accent that her friend had not been able to shake, even though she had moved to San Francisco from Chapel Hill, North Carolina over eight years earlier. Ryan was ready to be released, but Ally held on just a bit longer, mainly to let her know she was still on top. Ryan turned in her embrace and lifted her head just an inch to brush her lips against her friend's silky, soft mouth.

One of the things that Ryan loved best about Ally was the contrast between her external demeanor and appearance, and the soft, warm, womanly curves that were hidden under her workout clothes. Ally had rather large breasts and a delightful curve to her hips that Ryan loved to run her hands over. To Ryan's appreciative eyes, her external toughness just accentuated the hidden treasures that she loved to indulge in. "I've missed you, too, Ally," she said sincerely.

"How long has it been?" Ally stepped out of Ryan's embrace and reached around to pick up a french fry and toss it into her mouth.

"I was thinking about that on the way over," she said. "I think it was right after the AIDS Ride. I remember that my legs were stiff when I came over and that they stayed that way for another week thanks to you."

"You know I never guarantee not to bruise the merchandise," she purred as she backed Ryan up against the table. Ryan slid her arms around Ally's neck and allowed herself to be thoroughly kissed. Those big strong hands held her tightly around the waist as Ally worked on her mouth with a methodical intensity. She pulled back slowly and chuckled a bit as Ryan kept her arms twined around her neck, eyes tightly closed. "Aren't you hungry, sweet pea?" she asked softly.

Ryan mutely nodded, eyes still closed, lips slightly parted.

"You look like you're hungry for some love," Ally purred, bending to lavish another round of heated kisses on Ryan's hungry mouth.

Ryan couldn't stop a low groan from escaping as her mouth was claimed ravenously by her friend.

"Come on, sugar baby," Ally said softly as she pulled away from the embrace. "I need to keep my strength up to handle you all night long."

As they ate, Ryan reflected that their conversations centered almost entirely on working out, weight training and acquaintances that they had in common. Ally usually asked her a few questions about school, but it was clear that she did so to be polite. They hardly shared an interest in anything, Ryan mused. A Wynona Judd CD was playing quietly in the background, as if to highlight one area of difference. Ryan liked to listen to world music, with a particular fondness for Afro-pop or contemporary Irish artists, while Ally never varied from Wynona, Shania, Reba and Faith. Her apartment was devoid of personal mementos and books, the only reading material being fitness magazines.

Ally came from a big family, and she had left home almost immediately upon graduating from high school. She had been having sex with women since she was fifteen, but her orientation was a secret until an older brother caught her with another girl when she was a senior in high school. Her family made life nearly unbearable for her that last year, and she took off as soon as she could. After she left North Carolina, she maintained a relationship with one of her sisters who had also left home for good, but that was it. She had never been back home, and she had no contact whatsoever with her parents. Ryan was not even sure if her parents knew where she lived. She knew that there must be a lot of pain hidden behind her friend's sunny demeanor, but they never talked about it. Ally really preferred to dwell on current issues, and Ryan had decided long ago that she needed to honor her need for privacy if she wanted to maintain the relationship.

Perhaps because of her family situation, Ally also never inquired very deeply into Ryan's home life. She knew that Ryan lived at home, since they could never go there for a date, but she rarely asked after the rest of the O'Flaherty clan. Their relationship almost seemed to exist outside of their normal lives. Ryan mused that perhaps they got along so well because their relationship was untainted by any of the day-to-day issues that could have caused tension. There was clearly only one focus, and after five years, that focus seemed enough for both of them.

"So, tell me what's caused the change to your schedule." Ally said as she picked up Ryan's now-empty plate and carried it into the kitchen.

"I'm switching over to the East Bay location," Ryan began as Ally came back into the room and sat down right next to her on the couch. Her friend casually draped an arm around her shoulders and pulled her close, and Ryan smiled demurely as she automatically snuggled up against Ally's side. "Well, actually, a friend arranged the switch for me," she admitted, just to be accurate. "I'm gonna work exclusively with private clients, which is really a godsend." She smiled and revealed, "I'm gonna be making more money than I thought possible. I'm pretty jazzed."

"Huh. You just had a bunch of private clients fall into your lap? That's odd."

"No, no, my friend set me up. She got me seven new clients — I'm gonna see them for a total of fifteen hours a week. Cool, huh?"

"Is she as good a lay as she is a pimp?" Ally chuckled. "If she is, wanna share?"

Cuddled up against her, Ryan had begun to trace patterns on Ally's soft, cotton T-shirt. She laughed and said, "I don't know if she's a good lay. I never will, either. She's seriously straight."

"Are you giving her a cut of your fees?" Ally asked, clearly confused about the relationship.

"No, of course not. We're friends, Ally. She just wants to help."

"Does she work at the gym?"

"No, we go to school together. She's just a really nice person. Actually, I'm training her to do the AIDS Ride this year. She's very open-minded — although I have a feeling her fiancé isn't."

Ally gave her a pointed look and mused, "Open-minded straight girl who spends her free time finding you private clients. I'll bet her fiancé doesn't really mesh with her that well — but she meshes just fine with you, doesn't she, sweet pea?"

Ryan flushed a bit under her interrogation. "Uhm … well, yeah, we hit it off really great. We've … become very close."

"Is she cute?" Ally asked.

Nodding, Ryan said, "Very."

"Describe her for me," Ally urged, trying to get behind the smokescreen she felt Ryan was putting up.

"Mmm … about five feet six; thin, but with the potential to be really sturdy; blonde hair, worn pretty short. It looks almost messy sometimes, but that good kinda messy — like bed-head," Ryan added. "Green eyes that are a shade I can't begin to describe." She had a faraway look in her eyes as she tried to come up with the proper description. "Sometimes they almost look like jade, and other times they're the color of spring grass." She shook her head a little and went on, "Really nice features, nothing sharp or coarse about her. Everything's soft and smooth and round and very feminine." She shrugged her shoulders and said, "That's about it."

Ally gave her a gentle squeeze and chuckled, "If I were a police sketch artist, I could draw a picture that could pass as a photograph after that description."

"Thanks," Ryan said, missing the point entirely. "My powers of observation are pretty darned sharp."

"Oh, I know," Ally nodded, playing along. "So, babycakes, are your current clients gonna move with you?"

"A couple will, but two of them can't. Would you like to take them?"

"When do you see them?"

"I see Mark on Wednesday at 9:00 p.m., and Sunday at noon, and Vanessa on Sunday at 4:00. I think they would actually prefer to come on a weekday, though. Mark's a writer so he can make his own schedule, and I think Vanessa is either a sex worker or a dancer. We've never talked about it, but she's got a lot more silicone than I think you need for normal purposes," she said with a laugh. "She's a lot of fun — I know you'd like her."

"I'd love another couple of steady clients," Ally said. "Do you want to hand them off, or should I call them?"

"I was planning on finishing out the month with them. Would you be willing to come over on Sunday and meet them?"

"Sure. Why don't you come over tomorrow night, and we can have brunch on Sunday morning before we go over?"

Ryan gave her a lopsided grin as she made a small plea for moderation. "That works for me, but you have to promise not to wear me out too badly tonight. I've got a long bike ride scheduled for tomorrow, and I can't do it standing up. Plus, I need to reserve a little energy if you want me to come back tomorrow night."

"Okay," Ally said softly as she leaned over and started to nibble on her neck. "I'll go easy on you tonight, but tomorrow all bets are off," she said as she nipped her neck rather sharply in anticipation.

Ryan gulped audibly as she considered what she was in for. Ally never hurt her or forced her to do anything, but she took great pleasure in wringing every bit of desire from Ryan's body. She didn't use any elaborate bondage paraphernalia, but she did like to restrain Ryan, usually with her hands or sometimes just with her personality. Ryan knew exactly what it was like to be in Ally's shoes, since she behaved just like her when she was with other women. But it was a very big turn on for her to be the object of desire when they were together.

Ally could rarely let her off with just one orgasm, and since Ryan was not multi-orgasmic, she needed to rest for an hour or so between bouts. So, some of their dates turned into very long marathon sessions, with short naps or even a run to a twenty-four hour diner for a little sustenance to keep them going.

Ryan leaned her head back as she closed her eyes and gave her friend total access to her sensitive neck. Ally liked for Ryan to look a little butch on the outside, so she had worn a tight, black V-necked T-shirt with the short sleeves rolled up a few turns and carpenter-style canvas jeans. But under her tough girl outfit she also satisfied Ally's need for lacy, sexy underwear. A nearly transparent black lace bra and a scandalously tiny thong barely covered her most desired assets. Ally started to work her shirt out of her pants, and Ryan reflected that she had never undressed herself when they were together. Ally had a need to control the entire scene, from start to finish, and undressing her partner was a very important part in setting the stage.

After she had pulled Ryan's shirt free, she returned to her neck and started kissing down the v of her collar. She didn't like the angle she was working at, so she slid her arms behind Ryan's back and knees and effortlessly pulled her onto her lap. Ryan smiled serenely as she felt herself being lifted so easily. She was always the one to cradle a woman in her lap, and she loved the role reversal. There was something so freeing in just letting herself go and allowing Ally to make all the decisions. She briefly wondered if Ally had anyone to switch roles with, but all such thoughts flew from her mind as she felt her shirt being lifted from her body. "Ooo, I love this," Ally's voice burred against her ear as she ran her powerful hands all over Ryan's breasts.

She felt her nipples snap to attention as they were teased through the somewhat rough lace. She hadn't asked Ally to go easy on her breasts, and she shivered slightly as she imagined how thoroughly they would be loved. Ally was decidedly a breast woman, and it seemed that most of her arousal came from fondling Ryan's breasts. Even though they weren't Ryan's favorite erogenous zone, she greatly enjoyed Ally's attentions, partially because Ally got so much pleasure from them.

Ryan leaned languidly against Ally's neck as she continued to massage her breasts through her bra. A small moan escaped from her lips as she felt those big strong hands grasp and play with her increasingly aroused mounds, but she knew that Ally would go at her own pace, no matter how aroused she was. Ally clearly wanted to please Ryan, but her own pleasure was the focus of their interactions. She waited until she was ready to move on in their lovemaking, and Ryan knew that she might as well relax and enjoy the ride. Ally was driving, and she had no control over the route or the destination.

Ryan slid her hand around to grasp Ally's full breast, but she felt her hand being gripped firmly as her friend whispered, "Focus, sugar. Just feel what I'm doing to you." Ryan submissively complied with her instructions as she wondered whether she would be allowed to touch Ally this time. She was usually allowed to please her friend, but she normally had to wait until Ally had made love to her at least twice. There seemed to be a barrier that they had to cross in order for the larger woman to be receptive. Sometimes they would be together for two days with Ryan never being allowed to even kiss her breasts. But Ally clearly did not want to talk about her desires or her needs. Ryan assumed that she had been molested as a child, since there were certain ways that she could not tolerate to be touched. There were also certain positions that Ryan had learned never put her in. Ally could not tolerate being on her back with Ryan on top of her. Ryan had learned that lesson the hard way when she was nearly thrown from the bed when she tried it.

It didn't happen often, but they sometimes reached a level of intimacy that allowed Ally to shove down her barriers and welcome Ryan's touch without restriction. Ryan loved those times best of all. As much as she loved being touched, touching Ally seemed like a gift. She would focus all of her energies on pleasing her friend, and sometimes they would fly into a frenzy of lovemaking that was truly overpowering for both of them. But every time that happened, Ally would withdraw the next day and be unavailable for at least three or four months. Ryan reflected that the last time they had seen each other, they had gotten very intimate. Ally was more vulnerable than she could ever remember her being, and had, in fact, softly wept after Ryan made love to her. But the experience had obviously been uncomfortable, since she had not heard from her since June.

It was clear tonight that Ally did not want Ryan's hands to wander into restricted space. She slowly unbuckled Ryan's belt while she kept her gaze locked on her. Pulling it from the loops, she quickly wrapped it around Ryan's hands and gripped it tightly, completely restricting her ability to move her hands independently. She gently tossed her onto her back and tied the belt over the wooden arm of the sofa, causing Ryan's arms to be fully extended over her head.

Ryan sighed deeply as she felt her hands being removed from her control. She was completely confident in Ally's concern for her, and she knew that she would stop anything she was doing if Ryan asked her to. It seemed that she didn't restrict Ryan for her own pleasure as much as she did to remind her to relax and give up any desire for control. And Ryan had to admit that it worked perfectly. She opened herself up to Ally's desires and let her friend use her body to bring both of them the pleasure that they sought.

Ally moved down to remove Ryan's big, black lineman's boots and her thick, white socks. She had learned long ago that Ryan had a bit of a foot fetish, and she spent a long time massaging her feet, sending waves of pleasure up and down Ryan's spine. Ryan was so relaxed that her limbs felt heavy and weak. Ally decided to crank her back up a bit, so she raised the foot and began to sensually suck on her clean, pink toes. The feel of that terribly soft, warm mouth on her foot brought her right back up to her previous level of arousal. She started to slowly twitch her hips as she waited for her friend to make her next move. She sincerely hoped that it would involve her vulva, but she had a feeling that she was a long way from getting any release. Much to her surprise, Ally began to slowly unzip her. She slid her hand in and tickled her mound with just the tips of her fingers, letting the pads of her fingers press against the sensitive flesh. Ryan's hips shot off the sofa and tried to increase the pressure, but Ally knew all of her tricks. She lightened her touch every time Ryan thrust at her until she was touching only her panties.

She leaned over and whispered into Ryan's flushed ear, "Are you ready for me, sweetness?"

Ryan closed her eyes and ground her hips around in a little circle, nodding her head slowly.

"Talk to me, sugar. Tell me what you want," Ally urged.

Ryan took several deep breaths before she had the ability to express her needs. "I want you to touch me, Ally. I want to feel your hands on me, and I want your fingers deep inside of me."

"Mmm, I want that, too, sugar," Ally whispered. She captured the swollen bottom lip, and gently sucked it into her mouth, nibbling on the tender flesh for a moment before she moved on to explore Ryan's mouth with her tongue. After a few achingly long moments she pulled away, and gazed into Ryan's desire-filled eyes. "I promise you'll get all you can handle, sweetness. But I don't think you're ready yet," she informed her with a note of regret in her deep voice. "When you're really ready, you'll beg for my touch."

She climbed on top of Ryan, her heavy musculature pressing her hard against the couch. Dipping her head, she started to kiss her again. Ryan's mouth opened and welcomed Ally's warm tongue as it began to explore every surface. As the kissing intensified, Ryan had an overpowering desire to wrap her arms around Ally and toss her onto her back. She wanted to satisfy her primal urge to be on top, but her bound hands constantly reminded her that she was a bottom today and would remain so for the duration of the evening. She knew very well that it was the suppression of her natural urges that made their sex so hot — but she still struggled mightily.

89

After Ally had kissed her so thoroughly that her lips felt bruised, the taller woman shifted to the end of the sofa. She grabbed the hems of Ryan's pant legs and gave a powerful yank. The pants flew from her body before they were quickly tossed aside. The racy thong was pulled down inadvertently, so Ally gently tugged it back into place and patted Ryan's belly. Meeting the blue eyes, Ally leaned over and kissed all along the top edge of the thong, then she looked up and grinned. "Thanks," was all she said.

Her large, warm hands trailed across Ryan's body while she let her instincts guide her. The tempting breasts caught her attention, and she once again climbed on top and began to kiss Ryan's nipples through her bra. The pressure of her firm tongue made the material feel quite rough on Ryan's delicate skin, and her nipples puckered so forcefully that her areolas almost disappeared. Ally's hands were never still as her mouth worked away, running up and down Ryan's torso, touching her lightly, teasingly.

After a long while she sat up and gazed at Ryan for a moment. Cocking her head in speculation, she reached up and untied her hands, swiftly pulling her up to a sitting position. "Dance with me?" she asked, extending a hand. Ryan obediently grasped it and was pulled to her feet.

The large, powerful arms pulled Ryan close, and Ally held her tightly as she began to sway to the music. The rough feel of new, black jeans brushed across Ryan's bare thighs, and her hands slid around Ally's back to sneak under her short, cropped T-shirt. Ryan smiled when she considered the logo, which simply read "girl." She knew that Ally was often mistaken for a man, even though Ryan didn't understand how that happened, with those magnificent breasts proudly announcing their presence. Nonetheless, happen it did, and she admired the good humor that Ally maintained about the subject — including touches such as the public service message that she wore stretched across her spectacular chest today.

A slow, emotion-laden song was playing, and Ally wrapped her arm around Ryan's waist as she grasped her hand and held it to her breast. She began to move her slowly around the floor, keeping perfect time to the music. Ryan felt more naked than she would have felt if she were, in fact, naked. Something about dancing in lacy underwear with a fully-dressed partner seemed to have that effect on her.

Ally's black Doc Martens added to her height advantage — making her at least three inches taller than Ryan who appreciated the height difference, since it allowed her to get close by tucking her breasts just under Ally's. Ryan let her head drop to rest on Ally's broad shoulder, and she sighed as she felt her partner's head turn to gently press against hers.

There was something so intimate about this tender dance that Ryan felt a burst of emotion fill her. They continued to move with and against each other until the entire CD was finished, but neither was ready to release the other. They stood and swayed together for a few long minutes, until Ally finally lifted her head and kissed Ryan tenderly, just barely brushing their lips together. Her hand lifted from Ryan's back and gently held the back of her head as she slowly increased the intensity of the kiss, until she could feel her partner's knees begin to weaken.

With one powerful move that thrilled Ryan to the core, she swept her into her arms and started to carry her towards the bedroom. Ryan raised her hands to clasp behind Ally's neck as she leaned back and enjoyed the ride. She hadn't been carried to bed since she was a small child, and she smiled as she thought of all of the women she had done this to. *I hope they all enjoyed the ride as much as I'm going to*, she thought with an anticipatorily satisfied grin.

Hours later, the two women stood in the shower, leaning against each other like punched-out boxers in the ring — each of them too tired to speak. They dried each other quickly, then stopped in the kitchen for a snack. Ryan's eyes lit up when she found a pint of mint chocolate cookie ice cream, and they stood in the dark in front of the open freezer and fed each other by the dim light. The cold air that wafted down on their bodies was blissfully refreshing, and Ally started to get a little playful once again — chilling Ryan's tender nipple by holding a spoonful of the ice cream onto it for a few seconds while the dark-haired woman squirmed. Of course, the chocolate had to be removed, and Ally chose to do so the fun way. Before either knew what had hit them, they were slipping and sliding across the kitchen tile, chocolate ice cream slathered across their bodies.

After a long bout of sucking and nibbling the ice cream from tender flesh, they rested against each other until Ally asked weakly, "You know what we have to do now, don't you?" Cleaning the kitchen floor and taking another shower were the last things either woman believed she was capable of — but both were rather meticulous, so clean they did. As long as they were up and cleaning, they decided to change the soggy sheets. Finally, they crawled back into bed and cuddled up together to sleep.

Ryan was always amazed at how snuggly and affectionate Ally was when they slept together. She had every part of herself touching some part of Ryan as they settled down into a comfortable position. "G'night, Ryan," she whispered as Ryan felt herself begin to relax into the hug.

"Good night, Ally," she replied, turning her head to give her one final kiss. Moments later, she could feel the larger woman relax and lean against her heavily. Ryan sighed deeply, and joined her in sleep minutes later, feeling sated and protected in Ally's tender embrace.

⌘

Jack walked in to his apartment on Friday evening and smiled as his senses took in the smell of roasted chicken coming from the kitchen. *There is nothing better than coming home from school and having Jamie here making dinner for us*, he thought contentedly. He stopped in his tracks, however, when he came upon an obviously new, bright orange bike leaning against the wall in the hallway.

"Jamie, are you here?" he asked.

"Yeah, honey. I'm in here," she replied from the kitchen. "C'mon in."

He did as he was told, but his confused look remained. "Whose bike is that?" he asked as he pointed in the direction of the hallway.

"It's mine, silly," she replied as she made her way over to give him a proper greeting. "Who else's would it be?"

"I don't know," he replied. "I didn't know you liked to ride, and I didn't know you had a bike, so …"

"Well, I do and I do," she said simply, wrapping her arms around his neck, silencing any potential response by keeping his lips busy for several long moments.

He was not to be deterred, however. When she pulled away, he walked back into the hall and looked more closely at the bike. "Sure seems like a nice one," he said. "Is it new?"

"Yeah, I just got it this week."

"How come?" he inquired as he returned to the kitchen, carrying his mail.

"How come what?" she asked, although she knew what the question really was.

"How come you bought a new, expensive bike?" he said patiently.

"I want to get into riding," she said, as if this explained everything.

But Jack was his usual tenacious self, and he sensed there was more beneath the surface. "Why?" he asked firmly as he locked his gaze onto hers, giving her a clear signal that he wanted a complete answer.

"I've decided that I'm going to ride in this year's AIDS Ride in June." *That should satisfy him,* she thought.

With his voice rising, and his forehead contracting into a frown he asked, "Why on earth would you want to do that? Moreover, why are you avoiding my questions?"

She gave him a puzzled smile and said, "Why do you think I'm avoiding your questions? I'm answering them as quickly as you're asking them."

"Okay," he nodded. "What led you to decide to do something so out of character?"

"What's so odd about wanting to do something to support a worthy cause, Jack?" she replied. "We've both been lucky enough to have been unscathed by this disease. The least I can do is show my support by doing this ride."

He shook his head, frustrated that she was not really answering the questions he was asking. "Jamie, we both know if you wanted to support this cause, you could write them a check that would make them faint. That can't be the reason for doing something this stupid." As soon as it was out, he truly wanted to pull that last word back into his mouth. The urge got stronger when he saw the hurt look in her eyes. He reached out to her and tried to put his arms around her, saying, "I'm so sorry, Jamie. I didn't mean that to come out like that."

Jamie was having none of it. She turned her back on him, and struggled to keep the tears from flowing. His repeated attempts to touch her were roughly shrugged off while she tried to control her emotions. Finally, she turned around and regarded him carefully, her lower lip quivering. "Why would you say something like that? Are you *trying* to hurt me?"

"No, of course not, sweetheart," he insisted as he was again rebuffed in his attempt to touch her. He gave up and flopped down into a kitchen chair, dropping his head into his hands. He let out a frustrated growl, scrubbing at his face roughly. "I don't know what's going on, Jamie, but something is. I've known you for three years now, and all of a sudden you've started to withhold things from me." He shook his head and said, "Ever since we've been engaged, you've started to act distant. I feel … I feel left out," he grumbled with a dejected look on his handsome face.

Jamie could not resist the hurt puppy look, and she honestly had to admit that he was right. She was leaving him out of some important decisions, and she knew it was wrong to do so. Taking him into her arms, she murmured, "I'm sorry, Jack. I don't want you to feel left out. This is just something I decided to do recently. It's important to me, and I'd really like your support. I guess I sometimes forget to tell you things, but I'll try to do better."

He wrapped her in a fierce hug and held on for several minutes. "Don't shut me out," he murmured.

"I'll try," she whispered. "I promise I'll try. I hate to fight," she sighed.

He continued to nuzzle his head into her chest, and he broke the ice by asking, "Do you want to make up like we did last time?"

She laughed a little as she leaned her head back and gave him a tender kiss. "I would love to, but dinner's about ready. Let's eat and then go to bed early, okay?"

⌘

Over dinner she explained the ride more thoroughly. She was reticent to explain how Ryan was so intrinsically involved, but she was resolved to try to keep her promise to Jack. Her friend's name had not been mentioned since the big fight, and she felt a little guilty about developing such a close relationship without Jack's knowledge. The first time she mentioned Ryan's name Jack paused mid-bite, but he did not comment. Jamie dutifully told him everything. She told him about deciding to do the ride, about buying the bike, about training at the gym. She was chagrined to hear herself mention Ryan every five seconds, but she was determined to be completely honest.

Jack asked a few questions, but just generally let her talk. When she was finished, he sat back in his chair and regarded her for a long moment. "I would like to get to know this woman," he said simply. "She's obviously become a very good friend, and you seem to be spending quite a lot of time with her, so I would like to spend some time with her, too."

"How about tomorrow?" she asked tentatively. "She's bringing her bike down here, and we're going on a ride."

"Tomorrow it is," he said with a small smile.

⌘

They lay in bed together late that night. Jack was sound asleep, and Jamie watched him as he lay in peaceful exhaustion, his head pillowed on her breast. They had made love, and while Jamie was not physically satiated, she felt very peaceful and content lying next to her fiancé.

Jack had tried hard — too hard for Jamie's comfort — but she just wasn't able to relax enough to climax. She knew that the problem was a psychological one — that they were both too focused on her achieving an orgasm. As much as she tried, she couldn't reassure Jack that it was really all right with her if she didn't come every time. That concept seemed so alien to him that she had finally given up even trying to explain it. The fact was that she loved the closeness and the warmth their lovemaking provided, even when she couldn't reach orgasm. She often thought that her favorite time was after Jack had finished, and he lay collapsed in her arms. She felt so close to him then, kissing his forehead and holding him tight as she whispered softly into his ear.

It was the intimacy that she loved, and she worried that focusing on orgasm was beginning to destroy the intimacy. She knew that they had to do something to break this impasse, but she didn't have a clue what to try.

Deciding that she couldn't solve the problem that night, she waited until she was sure he was sound asleep, then rolled him onto his side. She snuggled up behind him and rested her head against his back, listening to his slow, strong heartbeat — letting the steady sound lull her to sleep.

⌘

Jamie had donned her new bike shorts and a lightweight, long-sleeved T-shirt that was designed to wick away sweat. She clomped around the living room in her bike shoes and did a few light stretches to loosen her hamstrings and quads. Ryan was due in a few minutes, and she knew she would be on time, as usual. Jamie was a bit nervous, and Jack seemed very quiet. *I hope this goes well. I know he will like her if he can just give her a chance.*

Just then the doorbell rang, and she went to let her guest in. *Well, I finally got my wish,* she sighed to herself as she took in Ryan's long form. *I've been dying to see her muscles, and there they are!* And she had to admit that the wait was well worth it. This woman was a truly amazing sight. She wore black, ankle-length bike pants that highlighted every firm muscle of her legs, and a tight, red, short-sleeved bicycling jersey covered with advertising logos. Her large, red bicycle was casually slung over her broad shoulder, and her black helmet dangled from the handlebar. Her black hair was slicked back off her face, and her face was flushed from exertion, which obviously included carrying the bike up three flights of stairs. She wore a bright smile on her beautiful face as she grinned down at Jamie. "Hi."

"Di … Di … Did you ride here?" Jamie asked incredulously as she struggled to resist the urge to catch the drop of sweat that was trailing down the side of Ryan's cheek.

"Yep. I figured that since I need to put in a hundred or so miles on the weekend, this would be an easy way to do it."

"C'mon in, and I'll get you something to drink. You look like you could use it," she laughed. "Honey, Ryan's here."

He emerged with a quizzical look on his face. He took in the figure before him and shook his head a bit. "Did you ride here?" he asked with a smile as he extended his hand.

Ryan struggled a little to remove her padded glove, finally got it off, and took his still-extended hand. "Sorry, I'm a little sweaty. That last hill was a killer," she admitted.

Jamie emerged from the kitchen with a cold bottle of water, which was gratefully accepted. Ryan tore the cap off and tilted the bottle up to her mouth. As she leaned her head back to chug the cold water, Jack stole a long glance. *Damn,* he marveled, *she could be a model. Well, maybe a model for a fitness magazine — she couldn't pull off the waif thing at all,* he mentally amended.

Ryan dropped the now-empty bottle to her thigh and breathed out a satisfied sigh. "Boy, that really hit the spot, Jamie. Thanks."

"You're welcome," Jamie grinned. "I'm surprised you didn't bring some along for the trip."

"Oh, I did," Ryan admitted. "But I drank it all halfway down here. Sometimes I don't pay attention to the weather change from the city to the Peninsula. It was cold and foggy when I left home this morning, and I didn't check the weather before I left. It must be twenty degrees warmer here than at home."

"Give me your water bottles, and I'll fill them for you," Jamie offered.

Ryan handed over her two spent bottles from their cages on her bike. "Can I make a pit stop before we take off again?" she inquired.

"Sure. It's right down the hall, next to the office," Jack directed.

Jamie retreated to the kitchen to complete her chore, and Jack followed on her heels. "God, Jamie, I didn't notice before how gorgeous she is," he whispered into her ear as she leaned over the sink.

"Maybe you just like the sweaty look," she said with a chuckle. *I know I do,* she thought wryly. "Do you feel the standard male urge to convert her to your team?" she asked with a giggle, right back into his ear.

"No, not me, but a lot of guys sure would."

"Why not you?" she inquired as her brow furrowed.

"One — because she's not my type. Two — because I've got my hands full with you. I can't take on any side work," he said as he bent slightly to kiss her smiling mouth. Jamie was a bit taken by surprise as he really began to get into the kiss. One hand moved up her torso as the other slipped down and palmed her Lycra-encased butt. She was about to push him away when she caught a glimpse of Ryan in the doorway.

⌘

Jamie thought about the kiss for a moment as she finished filling up the bottles, and Jack returned to the living room to chat with Ryan. *That was odd. He is normally so reserved around other people. It almost seemed like he wanted her to see that — like he was laying claim to me.* She briefly chastised herself, *You don't have to analyze everything, Jamie. Maybe he just felt like kissing you at that moment. And copping a feel right in front of your lesbian friend,* her suspicious side warned.

Ryan hoisted her bike onto a broad shoulder while Jack did the same with Jamie's. "Jack, I brought it up here myself," she argued, "I'm sure I can get it down the same way."

"I'm sure you can, sweetheart," he agreed. "I want to help."

As Jamie situated herself on the bike, he leaned over and kissed her goodbye. "I really might need your help when I get home," she admitted. "If I ring the buzzer will you come down?"

"Absolutely," he agreed. "Now you two be safe. There's a lot of traffic on Saturday."

"Okay, Dad," Jamie teased.

"I'll take care of her, Jack," Ryan said in the same teasing tone.

Jamie thought she saw the smallest flicker of irritation cross his handsome face, but she decided to ignore it.

⌘

They took off and began their short trek to the Stanford campus. "Have you been down here much?" she asked Ryan.

"No, not really," Ryan revealed. "I've been to a few athletic events, but that's it. I'm actually not sure that I've ever been here during daylight hours."

"Well, you're in luck because I know this place like the back of my hand," she declared.

"Why are you so familiar with Stanford?" Ryan quizzed as they rode along.

"Well, both of my parents went here, and my mother's family has a strong connection."

"Hmm," said Ryan with a knowing grin. "Given what you've told me about your family, I assume that means that some big buildings are named after you."

Jamie shot her a glance, but then laughed a bit as she admitted, "Surprisingly not. My family is more into sponsoring chairs in various disciplines. I think they felt that having a building named after you would be nice, but only people on campus would see it. But when a professor is the recipient of the 'Putnam Barrett Smith Chair of Humanities' he uses that title on all of his professional publications. Or she does," Jamie smiled. "Lots more notoriety," she informed Ryan with a roll of her eyes.

"Smith, huh?" Ryan said as she rode closer. "Could you be any WASPier?"

"Don't think so," Jamie admitted. "We are the epitome of WASPdom."

"You know, even if there aren't any big buildings with your name on them, I bet there's something around here that mentions you."

"Oh, I guess I can find something," she replied. They pedaled over to the main quad and hopped off their bikes, then walked over to an impressive, stone archway. Jamie led her inquisitive friend to a large plaque that had been placed on the interior of the arcade. "There you go," she said as she pointed to the plaque with a flourish.

The legend read that the archway was substantially retrofitted and repaired after the Loma Prieta earthquake by the generous contributions of the listed benefactors. Ryan scanned the names for a Smith, and pointed to a Roger B. Smith. "Is that your family?"

"Yeah. That's a cousin. But that's not what I wanted to show you." Ryan gave her a puzzled glance, so she pointed to the E's. After a few seconds of scanning, Ryan turned to her with a cute little grin. "Are those your parents?"

"Yep."

"Why are they listed separately?" Ryan inquired as she considered the entries for both James S. Evans and Catherine D.S. Evans.

"Hmm, I'm not sure," she admitted. "I assume they each made a contribution from their separate funds, and they didn't want to share the glory."

Ryan shot her a glance to see if she was kidding, but it was obvious that not only was her friend serious, she didn't seem to think this behavior odd. It was a struggle not to impart her own family's sense of propriety onto the Evans family, but Ryan could not understand why you would not want to have your name listed along with your spouse's. It seemed terribly odd to her, but she didn't want to make a big deal out of it, so she kept her opinion to herself.

They began to ride again, and Jamie pointed out some markers of her family history, including the spot under a beautiful redwood where her father had proposed to her mother. "That's really neat," Ryan marveled. "How old were your parents when they married?"

"Mother was only twenty when she had me, so I guess she was still nineteen when they married. Daddy was twenty-four at the time."

"How old is Jack?" Ryan asked thoughtfully.

"He's twenty-four," Jamie replied.

"And when is your wedding set for?"

"The summer after I graduate. I want to have the whole college experience as a single woman, and I want Jack to have a year's work out of the way."

"Does he know where he is going to work?" Ryan inquired.

"Yeah, pretty much. He really wants to clerk for a federal judge after he graduates this summer. He can't be too picky about the location, but he's trying for the Ninth Circuit Federal Court of Appeals. That would have him in the western region, but it could be Montana or even Hawaii. That's why I didn't want to get married right after he graduates."

"Wow, won't it be hard if he's that far away?"

Seemingly for the first time, Jamie considered that. "Uhm, I guess it will, but it's what he wants, and it will help his long term career prospects."

For the second time that day, Ryan bit her tongue rather than comment on the strange ways of these people of the Peninsula. "What are his plans after the clerkship is over?" Ryan asked.

"It's pretty obvious that he'll get an offer from Davis & Gray," Jamie replied, shifting her eyes so that she didn't look directly at Ryan.

"What firm does your father work for?" Ryan asked casually.

"That would be Davis & Gray," Jamie grumbled.

"I'm not prying, am I?" Ryan asked with a hint of concern in her voice.

"No, not at all. I know that Jack is really talented. It just seems like an ideal opportunity for nepotism, even though I know it's not. I guess I'm just sensitive to people perceiving me in a certain fashion."

"I certainly don't perceive you as anything other than a hard-working woman, who I am certain would never marry anyone other than a hard-working, talented man," Ryan said confidently. "Besides, the mere fact that your father works for the firm isn't that big a deal. I mean, it is a huge place, isn't it?"

Jamie rolled her eyes a bit as she revealed, "Yeah, it's huge all right … but my dad doesn't just work there. He's the managing partner. That's about like being the CEO of a business."

"Oh … uhm … well, I bet in a way that will make it a little harder for Jack. The last thing your dad wants is to hire some dolt and have everyone think it's mere nepotism."

"Thanks, Ryan," Jamie replied, quite relieved. "It's just that I know people think that everything comes so easily for me, and that my parents just get me everything I want. I worry that people will think that Jack got his job because I demanded it."

"I know that's not true," Ryan said gravely. "Money can't buy everything, Jamie. It can't buy you big quadriceps!" This last sentence came from over her shoulder as she put on a terrific burst of speed and left Jamie in her dust, a mellow laugh trailing after her.

"I thought the key to this ride was long, *slow* distance!" Jamie huffed as she finally caught up to Ryan's slowing form.

"It is, Jamie," she said seriously. "Why, do you want to go fast?" she asked with the most cherubic of faces.

"It's obvious that you were raised with brothers, Ryan O'Flaherty," she sulked.

"Yeah, sometimes it's painfully obvious!" Ryan teased, as she burst into another flash of blinding speed.

⌘

They completed the scheduled fifteen miles with just a few more sprints. By the time they returned to the apartment Jamie was definitely beginning to tighten up. "I don't think I could go another mile," she moaned.

Ryan looked fresh as a daisy, of course, and this slightly irritated Jamie. "You know, you could at least try not to look like you've been lying on the beach for the afternoon."

Ryan laughed and did her best to put on a tired and bedraggled expression. She dragged herself over to the buzzer and rang it several times. "I guess Jack went out," she finally said after three tries.

"And I was going to bribe him to carry me upstairs," Jamie whined mildly.

"Well, you're way too heavy for a poor, tired woman like me," Ryan teased. "But I could help you out with this." At that she leaned over and grabbed Jamie's bike frame with one powerful arm and hefted it onto her shoulder.

"Thank you, O Powerful One," Jamie intoned as she bent in praise once the bike was delivered.

"Oh, that's nothing," Ryan replied casually. "I probably could have left you on the darn thing, but it would have upset my center of gravity."

"Yeah, right!" Jamie teased along with a little poke in the gut. "Hey," she said seriously as she poked again and was met with a very firm resistance, "Maybe you're right," she marveled. "I thought you said your tummy was flabby," she chided.

"I'm quite sure I never said that," Ryan assured her with a chuckle. "I said that I have a thicker layer of abdominal fat than you have, but my abs are in great shape, if I do say so myself. Keeping them built up really helps with bike riding."

Jamie reached over to pat her again. "They are firm," she admitted, wishing that Ryan would lift her shirt for a peek. "How do you get them so firm? Do you do the same crunches you showed me?"

"Yeah, sometimes," she advised. "But I like to challenge myself a little, so I've devised some little tortures that I don't think you'd like," she said with a grin.

Jamie crossed her arms and glared at her friend. "Like what, tough stuff?"

"Well, my new favorite is to lie on a declining bench and do some crunches."

"That doesn't sound so hard," Jamie scoffed.

"No, that part isn't hard. But I have someone toss a medicine ball at my gut while I'm doing them," she said with a casual look on her face.

"*What?* One of those heavy, sand-filled, leather balls?"

"Uh-huh," she said as she blithely refastened her ponytail, trying to suppress a grin at Jamie's shocked expression.

"I don't think I believe you," she finally mumbled.

Ryan could never resist a challenge. She stood tall and gazed at her friend with a daring look and said, "Hit me."

"What?"

"Hit me," she repeated. "Hit me in the gut — hard as you can."

"Ryan! I wouldn't do that! I would hurt you!"

Ryan gave her a slight smirk as she scoffed, "Don't think so."

"You don't think I could hurt you?" she asked incredulously. "I'm not as weak as I look!"

"Prove it," she demanded, egging Jamie on.

"Fine!" Jamie fumed, quite insulted that her friend treated her like a weakling. Ryan tensed her abs and jutted out her chin defiantly. Jamie pulled her arm back and popped her right in the gut at about fifty per cent of her capacity. She had closed her eyes as she swung, since she did not want to see the pain in her friend's face. But when she opened her eyes Ryan was not only not in pain — she was laughing at her.

"Is that all you've got?" she scoffed.

"You want more? I'll give you more!" This time she kept her eyes wide open as she reared back and slammed her fist into Ryan's midsection with as much force as she could generate. But on impact it felt like she had slammed her hand into a brick wall. Only this wall was smirking at her.

"That was better," she advised. "Wanna switch?"

"You are truly mad!" Jamie fumed, outraged that she had been unable to hurt Ryan's body or her attitude. But just as that thought hit her, she slapped herself in the head. "You made me want to hurt you!" she gasped. "I've never hit someone with that intent before!"

Ryan slung an arm around her shoulders and gave her a sound hug. "Boy, you missed a lot not growing up with brothers! If one of us wasn't bleeding or crying at the end of the day, we just felt incomplete!"

"Well, I've had enough," she grumbled. "I don't ever want you to taunt me into hitting you again! Are you sure I didn't hurt you?"

"Yep," she declared. She reached out and grasped Jamie's right hand and closely examined the wrist. "You didn't hurt yourself, did you?" she asked solicitously.

The smaller woman shook her hand roughly a few times. "No, but it does sting a little. How on earth do you make your abs that hard?"

"Nothing but hard work." Ryan cast a glance at the slight quiver in Jamie's thighs. "Time for a little rub down," she ordered.

"Oh, my favorite part of any exercise," Jamie enthused.

⌘

Jack walked into the apartment as Ryan was finishing her massage of Jamie's hamstrings. His face was friendly, but a little impassive to Jamie's eyes. *Please don't let this bother him.* "Hi, honey. Where did you go?" she asked brightly.

"I had to run down to the bookstore for a few minutes. I'm sorry I wasn't here to help you bring the bike up."

"You should be, I really needed a hand," she lied. She glanced at Ryan to see if her lie would get a reaction, but Ryan's head was bent in concentration on her task. "Ryan's a massage therapist," Jamie added, even though Jack had not commented on their activities.

He forced himself to banish the thought of Ryan giving a woman an intimate, all-nude massage and said weakly, "Oh, that's nice."

Jamie was pleased that the rather intimate contact with Ryan didn't seem to bother Jack. *Maybe he's really getting used to her,* she hoped.

⌘

Late that night as Jack hovered over her, claiming her with a need that was foreign to their lovemaking, Jamie wondered if Ryan was the cause.

Whatever the cause, she thought, *this is a very good thing.* He was focused on his own desires, instead of being so solicitous of her, and she felt herself begin to respond a little more freely. She lost the feeling before she was able to orgasm, but she was cheered by the fact that she had gotten close. *I bet not many women wish their boyfriends paid less attention to them when they made love,* she smirked to herself.

⌘

Monday morning found Ryan lying beneath Ally's sprawled out body. They had spent the night making love with nearly as much passion as they had possessed on Friday and Saturday nights, and Ryan was almost ready to shut off her watch alarm and just stay cuddled up.

But the insistent alarm had woken them both, and Ally crawled off her to go to the bathroom while Ryan waged a small war with her well-hidden lazy side. When Ally returned, she reached for Ryan and started to stroke her belly in a very friendly manner. Ryan knew if they got started again she'd lose the whole day, so she gave her a kiss and softly patted her cheek. "Gotta go, babe," she murmured, forcing herself to slip out of bed, avoiding Ally's reaching hands. She stumbled into the shower, and when she came out, her friend was sound asleep again. Ryan checked the alarm clock to make sure it was set for 8:00, since she assumed Ally had to be at work by 9:00, and then she walked over to the kitchen table and left her a note.

> "Thanks for the marvelous lesson in how to fill up a weekend. I'll think of you all day — especially every time I have to sit down!
> Love,
> Ryan"

She hopped on her Harley with a grimace and rode directly to the Muni station to catch a ride to school. *I'll be much better off standing the whole way,* she grumbled. *Why did we have to try out every new toy she's bought since I saw her last? Will I never learn?*

⌘

She barreled into class about five minutes late and took a seat near the door. Jamie caught sight of the definite wince as she sat down and wondered if Ryan had hurt herself on their bike ride. But when she looked

103

at her again, she noticed how terrible she looked. She was very pale, and her eyes looked dull and bloodshot. Her hair was pulled back into a ponytail, and shoved haphazardly under a baseball cap. As Jamie cast another glance at her, Ryan's head hit her chest, and she jerked in her seat as she startled herself awake. *She looks injured all right,* she smirked, *but not from biking.*

After class, Ryan waited for her outside the door. She was leaning against the wall and looked like she might fall asleep right where she stood. "I don't want to belabor an obvious point, but you look like you could use some coffee," Jamie commented when Ryan forced her eyes open.

"I don't think coffee will help," she moaned. "I think I'm gonna find a nice shady spot and take a nap until I have to go to work."

"Don't you have your bio lab?"

"Yeah, but there's no way I could safely perform any experiments today. I don't want to endanger my fellow students."

"Come on," she said as she slipped her arm around Ryan's waist. "I can help you out."

After a relatively slow and silent walk they climbed the stairs to Jamie's house. "I take it that you figured out how to fill your weekend," Jamie asked casually as she led her friend up to her bed to allow her to crash.

"Oh, it got filled all right," Ryan said, thinking to herself, *Along with every other orifice.*

⌘ CHAPTER FIVE

AFTER A FEW WEEKS OF WORKING AT THE NEW GYM, RYAN REALIZED that her new schedule effectively precluded her from taking her early–morning bicycle rides. Jamie gave her dilemma some thought and offered to keep Ryan's mountain bike at her house. Ryan was then able to leave her motorcycle at Jamie's, and ride the bicycle to work and later to class. Cassie was not very happy to be roused from sleep every morning at 5:00 by the thrumming engine of the Harley, but she eventually stopped complaining when Ryan agreed to turn off the engine at the curb and walk the bike down the drive.

It was when Cassie learned that Jamie had given Ryan a key to the house that she really blew up. "Jamie, I don't want that woman to be able to barge in here whenever she pleases," she huffed. "Her bicycle is in the garage — why on earth does she need to come into the house, anyway?"

"She needs to come in to change out of her boots and jacket and put on her bike clothes. I'm not going to have her do that in the garage!"

"She can ring the bell like everyone else," the tall blonde grumbled.

Jamie sighed heavily and appeared to give in. "Fine. I'll never wake up from the sound of the bell, so since you're a light sleeper, you can let her in. I'll ask for the key back," she agreed, smiling sweetly.

"Fine, Jamie, just give all the sex-crazed lesbians in town a key to our house," she fumed. "You know, I talked to some people who know her, and they say she is a real slut. I can't believe that's the type of person you like to associate with."

She pursed her lips and regarded her roommate for a long moment. "Cassie, if all of my friends were as kind and as generous and as honorable as Ryan, I would be one happy woman," she stated with narrow, flashing eyes as she turned on her heel — hoping that Cassie understood the true meaning of the jibe.

⌘

As the term heated up, Jamie began to regret taking so many courses that required so much reading. Her nose was pressed into a book at every unscheduled moment, and soon she began to really look forward to any break in her schedule — which served as a strong inducement to ride as much as she could.

When she was on her bike, she was able to free her mind of every concern about her classes and her future. She didn't worry about her relationship with Jack or think about their life together. She merely put her mind on hold and let the wind fly past her face while she pedaled along the steep hills of Berkeley. Having been away from bike riding for so many years, she realized that she had forgotten the freedom that two wheels afforded. No matter how bad traffic was, she could scoot right past the stalled cars and be home in a matter of minutes, so she found that she took her car fewer and fewer places.

She had to admit, though, that the workouts with Ryan were what she really looked forward to. They worked together three hours a week, and they were among the most enjoyable ones of her week. Even though they spent lots of time together having coffee, or a quick meal, the workouts were when Jamie felt truly special.

When she really allowed herself to think about it, Jamie realized that she was the one who usually spent her time making other people feel special. Sometimes it seemed that her entire relationship with Jack was spent making sure that his needs were met: making him lunch and dinner, being with him while he studied, never making demands to go out to dinner or a movie and being available to him sexually. But for three hours a week, the world revolved around her and her slowly developing body.

One of the things she had grown to appreciate about Ryan was her ability to intensely focus on a task. As the weeks passed, she realized that focus was never more welcome than when it centered upon her.

Jamie had observed many other trainers during her weeks at the gym, but she had never observed anyone who concentrated so fiercely on her clients. Without a word from Jamie, Ryan would automatically remove five pounds from the weight stack if it was a tiny bit too heavy; she would order her to stop at nine reps instead of ten if she detected too much fatigue; she would skip a certain exercise if a related exercise was too difficult on a given day. All in all, she was just so highly attuned to Jamie and her body that, after a while, they spoke less and less during the sessions.

But when the session was over, Ryan invariably spent a few minutes giving her very specific praise for various aspects of that day's work. Jamie knew this was primarily to keep her motivated, but she ate it up greedily. She felt so unique and special when they spent this time together, that she began to wake up in a very happy mood on every workout day. *I would never have believed that I'd enjoy working out so much,* she mused one morning. *With Ryan's help, I'm certain that I'm going to be ready for this ride — no matter what.*

⌘

On a cool and overcast Wednesday, Jamie arrived at the gym for their usual four o'clock appointment. She looked around for Ryan, but did not see her hanging around the front desk as was her usual habit. She dropped her things off in a locker and entered the main part of the gym, looking for her friend. After she was about to give up and have her paged, she spotted her in the far corner of the gym.

Jamie had never even noticed the boxing equipment located on a slightly raised platform in the corner. But Ryan was standing in front of a heavy, leather-covered bag, banging the stuffing out of it with her hands, which were encased in bright red boxing gloves. She stood for a second and observed her friend, watching the sweat fly from her face as she delivered one strong blow after another. Jamie mused that she would not hit the bag the way her friend was doing it. But when she watched carefully, she could see that Ryan's technique was the proper one. She punched from her shoulder, getting the force of her entire torso behind each blow. Jamie noted that she was nearly standing on her toes while she punched the bag, and that her body followed her arm, with even her hips helping provide thrust. It truly amazed her that she could stand and watch her friend for such a long time without her being aware of her scrutiny, but Ryan was so intent that she was obviously unaware of anything other than her furious assault on the heavy bag. "Uhm ... mad at someone?" she finally asked to break the spell.

Ryan whirled to face her, sweat flying from her hair and hitting Jamie in a light spray. "When did you get ... what time is it?" she asked as she looked at her watch. "My God!" she gasped. "It's 4:15!"

"I know," Jamie said with a smile. "I've been watching you for fifteen minutes."

"You have?" Ryan asked with a truly perplexed look on her face.

As she said that, Jamie realized how odd it sounded to just be watching her so she explained, "I've never seen anyone work on a bag like that. I've always been fascinated by boxing."

"You have?" Ryan asked dubiously, grabbing a small towel from a stack and wiping her face and neck down.

"Yeah, I have. That was pretty impressive, by the way," she said with a smile.

"Thanks," Ryan said. "My three o'clock cancelled, and I wanted to do something aerobic for a few minutes. I thought this would be something that I could do and not sweat too much," she said as she looked at herself rather helplessly. Sweat was still running down her face and into her black shirt. Rivulets ran down her arms, and even her thick black golf shirt looked drenched.

"Uhm … you were wrong?" Jamie hazarded.

"Well, I started out just playing around with the speed bag," Ryan admitted. "But when I was finished I still felt kind of twitchy, so I thought the heavy bag would tire me out."

"Twitchy?"

"Yeah," she said, shifting her weight from one foot to the other, in what Jamie had come to recognize as a sign of Ryan's discomfort with a particular topic. "Sometimes I just need to … I don't know … like … let off some steam."

"I think you were successful," Jamie observed wryly. "Now, let's get to work, so I can look just as limp as you do."

⌘

After their very strenuous workout, Jamie asked, "Do you have time for dinner? I could whip something up."

Ryan appeared to consider the offer for a moment, but finally said, "I'd love to, Jamie, but I can't squeeze it in. My father made a brown bag dinner for me, so I'm just gonna go study."

"That's okay," Jamie said, trying not to sound like she cared. In truth, she cared a great deal. As much as she enjoyed the workouts, she equally enjoyed the post-workout massage and praise session. But she didn't feel comfortable admitting how much that special time meant to her, so she tried to appear casual.

Ryan perceptively caught the small look of disappointment on her face. "If you need some company tonight, I'll make time for you," she said, bending down just a touch so that she could see Jamie's eyes.

Jamie felt a little busted, and tried to cover it up with a casual reply. "No, I should study, too. I'm just looking for a reason not to."

"If you're sure, Jamie."

"Positive," she replied, immensely glad that Ryan cared enough to meet her needs.

⌘

Four hours later, Jamie was hard at work on a short paper for her psych class when she realized that she did not have a necessary book. *Darn, I must have left it at Jack's.* It was already nine o'clock, and she wasn't sure where to buy the book. She called around and found that the lesbian bookstore had the only copy in the area, so she hopped in the Porsche and drove to Oakland.

As she circled the block looking for parking, she noticed an unmistakable vehicle — a turquoise and cream Harley. *Hmm, what's she doing here — Little Miss I Have To Study?* She was a trifle annoyed at Ryan when she entered the bookstore side of the store. She looked around furtively but didn't see her friend anywhere. *Well, I guess there could be two people who ride that Harley. That is within the realm of possibility.* She found her book, stopped at the counter to pay for it and was getting ready to leave when she paused to take a quick look around the coffeehouse.

The room was quite a bit darker than the last time she had visited. A woman was on the small stage singing some contemporary ballads. Jamie scanned the crowd in the dim light and noticed that only three of the small tables were occupied — none of them by Ryan. As she turned her head slowly, trying to adjust for the differences in brightness between the two rooms, she caught what looked like a familiar form in the farthest corner of the establishment. Two women occupied a small loveseat in the very dark corner. You couldn't really say they were sitting, because neither of them was upright. An attractive black woman, with very close-cropped hair, was half-reclining on the loveseat, with Ryan partially lying on top of her.

Jamie stood slack-jawed in the bright light of the bookstore, staring in shock at the pair. Ryan was kissing the woman deeply and moving gently against her whole body as she did so. Jamie did not think she had ever seen anything that was more erotic, but every fiber of her being wanted to run out of the store and never think about the sight again. She watched as Ryan gripped the woman's face and kissed her even more passionately. Jamie could feel the desire radiating out from the pair, and even though she desperately wanted to flee, she was unable to stop watching.

Ryan began to sit up, and the woman came right with her, latched tightly on to her mouth. When they were both upright, Ryan put one arm around her shoulders and another under her knees and pulled the woman onto her lap. Jamie saw those strong, tanned hands begin to caress the woman all over her body, sliding across her ample curves. She knew she would faint if she did not look away, but she felt rooted in place. She watched as Ryan's hands again moved to either side of the woman's head and held her still as she began another round of deep kisses. Jamie saw tongues passing between mouths as they drew back an inch or two, and then fell right back into each other. The woman's hands slowly slid up Ryan's torso, and Jamie had to grasp for something to steady herself as she saw one small, dark hand firmly grasp Ryan's left breast and begin to knead it. Ryan's head rose slowly and dropped back against her shoulders as a look of absolute pleasure crossed her beautiful face. Jamie could see her chest heaving as she squirmed in her seat, and she felt a rush of sensation between her own legs as she stared at the fantastically arousing sight.

As the book slid from her now-nerveless fingers, Jamie heard a voice ask, "How ya doing kid?" The question, which came from directly behind her right shoulder, nearly caused her to scream. She used all of her composure to focus her attention in the direction of the voice. Babs, the owner of the shop and Ryan's friend, looked at her in sympathy. "Don't be mad at her, hon," she said. "Ryan's not a bad kid, but she just can't get tied down to any one woman. She's just not the type."

"What?" Jamie looked at her in total confusion. "Why would I be m ...? What?" Never in her twenty years had she felt so completely inarticulate.

"It's okay, kid. You aren't the first, and you won't be the last. Don't let it get to ya."

"B ... b ... but we're not ... she isn't ... I'm *not* ... I didn't ..." Jamie truly wanted to sink to the floor and cry. She was so frustrated with her inability to form a coherent sentence, and her chaotic feelings about Ryan, that she was truly at a loss.

"All I'm saying is that there are plenty of women who would love to date a good-lookin' girl like you. And most of them wouldn't give you up so easy as Ryan did." Shaking her head, she patted Jamie on the back and walked back into the coffeehouse.

Now, besides being painfully aroused, Jamie was totally mortified. *If Babs thinks we're together, do other people, too?* As if in a trance, her eyes traveled, of their own accord, back to the dark corner. She watched as Ryan and her date disentangled themselves from each other and stood on wobbly legs. The woman had her arm wrapped around Ryan's waist, and Ryan's arm was draped across her shoulders. Ryan's mouth was attached to the woman's neck as they stumbled through the door and out into the darkness.

In order to give herself time to collect her feelings, Jamie picked up her book and sat down at one of the small tables. She sat motionless and dazed for at least fifteen minutes with her mind a complete jumble. She was angry, puzzled, curious and more aroused than she could ever remember being.

Finally, she felt that she had enough control to drive. She walked outside and was very surprised to see the Harley still in its space. Making her way around the corner, she saw Ryan and the woman leaning up against a small import, continuing what they had been doing in the coffeehouse. The problem was that the car was right in front of Jamie's.

Now Jamie was able to sort out her feelings — she was angry. Intensely angry with both Ryan and with herself. *I want to leave for God's sake!* But even as she said this, she knew that she could walk right to her car and drive away. It was Ryan who should be embarrassed — not she. And if the throbbing in her groin had stopped for just a moment, she might have been able to convince herself of that.

Her quandary was solved a moment later when the woman opened the rear door, crouched down and slid across the seat. Ryan dove in and obviously landed right on top of her. Their heads immediately dropped below the windows, and Jamie felt that she could finally leave and not be seen.

Once at home and safe in her room, she considered the events of the evening. *It's not like I didn't know she was with a lot of women. It's just that actually seeing her with a woman was such a shock. But why did I feel so turned on?* She pondered that question for long minutes. *It must just be the thrill of seeing someone do something that is kind of forbidden. I'd probably get turned on from watching Mia and her boyfriend really go at it, too.* She could feel her body flush as she considered just how passionate Ryan had looked with her date. *God, she sure was going at it. She looked so powerful and strong when her hands possessed that woman. God, I wonder what they're doing now?* Her mind only paused a second before it delivered the obvious message. *What do you think, Jamie? They're having hot sex in the back seat of that car! Oh, God, why didn't I take abnormal psychology like everybody else?*

⌘

Jamie decided that speaking to Ryan about seeing her at the coffeehouse would serve no useful purpose, so she decided to let the matter drop. After class on Friday, they stopped for their customary juice break, but since the day was nice, they grabbed a couple of bottles of juice and went out to Faculty Glade to relax in the sun. As they got settled, Jamie was puzzled to see Ryan pull a brown bag from her book bag and begin to eat her snack.

"Uhm, Ryan?" she began.

"Mmrmfh?"

"Why are you a eating cold, dry pork chop?"

"It's cold because it was made last night, and I don't have access to a microwave. It's dry because cold gravy would make it even worse." After delivering her logical answer, she gazed at Jamie with an open, placid look on her face. This was one of Ryan's idiosyncrasies that Jamie both loved and hated. She invariably answered your question — she just answered it exactly as it had been asked. The thought passed through Jamie's mind that everyone she knew thought like a lawyer.

"You know that's not my real question," Jamie said as she gave her arm a little slap.

"Okay, I'll confess. I didn't call home by 3:00 p.m. to tell my father that I wouldn't be home for dinner. This," she said as she shook the chop, "is my punishment."

"Uhm, I guess that clears it up," she replied with a confused look.

Seeing that her explanation hadn't been very clear, Ryan continued, "Okay, my father expects each of us to be home for dinner at 6:00, sharp. It's no big deal if we can't make it, but if you don't opt out by 3:00, he cooks for you. If he cooks for you, you damn well better eat it. So, whatever you didn't eat for dinner, you get for lunch the next day."

"But you don't have to eat it, Ryan," Jamie laughed.

"Yes, I do," Ryan intoned seriously. "It's important to my father."

"What do you mean?" she asked, completely unable to understand how eating a cold pork chop could be important to anyone.

"When my mother died, he did his best to keep us functioning as a real family. Having meals together is a big part of what makes that work. When I break one of the family rules, there should be a price to pay. It's all about respect." Ryan was serious as she gazed steadily at Jamie.

"I would love to meet the man that you love and respect so much, Ryan," Jamie said as she covered Ryan's hand with one of her own.

"Why don't you come for Sunday dinner and meet everyone?"

"I would love to," Jamie replied enthusiastically.

"Sunday at 3:00. Don't be late," she threatened ominously as she gave her pork chop another shake right in Jamie's face.

⌘

Jamie left Palo Alto extra early to insure that she would be on time for Sunday dinner. Jack wasn't very happy to have her leave at 1:30, rather than after dinner as usual, but he didn't put up too much of a fuss.

She arrived at the stated address at 2:40 and found a fairly close parking space. As she approached the neat little Victorian, she heard music coming from the attached garage and decided to check there before climbing the exterior staircase to approach the front door. Two dark figures were lying on the floor, flanking a turquoise and cream Harley, as she approached.

Walking into the garage she tentatively asked, "Ryan?" still not positive that one of the figures was her friend.

"Hey, Jamie," replied a friendly voice. "Did you bring your overalls?" Ryan scooted out from beneath the bike and rose to her full six foot plus height. She wore her black hair in a neat braid that stuck out from beneath the bill of her backwards red baseball cap. A tight, white, ribbed tank top showed every dip and curve that delineated her torso. Very old, very faded 501's covered her long legs. The jeans bore large rips at each knee and small ones beneath the soft curves of her butt. As she stood, Jamie could make out gray underwear that seemed to extend well past the norm, visible through the rips. *What does she have on under those jeans?* she mused. *Does she wear boxers?*

Jamie could almost feel her chin hit her chest when the next figure stood. She was fairly certain that Ryan did not have a twin, so the tall man who now stood beside Ryan had to be a testosterone-laden clone. Looking at them together, Jamie marveled at the striking likeness, but where Ryan had smooth curves, the man had tight muscle. He was at least four or five inches taller and a lot broader in the shoulders, but his hips were narrow, much like Ryan's. He did not have an ounce of fat anywhere it did not belong, as his sister could also claim. His hair was identical in color and texture, but he wore it short around the sides of his head and a little long on top. His eyes were the same deep blue, and they had the same intensity as Ryan's, but Jamie quickly noticed that they lacked the gentleness that Ryan's often bore. His gaze seemed intimidating, almost predatory, while Ryan's usually seemed open and interested. He was dressed in a similar manner, but his T-shirt covered his shoulders, and his jeans had fewer holes.

Ryan looked thoroughly amused at the expression on Jamie's face. "Kinda creepy, huh?" she teased.

"Wha ... oh ... yeah," she admitted. "You aren't twins, are you?"

The man was busy wiping his hands on a towel. As he finished, he extended his right one in greeting. "She should be so lucky as to share my chromosomes," he said with a robust laugh.

Ryan punched him rather hard in the bicep. "This is my sweet, charming brother, Conor. Conor, this is my friend, Jamie."

"I'm pleased to meet you, Conor," Jamie finally got out, aware that she was still staring, but unable to stop.

"It's only gonna get worse, Jamie. Prepare yourself," Ryan warned.

The grungy siblings spent a few moments putting away their tools and neatening up the work area. Jamie watched them work, still unable to get over the astounding similarity. After they had finished, they all exited the front of the garage and hung a left to walk up the narrow staircase that led to the front entrance. When they reached the landing, she noticed a very nice flower-rimmed deck that obviously covered the two garages. "Nice," she said appreciatively, taking in the neat space.

"Yeah," Ryan agreed. "We've got the only deck on the whole block. Actually, one of the few in the whole neighborhood. It's a great place to sit out and get a fog tan," she chuckled, acknowledging the few clear days that her neighborhood was blessed with.

Conor held the door for her, and she stepped in before the siblings. "Your home is charming, Ryan," she enthused. As Jamie looked around, she thought to herself that part of the charm was the near Lilliputian size of the rooms. The house was only two rooms wide and two rooms long, and it seemed that every available space was filled with photos, trophies and other bits of family memorabilia.

As Jamie finished surveying the room, she was greeted by yet another of Ryan's clones. This one looked a bit older, and while he was also well built, he didn't leave the impression of raw power waiting to burst out of its skin that his siblings had. "Oh, Brendan, when did you show up?" Ryan asked as she crossed the room to give him a big hug and a kiss on the cheek.

"I came over about a half hour ago, but I've got good clothes on, and I wasn't going to let you grease monkeys talk me into ruining another pair of pants," he informed her.

"Brendan, this is my friend, Jamie," Ryan again began the introductions and was forced to add another, "and this is Rory," she said to Jamie as the last brother entered.

Well, at least he's not a clone, too, Jamie thought. Rory was shorter than Ryan by two or three inches. His hair was also lighter, and Jamie guessed that it would be a deep red in the sunlight. His eyes were a soft green, and they bore clear signs of intelligence as well as warmth. His skin was fairer than his siblings, but his features were quite similar, making him look less like a clone and more like a sibling.

"I'm pleased to meet you both," Jamie said as she shook hands with each in turn.

A voice rang out from the kitchen, "Dinner will be ready in exactly one half hour. Any people with a spot of grease on them will not be served."

Conor and Ryan cast guilty glances at each other. "Flip you for the shower," Ryan said. She produced a dime from her jeans, and Conor lucked out. "Please leave some hot water for me, Conor," she begged.

"What's it worth to ya?" he inquired.

"Well, it's you who has the most to gain, since I sit next to you at the table," she reasoned.

"Good point, stinky," he relented, "I'll hurry."

The voice boomed from the kitchen yet again. "Shi-vawn," it appeared to say, "use some manners and bring your guest in here."

"Shi-vawn?" Jamie mouthed to her friend.

Ryan looked a little sheepish. "It's my real name," she admitted. "I changed it long ago, but my father doesn't acknowledge it."

They walked through the dining room and turned right into a very large kitchen. The room was rectangular in shape and ran about fifteen feet to a screened door at the rear. It was only about nine feet in width, but the high ceilings and bright tile made it look much bigger. The kitchen was not what Jamie was mesmerized by however; that distinction fell to the older male clone stirring a pot on the stove.

Gee, I guess they're not adopted, thought Jamie. This specimen was clearly the original from whom the little O'Flaherty copies sprang. He was a good four inches taller than Ryan, with a bit of gray at the temples of his otherwise black hair. His physique matched that of Brendan, and from a distance he could have been thirty years old. But up close his face had the small lines and weathered skin that befitted a man who worked at a dangerous profession. His eyes, however, were exact copies of Ryan's — deep blue, warm and friendly.

"Da, this is my friend, Jamie," Ryan again made the introduction.

"Ahh, Jamie," he said warmly with a more than a hint of an Irish accent. "Siobhán speaks of you well and often. I'm very pleased to make your acquaintance, but I wish it had been weeks earlier," he said as he shot a glare at his smirking daughter.

"If she speaks half as well of me as she does of you, Mr. O'Flaherty, then I'm a lucky woman," Jamie replied with a twinkle.

"Siobhán, are you certain this little one is not from the old sod?" he said with a laugh. "She seems to have kissed the Blarney Stone rather recently. There is no Mr. O'Flaherty here, darlin'. You may call me Martin or Marty, whichever you choose."

"Which do you prefer?" she inquired.

"Pay attention, Siobhán," he said with a grin identical to the one Jamie had seen hundreds of times on her friend. "The child has manners." He turned to Jamie and looked a bit pensive as he finally said, "I suppose I prefer Martin. It's the name my parents gave me, and I can't think of a reason to change it." This last was directed at Ryan, who rolled her eyes. "Another lesson you could take from this one is how to dress for dinner," he said as he regarded Jamie's outfit. She wore a forest green cashmere crew neck sweater, and a pair of wide-wale corduroy slacks in a soft, buttery, cream color, looking just perfect for a Sunday afternoon dinner.

"I'll try, Da," Ryan agreed. "But I don't think even Jamie could do much for my sense of style." She cocked her head in concentration. "I think Conor's out of the shower. Wanna come to my room to give me some pointers, Jamie?"

"Sure, Ryan," she replied a little hesitantly. Even though she was very interested in seeing what was under those jeans, she knew it was not the wisest course of action. But she put her cautions to the side and followed right on Ryan's heels. They walked back to the small entryway and opened a door that Jamie had not noticed. As they descended a low-ceilinged staircase, Ryan was forced to duck her head severely. The room was surprisingly bright as it was above ground even though Jamie supposed it was technically in the basement. A large casement, double-hung window loomed over the bed and faced the small, neat backyard. Jamie could see a large, black dog looking through the window with a quizzical look on his face.

"Hi, Duffy," Ryan said as she knelt at the head of her large bed and opened the window. "Duff, this is Jamie," she said as she pointed at her amused friend. "She's my very good friend, and I want you to greet her gently." The dog cocked his big, black head and gave her a stern expression that seemed to imply agreement. "We'll be out soon, so you go practice," she said as she closed the window and the dog trotted away.

"He's awfully cute, Ryan," Jamie said. "What kind of dog is he?"

"He's half black Lab and half standard poodle. I got him from a client three years ago. Best tip I ever got," she said proudly.

Ryan rose from the bed and crossed the room to a well-built set of drawers and doors that lined the entire side wall of her room. She began to open the doors and look at her wardrobe. Jamie walked up next to her and marveled at the way everything was organized. Each drawer was labeled neatly: T-shirts L/S, T-shirts S/S, T-shirts N/S, Sweats, Socks, U/W, etc.

"Got enough T-shirts?" Jamie asked casually as she opened the N/S drawer to confirm that, indeed, the shirts stored inside did not have sleeves.

"Hey, I'm a dyke," she said defensively. "T-shirts are part of the uniform."

"Do you need help, Siobhán?" Jamie asked innocently as her friend seemed at a loss.

"Don't start," she warned with a smile.

"God, Ryan, I think I know you so well, but I don't even know your real name."

"I haven't used that name since I was seven," Ryan replied. "Only Da and my grandparents use it; even the boys stopped when I beat them up," she admitted. "And you do know me, Jamie," she said sincerely. "You know me very well. I wouldn't have invited you here otherwise."

Jamie remembered that Ryan's mother had died when she was seven. Thinking there might be a connection, she chose not to pursue the matter. "I'm sure I know all the important parts," she admitted. "Besides, a touch of mystery becomes you."

Ryan laughed and resumed her task. "My big problem is that I don't have any nice pants," she moaned. "Every time I decide to buy something nice, I find some new bike pants or a new warm up suit that I know I'll wear ten times more often, and I buy that instead."

She pulled out a perfectly acceptable pair of navy blue, wool slacks and a cream-colored, cable-knit sweater. She laid her selections out on the bed and sat down to unlace her boots. Jamie's nerve deserted her as she considered watching her undress, so she said, "I think I'll offer to help your father while you get ready."

"He won't let you help, but he'd appreciate the offer," Ryan predicted.

As she turned to leave, she remembered something that had puzzled her. "Why do you call him 'Da'?"

"It's the Irish equivalent of Dad. Many kids call their parents Ma and Da rather than Mom and Dad."

"It's kind of cute," Jamie offered as she began to walk up the stairs.

⌘

As Ryan predicted, Jamie's offer to help was rebuffed by Martin. "You go play with the children," he said as he directed her to the door off the living room. The relatively big bedroom facing the street was filled by a king-sized bed, a well-worn upholstered chair and three men lounging in various positions as they watched the '49ers battle the St. Louis Rams from a TV set located in another lovely built-in cabinet lining the wall.

Jamie sat on the floor, after refusing the offer of the chair.

Ryan joined them as halftime was just beginning, freshly scrubbed and shockingly beautiful in her dress up clothes. She sat next to Jamie on the floor and watched a little challenge that Conor had obviously just made with Jamie. They were each putting $5 up, and Rory was acting as judge. Jamie scrunched her face up, deep in thought. "Well, there has to be an 's,'" she said. "And an 'h'?" she asked hopefully.

"Two for two!" said Rory.

"How about an 'a'?"

"Three for three!"

"A 'w'?"

"Nope, one wrong," he replied.

"S-i-o-b-h-a-n" Ryan enunciated as she handed each contestant back his $5.

"No fair, Ryan," said Conor, a little perturbed.

"I don't like people to play games with the spelling of my name," she said seriously. "It bothers me," she said softly as she looked at the floor.

"I'm sorry, Ryan," Conor said quickly as he rose from the bed and squatted down to look into her eyes. "I wouldn't have done it if I knew it would bother you."

"Well," she admitted, "It doesn't bother me much, but it did get you off the bed and into my evil hands," she laughed gleefully as she began to tickle his sides unmercifully. He quickly lost his ability to remain upright, but she stuck right with him as he rolled around on the floor.

"Please, please, no more, I can't take it," he pleaded as he giggled hysterically. "You win, you win!"

"I always win," she said proudly as she helped him straighten up. "I'm the little sister."

"Just our luck boys," he addressed his laughing brothers. "To have a little sister who can kick all of our butts."

The game began again just as Martin called them all to dinner. Brendan rose and hit the record button on the VCR, and they all walked into the dining room without a word of complaint.

Jamie could not remember ever having a better time at the dinner table. Meals at her home were always pleasant enough, but there was never much spark.

The O'Flaherty clan, however, spent their mealtimes in a boisterous mélange of funny stories, jokes and constant teasing. Jamie was pleased that they seemed to welcome her into the group seamlessly. They teased her often, but gently, much the way they did to each other. By the end of the meal, Jamie had formed some tentative impressions of each of the O'Flaherty men.

Martin was clearly in charge. All of the children seemed to respect and admire him, but she did not detect even a glimmer of fear. When he told one of them to stop a tease that was becoming too sharp, he did so immediately. He had quite a flair for storytelling, and Jamie noticed that each of the kids listened to him raptly even though she imagined they had heard his stories many times. The number of repetitions was obvious when he finished one, and all of the children complained that he had changed the ending. "How else can I keep the lot of you on your toes?" he explained with a laugh.

Brendan was the most serious of the group. He was a lawyer with a small, public interest law firm, working to secure the rights of people with disabilities. The other boys and Ryan looked to him as a bit of an arbiter also. He was quite adept at keeping the rest of them in line with his wit and easy laughter, and his teasing was very gentle and sweet.

Conor was clearly the troublemaker of the boys. He seemed to love to get under everyone else's skin. Jamie could just imagine the practical jokes he must have played on the others when they were growing up. She wasn't surprised when Martin told of the number of times he had to leave work to bail young Conor out of the principal's office.

Conor worked as a carpenter, a trade that he loved and was obviously very good at. He had built Ryan's wall-to-wall closet and Martin's bookcase, and the work was immaculate. He worked for a firm that did renovation work in the city, and he took obvious pride in talking about the historically accurate work his firm did on the city's many Victorian homes.

Rory was very boyish and a little shy. He was a musician and played in a band that often performed at various pubs and clubs in the city. Ryan explained that his group played primarily traditional Irish music. Jamie wasn't sure what that meant, but she hoped to find out. He traveled quite a bit when his band toured with bigger name acts, but he would be at home for several months this winter, playing around the city. He would occasionally lapse into a soft, Irish brogue that one of the others would call him on. Ryan explained that he spent most of the summer in Ireland every year, playing all over the country, and that the brogue lingered. Ryan seemed particularly fond of Rory, and she boasted to Jamie about his considerable talents as a musician. He just blushed, and shook his head at the compliments, but it was clear that he appreciated them.

When dinner had ended, Jamie was amazed at what happened next. With nary a word from Martin, or to each other, each child got up and began to perform a particular task.

Brendan began to clear the counters, while running water in the sink.

Conor cleared the table, while Rory got out a towel to dry the dishes with. Ryan busied herself removing the linen tablecloth and placemats, taking them into the kitchen to pre-spot any food stains. Jamie offered to help, but Ryan refused her offer saying, "Once we get going, you could get hurt if you tried to step in."

The multiple tasks were quickly finished, and in less than twenty minutes every dish was put away neatly. Ryan had the final job of sweeping and mopping the floor, and she backed herself out of the back door as she finished. Minutes later she re-emerged, via the front door, accompanied by Duffy.

Duffy tried his best, but gentle was not the term best used for his initial greeting of Jamie. He placed his big, black paws on her waist and whimpered until she lowered her face enough to be thoroughly licked. "I guess I should have asked if you like dogs," Ryan drawled.

"Lucky for you, I love them," Jamie enthused.

Duffy was obviously in love with every member of the family. He went to each of the brothers in turn and joyfully licked each face. Martin made a show of disliking the attention, but he giggled as Duffy worked away, despite his complaints.

As Ryan sat down on a love seat, Duffy climbed right up next to her and dropped his head in her lap. "Duffy, we have company," she gently rebuked him. "You know there are only enough seats for the humans." With a baleful stare, Duffy lay on the floor, his big, black head resting on Jamie's foot.

After a few minutes of chat, the boys decided to watch the rest of the game, but Ryan caught Jamie's eye and indicated that she wanted to go downstairs.

"So, what do you think?" Ryan asked as she flopped down on her big bed. Jamie sat on Ryan's desk chair, pulling it next to the bed and putting her stocking feet up on the comforter.

"About what?" she asked innocently.

"You know what — what did you think of my family?" Ryan stated the obvious.

Jamie gave her a big smile as she admitted, "I don't remember when I've met a nicer group of people."

"You must not get out much," Ryan drawled, but she was obviously pleased by the compliment.

"I get out plenty, Ryan, and believe me, you are one lucky woman. Your brothers clearly adore you, and your father's face lights up every time he looks at you."

Ryan gazed at her in contemplative silence for a few minutes. "I really do know how lucky I am, Jamie," she said softly. "I spent a couple of years feeling sorry for myself during puberty. I missed my mother so much, and it was hard going through that with a bunch of clueless men. But once I got a little older and saw how few people share the kind of love we have for each other ..." She let out a sigh, "I thank God every day for all that I have".

"Do you really?" Jamie asked, interested in this new facet of her friend. "You've never talked about your spirituality."

"Yeah, I really do," Ryan admitted. She looked a little bashful, but continued tentatively, "I wanna tell you something that I've only told Da." She locked her clear eyes on Jamie, obviously waiting for permission.

Jamie returned her look and gave her an encouraging smile, "Please do."

Ryan cleared her throat a little nervously as she began. "As I've told you before, my mother died when I was seven. I was just starting second grade when it happened, and we were beginning to receive religious instruction. The nuns told us about letting Jesus into our hearts, and all of the standard religious stuff they think seven-year-olds can comprehend. But what struck me the most was when they talked about the Virgin Mary. Sister Kevin explained that we could talk to Jesus directly, but we could also get a message to him via his mother. She said that Mary would always watch over us just like our own mothers would." Ryan looked down at her folded hands and wiped a tear from her eye. Jamie took this opportunity to get up and sit down right next to her, reassuring her by her presence.

"I figured that since my mother was already with God, I didn't have to go through the Virgin Mary. I had an insider to listen to my prayers and direct them to the proper party." She laughed a little at the memory of her childish self. "So, from then on I prayed to my mother instead of to God or Jesus. I knew that no one would ever care more for me than she did, and I knew she would always be there to watch over me. I still do that every night," she admitted with a catch in her voice as the tears began to flow in earnest.

Without allowing herself a moment to second-guess her actions, Jamie scooted even closer and wrapped her arms tightly around Ryan's sobbing shoulders. "Shh, shh," she cooed into her ear, rocking her gently while she caressed her head.

They sat like that for a few long minutes, Ryan seemingly at ease with exposing herself so totally — Jamie touched beyond words at the trust that Ryan showed by her actions. After a bit Ryan leaned away to grope for a box of Kleenex on her bedside table. She took several for herself and watched as Jamie did the same, clearly having been moved by the story.

"Does it bother you to talk about her, Ryan?" she finally asked, still sniffing away a few tears.

Ryan closed her eyes and leaned her head back for a moment. Then she took in a breath and said, "No, not with you or my family. I miss her more than I can express in words, but she loved me so well that I can still feel her presence. She's in my heart — in my soul. Do you know what I mean?"

Nodding briefly, still struggling with her feelings, Jamie relaxed against Ryan when the larger woman tucked an arm around her waist.

"It makes her come alive again to talk about her with people that I'm close to," she murmured.

Jamie was enormously pleased at this revelation of Ryan's feelings for their friendship. She leaned over and gently kissed both of her moist, pink cheeks. "I'm sure she would be proud of the woman that you have become, Ryan," she whispered.

Ryan gazed at her with the most adorable little grin that Jamie had ever seen on a human being. Her eyes were a little hooded, and she looked just a bit embarrassed, saying, "Thanks, Jamie, that means a lot, coming from you."

After they sat in companionable silence for a few more minutes, Jamie got up from the bed and walked around the room, examining it closely. The room looked very much like Ryan; clean, neat, organized and fairly utilitarian, but with a little color here and there. A large built-in bookshelf covered the wall opposite the closet and it was filled with science texts, magazines, awards, trophies for various sports and photos. Jamie was struck by one such photo, and after staring at it for a few moments, she turned back to Ryan with tears in her eyes again. "You knew, didn't you?" she inquired plainly. Ryan rose and came to stand next to her, and she put an arm around Jamie's shoulders while she looked at the very familiar picture.

The three by five color photo in the simple frame showed a very ill woman holding a small, very melancholy-looking child. Ryan's big, blue eyes stared up at the camera and revealed all of her fears. The woman, who Jamie guessed was quite beautiful before illness had ravaged her, also stared directly into the lens. She had a stoic, calm look on her face, and it was clear that she still possessed a fiery spirit. Little Ryan was holding on to her tightly, her small arms wrapped around the frail waist. Ryan's head was resting on a bony shoulder, and a painfully thin hand held the back of her small head.

"Yes, I knew how sick she was. This was my seventh birthday," she said wistfully. "I didn't understand what death was, but I knew that she was going to leave soon, and I knew she wasn't coming back. She died about a month after this picture was taken," she said with a flat voice.

"Oh, Ryan, I'm so sorry you had to feel all of that pain," Jamie said as she turned, and was enveloped by Ryan's strong arms.

"Everybody feels pain like that if they really love someone. No one gets out of here alive, you know," she whispered into Jamie's ear.

"I know, but you were such a baby, Ryan. Look at that precious little face," she lamented as she looked at the photo again.

"I'm not saying that I didn't have a difficult time, Jamie; I know I did. It was incredibly tough for a little girl not to have her mother. There were times that I felt so lost that I didn't think I could survive. The pain was just so great. But I got through it, and it made me stronger, and it enhanced the connection that I have with my brothers and my father. That's what I'm the most grateful for. Death tears many families apart, but it made ours much stronger."

"You don't have to answer this if you don't want to, Ryan," Jamie said as she pulled away from their embrace, "but why did you change your name?"

"As I'm sure you've guessed, it was because of my mother. She loved the name Siobhán, and Da said she was ready with the name for each of the three boys. I liked it, too, mainly because it was different. I got through first grade okay because everybody was just getting used to each other, and having an odd name was hardly noticed. But right after I came back to school after my mother died, a little boy started making fun of my name. We were just learning to read using phonics, and as you found out today, that's one name where phonics doesn't apply. The other kids kind of picked up on his teasing, and I just flipped out. It was probably too soon for me to be back at school, but there I was, and I had kind of a little episode. In retrospect, it must have been a panic attack, and from that day forward, every time a person outside of my family called me Siobhán, I got hysterical. Nobody knew what to do with me. It had only been a couple of weeks since my mother died, and everybody in the family had their own issues they were trying to deal with. Luckily, Sister Kevin sat me down and asked me what I would rather be called. Most of my ideas were unacceptable, running along the lines of things like Tigger as I recall," she said with a gentle laugh.

Jamie let out a little laugh of her own as she continued to look at the picture, unable to take her eyes from the heart-breaking look on the adorable little face.

"Finally, and with a lot of prompting from Sister Kevin, we settled on Ryan. It was my middle name, and my mother's maiden name, and Sister Kevin pointed out how that would keep her with me every time someone spoke my name. That was about the only time that Da just wasn't able to support me," she admitted sadly. "He was really invested in the name since my mother had loved it so. But he didn't put up too much of a fuss after Sister Kevin explained it all to him. The side benefit, of course, is that I don't have to spell Siobhán several times a day," she said with a little smile.

"Wow, Sister Kevin sounds like a neat lady," Jamie said.

"Yeah, she really was. I lost touch with her when her order left our parish, but I still think of her often," Ryan said.

"I do have one more question," Jamie finally said. "That balletic performance of cleaning the kitchen was something to behold. How did that come about?"

"That's another effect of my mother's illness. When she was too ill to cook or do housework, we were all assigned jobs. I was so little that I had to do the jobs closest to the floor. Brendan helped me with the mopping for years, but I think it was important that they made me feel a part of it," she smiled at the memory. "After my mother died, we just kept to the same tasks. Da transferred from active fire fighting and became a cook. He did it mostly because he just wasn't willing to risk his life anymore. We couldn't afford to lose him, too. He became a good cook, and we just drifted into his doing all the cooking and our doing all the cleaning. It's a little militaristic, but that's how a firehouse is run."

Jamie spent a few more minutes looking at the photos placed all over the room. She found one of Ryan's mother when she was about Ryan's age. "Wow, she was a great-looking woman," Jamie said.

Ryan grasped the picture in her hand and looked at it for a few moments. "Yeah, she was," she said softly. "I used to wish I looked more like her. She was small and delicate, fair-skinned, with auburn hair and vivid green eyes. She had a lovely soprano singing voice and just the gentlest touch you could imagine. When I was going through puberty I felt so big and awkward that I wished I had inherited her bone structure. But it all worked out in the end," she admitted.

"Yeah," Jamie agreed with a chuckle. "I don't think you'd get much sympathy complaining about your looks, Ms. O'Flaherty."

Ryan's eyes darted a little and she changed the subject quickly. "Let's go see what the boys are doing," she suggested. As they returned to the first floor, Conor came out of the bedroom and asked with a hopeful look, "Jamie, Ryan said you have a Boxster. Could I take a look at it?"

"Sure, Conor, you can drive it if you want."

"Can I really?" he asked with delight. "I've never driven a Porsche. Cars are kind of my passion, but I have to drive a truck for work."

"Here are the keys," she replied as she tossed him the set.

"Aren't you gonna go with me?" he asked as his baby blues lit up.

"I will if you want me to, but it's okay if you want to go alone."

"I don't want to hurt anything. You can show me where all the buttons are," he grinned.

As they began to make their way to the stairs, Ryan grabbed Jamie's arm and whispered, "Be careful. He thinks he's God's gift to women."

Jamie wrinkled up her nose and whispered back, "And you don't?"

⌘

Conor drove very quickly, seeming to have a route in mind. Jamie was trying to keep up a conversation while praying that he didn't crash the car with his aggressive moves, and before she knew it, they were nearly in the financial district. He turned around to head back home, and as they passed a coffee bar, he turned to Jamie and said, "You look chilled. Why don't you pop in and get us each a cup of coffee or cocoa?"

"I am a little frozen," she admitted. "You don't want to come in?"

"Nah. No parking. I'll just idle here until a cop comes up."

"Okay, but I think I'll call your house to tell Ryan we'll be gone awhile," she said as she pulled her Startac from the glove box.

He reached into his pocket and pulled out a twenty dollar bill. "You go on in and order me a cocoa. I'll call and then put the top back up. Go get warm," he said firmly.

As Jamie hopped out, he dialed the little phone. Ryan answered on the first ring. "Hi, sis, it's me."

"Where are you?" she said crossly. "You've been gone over an hour."

"You sound a bit possessive, Ryan. I thought this one was on my team," he laughed.

"She is on your team, but she's somebody else's starting pitcher — so keep your mitts off her," she warned.

"I have no intention of touching her ... unless she asks me to, of course. We stopped for coffee to warm up a bit. We'll be home soon. Now don't wait up if you get tired. I'll make sure she's well taken care of."

"Conor, if you harm one hair on her head, I'll kick your butt all the way down Market Street," she threatened.

"How can I hurt her getting a cup of coffee?" he asked innocently.

"Just bring her back in one piece — and still engaged!" she said as she hung up.

"Gotcha!" he crowed as he shut the phone off.

⌘

On Thursday night Jamie was riding her bike home after a long night at the library. It was about nine o'clock, and the wafting scent from Hallowed Grounds called to her. She locked up her bike and walked into the warm space. As she stood at the counter waiting for her latte, she spied Ryan sitting in the corner, her head bent in conversation with a young woman. A very young woman. A very, *very* young woman. *Boy, does she not fit the mold.* The woman had a shaved head and a riot of piercings on her ears and eyebrows. *I bet she's got some that are hidden, too.* That bet was quickly resolved when she got up to go to the restroom. She walked right by Jamie, and fairly large rings clearly showed their shape upon her nipples through her thin tank top. Jamie stared at her in shock. *She couldn't be out of high school!* She turned her gaze to Ryan who was staring at her with a bemused expression on her face. Jamie marched right over to her, her outrage growing with each step.

"Gee, Ryan, isn't it a school night?" she asked with syrupy sweetness. "You don't want your date to be late for the bus in the morning!"

"What do you mean, Jamie?" Ryan inquired with a look of pure innocence on her face.

"That woman doesn't look like she's even out of high school!" she fumed.

"Don't be ridiculous, Jamie," she said with a big grin. "Jennie isn't in high school."

"Well, you could have fooled me ..." she began but was cut off by the woman's return.

"Jennie, Jamie thought you were in high school," she laughed.

Jennie laughed, too, and mumbled, "I wish."

"Jamie, Jennie is in grade school," she said with a guileless expression. "She just turned thirteen."

Jamie felt as though her head would burst. She knew her face was bright red, and she felt completely unable to form a word to express her outrage that her friend was obviously a child molester.

Ryan turned to Jennie, "You don't mind if I tell Jamie about the nature of our relationship, do you?"

"Nope," Jennie replied easily as she smiled up at Jamie.

"I work with Jennie though a group called Gay Teens in Crisis. She's had some tough times at home and is currently living in a group home here in Berkeley. She's kind of my little sister," she said as Jennie beamed at her.

Jamie felt all of the color drain out of her face. Struggling mightily, she pulled out a chair and sat down before she fell down. As soon as she looked up at Ryan's sweet smile, she felt her color rise again, this time reflecting her profound embarrassment.

"Did you order something, Jamie?" Jennie asked, looking at the empty space in front of Jamie.

"Uh-huh, a latte," she mumbled in reply.

"I'll get it for you. Then I gotta take off, Ryan. Nine thirty is my curfew."

Jamie stared at Ryan who just looked back at her placidly. They sat that way until Jennie returned. She kissed Ryan on the cheek and picked up her book bag and her bike helmet. "Put it on," Ryan ordered.

"It's so rank, Ryan. I've got an image to maintain."

"Well, I happen to like your brain," Ryan said as she stood and plunked the helmet on the stubbly head, "and since you don't even have hair to cushion it, you've gotta wear this."

"Okay, you win," Jennie said as she gave Ryan a quick hug. "Good to meet you, Jamie," she said over her shoulder as she hiked up her huge khaki pants and left the shop.

Jamie dropped her head to the table with an audible thunk. "I am such a jerk!" she moaned into the wood.

"It's okay, Jamie," Ryan replied as she patted her back. "It's not like it's outside of the realm of possibility that I would be with a younger woman," she admitted. "Although thirteen *is* a little young, even for me. I like my women to at least be able to go to an R-rated movie with me," she teased.

"I am such a jerk!" Jamie repeated, still not lifting her head from the table.

"You are most definitely not a jerk, Jamie. I was taunting you a bit. I made it worse, and I'm sorry." After a moment she added, "As long as you've got your head down there, can I ask you something?" she inquired.

"Sure," she mumbled from her new tabletop home.

"Were you at the bookstore last Wednesday night?"

"Oh, God," she moaned and sank even lower in her chair. "Is there no end to my humiliation?"

"What did you see?" Ryan asked gently as she again placed her hand on Jamie's back and gave it a reassuring scratch.

"I saw you ... uhm ... talking to someone," she said as she lifted her head, hoping that Ryan did not know what she had seen. "How did you know I was there?"

"I saw your car when I went outside. I figured you were there, but I was kind of, uhm … occupied," she admitted with her own flush rising to her cheeks. Suddenly, this information made Jamie feel much better, since all indications were that Ryan hadn't seen her staring. She was beginning to get her normal color back and had risen to sit upright in her chair. But Ryan decided she needed to be completely honest with Jamie, so she told her the rest. "Plus, Babs told me she saw you," she admitted.

As Jamie's color rose, her body sank until she was again face down on the table. "Shoot me now, please," she moaned. "What did she tell you?" she asked with a quavering voice.

"Uhm, she was under the impression that we had been … uhm … dating," Ryan explained. "And she said that you looked kind of upset," Ryan paused a bit. "I wasn't going to say anything, but I thought that maybe that was why seeing Jennie bothered you," she revealed.

"Yeah, that's probably true," she said with her muffled voice.

"Why didn't you say something, Jamie? I hate to think that my behavior upset you in any way. Tell me what happened," she said gently, lifting Jamie's head with both hands.

Jamie sat up straight and cleared her throat. "I had to pick up a book for that report we were doing. I went and was just leaving when I saw you. It was like watching a train wreck, Ryan!"

"Uhm … I don't think I get the analogy," she said with a confused look on her face.

"You know, when something happens that you know you shouldn't see, but you can't help it. I saw you getting kind of, uhm … frisky, and Babs came up behind me. I felt like I had been caught doing something wrong. She jumped to all sorts of conclusions, but I was too embarrassed to set her straight. I just stood there unable to explain a darn thing."

"Go on," Ryan reassured her.

"Well, I was mortified to have her make those assumptions and to have been caught staring at you, so I went out to my car, and you were, uhm … occupied, right in front of me. I felt like I was stuck there because I certainly wasn't going to interrupt you at that point." She blushed fiercely, even while receiving a warm smile from her friend. "But you got in her car, and I was able to leave," she said as she let out a big breath.

"So … does it bother you to see me with a woman?" she asked slowly.

"No, I don't think so. I saw you with Chitra from class that time, and it didn't bother me at all."

"That's true," she mused. "But you didn't know me very well then. Do you think that made a difference?"

"That might be part of it," she admitted. "But I think the bigger issue this time was that you didn't know you were being watched. I felt like a voyeur," she confessed. "I'm really sorry I saw you and that I didn't turn away immediately, Ryan."

"And I'm sorry that I embarrassed you, Jamie. Robin lives at home, too, so we don't really have anywhere to go to be, uhm ... alone. I don't usually let myself get that carried away in public," she dipped her head and her cheeks colored brightly. "But things got out of control, and I just lost my head. Like I said at the gym on that afternoon, I was feeling a little twitchy."

"I'm sorry, Ryan, that must be difficult for you," she said sincerely.

Ryan grinned broadly. "You don't know what difficult is until you try to do it in the back seat of a Hyundai when you're over six feet tall," she drawled.

"Well, I hope it all worked out in the end," Jamie teased back.

"Yeah, we reached our destination," she divulged, "but my neck's still stiff." She laughed as she rubbed the part in question. "I've got to start inquiring about living arrangements before I accept dates," she said with a grin.

"Hey, don't rule out girls with big cars, either," Jamie reminded her. "The SUV craze ought to be good for something!"

⌘

After class on Friday, Ryan was bubbling with energy. Always vaguely hyperactive, she was bouncing around in her seat, looking for something to keep her occupied.

"How did your father harness your energy when you were a kid?" Jamie asked, giving her a fond smile.

"Sports — lots of sports," she revealed. "Plus music lessons, gymnastics, karate, various clubs at school and church. Just the usual. I think I'm a little wacky these days because I'm getting too much sleep. This is my normal state," she decided. "Scary, isn't it?"

Her new schedule allowed her to sleep an extra two and a half hours a night, or even go out occasionally, something that had not been possible for years. "You know, Jamie, you have allowed me to have a quality of life that I didn't think was possible. Getting me that job at the gym has allowed me to feel more rested than I have in years."

Jamie regarded her friend carefully. Ryan did look better than she had ever seen her. *Not that she had ever looked truly bad,* she thought with a laugh. But Ryan now looked completely relaxed and was childlike and very playful the vast majority of the time. The little lines of tension that sometimes nestled between her eyebrows were completely gone, and Jamie also noticed that Ryan's chronic habit of rubbing her eyes had almost stopped.

"Did you hear Linda say that we didn't have class on Monday?" she asked, changing the topic.

"I have never missed a teacher canceling a class," Ryan replied lightly. "I could sleep till noon if I wanted to," she said happily. "I'm all caught up on my lab work, so I don't have that on Monday, either."

"I have a little idea for how to occupy your morning, if you're up to getting your butt kicked," she offered.

"I guess that depends on who is doing the kicking," she mused.

"How about me?" Jamie replied.

"What method are you planning on using for kicking my butt?"

"Golf clubs," Jamie replied fiendishly.

"I think my butt is in big trouble," Ryan replied with a grimace.

⌘

Jamie pulled up in front of Ryan's home at 6:00 a.m., sharp, driving an enormous, claret red Range Rover. Ryan popped out of the front door looking absolutely perfect for a day on the links. She wore a navy blue turtleneck under a navy blue, emerald and white argyle cardigan. Navy blue poplin slacks covered her long legs, and her hair was in a neat braid that hung down her back. She looked at Jamie with a quizzical grin. "Uhm, Jamie," she said across the roof of the big car, "Something ate your car."

"As much as I love my little car, golf clubs do not fit well," Jamie replied. "My father has an apartment in the city, and he keeps this car there. I called him, and he wasn't planning on using it, so here we are."

"Pretty nice spare," Ryan replied as she looked the car over thoroughly.

Jamie tossed the keys to her without a word. Ryan gave her a winning grin and trotted around to the driver's side. "You know me too well, Jamie. I have to learn to keep some secrets from you."

"I don't think you can ever learn to keep that grin off your face," she replied fondly.

Ryan looked like she belonged in the big car. The scale of the car fit her perfectly, unlike Jamie, who looked a bit lost in it. "So, where to?" she inquired brightly. "I hope it's far," she added as she gripped the wheel and got a devilish look in her eyes.

"We're going to the Olympic Club," Jamie replied.

"The Olympic Club?" Ryan nearly shouted. "I've never played before, Jamie. They hold the U.S. Open there!"

"I'm well aware of the history of the club, Ryan. My mother's family has belonged for generations," she stated honestly. "But don't worry your pretty little head. We'll get warmed up on the driving range, then we'll get a cart, and you can caddy for me if you don't feel comfortable."

"Do I get to drive the cart?" she pleaded. "I've always wanted to drive one of those little things."

"Yes, you can drive the cart," she replied indulgently as she smiled at Ryan's hopeful look.

"Okay, let's go!" she responded gleefully.

As she glanced into the rear of the car Ryan noticed only one set of clubs. "Did you bring some clubs for me?" she asked.

"Yep, those are for you. If you can play with right-handed clubs, that is. My father keeps a spare set at the apartment for guests or when he wants to play another course. He's about your height, and you're easily as strong as he is, so I thought they would fit you," she explained.

"Well, since I've never struck a golf ball, I guess I can do it equally poorly from either side, so right-handed clubs should be fine."

"Well, it's a little more complex than that, Ryan. Is your right hand dexterous?"

A rakish grin and a tilt of the head was her devilish response.

"Come on, silly. Be honest with me. I'm sure we can rent a set of left-handed clubs at the course if we need to."

"No, Jamie. Right-handed ones are fine. I'm a natural lefty, but I switch-hit when I play softball, and I can throw with either hand."

"You are quite the jock, aren't you?" she observed as she cast a sly glance at Ryan's athletic body.

"I do all right," she said with a touch of smugness.

A few minutes later, Ryan pulled up to the attractive clubhouse as an attendant in a white shirt and pants dashed out to greet them. "Good morning, Miss Evans," he greeted Jamie cheerfully. "Are you joining Mr. Evans this morning?"

"No, my friend and I are going to play alone today," Jamie replied as another attendant ran to open Ryan's door. The first young man trotted around to the trunk and lifted the gate. "Will you be having breakfast first?" he inquired.

"No, but I would like a large hot chocolate," she said, rubbing her hands together against the morning chill. "How about you, Ryan?"

"Sounds great. I'd love one," Ryan replied.

"We'll be over at the range, Charlie," she replied as she led Ryan into the clubhouse.

"What size shoes do you wear?" Jamie asked curiously.

"It depends on the shoes," Ryan replied. "My gym shoes are usually elevens, but some of my loafers are size ten and a half. Why?"

"Come with me," Jamie replied mysteriously.

They walked into the opulent pro shop. Ryan gazed around the overstocked shelves a bit in awe. "Hi, Jason," Jamie called brightly.

"Morning, Miss Evans," he replied. "What can I do for you today?"

"My friend here," she indicated Ryan, "needs a couple of things. Hold up your left hand," she instructed as Ryan dutifully complied.

"Hmm," replied Jason. "Looks like a cadet medium. What color?"

Jamie replied for her, "Navy," she replied firmly.

He handed Ryan a navy glove which she slipped onto her left hand. "Seems perfect," she replied as she got the idea and held up her hand for Jason's inspection.

"What else?" Jason inquired.

"A pair of FootJoys, ten and a half, leather soles, this style," she lifted her own foot for him to see. This got her a wide-eyed look from Ryan, but Jamie just winked at her and said, "Trust me."

Jason brought the shoes out, and Ryan sat down and removed her gym shoes. "Would you like to wear two pairs of socks, ma'am?" he inquired. Ryan looked to Jamie who again replied for her. "Yes, a pair of FootJoys."

As he left to find the proper socks, Ryan said in a whisper, "What are you doing? I can't afford this, and I don't want you buying all this for me."

"You can't judge if you like the game if you don't have the right equipment. Now be quiet, or I'll buy you golf clubs!" she threatened. Ryan closed her mouth abruptly and kept it closed. With two pairs of socks she needed the size eleven shoes, but she nodded her assent when Jason asked about her comfort.

They clomped out of the pro shop and walked in silence to the rear of the building. Exiting the rear door, they walked the short distance to the driving range where their clubs were set up neatly on bag stands. Large buckets of clean white balls stood near each set of clubs. A golf cart sat about five feet behind the clubs, and Ryan could see two large insulated mugs in the drink holders.

"So, this is how the other one half of one percent lives," she mused. Giving Jamie a stern look, she said, "I don't want to seem ungrateful, but I wouldn't have accepted this invitation if I had known you were going to spend this much money on me," she chided.

"Well, Miss O'Flaherty," she replied logically, "why do you think I didn't tell you beforehand?"

"It really does make me uncomfortable," Ryan revealed seriously. "I'm not used to my friends spending money on me."

"Look, Ryan, let's get this settled," she said as she sat in the cart and patted the seat next to her. Ryan gamely joined her and met her eyes. "I will personally have so much money one day that I don't believe I could spend it all in my lifetime, unless I started buying military aircraft."

"But ..." Ryan started but was cut off.

"I wanted to come here to play today. It's much more fun for me to have you with me. You'll enjoy the day more if you have the correct shoes, and you'll not get a blister on your hand if you wear a glove. The membership here belongs to my father, and he's happy that I brought you here. He figures that if I have a friend to play with, I'll play more. If I play more, I get better. When I play well, it gives him enormous pleasure. So, really, you've made my whole family happy by being my guest," her face curled into a cute little grin that Ryan had no defenses against.

"Well, if it makes the whole family happy, I guess I can't turn it down," she grumbled.

"Ryan, you are the last person who would want to be my friend because of my money. But it gives me pleasure to spend just a tiny bit of it on you. Will you let me do that once in a while?"

She took a deep breath, gazing into Jamie's eyes and found herself saying, "Yes, Jamie, I will. I promise I will not bring it up the rest of the day. I will just sink into the lap of luxury and enjoy."

⌘

After a long time at the range, Jamie's patient instruction began to pay off, and Ryan was able to make a very passable swing at the ball. They decided to play a round, but Ryan didn't even try to chip or putt, choosing to watch Jamie's form, rather than trying those things herself just yet. After the round they had lunch, and Jamie signed for the bill as she had all day.

Ryan pondered how she would repay her and finally reached a decision. "Jamie, I can't tell you how much I've enjoyed today," she said sincerely. "But our friendship has reached a close enough level that I feel uncomfortable having you pay me to train you." She held up her hand to stop Jamie's protest. "Yes, I know that this is my profession, and that I would be able to work with a paying customer if I weren't working with you. But I want to give my talents to you, Jamie. I don't want you to pay for them anymore."

"But, Ryan," she protested, "that's $375 a week you could be earning."

"I'm well aware of that, Jamie," she said, appraising her friend. "But money isn't an issue between us. If we weren't working out together, I'd still want to be with you, just hanging out. I really enjoy our workouts — I actually look forward to them. So, please don't ask me to accept money for spending three enjoyable hours with you a week. At this point in our relationship, I just can't accept it."

"Okay," Jamie agreed reluctantly. "I can tell that you've made up your mind. Can I bring you to play golf every once in a while, so I don't feel like I'm completely abusing you?"

"Deal," Ryan replied as they shook hands on the agreement.

Ryan had just enough time for Jamie to drop her off at home. As Jamie pulled up to the house, Conor was maneuvering his big, black Dodge Ram into a nearby parking space. *Boy, he looks good in that*, she mused. He came over to the Range Rover as Ryan got out and dashed in the house to change. "Gee, Jamie, do you have a different car for every day of the week?"

"No, Conor. I actually only have one. This is my father's. We borrowed it so we could play golf this morning."

"Golf? Ryan played golf?" he said in amazement. "I started playing about five years ago, and she hasn't stop teasing me about it since. Thanks for the ammo, Jamie," he said. "So, where did you play? Tilden?"

"No, we played at my father's club," she replied, hoping he wouldn't pursue the point.

"Which is ...?" he inquired.

"Olympic," she said without embellishment.

"You took Ryan to play at the Olympic Club?" he said, his mouth hanging open in shock. "Are you still a member, or did they throw you out?" he teased.

"She did very, very well, I'll have you know. I've been playing since I was six, and I'll bet she could beat me within the year if she worked at it. She's such a gifted athlete," she said admiringly.

"Oh, she'll work at it, all right. She owes me at least twenty rounds after all the teasing I've put up with. That gives me an idea for her birthday, though."

"Her birthday? When is it?"

"It's Friday. She's going to be twenty-three."

"I had no idea — the little rat!"

"Well, you've really helped me out. I didn't have any ideas for a present for her until now. Hey, it would be fun if Brendan and I could play as a foursome with you two sometime," he added.

"I'd like that," Jamie agreed.

Ryan was barreling down the stairs to fetch her motorcycle when she spotted Conor still at the driver's door of the Range Rover. "You can't drive that one, Conor. It's her father's," she stated with authority.

"Did you drive it?" he questioned.

"Yeah, but I'm trustworthy," she stated in a superior manner.

Jamie laughed and said, "Sorry, Conor, I've got to get back to Berkeley before traffic gets bad. But next time, I'll let you drive it," she promised.

Ryan grabbed her bike from the garage and walked it up next to Conor. "Gotta run." She smiled warmly and said, "I really had a fabulous day, Jamie." After a beat she added, "Have we ever had a bad time together?"

"Nope. But I'm sure I'll wear on your nerves over time."

"Don't count on it, buddy," Ryan said as she patted Jamie's cheek with an affectionate smile on her face.

⌘ CHAPTER SIX

ONE OF THE CLASS PROJECTS RYAN AND JAMIE HAD AGREED TO TACKLE
involved spending some time volunteering at a lesbian-centered community
organization. Ryan had a long association with one such outfit, and she
agreed to arrange for two evening volunteer sessions at the Gay and
Lesbian Teen Talk Line.

Jamie picked Ryan up from the biology building at 6:30. They generally
didn't see each other on Tuesdays, and Jamie knew that it was Ryan's
busiest day. She also knew that she had a tendency to ignore her own
needs in order to be early for her appointments. "Have you eaten?" she
inquired sternly.

"Yep," Ryan replied as she patted her flat belly. "Da fixed me a
delicious spaghetti dinner, which I ate with gusto."

"Good. Then let's get over there early, so we can get set up." Jamie
always felt more comfortable when she was early for an appointment, and
she knew that Ryan had the same quirk.

They drove through the streets of Berkeley and crossed over into
Oakland. When they reached a rather seedy neighborhood, Ryan pointed
out the building and Jamie pulled up in front. A small sign read,
"G.L.T.T.L." "That's certainly unobtrusive enough," Jamie remarked.
"Do you think they get harassed here?"

"Not that I've ever heard of," Ryan replied. "It's not a bad idea to be
cautious, though."

As they went into the small building Jamie noticed several cubicles
each about six feet in height. She could hear soft voices coming from
them, and she assumed that people were within each one, taking calls.
Ryan confirmed this as they walked into a small office near the rear of the
building. A large, redheaded woman rose to greet Ryan with a big smile
on her expressive face. "Ryan, I have missed you," she said as Ryan
enveloped her in a hug.

"I've missed you, too, Yvonne. I feel guilty for not having been here in a
year."

"Honey, I think you still hold the honor of logging the most hours of
any volunteer we've ever had. Your name is still up on the plaque," she

136

reminded her, indicating a little wooden sign that listed the most loyal volunteers. "We're just glad to see you again," she said as she patted Ryan's back.

"Oh, Yvonne, this is my friend, Jamie." Jamie nodded at Yvonne as Ryan continued, "I thought I could take calls, and Jamie could listen in. Even though it's been a while, I think I can get up to speed quickly."

Yvonne smiled at her, used to Ryan's self-effacing manner. "You took every training class we offer and taught a few classes for over a year, honey. I think you can manage to take a few calls and not screw up completely."

Ryan just shrugged her shoulders and looked down at the floor for a moment, then met Yvonne's eyes and said, "Yeah, I guess I can handle it."

Ruffling her hair, Yvonne sent them on their way. Once in the cubicle they'd been assigned, Ryan set to work to locate all of the pertinent reference materials, talking the whole time. "The calls can cover anything. I've asked the operator to steer us calls from lesbians tonight, and I promise you that they can run the gamut. I've had people ask me how to use a microwave oven," she laughed. "But about ten percent of the calls are really serious. I do my best to make appropriate referrals, but sometimes the kids' stories are truly heartbreaking. If any of the calls bothers you, just let me know, and we'll stop for a while to decompress, okay?"

Jamie was truly touched by Ryan's concern for her. "Thanks for looking out for me," she said with a smile. "I'll let you know if anything gets to me."

When she felt comfortable, Ryan pressed a button and told the operator she was ready. Less than a second later, the phone rang. "Gay and Lesbian Teen Talk Line, this is Ryan. How can I help you?"

The first two hours passed more quickly than Jamie could believe. She was truly amazed at the astounding variety of issues that kids called about. And most of the callers were kids, she realized. They took calls from girls as young as twelve, which truly shocked her. One young girl had kissed another girl at a party, and she wanted to know if that made her gay; a sixteen-year-old was sure she was gay, but her Orthodox Jewish parents prohibited her from going out without being chaperoned; a nineteen-year-old wanted help with a paper she was doing for school. Ryan didn't spend a lot of time with that call, but she knew who to refer her to, and she gave her some interesting sounding web sites to look up. Ryan handled each call with professionalism and an amazing amount of empathy. She dispatched the calls as quickly as possible, but let kids ramble on if she thought they needed to. *God, she has an amazing amount of patience,* Jamie thought when a particularly non-verbal young woman could not spit out her question. Jamie jumped to her feet several times to write questions for Ryan on a white board, and each time, Ryan incorporated them into the call. She would generally mouth a thank you or give Jamie a grin when this happened, looking so calm and self-assured that Jamie once again found herself envying Ryan's confidence.

After two hours Ryan buzzed the operator to take a break. After yawning loudly, Ryan stood and stretched thoroughly. Then she lay down on the floor and stretched her back out even more systematically. Jamie did the same, but with much less efficiency. Ryan gave her a little smile and asked if her back was stiff. When she nodded, Ryan said, "Come here and put your hands around my neck." Jamie gave her a puzzled look, but did exactly as she was told. She got close and placed her hands around Ryan's neck as the taller woman leaned over to accommodate Jamie's height. "Now, lock your hands together tightly," she said from mere millimeters away. Jamie again followed her instructions and was surprised to feel Ryan rise to her full height. She felt and heard the pops as each vertebra seemed to slip back into place.

"Ooo, God, this feels good," Jamie moaned in pleasure.

"All better?" Ryan inquired with a satisfied grin.

"Pretty much," she agreed as she twisted around a little bit. "Except for one spot right in the middle," she said as she rubbed the spot with her hand.

"I've got another one for that," Ryan replied confidently. "This time, put your elbows around my neck," she instructed. Jamie felt her mouth go dry as she contemplated this move. She stood close, and Ryan leaned over so far that they were breathing the same air. The warmth of Ryan's breath on her cheek caused her heart to pick up its beat, but she gamely stood her ground and placed her arms just as Ryan had instructed. This time, when Ryan rose, she was draped along her body, and her chin rested right on the broad chest. She turned slightly, so that her face lay on Ryan's clean-smelling, white T-shirt, and she made the mistake of breathing in deeply. The delicious scent of her friend filled her lungs, and Jamie sucked it in greedily, having never smelled anything quite so delicious. They both heard an audible snap, and Ryan's low laugh rumbled right through her entire body. Jamie hoped fervently that her legs would hold her when she was returned to earth, even though she knew it was doubtful. The low voice rumbled through her again. "Ready?" it asked.

"For what?" was her mumbled reply into the strong pectoral muscle.

"For me to put you down," Ryan chuckled deeply.

"If you must," she heard herself reply after a deep sigh.

Ryan wore a bemused grin as Jamie got her legs functioning. "You really are a pleasure hound, aren't you?" she inquired with a light tone.

"Uhm, I can't say that I knew that about myself, but I guess I am," she replied with an embarrassed grin.

"Lucky for you that pleasure hounds are my favorite animals," Ryan intoned as she tweaked her nose.

I'm gonna have to sit on uncomfortable chairs more often, Jamie decided immediately.

After their little break, the first really tough call of the evening came in. It was from a fourteen-year-old girl who had been raped by her mother's boyfriend — apparently because he thought she was gay. Karen related that the man had been with her mother for about a year and had been harassing her because she didn't have a boyfriend yet. She claimed that he drank a lot and that his abuse got worse when he was drunk. Her mother worked nights as a waitress, and Karen was often left at home with the boyfriend, even though she told her mom that the man scared her.

She said that he had come into her room on Sunday night and demanded to know why she never had boys calling. She tried to get rid of him with a flippant answer by telling him that she was a lesbian. He had flown into a rage, beaten her severely and then raped her, telling her that he wasn't going to have a queer living in his house.

She was terrified to tell her mother because she was afraid that, despite her bruises, her mother would believe him rather than her, and from her description of her mother's reactions, that sounded like a distinct possibility to Ryan. During the call the girl was periodically hysterical, which was absolutely normal, given her situation. But the hysteria was followed by long periods of silence which frightened both women. Ryan asked her directly, "Have you had any thoughts of death or killing yourself, Karen?"

Jamie looked at her with wide eyes. She thought it was a very bad idea to suggest such a thing to the girl, afraid that it would give her an idea that she didn't currently have. But after a long pause Karen finally answered. "Yes," she said softly.

"Tell me about them," Ryan urged.

"I keep thinking about my funeral. I think about how sorry my mom's gonna be for having him in the house. And I think about the kids from my school finally understanding how much this hurts," she gasped out.

Ryan quickly placed the call on mute and told Jamie, "I hate to do this, but we've got to trace this call. I think she may have already taken something. Go talk to Yvonne and tell her what's going on."

Jamie dashed into Yvonne's office and hastily told her about the call and Ryan's assessment. She ran back in after Yvonne immediately agreed to ask the police to trace the call. During one particularly long period of silence, Ryan caught a look of Jamie's terrified face and grabbed her hand, holding it tight while she continued to talk in quiet, reassuring tones, hoping to draw Karen out again. At least ten more minutes had passed, and by now, Jamie agreed with Ryan's assessment of the severity of the girl's mental state. Her voice was becoming slow and dreamy when she wasn't crying uncontrollably. Ryan had been letting her lapse into absolute quiet for a few minutes, but after another interminable silence, Jamie could see the tension in Ryan's face and feel the pressure of her hand becoming more intense.

As the minutes ticked by, the tension in the room was unbearable. Jamie could feel beads of cold sweat running down her back, and Ryan finally stood up and started to pace in a small circle. She started to talk in a louder voice, "Come on, Karen, talk to me. Please talk to me," she pleaded. Finally, she couldn't take the silence anymore, and she yelled in a frustrated plea, *"Karen, for God's sake! Please talk to me!"*

Every muscle in Jamie's body was coiled with tension. Ryan was pale and rigid as she stood in place with her eyes tightly shut. Just when Jamie was sure they had lost her, Ryan heard the commotion that signaled help had arrived. The voices were loud at first, and she heard a few sharp commands, obviously from one paramedic to another. After a moment the sounds grew quieter, and Ryan could sense the tension in the paramedic's voices begin to fade. Finally, after what seemed like hours, an older female voice picked up the phone and identified herself as an Oakland Fire Department paramedic. "Is this the crisis line?" she asked.

"Y ... yes," Ryan said, her voice shaky.

"We've got her stabilized," she announced. "We're taking her to Oakland Memorial. You can call later to get her status."

"Thank you," Ryan sighed, the relief nearly overwhelming. She hit the disconnect button and sank into her chair. Her head dropped into her hands, and she sat motionless for many long moments. Jamie was shaking all over and felt like she was freezing to death. When Ryan finally looked up, she saw the pallor of Jamie's face and immediately got up and shoved Jamie's head between her knees, simultaneously grabbing a paperweight from the desk to fling against the wall. Yvonne came running, and Ryan instructed her to get a cold cloth. She returned seconds later with the requested item, and Ryan told her she could leave, thinking that Jamie would respond better to her alone. She placed the cloth on the back of her clammy neck and slowly massaged her tense muscles. After a few minutes, she felt her begin to stir, and finally, she helped her sit up.

Jamie was still stark white, but she was shaking less, and Ryan guessed that she was in no danger of passing out. She helped her to her feet and guided her out of the small office. As they passed Yvonne's office, Ryan said quietly, "The paramedics took her to Oakland Memorial. I'll call in an hour to see how she is." Yvonne mouthed a thank you, and Ryan nodded her acknowledgement.

Jamie's color had not improved, and as Ryan managed to get her into the car, she began to worry that she should not have moved her. She appeared to be in shock, and Ryan hoped that being in familiar surroundings would calm her down. She had a rather vacant look in her eyes, but she seemed cognizant of where they were, so Ryan thought it was worth the risk to drive to Jamie's house.

The blonde was beginning to stir as they approached her place. She moaned slightly and shifted a bit as Ryan pulled into the drive, the dark woman letting out a sigh of relief. "Please let no one be home," Ryan prayed aloud.

She went to the passenger side and squatted down, looking into Jamie's hazy eyes. "Are you okay?"

A small shake of the head and a lurching movement were the only warning that Jamie provided before she turned and vomited, catching Ryan's leg in the process. The dark woman swallowed the bile that was rushing up her own throat and did her best to comfort her friend. When Jamie was finished gagging, Ryan slid one strong arm behind her shoulders and the other under her knees. She grunted from the strain as she rose to a standing position. *Boy, I wish we had the Range Rover tonight — this would have been a lot easier.*

She struggled to carry her friend up the walk and shot a concerned look at her as she moaned softly. Her diverted attention caused her to stumble just a bit on one of the stairs. *Please don't drop her,* she pleaded with herself. She hoisted her burden higher on her chest to free her right arm and managed to get the key in the lock and turn the knob. She was overjoyed to find the house dark and still. She crossed the threshold and laid her friend down on the sofa. "Jamie?" she said quietly. When she got no response, she lightly slapped her face. *Great! Now she's unconscious!* After making sure that she would not tumble off the small sofa, she dashed into the kitchen to fetch a dishtowel, which she wet and filled with a few handfuls of ice. Flicking on the overhead lights as she returned to the sofa, she sat Jamie up again and gave her a brisk ice massage on the back of her neck.

She began to respond and finally muttered, "What happened?"

"You passed out. You're in your living room now. How do you feel?" Ryan dropped to her knees and held on to her shoulders to steady her and looked closely at her eyes.

"Okay, I guess. A little sick to my stomach, though. How long was I out?"

"Not long," Ryan said as she exhaled deeply and rubbed her eyes in her familiar gesture of fatigue. "But a lot longer than I'm comfortable with. Has this happened to you before?"

"Yeah. I …" she started, but Ryan saw the green tinge return to her face. She scooped her up and began to climb the stairs quickly, feeling beads of sweat pop out on her forehead as she struggled with the weight.

Carrying her friend into the bathroom, she urged her to kneel on the floor. Moaning pathetically, Jamie rested her head on her folded arms, crossed upon the toilet seat. Another round of gagging followed, and after a few quiet minutes Ryan helped Jamie to her feet and guided her into her room.

"What did you have to eat today?" Ryan inquired.

Jamie thought for a minute, trying to order her muddled brain. "I don't remember. Didn't we eat together?"

"No, that was yesterday," Ryan said as another look of worry crossed her face. "Jamie, I want you to think about today. This is Tuesday. Tell me about what you did today."

"Uhm, did we have psych today?"

"No, that's on Monday. This is Tuesday. You have your romantic poets class on Tuesday. Did you go?"

Jamie concentrated hard, and after a few minutes, her memory came back. "Yeah, I did. After that I went to the library, and then I got some lunch."

"What did you have?" Ryan asked.

"Uhm, I felt a little funny so I just had some soup and a couple of crackers."

"No breakfast?"

"Uhm, I don't think so. Oh, no, I was running late so I just had a Diet Coke."

"Okay, then what did you do after lunch?" Ryan continued.

"I had my next two English classes, back to back. Then I went back to the library and got really engrossed in reading for my class. My watch alarm went off at 6:00, and I rode my bike home and got my car. I drove back and picked you up at 6:30." She gave Ryan a little smile, proud of her accomplishment of remembering her day.

"So, you asked if I had eaten, but you didn't tell me that you hadn't," she chided her gently. "I guess you need someone to look after you, too," she said as she ruffled Jamie's hair. "I'm going to call your parents to let them know about this. I think you should see your doctor."

"*No!*" she cried. "Don't call them, Ryan! Please!" she begged with a note of panic in her voice.

"Okay, okay," Ryan said as she gently caressed her cheek. "But we've got to get something into your tummy. Do you think you have any ginger ale?"

"Maybe, but I'm not sure."

"Do you feel like I can leave you for a minute or two?"

"Yeah. My stomach is still bad, but I don't think I'll pass out again."

When Ryan returned with a glass of ginger ale, she resumed her questioning. "Tell me about when you passed out before."

"It's kind of embarrassing, but I tend to pass out when I'm under stress. My blood pressure is kind of low, and I just go out."

"Do you get any warning?" Ryan asked.

"Yeah, like tonight, I could tell that as soon as you disconnected the phone ..." Her voice got fainter, and she began to lose her color again. Ryan reached over quickly and removed the glass from her weak hand.

"I'm gonna get you into bed. Then we're gonna talk about this a little. What do you wear to bed?"

"A T-shirt," Jamie replied as she pointed to her chest of drawers. Ryan lowered her to the bed then walked over to the chest and picked out a very large, light blue T-shirt, obviously one of Jack's. She returned, holding the shirt up for Jamie's approval, receiving a nod in return.

Ryan stood at the foot of the bed and began to unlace Jamie's brown leather ankle boots. Touching a sock, she asked, "On or off?"

"Off," was the weak reply.

Shaking her head in concern, Ryan sat on the edge of the bed and began to unbuckle Jamie's brown leather belt. "I can do that, Ryan," she insisted, trying to sit up.

Ryan let her give it a try, but she flopped back down again in seconds. "God, why am I so dizzy?"

"Because you've been vomiting, and you had almost no food in your stomach to start with. You're probably a little dehydrated. Let me get you undressed, and then we'll try to get some fluids down you, okay?"

"I'm embarrassed," she admitted with a small voice.

Looking like she'd been struck, Ryan sat down next to her on the bed. "Jamie," she said softly, "I ... I'm not trying to ... I mean, I don't want to ..."

All at once, it dawned on Jamie why her friend was looking so wounded. "No, no, Ryan," she said, her voice rising to full strength, "please don't think I'm worried about *your* seeing me naked. I'm just shy ... around everyone," she insisted. "I'm finally at the point where it doesn't bother me if Mia's in the room, and I'm even a little reticent with Jack."

Ryan nodded her head, looking rather helpless until Jamie sighed and said, "I'm being silly. Please help me."

Trying to keep the stiffness from her body, Jamie lay back and let Ryan do her job. The larger woman began to undress her quickly, getting her chinos and her shirt off without trouble.

Ryan pulled her up into a sitting position, braced against her own body. "Are you okay?" she asked gently.

"Yeah," she said weakly, but it was clear that she was feeling queasy again. Trying to move quickly, Ryan put her arms around Jamie's torso and unclasped her peach–colored, silky bra. She slid it off her shoulders and tossed it away, being careful to avert her eyes as much as possible. Gathering the blue T-shirt, she bunched the fabric together, pulled it over Jamie's head, then pulled an arm through each sleeve and placed her back onto the bed.

Jamie's color was much better once she lay back down, and she reached for Ryan's hand and gave it a squeeze. "Thanks for helping me get through that little bout of insecurity."

"My pleasure," Ryan assured her. "Just relax for a minute, okay? I need to make a couple of calls."

Yvonne answered the main number at the help line, and Ryan anxiously asked if they had received word on Karen yet.

"Yes, about ten minutes ago. They pumped her stomach and have stabilized her. They seemed quite confident that she'd be okay. Physically, at least," she added. "How's your friend?"

"She's okay. That was not an uncommon reaction apparently." After a few more words, Ryan hung up and went back to the bed. Jamie's color was nearly normal, but now she was quietly crying.

Ryan kicked her shoes off, then finally pulled off her leather jacket and draped it over a chair. She had to get her sodden jeans off, but she didn't want to leave Jamie unattended, so she just shucked them and looked in the dresser for some sweats or pajama bottoms. Luckily, she found some thin, flannel pajama bottoms that must have been Jack's. She slipped them on and shimmied out of her bra without taking off her T-shirt, just to avoid making Jamie uncomfortable. She climbed into bed and pulled Jamie into the crook of her shoulder. The blonde head dropped onto Ryan's breast, and she shook with quiet sobs for a long while.

"How could someone be so cruel to a child?" Jamie finally gasped out. "How could you rape a little girl because you think she's gay?"

"I can't answer that, Jamie. I can't imagine abusing anyone, especially someone so vulnerable." She was quiet for a moment, then sighed and said, "The really awful thing is that Karen's innocence is destroyed. She might get through the trauma, but she can't reclaim her childhood. That's gone forever."

"I'm so proud of you, Ryan," she murmured. "You saved her life. You really saved her life."

"No, a paramedic did that. I just knew enough to call them."

Jamie began to calm down after a few more minutes of sobbing with Ryan holding and patting her the entire time. The stress of the evening began to claim her, and she was sound asleep within moments, leaning heavily against Ryan's body. Once Ryan was sure she was in a deep slumber, she rolled her onto her back and got out of bed to call her father. "Hi, Da. It's me," she said when he answered.

"What's wrong, Siobhán?" he said with a note of concern.

"Nothing big. Jamie and I went to the teen talk line tonight, and we had a really stressful call. A young girl overdosed, and we got to her just in time. Jamie hadn't eaten, and she passed out from the stress. None of her roommates are here, so I'm gonna stay over to watch her."

"Oh, the poor lass. You take good care of her, Siobhán; she's a lovely little thing."

"Thanks, Da. Will you let the boys know I won't be home?"

"Sure thing, sweetheart. I love you, Siobhán," he said softly. "And I'm proud of you for helping that child tonight."

"I love you, too, Da. See you tomorrow."

Taking a small quilt lying on a chair, Ryan flipped off the lights and got onto the bed, placing the quilt over herself. She lay in that position for a long time, unable to relax enough to sleep, images of a young, desperate girl filling her head.

⌘

Waking from her tormented sleep, Ryan took a quick shower and went downstairs to see what she could rustle up for breakfast. The cupboards were bare, so when she'd rinsed the leg of her jeans out, she struggled back into the wet fabric and grabbed the keys to Jamie's car. After a $50 trip to the market, Ryan returned to the house to start breakfast.

The first order of business was getting her own stomach filled. Ryan assumed that Jamie would not be up for some time, but she could hardly wait another minute.

With her usual methodical style, she quickly prepared her meal, then pulled out one of her textbooks so she could study while she ate. The time flew by, and she was astounded when she realized it was ten o'clock. *I guess I'm skipping my bio lab, as well as our psych class*, she thought. *Good thing I'm pretty well caught up.*

Moments later, she heard Jamie get out of bed. She gave her a few minutes to go to the bathroom, and when she didn't hear the shower, she walked back up the stairs to see how she was.

"Come on in," Jamie replied when Ryan knocked softly.

"Are you going back to sleep, or are you ready for some food?"

Jamie recoiled at the mere thought. She scrunched up her face in distaste and moaned, "I'm never going to eat again."

"Oh, yes, you are," Ryan insisted. "Your stomach will not feel better until you get something in there. You can have tea and toast or cereal or oatmeal or French toast or pancakes or scrambled eggs. But you're putting something in there if I have to hold you down," she said with her hands on her hips.

Jamie had to laugh at her fierce demeanor. "Joke's on you, Ryan. We don't have anything to eat around here except popcorn."

"You do now," she informed her. "I went to the store. Now, what can I make you?"

"I tend to like sweet things when I'm sick. Do you think I could keep French toast down?"

"I think you could if you don't put too much syrup or butter on it. You stay in bed until I'm ready for you, okay?"

"Okay," she agreed as she let out a massive yawn. "I'm still a little tired."

Ryan ran downstairs and prepared Jamie's meal, then put it on a tray and added a small pitcher of syrup, a mug of sweetened tea, silverware, a linen napkin and a bud vase with a bright yellow Gerber daisy that she had purchased at the market. She expertly balanced the tray as she opened the door to Jamie's room. "Breakfast is served," she said cheerily as she entered.

Struggling to sit up, Jamie's face curled up into a delighted grin. "That's so sweet, Ryan! I just can't believe how thoughtful you're being."

"You were really in a bad way last night, Jamie, and I feel responsible for it. I feel like I should have better prepared you for the types of calls we got, or at least asked them to give us easier calls."

"No way, Ryan," she said as she shook her head. "This is just me. There's no way you could have known that I had a tendency to pass out under stress. I should have warned you," she admitted. She took a bite of the toast and closed her eyes in pleasure. "Thanks for making this. It's just perfect for my sad little tummy."

Ryan was still quite concerned about her and peppered Jamie with questions about her health, as the now-ravenous woman diligently worked away at her breakfast. "How many times have you passed out?" she inquired.

"I would say it's happened to me four or five times."

"Have you ever mentioned this to your physician?" Ryan continued.

"Yes, I have. I had to have a physical before I was admitted here, and she asked me if I had ever fainted. She didn't think it was a big deal."

Ryan mulled over her answers for a few moments, then latched onto a little detail that had been rolling around in her head. "You said that you felt funny at lunch yesterday. What did you mean?"

"I just felt queasy all morning." Jamie looked thoughtful for a moment then shrugged her shoulders. "Now that I really think about it, I've been feeling a little off for a while. Maybe I'm not getting enough sleep or something."

Ryan gazed at her for a moment, then placed her hand on Jamie's shoulder, keeping it there until the younger woman looked up at her. "I don't want to upset you, but is there any chance that you might be pregnant?"

Jamie's face was drained of all color in less than a second. Ryan could see her hands grip the edges of the tray so tightly that her knuckles turned white. Her eyes were wide, and Ryan was very concerned that she would pass out or vomit again. After she sat for a minute in shocked silence, she tried to answer but couldn't find her voice.

"I'm gonna take that as a yes," Ryan said as she raised her hand to gently stroke Jamie's cheek. "I'm sorry I brought it up, since it's obviously upsetting you, but if it's a possibility you really should be seen by your doctor."

Jamie pushed the now-empty tray away from her lap and let her head fall back against the pillows. "Please, God, make it not be true," she begged. "I don't know what I'll do if I'm pregnant, Ryan," she said, with a nearly despondent expression.

Ryan sat closer and wrapped her arms around her tightly. "Don't worry about it, Jamie. Let's get you dressed and go to your doctor. You'll get the results in just a few minutes — then you can put your mind at ease. Do you want to call Jack and have him go with you?"

"No, no, I really don't. Won't you go with me?" she asked, looking like a frightened child.

"Of course I will. I'll call the doctor and make sure he can see you. Do you have the number handy?"

"Yeah, and he's a she. I have her business card in my wallet."

Ryan found the number and instructed Jamie to get dressed while she went downstairs to make the call. She didn't want Jamie to hear her cancel her one and two o'clock clients, or to hear what she said to the doctor, so she hoped it would take her a few minutes to get ready.

Both women were silent during the entire ride. Seeing the anguished look on her face, Ryan instinctively grasped her hand and placed it on her thigh, reaching down to cover the cold skin whenever she could free her right hand for a moment.

When they pulled up to the charming, two-story brick building that held her physician's office, Ryan pulled over to the curb to let her out. "I'll park and be right in," she reassured her. Jamie looked hesitant, but Ryan insisted that she get in before the doctor left, since the receptionist said she was only going to be in the office for a short while.

After parking, Ryan ran all the way back to the office and was pleased to see that Jamie had already been shown to a room. The waiting room was empty, and she started to sit down to read a magazine when the door opened and a nurse beckoned her in. "She's in room three," she said as she pointed Ryan towards the room.

"Does she want me with her?" she asked in surprise.

The nurse looked at her like she was slow. "How else would I have known to come get you?"

Ryan just shrugged and walked down the hall to the examining room. Jamie had already taken off her clothes and was sitting on the examining table with just a green paper gown on. She looked small and scared and very cold. Ryan looked at her for a moment and felt totally helpless — then decided that she could relieve at least one problem that was bothering Jamie. Going to her side, she wrapped her in her arms and rubbed her arms briskly, trying to warm her as much as possible. Jamie seemed very grateful for the comfort, and she nestled her head right into Ryan's neck. "I already gave them a urine sample," she mumbled. "They're doing the test now."

After a perfunctory knock, the door opened and a very young-looking doctor entered. She looked a bit surprised to see Ryan, but she recovered quickly. "Hi, Jamie," she said with a friendly smile. "I hear you've had a tough day."

"Yeah, pretty tough," she agreed. "This is my friend, Ryan. She was with me last night, so she can answer any questions that you might have, since I was so out of it."

"Hi, Ryan," she said as she extended her hand. "I'm Alison Atkins."

They shook hands, then Alison snapped on a pair of latex gloves and sat down on a small stool. "Have you had any adverse reactions to the new pill, Jamie?"

"No, I haven't had any side effects from it," she said. "But I haven't been on it for a full month, so it might be too soon to tell," she admitted.

"Have you been using condoms?"

Jamie blushed deeply as she admitted, "Usually. But there were two times when I had sex without one. Both times were on the same weekend, but I'm not sure of the date."

"The date of your last period was ..." she looked at Jamie's chart and commented, "forty days ago."

"Yeah." She gulped and stated the obvious. "I'm late."

Alison moved her stool into position at the end of the table. "There are many, many reasons to be late," she assured her. "That certainly doesn't mean you're pregnant." She placed her hand on Jamie's knee for a second, then said, "I'd like to do a pelvic exam. Okay?"

Jamie scooted down into her least favorite position, and Alison quickly examined her. "Hmm," Alison said as she stripped off her glove and tossed it away. "You can scoot up now," she said as she lightly patted Jamie's leg. "Everything seems normal. But it's too early for me to detect much if you are pregnant. Tell me about your symptoms."

"I've felt a little lethargic for a month or so. My sleep has been off a little bit, too. I've been queasy in the mornings for about a week."

Alison was staring at her intently as she listened to her description of her symptoms. "Are you urinating more than normal?"

"No, no difference."

"How do your breasts feel? Any tenderness?" she asked as she lightly palpated them.

"Yeah, they're tender, but they always are before my period."

"Tell me about last night," she said.

The pair collaborated to tell the story, since Jamie was unconscious for part of it. When they finished, Alison looked thoughtful for a moment and asked, "Any other symptoms? Have you changed your eating habits, or your activity level?"

Jamie started to say no, but Ryan butted in. "Yes, she has. She's decided to ride in the AIDS Ride this year, and I'm training her. She rides fifty to seventy-five miles a week, and she works out three days a week with weights."

"I'm a little concerned about your weight, Jamie. I notice that you're significantly lighter than the last time you were in. How have you changed your diet to accommodate your increased activity?"

"Uhm, I haven't?" she admitted weakly.

"I think you'd better consult with a nutritionist, Jamie. You need to make sure you're getting enough nutrients to make up for the increased demands you're putting on your body. I'll give you a referral and run some tests on your blood. I'll have the results by Friday, okay?"

"Okay," Jamie agreed.

"I'll be right back," Alison said as she opened the door. "You can get dressed, Jamie."

Looking up at Ryan she mumbled, "I feel like a condemned woman waiting for the call from the warden to see if they're going to execute her."

Shaking her head in sympathy, Ryan wrapped her in her arms again, holding on tightly while doing her best to reassure her. "It's gonna be fine, Jamie. Try not to worry."

Minutes later, the doctor knocked as she came in again. "You didn't want to be pregnant, did you?" she asked with a smile.

"God, no!" Jamie shouted.

"Then I have good news," she announced. "You are officially not pregnant."

Jamie threw her arms around Ryan's neck, breaking into tears. Alison just nodded to Ryan and backed out of the room quietly. Jamie cried for a few minutes as Ryan rubbed her back. She finally lifted her head and said, "Thank you so much for being with me today. I don't know what I would have done without you."

"That's what friends are for, Jamie. I'm honored that you asked me."

⌘

When they were back in the car, Jamie looked a little embarrassed as she said, "Was it okay to be in the examining room with me? I mean, I know I should have asked you first, but I just didn't want to be alone."

"Of course it's okay. It feels nice that you trust me enough to want me to be with you. I'll admit to being surprised that you wanted me there, though. You seemed so embarrassed last night to have me help you undress."

"Oh, I'm just a big baby sometimes. Today I had to decide what was more important — being embarrassed about having my legs in the stirrups or being scared to death. The scared part won." She gave Ryan a wry grin and admitted, "It was kinda weird when she was asking me about having sex, though."

Ryan patted her now-relaxed hand and said, "It's okay, Jamie. It's perfectly natural to have sex with your fiancé."

Jamie blushed deeply. "I know; it's just embarrassing to talk about it."

"Now you know how I felt when you saw me practically having sex in public," Ryan teased.

"There was nothing practical about it, Ryan, you *were* having sex," she teased right back.

Ryan shot her a small grin and changed the subject. "As soon as you get home, you'll call the nutritionist, right?"

"Right," she nodded. "Speaking of eating, do you want to have dinner together on Friday?"

"Uhm, sure," Ryan said as she shook her head slightly at the abrupt change of topic. "I don't have any dinner plans. Where do you want to go?"

"My house. I want to cook for you to thank you for taking such good care of me last night. What's your favorite food?"

"Well, you certainly don't have to do that, Jamie. You're my friend — and my duty as your friend means that I take care of you when you need my help."

"I know that, Ryan, but I want to do this. Now spill it."

"My favorite food — no restrictions?" she asked with a familiar look of contemplation on her beautiful face. She leaned her head back and closed her eyes then cocked her head just a little and met Jamie's amused gaze. "Lasagna," she said with finality.

"Lasagna it is," Jamie agreed.

⌘

When they reached the O'Flaherty home, Jamie gave Ryan a broad smile as she said, "Thanks again for being there for me. I just realized that today is Wednesday, and you missed all of your clients. Can I pay you back for that?"

"Yes," Ryan said quickly, surprising Jamie a bit. "You can go home and make yourself a nice dinner with the things I bought from the store this morning. Then you can call the nutritionist and make an appointment. After that, you can take a long nap and pamper yourself for the rest of the day. If you do all of that, we're even," she grinned.

"You're the best friend I have, Ryan," she said softly as she gave her a gentle smile.

⌘

At around 9:30 the phone rang. Ryan's deep voice asked, "Did you speak to the nutritionist?"

"Hi, Ryan. Yes, I dutifully followed your instructions. I'm meeting with her on Monday, and I've eaten so much today I could burst," she laughed.

"Was this your first pregnancy scare?" Ryan inquired a trifle tentatively.

"Yeah, it was," Jamie said. "And I certainly hope it's my last."

"One more reason to be thankful I'm a lesbian," Ryan teased. "I'd probably have ten kids by now if I were straight."

"Well, you do seem to have a few things in common with bunnies," Jamie laughed.

"You're just lucky I can't reach you from here," Ryan replied threateningly.

"Where are you anyway? It sounds loud."

"I'm at a bar in Oakland. I've kinda got a date waiting for me, so I'd better go."

"Okay, you little rabbit. Don't do anything I wouldn't do," she teased.

"Don't count on it, Jamie. They don't call it the luck of the Irish for nothing," she said as she hung up.

⌘

After class on Friday morning, Ryan fixed Jamie with her penetrating gaze. "So," she began, "tell me how you're feeling."

"I feel pretty good. I've really cranked up calories, and I think it's helping already. My stomach is back to normal, too, so I think I'm ready to start working out again."

"I still want you to take the day off," Ryan said firmly. "You need a few days to get your strength back after being as sick as you were."

"Okay, Doc, I'll stay home and get your dinner ready," she said with a smile.

"Can I ask you something pretty personal?" Ryan asked tentatively.

"Sure, I don't have any secrets from you," she replied.

"Why were you so devastated when you thought you might be pregnant? I mean, I could see why if you weren't in love with the guy, but you are. And you're getting married in a year and a half. So, what's up?"

Jamie sat in silence for a few minutes. She was obviously thinking, so Ryan didn't interrupt. She finally looked up and said, "I'm not sure I know, but it felt absolutely horrible. I felt just like I would have when I was sixteen."

"That's kind of odd, don't you think?" Ryan continued. "I also wondered why you wouldn't tell Jack. Shouldn't he be involved?"

"I don't know," Jamie admitted. "It just didn't feel like something he could be helpful with. I mean, I know he loves me, but he's not very good at the emotional comfort thing. I think he would have been upset — probably with me — for having sex without a condom."

"Are you on the pill now?"

"Yeah. But I had trouble with the first two types I took. I got breakthrough bleeding with one, and the other made me terribly nauseous. I had to wait almost a month before I started this new one. Alison told me to use a condom during the transition, but we got carried away once, and he snuck up on me early in the morning the other time," she said as she looked down at the table in embarrassment.

Ryan slid her hand over and patted Jamie's. "I'm sorry if I'm prying. I'm just a little worried about you."

She gave her a broad smile and replied, "It's okay. I know I've got some issues that I have to work out with Jack. I guess I just want to make sure that we don't start our family until we get them resolved. I think we have quite a few years of growing up before we're ready."

"I think you're awfully mature for a twenty year old," Ryan revealed. "But having kids is a whole new world."

CHAPTER SEVEN

AS SOON AS HER CLASSES WERE OVER, JAMIE RUSHED HOME AND dove into the preparation of Ryan's birthday dinner. She didn't cook elaborate meals very often, but she really enjoyed doing so when she got the chance. She actually enjoyed making something difficult a lot more than just making an ordinary dinner, especially when she was feeding someone who really enjoyed food — and she didn't know a soul who enjoyed eating more than Ryan.

She had decided to make her favorite lasagna — one she had first tasted at a small restaurant in Bologna. Store–bought noodles were entirely unsatisfactory, so she not only had to make a ragú and a béchamel sauce, she had to make the spinach noodles by hand. The process was a laborious one, made even more labor intensive when she decided to also make gelato. She worked without pause until 4:45, and since she knew Ryan would be on time, she had to really rush to be ready.

As expected, the doorbell rang at 5:00 on the dot. After hiding the small presents she had rushed to wrap, she dashed over to the door, running her hands through her hair to order it.

She was greeted by a broadly smiling Ryan who leaned over to give her a hug. They had recently begun to hug when they hadn't seen each other for a few days. Jamie found that she felt very comfortable with the increased intimacy and noted that she missed the contact on the occasions Ryan didn't offer it. She was a bit surprised to receive a hug now, but only because they had seen each other earlier at class.

"You certainly look happy," the blonde smiled up at the beaming face.

"You are cooking, aren't you?" Ryan asked logically.

"Yes, I most certainly am."

"Then I am most certainly happy," she stated with an even bigger grin. She leaned over again and gently brushed her thumb across Jamie's cheek a few times. Holding her hand up close to her eyes, she nodded her head and said thoughtfully, "Flour."

"I get a little wild when I cook. God knows what's hiding in my hair."

"It smells very good in here," Ryan said, her nose twitching reflectively. "Hmm … something sweet as well. Do I get dessert, too?"

"Yes, you get dessert, too. I don't believe in making a partial thank you dinner."

"Far be it from me to turn down a special meal ... okay, far be it from me to turn down any meal," she chuckled, "but you don't owe me any thanks, Jamie." She slung an arm across her shoulders and said, "We're friends, and I take my friendships very seriously. You were really out of it on Tuesday, and I felt responsible for you. I know you would have done the same for me."

"Well, conceptually you're right, Ryan. But I was thinking about that night, and I don't remember walking on my own volition at any time after that phone call."

"Mmm ... you walked to the car, but I had to carry you into the house and up the stairs to your room."

"Okay, now let's switch roles. Where would we be if *you* had passed out that night?"

"Uhm, still lying on the floor of the building, I guess," she said, grinning widely. "It would take two men and a strong boy to pick me up."

"My point exactly. My spirit would be willing, but my flesh is weak. So, the bottom line is that I'm very thankful not only for your friendship, but your big muscles are awfully nice to have around, too."

"So, you're just replenishing all of the calories I expended, huh? I guess that does seem fair," Ryan decided. "I'd do it over again in a minute, Jamie, but I will admit that I would have given a lot to have had the Range Rover that night."

"Why's that?" Jamie asked, confused.

"I had to power you up from a deep squat to get you out of the car. I'm gonna have to do some more work on my quads if I'm going to continue to pick you up off the floor," she teased as she slapped her ample thigh muscles.

"Maybe you shouldn't try to get my weight back up. It might be to your detriment."

"I think I would rather make sure you don't get stressed out that badly again," she decided, dropping her arm to curl around Jamie's waist and lead her into the kitchen.

Ryan offered to help with the last of the dinner preparations, so Jamie set her to work on setting the table and choosing some music. Ryan bustled around the large kitchen, finding out for herself where everything was kept. She was just about finished when Jamie asked, "How do you feel about anchovies?"

"I feel very kindly towards them, so long as they lie still while they're being eaten," she replied with a laugh. She walked up behind Jamie and enthused, "Ooo, Caesar salad, my favorite."

"Ryan, I swear that almost everything you eat is your favorite," she playfully admonished her.

"Well, it is," Ryan gamely defended herself. "I have tons of favorites, but what I choose to eat at any particular time becomes my favorite. Caesar salad is my favorite Italian-style salad; particularly when served with anchovies and followed by lasagna."

"Sounds like the way you choose your dates," Jamie joked.

Ryan looked thoughtful for a moment, finally saying, "Not a bad analogy. Whoever I'm with is my favorite — at that moment in time. I never sleep with anyone that isn't my ideal choice for that night."

"Small comfort," Jamie said quietly, still slightly bothered by Ryan's serial dating.

Ryan came up behind her and placed a hand on her shoulder, waiting for Jamie to turn and face her. When she was looking into her eyes, Ryan said, "That's the best I can give. All of myself — fully committed to being completely present and emotionally available — for the time we have together. It might be just one night — it might be many. But no matter how much time we have together, she knows that she'll get all of me." She cocked her head, still gazing deeply into Jamie's eyes. "Many people never get that much from their spouses, much less a casual date."

Jamie's heart was thudding in her chest — thudding so loudly that she was afraid Ryan could hear it. With a flash of clarity, she acknowledged, for the first time, that she had rarely been fully present when she and Jack were having sex. *My God, I criticize her for sleeping with so many people, but she's more emotionally available to a near–stranger than I am to Jack!* This revelation was making her head hurt, so she did her best to stow it away for later examination and forced herself to concentrate on Ryan. "I'm sure that however you choose to live your life works just fine for you," she said, giving her a fond smile. "Maybe I'm just a little jealous, since I've not really sown my wild oats."

"I've sown enough for both of us," Ryan smiled. "I'd trade all of my wanderings for someone who loves me unquestioningly."

"Really?" Jamie gawped. "You would?"

"Yeah, I would," Ryan insisted. "In five or ten years, I really would."

That earned her a playful slap in the gut, Jamie's hand bouncing off the rock-solid abs.

Ryan's tasks were finished, so she sat down at the kitchen table to watch Jamie get a few final things ready. "Where did you get your recipe for lasagna, anyway? Is it a family secret?"

"I come from a family of diners, not cooks. My mother could probably make a peanut butter sandwich, but I've never actually seen her do so," she admitted. "And come to think of it, I'm certain she would never eat peanut butter, so it really would be a pointless exercise."

"Are you really being serious?" Ryan asked as she stared, absolutely dumbfounded.

"Completely," Jamie replied. "I have never eaten a meal that my mother prepared for me. Come to think of it, I wasn't even breast fed," she laughed.

"Not even tea and toast when you were sick?" Ryan asked incredulously.

"Nope. I had a nanny who took care of me when I was sick. My mother didn't really get involved in the day-to-day caretaker stuff."

"God, Jamie, I find that so hard to believe!" Ryan was truly shocked, and her astonishment showed clearly on her expressive face.

"Well, it's true. Our relationship has always been friendly and pleasant enough, but distant. She traveled and enjoyed delving into various interests, but child rearing wasn't really one of them," she admitted.

Friendly? Pleasant? What kind of words are those to use for your relationship with your mother? "So, how did you learn to cook?" Ryan asked, trying to change the depressing subject.

"We had a great cook named Marta. She's still with us, as a matter of fact. She's from Spain, but she can cook anything. She does a lot of northern Italian cuisine because that's my mother's favorite, but she can also do classical French and some great spicy, Spanish dishes for my father and me."

"Did you just watch and learn?"

"No, she was a really good teacher. She knew I was interested, and she spent a lot of time with me, teaching me the fundamentals. My mother found it odd that I wanted to spend my time chopping vegetables into julienne pieces, but she didn't mind much as long as I was entertained. Actually, Marta was one of the best teachers I've ever had. She didn't have any children, and we spent a ton of time together, just talking and hanging out."

Ryan was enormously saddened to hear her friend speak of this emotionless upbringing. The thought of young Jamie having to get her parenting from the hired help was just too much to consider, so she changed the subject again. "So, you know my favorite food; what's yours?"

Jamie turned thoughtful as she finished tossing the Caesar salad. "I think my favorite is a good steak and pommes frites from a French bistro. I've had some extraordinary meals at Chez Panisse. Have you been there?"

"No, but Conor has. He said he liked it, but the portions weren't big enough. Not that that is surprising!" she laughed.

"I think we're ready to eat. Hungry?" she asked needlessly.

"I was hungry when I got here, but smelling that lasagna has put me into a whole new classification of hunger. It's beyond famished ... bordering on starvation, I believe."

"Just what I wanted to hear. I'll take the lasagna out so it can cool for a minute." She went to the oven and pulled out the pan, noticing that Ryan got up and trotted right behind her, looking over her shoulder, mouth watering.

"God, Ryan, you look like a hungry wolf with a wounded animal in its sights," she said of Ryan's intense gaze.

"That's exactly how I feel at the moment," she replied, never taking her eyes from their bubbling target. "I think I'm willing to risk the burns to my mouth to eat that right now," she threatened as she leaned over her prey.

But Jamie grabbed her by the shoulders and turned her firmly around to face the kitchen table. She gave her a push and said firmly, "Sit. Now." Ryan complied, grumbling the whole time. "Would the Caesar salad placate you for a few minutes?" Jamie asked, taking pity on the poor creature.

"I suppose," she moaned, letting out an aggrieved sigh.

With her first bite, Ryan's face became a study of various levels of pleasure. She started at mere happiness, and by the fourth bite, had progressed to ecstasy. "My God, this is good," she moaned from her state of bliss. "You have ruined me for life, Jamie. All other Caesar salads will be but pale imitations. I'll never be satisfied with another!"

"Then you'll just have to come here when you need a fix," Jamie replied, enormously pleased at the effusive compliments.

Ryan mopped up every bit of dressing with a piece of crunchy, Italian bread. "Is it considered rude to lick the salad bowl?" she asked.

"There is just a tiny bit left, but I don't want you to be too full for your entrée," Jamie warned.

"My physiology is just like a cow's," Ryan informed her. "I have six stomachs, all in different stages of digestion. I'll just put the entree in another stomach." She was already on her feet, moving towards the salad bowl, and as she passed the cooling lasagna, she leaned down and gave it a hearty sniff. "You're next," she growled.

Jamie regarded her friend as she walked back to the table, holding the salad bowl possessively. Ryan was so full of life, so immersed in the pleasure of whatever she was involved in, that it was impossible not to enjoy being with her. Jamie thought of all the women that Ryan had been with and felt a little sorry for them. She knew how much they must crave further contact and how few of them got it. With a satisfied smile, she recognized that she was gifted with much more of Ryan's time than any of her dates were, and she decided that she was very lucky to have it.

Ryan polished off the remnants of the salad right from the serving bowl, using more bread to capture every bit of dressing and every tiny green leaf that tried, in vain, to escape.

"I don't think I've ever met anyone who enjoys food as much as you do. You just seem so immersed in the whole experience. It's fun to watch!"

Ryan's face grew serious. "Honestly, that's my whole philosophy of life. I try to be fully involved in whatever I'm doing because the simplest task is made beautiful if I'm fully in it. When I eat I try to exploit every sense. That's why I love to eat with my hands. I love the feel and the color and the texture of food. I even enjoyed the crunch the croutons in the salad made." She grinned up at Jamie with a slightly embarrassed smile. "I know that sounds kinda nutty, but that's how I approach life."

"That is the least nutty thing I've ever heard," Jamie replied. "You're really teaching me a lot about savoring life, Ryan, and I want you to know how grateful I am for that," she said simply.

"I didn't realize that, Jamie, but I'm glad it's helpful for you. I made up my mind when I was a teenager that I wasn't going to let life pass me by. I know that every day we have is a gift, and I intend to make the most of those gifts."

"Well, speaking of gifts," Jamie said as she rose and walked to the counter, "happy birthday, Ryan." She lit the candle that she had placed in the lasagna and carried the large pan to the table. She leaned over Ryan's shoulder and gave her a small kiss on a flushed cheek.

Ryan was truly stunned. "How did you know? I'm sure I didn't tell."

"No, you didn't, you big dope. I'm a little miffed that I had to find out from Conor."

"You know, you're right, Jamie. I should have told you. I usually spend the day with my family, and sometimes I forget to include the other people I'm close to. I kind of hate to have a big deal made out of it, but I should have included you. I'm really glad that Conor told you."

Jamie served up a steaming plate of the lasagna, and Ryan loaded up her fork, pausing to gaze at the big bite for a moment to let it cool. When she put it into her mouth, she was silent as she closed her eyes, deep in concentration. Jamie could just imagine each of her senses kicking in, feeling and tasting and smelling the delectable bite.

"If I hadn't believed in God before today, I would now. This," she waved another forkful of the dish at Jamie, "is a clear sign that God loves us and wants us to be happy."

"I'm so glad I could make you something that you enjoy so much," Jamie replied as she tried to control her beaming smile.

"I have eaten lasagna at least two hundred times in my life. I order it every time it's on the menu. But I can truly say I've never tasted lasagna before today."

Jamie just grinned in response.

They ate in silence for a few minutes to allow Ryan to concentrate. Finally, she looked up from her plate. "I need to know how you made this. There is nothing about this that I recognize — not the noodles, not the sauce, nothing! Most of the time lasagna is heavy and overly rich. This is just so light and delicate tasting."

Jamie explained the entire process, while Ryan watched her in rapt fascination. Finally, she shook her head, locked her eyes on her friend and asked, "You did all that just for my birthday?"

"Yep. And I'd do it again in a minute to see you enjoy yourself so much," she replied truthfully.

"Do you cook like this for Jack?" Ryan asked after a moment, a bit off topic.

"I do cook for him, but I don't think I've ever done anything very elaborate. He doesn't care about food a lot. He thanks me for cooking, but in the same way he thanks me for vacuuming. I think he eats to live, and that's about it."

"Well, anytime you need an enthusiastic taste tester, you know where to find me."

"I'll keep your name on file," Jamie replied with a grin.

After Ryan had eaten much more than Jamie thought wise, they sat together in the living room with large cups of cappuccino. "Is there anything you don't cook well?" Ryan asked as she sipped her coffee.

"I'm sure I've screwed up my share of meals. I just had a good day," she replied. "But I must admit, cooking for an appreciative audience is really pleasurable."

"If I were any more appreciative, I'd be on the phone to the Vatican, petitioning for your early sainthood," Ryan said.

Jamie just smiled at her, very pleased by the enthusiastic praise.

Ryan's face grew serious, and she said, "Yvonne from the talk line called me today. She's been following up on Karen, and she talked to her social worker today. The doctors were afraid that she'd have kidney damage, since she OD'd on painkillers, but they're confident that she's okay."

Jamie shook her head, still unable to get her mind around the violence that had been perpetrated upon the girl. "You were so good that night," she said reflectively. "How did you first get involved with the talk line?"

Ryan was silent for a few moments. She looked down at the floor as she said softly, "It's a long, sad story. Are you sure you want to hear it?"

"Only if you want to talk about it," Jamie replied.

Ryan fidgeted in her seat for a moment, then, looking like she'd made a decision, she nodded her head. "I like to reflect on my life on my birthday, and I haven't had a spare minute to do so yet. I guess this is as good a spot to consider as any." She gave Jamie a thoughtful look and said, "It all revolves around Sara." Such a wistful expression crossed Ryan's face that Jamie was ready to tell her that she didn't have to talk about the topic if it was too painful. But Ryan was already launching into it, so she just sat quietly and observed her.

"She was my best friend all through grammar and high school." Shrugging her shoulders, a small smile tugged at her lips. "That's not nearly a strong enough word, but I don't know how else to explain how I felt about her — other than to say that I loved her more than I thought possible." Ryan glanced up and said, "I've never felt like that about another woman — before or since," she admitted, her hooded eyes dark.

"Is this how you realized that you were gay?" Jamie asked, her voice as soft and low as Ryan's was.

"Mmm ... yes, I suppose this cemented the feelings I'd always had," she admitted. "It's hard to explain, Jamie. I mean, I knew that I was different from my friends, but it honestly didn't bother me. I thought I was just unique," she said as she gave Jamie a crooked little grin. "I didn't ever have a crush on a guy or have any desire to go out with one. Luckily, we didn't have the pressure of having guys around all the time, since I went to an all-girls school; the issue was never forced. I honestly never applied the word lesbian to myself, though. I just thought I was ... me. I thought everyone had crushes on her girlfriends and teachers and scheduled her week around 'Cagney and Lacey,'" Ryan said with a small laugh at the memory.

Jamie didn't understand the reference, but she nodded to encourage Ryan to continue.

"Anyway, as the years passed, I began to feel more than close to Sara. I wanted to be with her, even though I didn't really know what that meant, or how to go about it. I was stunningly naive when it came to sex. That was one area that Da did a pretty crummy job with, and the boys were certainly no help. It might have been different if I'd been a little worldlier, but my whole universe was sports and Sara. I was just not clued into lesbianism, even though we lived in a very gay section of town."

"You must have been so confused," Jamie empathized.

"In a way I was, but in another way I assumed Sara felt just like I did. We were so close, it was like we shared a soul." Ryan dropped her head a little, but continued. "I was finding the temptation just to touch or kiss her overwhelming. She was all that I thought about, Jamie. I wanted to let her know how I felt, but I was so confused about what this thing was, that I didn't feel able to."

"I can't imagine how confusing that must have been for you," she said, her heart aching with empathy for her friend.

Ryan nodded briefly, her head barely moving, wisps of black hair dropping into her eyes before being brushed aside by a quick hand. "One night I was staying over at Sara's. We did that a lot — so much so that most mornings my father would shout downstairs, 'Breakfast for one or two?'" Ryan squirmed in her chair and cleared her throat as Jamie realized that she was trying to keep from crying. "It was May — the end of my junior year. Sara was a year older, and she had already accepted a soccer scholarship at Cal, and I was going to go to Cal, too. To prepare herself, she was going to go to a soccer camp in San Diego as soon as school was over. I was panicked at the thought of her going away, even for just a few weeks." Ryan shifted again and shook her head, then said, "I let my fear of being away from her override my fear of expressing myself."

Jamie cringed, knowing right where this was heading. She reached out and tenderly stroked the bunched muscles in Ryan's thigh, amazed at how tense her friend was. "You don't have to tell me any more," she murmured. "I can see how painful this is for you."

Ryan nodded quickly, closing her eyes for a few moments while she cleared her throat once again. "I, uhm … I don't talk about this," she whispered. "I do my best not to think about it, either, but I'm not always successful."

"It's okay," Jamie soothed gently, still stroking her leg, feeling the soft, worn cotton of her chinos slip under her fingers. "This is your birthday, Ryan. I don't want you to have to revisit this today."

"No," she said quietly, her dark head shaking slowly. "I'd like to talk about it." She looked up at Jamie and said, "I've never told the whole story to anyone — it might help me let it go." She spoke with so much sorrow that Jamie was on the verge of refusing — afraid of the emotions that she knew the story would create in her. But she couldn't turn down Ryan's request. Offering a faint squeeze to her knee, she met her eyes and nodded briefly.

"We got into bed, and before I could stop myself, I started talking. I told her everything, Jamie. How much I wanted her, how I dreamed about her, how she meant everything to me. She was kind of quiet, but the look in her eyes showed me that she felt the same way. After a minute I reached for her, and I kissed her." Ryan's shoulders slumped, and she sank down into the sofa, obviously trying not to cry. "My God, Jamie, nothing before or since has ever felt that good to me."

Jamie reached out and grasped Ryan's hand, linking their fingers, then nodding to urge Ryan to continue. "I thought she was enjoying it as much as I was," she said with a rasp in her voice. "No, I know she was enjoying it. I know it," she said firmly as she closed her eyes tightly. "In my fumbling, terrified way, I continued. I don't know where I got the courage, but I got more and more aggressive. I guess all those years of yearning for her propelled me forward. I explored every inch of her body with my hands. After a long time of totally tender touches, we began to get more passionate. And it wasn't just me. She didn't touch me intimately, but she kissed me with so much emotion …" Ryan closed her eyes again. "I can still taste her lips," she whispered as she shook her head and took in a deep breath. Once again she seemed on the verge of tears, but she gathered herself and continued. "Eventually, I discovered what she liked and brought her to orgasm. I cannot tell you how that made me feel, Jamie. I can honestly say that was the happiest moment of my young life. I felt closer to her than I thought possible. I had used my hands and my body to give her such pleasure. She seemed so satisfied, and a few moments later, she kissed me with so much love in her eyes. As she fell asleep in my arms, I held on to her with all the strength and the tenderness that I possessed."

Ryan blew out a big breath, and Jamie steeled herself for the inevitable.

"I didn't sleep much that night. It felt so wonderful to be that close to her. I can't describe it as anything other than feeling like I was finally home. I watched her sleep and occasionally would give her a light kiss. I decided that night that when I followed her to Cal, we would live together and start our lives together." She smiled sadly at the memory.

A grim, self-mocking smile signaled that the story didn't have a happy ending. "In the morning Mrs. Andrews came to wake us up. Sara acted very flustered when her mom was there, and I figured she was uncomfortable about us getting caught. She came up with some lame excuse and told me I should go to school without her. I felt a little funny about that, but I wasn't really worried." She fixed her eyes on Jamie's and muttered, "I should have been worried. That was the last conversation we ever had."

Jamie sat in the starkly silent room with her hand on Ryan's knee. She knew the depth of the hurt — could see it on Ryan's face and hear it in her voice. But she had no words to heal the old pain. Instead, she just gently touched her in sympathy and understanding.

"Later that day at school, she wouldn't even make eye contact with me. I chased her from class to class — waiting like a dog outside the door as she exited." Ryan leaned her head back and stared up at the ceiling. "She shrugged me off like a bag of trash." Picking her head up, she gazed at Jamie for a moment. "I honestly almost lost my mind that day. I've had pain in my life, but the gut-churning terror I felt was something I wouldn't wish on another soul." Her voice dropped into a near-monotone, and she finished the rest of the story quickly. "She disappeared at the end of the school day, so I went to her house. Her mom told me that Sara didn't want to see me anymore, and she asked me to never call their house or try to contact her again."

"How unspeakably cruel!" Jamie shouted in indignation. "How could she do that to you?"

"Actually, that was what made it even harder. I was really close to her mom. She was one of my mother substitutes, and I relied on her for a lot of help and guidance. I never saw her again, either," she mumbled. Looking at Jamie guilelessly, Ryan said, "I don't blame her. Sara was obviously really upset, and I guess her mom didn't want it to get any worse. Sara must have told her what had happened because her mom told me that she hoped things worked out for me, but that Sara wasn't like I was. I don't know," she said softly, "if my daughter had been in the same situation, I might have done the same thing."

"I don't believe that for a minute," Jamie said, her eyes boring intently into Ryan's. "If you were her mother, you would have found a way to be supportive of a child who was going through a very difficult time. You would not turn your back on a child who needed you!" Jamie continued to stroke and pat her leg, and Ryan finally gave her a small smile.

"It was a terrible time for me. After the loss of my mother, and my cousin's death, this was the worst thing that had ever happened to me. It screwed up the way I felt about myself for a long time. I reasoned that if people as wonderful as Sara and her mother thought I was sick, I must be."

"You're not sick," Jamie whispered, tears overflowing her lids.

Smiling gently, Ryan said, "I know that now. I just didn't know it then. I started doing some crazy stuff — hanging out in Castro and going to bed with older, much more experienced women. I was almost seventeen, but I looked older, and my fake ID's got me in anywhere I wanted to go. I had no boundaries to speak of, and I'd go home with anyone who wanted me.

164

But I didn't really get anything out of the sex. I just wanted the contact, so I didn't feel so alone. I wanted to be with other freaks like me."

Jamie looked up at Ryan, nearly wincing from the pain in her friend's eyes. "Is that when you got involved with the teen talk line? Did you call them for help?"

"No, I wish I had, but I didn't know about it. My experiences are what made me volunteer as soon as I did learn about it, though. This is hard for people to understand, but it's really, really rough for so many gay kids. We don't get a chance to develop like straight kids do. Not many of us get to have normal dating relationships at the appropriate age. We often go from a crush to having sex, like I did, and that's really harmful for kids. It's too overwhelming to have your first kiss immediately followed by your first time making love."

"How did you come out of it?"

"It took a while. The next school year things got quite a bit worse. I'll save the details of that little fiasco for another day — preferably after quite a few drinks." She grimaced, and Jamie could see her shiver.

"Couldn't you talk to anyone?" Jamie inquired gently.

Ryan nodded. "Eventually, Brendan got me to talk about what was going on. Luckily, the whole family was supportive, and I started to get back to my old self."

"I'm so glad they were all supportive of you, Ryan. That must have really helped."

"More than I could have imagined. But I had screwed up at the worst possible time. My scholarship to Cal was withdrawn, and I had to come up with another plan."

"Oh, Ryan," Jamie sighed heavily. "What did you do?"

"Well, I'd been hanging out at the gym with Conor, and I really got into it. After I graduated, I spent the summer taking classes to become a trainer. I had been accepted at the University of San Francisco as my fallback school, but it was really expensive, so I had to work full time to be able to afford the tuition. So, after I got certified, I started to work full time."

"But why go somewhere so expensive? Couldn't you have gotten in somewhere else?"

"Getting in places wasn't a problem," Ryan assured her. "But I had such a hard time during my senior year that I couldn't bear to live away from home. Besides, after all of the problems I had in school that year, taking a couple of years off seemed really appealing."

"Do you regret it?" Jamie asked.

Ryan shrugged her shoulders and said, "In retrospect, it was a foolish decision to waste two years and have to pay my own way, but I was so heartbroken over not being given my scholarship that I just couldn't bear to attend Cal. And the thought of seeing Sara around campus was just something I couldn't risk. After I'd completed two years at USF, I decided that I had sulked long enough, and I transferred. Cal is where I'd always dreamed of going, and I finally decided that I was only hurting myself by not going there."

Impulsively, Jamie slid her arms around her friend and wrapped her in a warm hug. "You've been through some very hard times," she whispered, "but they've made you stronger."

"Yeah," she murmured, her warm breath tickling Jamie's neck. "I feel pretty darned good about myself now. I mean, I must be doing something right to merit a friend like you, right?" She pulled back from the hug and met Jamie's compassion-filled gaze.

Soaking up the words of friendship that Ryan so easily offered, Jamie mused, *I do not understand why she isn't in a relationship. It seems so easy for her to open up and show her feelings. Is she really that different when sex is involved?*

⌘

After Ryan had digested enough of her dinner to allow for dessert, Jamie led her back into the kitchen. "I hope you like what I made for dessert. I know you say you like everything, but this is a little different," she said with a smile at Ryan's interested expression. "The last time my mother and I were in Bologna, we had this at the same restaurant that made this style of lasagna. It's really the prototypical dessert of the region, and I thought it would be a perfect compliment to dinner."

Ryan watched with wide eyes as Jamie scooped a healthy serving of a frozen concoction into each of two bowls. "You *made* ice cream?" she asked, a confused look on her face. "I thought you had to be Ben or Jerry to make ice cream."

"No, it's a feat that's easily accomplished if you have a good ice cream maker," Jamie replied.

"You know, you are the last person in the world who should be underweight. You obviously don't cook much for yourself," Ryan observed as she playfully tried to pinch her waist.

"No, I really don't," she giggled, dancing out of the way. "I prefer to cook for others, I suppose."

"If you don't stop saying that, you're gonna find me on your doorstep every evening," Ryan threatened. Ryan focused on her bowl as she took her first big bite of the gelato. With a sensual moan, she dropped her head to her chest while both hands lifted and balled into fists. She lightly pounded on the table for a few beats then looked up at Jamie in wonder. Not a word had been spoken, but Jamie knew that she was being lavishly complimented. After every bite Ryan would look at her with a delighted expression of amazement and another little shake of her head. Finally, when her bowl was clean, Ryan muttered softly, "I have no words." She shook her head again and looked rather helpless as she said, "If I could have another bowl, I'd be forever grateful."

As her second bowl was presented, Ryan predicted, "I'm sure I'll be more erudite after my second helping." She dug in again, but was once again totally silent. Her brows knit in concentration, and she looked very reflective a couple of times — as if she had a point to make. But she would again shake her head lightly and shrug her shoulders in a small sign of defeat. She regarded her friend once again and admitted, "I just can't form a cogent thought. I truly want to do justice to that ambrosia, but I'm unable to come up with a compliment that's effusive enough."

"None needed," Jamie replied as she gently patted her cheek. "Just watching you eat is the supreme compliment." As she spoke she rose and crossed the room to retrieve the hidden presents.

"Jamie, you certainly didn't have to buy me presents after all this!" she protested.

"I know I didn't have to. But I wanted to. It really gave me a lot of enjoyment to be able to buy you a few little things," she replied.

"Okay, you win. If you get pleasure out of doing this, then I'm going to shut up and just let myself enjoy it," she decided as she grabbed the first box.

Jamie watched her face take on a childlike glee as she shook each box in turn. "I like to guess. Can I?" she asked.

"Of course, birthday girl. You can do anything you want."

"What I want is for you to be my personal chef," she said with a grin, "but I'll settle for opening my presents." She shook a box that was about nine inches square, and it gave a funny little rumble. "Hmm," she mused. The next box was square, but smaller. A muffled, wooden clicking sound emanated from it. Yet another was small and completely silent. The last gift was small, almost flat and rectangular. It was no more than a quarter inch thick and made no sound when shaken. "I think I'm ready," she finally pronounced. "I believe there is a common theme?" she said, a question in her voice.

"Yep, sure is."

"So, one box will lead me to guess the others?"

"Most likely."

"Okay," she said as she waved the long thin package. "I think this one is a golf glove," she stated with authority.

"How did you do that?" Jamie inquired, quite amazed.

"Well, you did just buy me one, and I remember the shape of the package it came in. Plus, I can detect a leather aroma. See?" She offered the package up to Jamie's nose.

"Wow, how good is your sense of smell?" Jamie wondered.

"It's pretty good, I guess. I don't realize how good it is until I can catch a scent several minutes before anyone else. Sometimes I even beat Duffy," she said proudly. "And I'm the official smeller of anything suspect in the refrigerator." She quickly tore open the little package. "Ooo, a white one. Now I won't clash when I wear another color." She opened the cardboard cover and slipped the glove on. "You remembered my size!" she said with delight. "Thanks, Jamie." She half got out of her seat and leaned over to kiss her on the cheek.

Jamie knew that she should not feel a flash of pleasure tear up her spine, but she quickly convinced herself that the excitement of watching her friend's joy had just become contagious, and her conscience chose to believe her.

Ryan tore through the rest of the neatly wrapped presents, correctly guessing the two dozen golf balls and the little box of tees. She had not guessed that the tees were personalized however, and this little detail delighted her to no end. "These are the bomb, Jamie," she said as she shook the little box. She hopped up once again to kiss the other cheek, and Jamie briefly wished that she had wrapped each of the tees separately. "I'm gonna feel like a pro with all my cool stuff."

Her glee continued when she opened the last little box. It was a small set of ball markers and a divot tool in a gold tone. Each was neatly monogrammed with "S.R.O." Ryan jumped up and came over to Jamie's side of the table. She grabbed her hands and pulled her to her feet. "This is all so nice," she enthused. "I can't thank you enough." They stood toe-to-toe, Ryan's hands on Jamie's shoulders, smiling faces locked onto each other. Ryan bent to kiss her cheek just as Jamie turned her head slightly. Their lips brushed just a tiny bit, no more than a quarter inch. The kiss was absolutely chaste, but Jamie felt a jolt of pleasure shoot down her spine, and she had a much more difficult time explaining this one away.

Ryan didn't seem to notice her reaction, as she wrapped her in her powerful arms for a generous hug. Suddenly, Jamie felt her friend's body stiffen noticeably in the middle of the embrace. She pulled back and watched Ryan's face close as she backed away, and in the next instant, the kitchen door opened and Mia walked in.

"Wow, what smells so good?" she inquired brightly. "Hi, Ryan, Jamie."

"Hi, Mia," they both replied nearly in unison.

Mia walked over to the pan of the now-cooled lasagna. She grabbed a knife from the drawer and carved off a piece, stuffing the whole, big bite in her mouth. "This is great. Did you make this?" she pointed at Jamie.

"Yeah, I did."

"What gives?" Mia asked as she looked at the gift-laden table. "Is it your birthday or something, Ryan?"

"Yep, it sure is."

"That's cool. Happy birthday," she said as she surprised Ryan by walking over to her and giving her a hug.

"Thanks. It has been a very happy birthday so far," she conceded as she grinned at Jamie.

"Oh, that reminds me," Mia added. "Jamie tells me that you've got available time on Monday, Wednesday and Friday afternoons. I think she's started to look great, and I don't want her to get too far ahead of me in the looks department." She shot Jamie a grin, adding a wink. "Would you be willing to work with me?"

"Absolutely, Mia. Do you know what my rates are?"

"Yeah, Jamie told me. That's not a problem. Can we start on Monday? I want to look good for this summer when I go to L.A."

Ryan marveled at the financial freedom these women enjoyed. Dropping $375 a week on a whim was not something she could ever imagine doing, but she was glad that Mia could.

After Mia left, Ryan gave Jamie another winning grin as they sat back down at the kitchen table. "You couldn't stand not to have me get paid for those hours could you?"

"Nope. You're gonna be swimming in dough when I get through with you," she laughed. "Hey, I forgot to ask why you were available today." Jamie said. "I figured you'd be with your family."

"Da had to work tonight, so a bunch of my relatives are coming over for a barbecue tomorrow." After a moment she looked at Jamie and asked, "Would you like to come? I'd love for you to meet the rest of my family."

Jamie was very tempted to immerse herself in a whole sea of O'Flahertys, but since Jack had been none too happy about her absence that evening, she thought she had better not . "I wish I could, Ryan. But I need to go down to Palo Alto."

"No big deal. You'll have plenty of opportunities. Actually, I was a little surprised that you were available tonight. I've never seen you spend Friday evening in Berkeley."

"That's because you never had a birthday on a Friday evening, silly," she said as she grinned over at her friend.

"Did you really stay in town just for me?" she asked with a shy little smile.

"Well, yeah," Jamie replied as if the answer should be obvious. "I was going to have you over next week to celebrate, but when I found out you were free on your actual birthday, I decided I had to move it up."

Ryan gazed at her for several minutes, her eyes never wavering from their hold on Jamie's. "You are so thoughtful and so giving ... I hope Jack appreciates you like he should," she said as she patted her friend's hand.

"I ... I ... think he does," Jamie stuttered, as she tried to appear casual. She fought to regain her composure as she said, "My birthday wish for you is that you find someone who truly appreciates how special you are."

"Thanks, Jamie," she said as she continued to hold her gaze. "I hope so, too."

"So, what are your plans for the rest of the evening?" Jamie inquired, trying to lighten the mood. "Surely, you won't be without female companionship?"

"I guess I could be wrong, but you certainly seem like a female to me," Ryan replied, letting her eyes playfully linger on some of the more defining signs of her friend's femininity.

"That's not the type of companionship I mean, and you know it," Jamie scolded, giving her a slap.

Ryan giggled, fending it off. "Okay, okay. I did have tentative plans to meet someone later," she admitted.

"Anyone special?"

Shrugging her shoulders, Ryan said, "No, not really."

"Gee, that must make her feel good," Jamie chided.

"That's not what I meant," Ryan said, clearly embarrassed. "I just mean, well, you know what I mean," she looked to Jamie for understanding, but found a blank face instead. "I'm still seeing that woman you saw me with at the coffeehouse. I like her, I really do. I don't sleep with people I don't like," she defended herself. "But I don't see this progressing very far. It's just fun."

"Why?" Jamie asked simply.

"Why?"

"Yeah, why won't this last?"

"One big reason — and I think it's a good one," Ryan replied with a chuckle. "She doesn't think she's gay."

"Really?" Jamie asked, rather shocked.

"Really. Robin has a boyfriend who goes to the University of Washington. He's actually on the football team, so I hope he never finds out about me," she said with a crooked smile. "I don't think I'd look good with two black eyes and a few broken bones!"

"Uhm … doesn't that bother you at all?"

"What? That she's bisexual, or that I'm cheating with some guy's girlfriend?"

"Uhm … either, I guess," she said hesitantly.

"Well, it doesn't bother me a bit that she's bisexual. I think we're way too hung up on labels for people. And she claims that they both date others during the school year. They're just monogamous when they're in the same city."

"Would it bother you if she were really cheating?" Jamie asked, knowing that she was treading where she did not belong.

"Uhm … I guess it depends. I would never try to get someone to cheat, and I would never seek out someone I knew was in a relationship, but I have slept with women who were involved with someone else, and it didn't really bother me. It's their relationship, and if they want to screw it up, I feel like it's not my business. But I will admit I could never be serious about a woman who cheated. If she does it to someone else, she'll probably do it to me."

"Yeah, I can see how that would prevent you from trusting someone," Jamie agreed. "So, it doesn't bother you a bit that she has a boyfriend?"

Ryan pursed her lips and gave the question some serious thought. "Well, I guess if I'm completely honest, there is one thing that bothers me. I don't mind that she has a boyfriend, but it does bother me that she doesn't really want to be seen in public with me."

"*What?* She's ashamed of dating you?"

Ryan gave her a delightfully crooked grin and said, "That outraged tone was a very nice compliment, Jamie. Thanks for the props."

"Well, really, Ryan," she huffed. "What kind of idiot wouldn't want to be seen with you?"

"I think her concern is that she doesn't want her boyfriend to find out about me. He doesn't know that she dates women," she advised.

"Ohh," Jamie replied with a slight head nod. "So *he* doesn't know she's bisexual."

"Correct." Ryan stood and extended her hand to Jamie. "Enough of this serious talk," she said with a wide smile and a randy wink. "I think it's time we went to our respective lovers and had some fun!"

Jamie gave her a hard bump with her hip as they neared the door. "You get a lot of pleasure out of being bad, don't you?"

"Go with your strengths!" Ryan said with a confident leer.

⌘

When Jamie walked into Jack's apartment a little before 10:00 p.m., the look on his face said more about his displeasure than she wanted to know. "Hi, honey," she called out in greeting as she placed her overnight bag on the floor.

"Hi," he replied, barely looking up from his book.

"Did you have dinner? I brought you some lasagna," she offered.

"Yeah, I made myself a sandwich," he said without elaboration.

"Is everything okay, Jack?" she asked, even though she really didn't want to get into a fight.

"Sure, why wouldn't it be?" he coolly replied, again not lifting his head to look at her.

She was already sick of this act, so she turned the tables on him a bit. "No reason," she said in a sweet tone. "I'm going to get ready for bed. Be back in a minute," she said lightly as she passed by and kissed his cheek. She could feel his eyes burning into her as she walked down the hallway, but she refused to goad him into talking if he didn't want to.

She brushed her teeth and washed her face, both at a leisurely pace. Stripping off her clothes, she put on one of Jack's T-shirts, then picked up a novel by Djuna Barnes that she had to finish by Monday.

As she walked back into the living room, she asked if he needed anything while she was up. He definitely muttered something under his breath, and it sounded like "a full time fiancée." She acted as though she had not heard a word even though she was seething inside. She gave him a completely fake smile and sat down on the end of the couch to read. Just to piss him off, she put her feet up on his lap and refused to let his cold disregard penetrate her outer demeanor. Luckily, her novel was mesmerizing, and she was fully engrossed for almost two hours. True to his always stubborn form, Jack did not loosen up one bit, and at around midnight, he stretched and announced flatly, "I'm going to bed."

The rigors of the day caught up with her, and she decided to turn in also. She turned off the lights and followed him into bed, where she expected the tension to remain.

Much to her shock, as soon as he got into bed he started to make sexual overtures. Amazed to hear the words come from her mouth, Jamie snapped, "Oh, please! You can't say a civil word to me, but now you want to screw me?"

Fixing her with an intense glare, he shook his head and growled, "Not anymore I don't. Forget it."

"Jack, please, can't we talk about this?"

"There's nothing to talk about. You spend your evenings like you want, then you come down here for a nice celibate sleepover. No problem." He rolled onto his side and put his pillow over his head, giving a clear signal that the discussion was over.

⌘

When Jamie woke at 7:00, she was dismayed to find that she was alone. There was a note on the kitchen counter that read, "Law review deadline on Monday. Be back late — don't expect me for dinner, Jack." *Well, that says it all,* she thought glumly. *No 'Love, Jack,' no 'I'm sorry,' no 'I'll call you later.'*

After a few minutes of just staring into space, she picked up the phone and dialed Ryan's pager.

"Jamie?" asked the deep voice when her call was returned.

"Hi. I didn't wake you up, did I?"

"Heck, no; Duffy and I have already been for our run on the beach. He won, of course, but I still had fun. What's up with you at this time of day?" she inquired.

"Is that invitation to your party still open? I'm unexpectedly free today," she stated, giving the partial truth.

"Absolutely. I'd love to have you," she replied easily. "Are you okay? You sound kind of down."

"I am, but just a little. Jack's tied up all day, but I didn't learn about it until this morning. I just don't want to sit here alone."

"Well, you're never alone at the O'Flahertys," she replied. "Not even when you want to be."

⌘

Ryan gave her all the details of the party and steadfastly refused her offer to bring anything. Jamie signed off and immediately felt better. *I've known her for two and a half months, and she can tell in two sentences that something*

173

is bothering me. I've been dating Jack for two and a half years, and I have to hit him over the head to even get his attention. Do I just need more than he's able to give me? Can any guy make me feel understood like Ryan does? Maybe I just want things I can't have.

When Jamie arrived at the party, Ryan answered the door and gave her a delighted smile. *Wow!* Jamie marveled, *she looks absolutely fantastic.* She mused that she didn't often step back and just look at Ryan objectively anymore. They had grown so close that she saw her inner self more than her package. But occasionally she just looked at her and enjoyed the wrapper, and this was one such day. Her beautiful friend was wearing a black, knit, silk T-shirt, which clung to every curve. Black, linen, pleated slacks, and soft, black loafers completed her monochromatic look — highlighting all of her essential traits. She looked tall, sleek, graceful, athletic and terribly, terribly sexy. "Hi, I'm really glad you decided to come," Ryan said enthusiastically, giving Jamie a big hug.

"You did say 2:00, didn't you?" she looked around the house, which was bursting with people.

"Yeah, that's when we wanted people to come. But in this family, they show up when they want to. We've had people show up at 9:00 a.m. for Thanksgiving dinner," she laughed.

As Ryan guided her into the teeming mass of people, Conor swooped down from his place on the staircase. "My, my, my, don't you look lovely today?" he said as he looked Jamie up and down. "Isn't that a gorgeous outfit?" he said to Ryan as he continued to appraise Jamie like a new Ferrari. Jamie was wearing a very slim-fitting, sleeveless shell of textured silk in tangerine and gold that just brushed her waistline. Tapered slacks of the same material showed off her trim legs. A silk knit sweater in the same tangerine was draped around her shoulders, and delicate, woven loafers in a dark tan finished the ensemble.

Slightly embarrassed by their joint assessment, Jamie patiently waited as the two siblings conferred. "Yes, Conor, I would agree that Jamie looks marvelous today," Ryan said with a big smile, "but I've yet to see her look less than lovely, so I'm hardly surprised."

"How about a tour of the rest of the house?" Conor asked. "I bet you haven't seen the upper floor."

Ryan rolled her eyes, but let her brother try to work his charm on her friend — knowing it was futile. When they returned, Ryan was sitting on the third step, leaning casually against the wall with her long legs effectively blocking their path. "Did our house just get a lot bigger, or did you show Jamie the roof?" she asked sweetly.

"No, the house is the same. Jamie was just interested in my mandolin, and I played a bit for her," he replied casually.

"Right," she replied suspiciously. "Well, I've been working on my manners while you were gone, and I realized that Jamie has not been properly introduced to the rest of the clan." She removed Jamie's hand from Conor's arm and placed it on her own. "I plan to rectify my error immediately." She gave Conor a twitch of her long, black hair and moved off with her friend firmly in tow.

"You two never stop, do you?" Jamie asked her with a giggle.

"No, we don't," she admitted. "We've always been competitive. I guess you just stick with familiar patterns as you grow up. But it's funny," she reflected, "we all played together growing up, but only Conor and I were ever really competitive with each other. It doesn't make sense, but that's the way it worked out."

As they moved through the house, Jamie mused that when she was with Ryan and her brother, they treated her like some prize they were fighting over. *Ryan seems much more aggressive when Conor's around. And it feels a lot more like she's flirting with me*, she thought. *No, that's not it*, she corrected herself. *She's not flirting — she acts like she's already won! She actually acts like I'm her little prize. Damn, it would piss me off if Jack acted like that! I wonder why it doesn't bother me in the least when Ryan does it?*

They maneuvered through the small house and eventually broke through the crowd in the kitchen to reach the tiny porch that overlooked the back yard. There were more than a dozen men in the yard, all gathered around two big Weber kettles. Ryan began to point them out. "I thought I would give you an overview before I boggle your mind with introductions," she explained. "This is the male side of Da's family; that's my Uncle Patrick," she indicated a man slightly smaller than Martin, but just as handsome. "That's my Uncle Francis." She pointed to an equally handsome, but slightly older-looking man who was very muscular and brawny. "And that's my Uncle Malachy." She indicated a man who looked like a slightly older Conor.

"Wow!" was all that Jamie could say.

"Now, for the next generation." She ticked off her cousins one by one. "Uncle Patrick has Niall, Kieran, Colm and Donal," she indicated each of the dark-haired men in turn. "Declan, Dermot, Liam and Padraig belong to Malachy, and Frank, Sean, Seamus and Brian are Uncle Francis' boys."

"Is anyone in your family less than gorgeous?" Jamie finally uttered as she shook her head in amazement.

"Uhm, what do you mean?" Ryan responded blankly.

"Do you mean to tell me that you don't know how beautiful everyone in your family is?" Jamie asked, bewildered.

"Well, no, not really," Ryan replied. "I guess I never thought about it," she said as she fidgeted a bit in obvious discomfort.

"You never thought about the fact that your uncles and cousins and brothers all look like Calvin Klein underwear models?" Jamie had to laugh at Ryan's perplexed expression.

"No, I never did," she finally said. "Looks are not a big deal in my family. I mean, I know that we're not exactly ugly," she said with a grin, "but we were never encouraged to feel good about ourselves because of how we looked." She looked thoughtful for a moment before she continued, "Da always told us to never feel proud or ashamed of our gifts or liabilities. He said that what you did with those gifts, and how you overcame your liabilities, was all that mattered. Everything else was just genetics." She shrugged her broad shoulders slightly and looked to Jamie for comprehension. "He also told me to be very suspicious of someone who spent a lot of time complimenting my looks. He said if someone was very focused on the outside of me, they wouldn't have any time to look at the inside."

"That is a wonderful view of the world. It's very different from how I was raised, but I like it a lot better," she grinned in appreciation at Ryan.

"Were looks a big deal in your family?" Ryan asked with concern.

"Not just looks, although that was important, but appearances were the big thing for us," she replied. "You know, wearing the right clothes, being seen with the right people, driving the right car. That sort of thing." She grew thoughtful for a long moment. "I'm going to try to adopt your philosophy for my children," she told Ryan sincerely.

"You can thank Da for that bit of philosophy. Ready to meet the crowd?"

"Ready as I'll ever be," Jamie smiled.

After the extended introductions, Jamie's head was spinning when they entered Ryan's room. "I don't think I can remember one person's name," she moaned. "There were so many of them. And they look so much alike!"

"Well, there are two sets of twins," Ryan mentioned.

"Two?"

"Yeah. Sean and Seamus, and Declan and Dermot are twins."

"At least I'm not totally losing my mind," she laughed.

"Do you really want to remember them all?" Ryan asked with a puzzled look.

"Yeah, of course I do. Will you go over them again and quiz me?"

They knelt at the head of Ryan's bed and looked out the big window at all of the assembled men. After four or five tries, Jamie had them all pretty well sorted out. "Okay, Ryan. I want you to lean over and quiz me all day. That's the only way I'll learn. But it might help if you wrote them down for me, too. I remember things better when I see them."

"I'm not sure that will help you," she advised. "Take Padraig for example. How would you spell that?"

"I guess it would be P-o-r-i-c?"

"Nope. P-a-d-r-a-i-g." She smiled as Jamie tried to get her mind around the odd spelling.

"Are they all that bad?"

"No. I'd say Kieran, Padraig, Niall and Siobhán are the worst of the bunch."

"I don't believe you've told me your mother's name," Jamie said softly.

"Fionnuala," Ryan replied even more quietly.

Jamie placed her hand on Ryan's shoulder and forced eye contact. "It's beautiful," she said sincerely.

Ryan was totally charmed and touched by how interested Jamie was in her family. After they'd completed a few more rounds of "guess the cousins," she pronounced her ready to meet the rest of the family. "You need to meet the O'Flaherty aunts and the Ryans. But don't worry," she reassured her, "there are far fewer of them, and their names are more American."

"I must admit, I've never heard so many Irish names in one place." She paused a moment to reflect. "You've never told me about how your family came to America. I mean, were your parents born here?"

"Not hardly," Ryan replied with a laugh. "As a matter of fact, I wasn't born here."

"Are you serious?"

"Quite," Ryan replied, "but that was a bit of a fluke. My mother came to this country in about 1965 or so, and she married my father a couple of years later. The boys were all born here, but when she was seven months pregnant with me, her mother in Ireland became very ill. She felt like she had to go home even though it must have been hell on Da to be left with three little boys. And I suppose it was pretty bad for her, too, having to travel that far when she was huge with me. After she was there for a month, I surprised everyone by arriving almost a month early."

"So, are you an Irish citizen?" Jamie asked, not sure of citizenship requirements.

"Actually, I have dual citizenship. The boys could have it, too, and

Rory went through the process, but Conor and Brendan don't have much interest."

"So your father was born here?" Jamie asked.

"Correct, but with an explanation. He and all of his brothers were born here. Their parents had immigrated during World War II. But after the war my grandfather couldn't keep a job because of all the returning vets, so they eventually went back home. I think they left here in 1950 or so."

"So is your father a citizen?" Jamie asked, still a little confused.

"Yes, he is. But my mother was illegal. She was just here on a tourist visa, and she overstayed it to be with Da. His brothers still tease him that she married him only for his citizenship status."

"I think your father could convince many a woman to leave her home, Ryan. He's adorable!"

"I think he's a pretty good catch, too," she smiled. "Ready for the rest of the family lineup?"

"I guess I got through the tough part, so bring it on!"

When they returned to the main floor, Ryan looked around and spotted her prey. "You must meet my favorite relative," she said, leading Jamie through the growing mass of people. "There she is!" Ryan said with delight as her eyes locked onto the object of her affection.

Ryan held out her strong arms, and a tiny face looked up at her confusedly.

"Is this the most perfect child you have ever seen?" Ryan asked in a tone that brooked no dissent.

Jamie studied the little person. She was very small, maybe a month old, and fair skinned with a sparse, fine covering of white-blond hair. Beautiful, pale eyes looked around absently as she nestled her little head in the crook of Ryan's broad shoulder. "I would have to agree with you on that one, Ryan. What is this little beauty's name?" she asked as she tickled a perfect foot.

"This is Caitlin," Ryan pronounced as she gave the precious bundle a kiss on the cheek. "She's my cousin Tommy's baby." She looked around the room for the proud parents. "That's Tommy, there, and his wife, Annie, is right there," she pointed in one direction, then the other as Jamie confirmed the sightings. "You know, Jamie," she said as she held Caitlin up next to Jamie's face. "I've been thinking that there was something familiar about the way you look. She looks more like you than she does her parents."

Jamie looked at the tiny face and fervently hoped that she and the indistinct-featured child did not resemble each other, since the child didn't yet look fully human. Ryan noticed her hesitation, and she assured her, "I just meant her coloring," she whispered. "I know she looks more like a doll than a person at this point."

Smiling at the reference, Jamie was paraded around with Ryan holding the baby next to her face to ask for an opinion from the assembled relatives. But when she was introduced to the baby's grandmother, Ryan's aunt Maeve, the agreement was beyond enthusiastic. Maeve made over Jamie as if she were sent directly from heaven. She looked at her from every angle and finally wrapped her in a big hug and said that Caitlin would be lucky indeed to continue to resemble Jamie as she got older.

To get away from the crowds, they decided to go downstairs to play with the baby. She was too young to be able to do much, but she seemed to respond to being talked to and held, something Ryan was all too happy to do.

"Do you want to put her down on the bed?" Jamie asked after Ryan had carried her all around the room, cradled gently in her arms.

"Nah, I really like holding her," she replied a little sheepishly. "I've seen her four or five times a week since she was born, but still, she's different every time. She's growing so fast; I won't be able to do this for long. I really want to enjoy it while I can."

"Right," Jamie laughed. "That baby couldn't weigh more than fifteen pounds, and with your muscles, you could carry *me* around on your hip. I think Caitlin will be able to enjoy a ride on your shoulders until she's in high school!"

"Yeah, but she won't want one then," Ryan chuckled. "I've gotta exploit every opportunity."

After a few moments of watching Caitlin sleep on Ryan's chest, Jamie asked quietly, "Do you want to have children?"

"Yes. I do," she said confidently. "I actually can't imagine not having them," she admitted. She paused for a moment, "I'm not sure how I will do it, though," she added.

"Do you mean technically?" Jamie asked tentatively.

"No, I mean whether I would physically have them or adopt or just co-parent with another woman," she laughed.

"How would you do it, uhm, physically," she persisted.

"Lesbians have the same parts that you do, Jamie," she teased.

"That's not what I mean, and you know it!" she said as she gave her a little slap on the head. "I mean, would you, uhm ... use somebody that you know? Would you do it the old fashioned way or what?"

"I don't really have any desire to experience that particular union," she said with an involuntary shudder. "I would probably either be inseminated from a known donor or use a sperm bank."

"Would you want the, uhm … donor to have a role in raising the child?"

"That is where it becomes tricky for me," she admitted. "I wouldn't want to deprive my child of having a wonderful father like mine. But I'm not sure how to do that in a way that makes everyone happy. I must admit, that's the only part of being straight that I envy," she teased. "Well, that and the marriage laws."

"That is one of the perks," Jamie admitted. "But the downside is that you have to use birth control most of the time." Jamie made a sour face at this.

"I guess having kids is a big deal for everyone," Ryan agreed. "What about you? I assume you and Jack are planning to reproduce, although you made it clear you're not ready yet."

"Yeah," Jamie agreed. "I think we both want a few kids. But I want to be significantly older before I do that."

"What do you want to do before you have kids?" Ryan asked.

"I'm not sure. But I want to do something for myself, like graduate school or maybe I'll write for a while."

"I don't know, Jamie. A little one of these," here she tipped the sleeping baby towards her friend, "can be awfully tempting."

⌘

After a few minutes, Ryan offered to go upstairs and fetch some drinks and something to snack on. To avoid waking Caitlin Jamie sat down on the bed as Ryan transferred the precious cargo to her. Caitlin stirred just a little as she adjusted to her new home. Her little, blonde head was comfortably resting on Jamie's breast as she slowly moved her thumb into her mouth. "I see your point about the temptation, Ryan," she admitted as she gazed down at the baby. "I can feel my ovaries aching already."

Ryan smiled as she took in the scene. "I think motherhood would suit you, Jamie. You two look perfect together."

⌘

Ryan had been gone just a minute or two when there was a quiet knock on the door. Caitlin's grandmother poked her head in and said, "I just wanted to check to make sure you didn't need anything."

"Nope. Everything's just perfect," Jamie said as she smiled up at the proud grandmother. "I must say, this is one lucky baby," Jamie stated.

"Well, I do know that she's loved beyond words," Maeve agreed as she retrieved a clean diaper from the bag she carried. She placed the cloth on Jamie's shoulder to protect her blouse as she casually asked, "How long have you and Ryan been seeing each other?"

"Uhm, Maeve," she said when she recovered from her shock, "Ryan and I aren't together ... in that way," she quietly stated. "We're just close friends."

"Oh, dear, I hope I didn't embarrass you. I'm sorry for making assumptions," she patted Jamie's arm reassuringly. "It's probably just wishful thinking on my part," she admitted.

"What do you mean?" Jamie asked, her interest piqued.

"I was so pleased that Ryan had brought someone home to meet the family," she explained. "She's never done so before, and I just assumed you were someone special to her."

"She is," came the quiet voice from across the room. "She's very special to me." Ryan was crossing the room now, with a small smile on her face. "Regrettably though, she's not my girlfriend," she stated as she shot a grin at Jamie.

Jamie was enormously pleased at this expression of their growing bond. She grinned up at Ryan broadly. "You're pretty special yourself, kiddo."

"I'm sorry for jumping to conclusions, Ryan," Maeve said. "I just hope that when you do bring someone home, she's as special as young Jamie here."

"The odds of that are not good," Ryan intoned seriously. "Jamie is truly one of a kind."

⌘

Dinner was just about ready when Jamie's cell rang. She debated not answering, but she thought better of that idea and scampered outside so she could hear. "Hello?" she said as she answered on the fifth ring.

"Hi," Jack replied, sounding a little small.

"How are you, sweetheart?" she said with as much warmth as she could generate.

"I'm okay. Where are you?" he asked.

"I'm back in the city, honey." She knew that she was intentionally misleading him, but she refused to give him ammunition to continue the fight. "Are we okay, or are you still mad at me?"

"I'm not mad, Jamie. You've just been so different lately; I'm really confused."

Jamie was dismayed to hear him sounding so sad. "Do you want to be alone, or would you like me to come back down?" she offered.

"Would you do that?" he asked hopefully. "I really do want to see you, Jamie. I miss you, sweetheart," he added quietly.

"I'll be there by eight o'clock," she promised. "What would you like me to bring for dinner?"

"I don't care about dinner. I just want you," he said wistfully.

⌘

Ryan was watching as Jamie picked at her food. They were sitting nearly at the top of the staircase that led to the upper floor, all of the other stairs already being occupied. The baby was still being held by one strong arm, while Ryan tried to get a bite or two of dinner into her own mouth. "Was that Jack on the phone?" she asked.

"Oh, yeah, it was. I think I'm gonna go back down to Palo Alto," she replied.

"Are you two having trouble?" Ryan asked with concern.

Jamie regarded her for a minute before answering, "Yeah, I guess we are. Things just haven't been great for a while now."

Ryan looked at her with sympathy and said, "If you need someone to listen, I'm always here for you."

"Thanks, Ryan. I appreciate that." She removed Ryan's plate from her hand and said, "If I don't help you out here, you're going to starve." She balanced Ryan's sturdy paper plate on her knees and cut up her turkey into small pieces. Then she speared bites of turkey and vegetables, and fed them to her friend, one at a time.

"I guess this is why it's so hard to be a single parent," Ryan stated as she removed Caitlin's little hand from her hair.

Conor, Rory and a few cousins sat on the other side of the room. Conor leaned over and quietly asked his brother, "So what do you think about Jamie?"

"I like her a lot. She seems like a good friend for Ryan," Rory replied.

"No, I mean do you think Ryan's going to make a play for her." he explained.

"Why do you want to know?" Rory asked suspiciously.

"Because I think she would be perfect for me," he said smugly.

"I'll make you a friendly little wager on that, Conor," Rory replied. "If Jamie is swayed by any O'Flaherty, I'm putting my money on Ryan."

"You're on, Rory. Let's make it interesting — say $50?"

They shook hands to seal the bet, with Rory casting a glance at the pair to watch Jamie carefully feeding his sister. *It would be a lot easier for Jamie to just hold the baby while Ryan fed herself*, he thought to himself with a smirk. *My money is as good as won.*

⌘

Jamie had to leave well before the party was over. Caitlin was asleep on Ryan's chest again, and Jamie leaned over to kiss her sweet-smelling little head. "I had a great time, Ryan. Thanks for letting me meet your family."

Ryan pulled Jamie back down by gently placing her hand behind her neck. She kissed her cheek lightly as she said, "Thank you for coming, Jamie. You made the day special for me."

⌘

On the drive to Palo Alto, Jamie tried to remind herself that it was perfectly normal to feel affectionate with her female friends. An annoying little voice kept asking, *Is it normal to feel tingles down your spine when they kiss your cheek?*

She arrived at Jack's just before 8:00 after having stopped to buy dinner. Jack was very glad to see her, immediately wrapping her in a big hug. He had his face pressed against her neck for a long time, finally murmuring, "Do you still love me, Jamie?"

"Of course I do, Jack," she gasped. "I'm unsure about a lot of things, but I know that I do love you," she said fiercely. She wrapped her arms around his neck as he bent to kiss her; they slowly progressed in their intimacy until they stumbled towards the bedroom, dinner left to cool on the counter.

CHAPTER EIGHT

JAMIE'S CELL PHONE RANG JUST AFTER 8:00 A.M. SHE SCRAMBLED OUT of bed and found the little phone as it rang for the sixth time. "Jamie?" rang out the deep familiar voice.

"Oh, hi, Daddy," she said, trying to sound awake.

"Did I wake you, sweetheart?"

"No, not at all," she lied, walking through the rest of the apartment, trying to find Jack.

He was sitting in front of the computer in his office, and when he spied her, he let his gaze travel slowly up her naked body. Even though they had been intimate for five months, she still felt a little shy about being naked around Jack when she was just walking around the apartment, and she tried to inconspicuously cover herself by moving behind a chair and strategically draping an arm across her breasts.

Sneaking a glance at her fiancé, she saw the longing in his eyes, and she shuddered a bit at the prospect of what she was certain would soon occur. When they had gotten into bed the previous evening, Jack was clearly willing to forget their small tiff. But Jamie still smarted from it, and she had been a little removed during their lovemaking. Her emotional distance logically affected her arousal and her receptivity — and she had spent most of the time just wishing he would finish. He had begun to touch her again before dawn, but she had feigned sleep to avoid another encounter.

"How about a round of golf this afternoon?" her father asked.

"Hold on and let me ask Jack." She was still uncomfortable having her father know that she stayed at Jack's on weekends, but he had never commented on their physical relationship, so she tried not to let if affect the way she acted.

She placed the phone on mute and said, "Do you want to play golf with Daddy this afternoon?"

"Yeah, that would be fun," he agreed. "I feel like I haven't been outside in weeks. I need to work until noon or so, though. Is that too late?"

"I'll see," she said as she spoke into the phone again, "How about one o'clock?"

"That's great, honey. I'll call and make a tee off time. See you at the club."

After she hung up, Jamie started for the bedroom, feigning a yawn. "I'm going back to bed," she said, smiling at her fiancé over her shoulder. "You really wore me out last night."

He was on her before she could take a step. "Would you like me to help you relax?" he asked as he slipped his hands around her small waist, and turned her towards him. Bending, he rubbed his face against her breasts, and she giggled involuntarily as his unshaven cheeks tickled her bare skin.

"Honey, I won't be able to walk if we make love again," she insisted.

"Oh, come on," he teased. "It's been over a week, baby. One time shouldn't make you sore." Laughing gently, he cocked his head and asked, "Are you just trying to stroke my ego?"

"No, not at all," she demurred. "You were inside me for quite a while, though …"

"You're complaining about my stamina?" he asked, stooping down to try to meet her eyes, which were gazing at the floor. He was clearly being playful, but Jamie was starting to feel trapped.

"I'm not complaining about anything, honey," she said, placing her hands flat against his chest and pushing him away slightly. "I'm just still tired, and I don't want to look like heck today."

"You know," he said thoughtfully, "I really like the way you look lately." He stroked her concave stomach with the back of his hand. "Working out has really improved your body." He gave her another assessing look and said, "But you are getting a little thin. Are you going to try to put some weight back on?"

"Yeah, I'm going to start working with a nutritionist so I can learn to eat right. I'm using a lot more energy, and I need to be able to fuel my body more efficiently."

Jack placed his hands under her breasts and hefted them, making her squirm under his inspection. "I just don't want you to lose any more weight here," he said with a wicked grin. "These are just perfect."

"Thanks," she said weakly as she walked back into the bedroom. She fell into the bed and stared at the ceiling for a long time, no longer tired, but too depressed to do anything else.

I can't believe that we still haven't talked about our fight. He honestly thinks that making love solves all of our problems! I guess the only thing that really matters is that my breasts don't get too small! After stewing for a long while, she finally drifted off into a fitful slumber.

⌘

They teed off at around 1:30 after spending a few minutes warming up on the driving range. Jamie had not played since that day with Ryan, but it had been a lot longer for Jack. She was beating him handily, and by the sixteenth hole, she was ahead by eight strokes. Usually he didn't much care how he played, but today it obviously bothered him. She was consistently out-driving him, and when she teed off, her ball lay a good thirty yards farther than his.

"Have you been playing much, Jamie?" Jim asked, beaming with pride.

"No, not really. I guess I'm just in the groove today."

"I sure was pleased when you asked if you could bring your friend to play," he smiled. "I hope you can start to play more regularly. Hey! We could enter the father/daughter tournament this year if you're interested."

Jack was facing away from Jamie, but she saw him visibly tense at this comment. He turned to her and asked neutrally, "Who did you bring to the club, Jamie? You didn't mention that you've been playing."

"I brought Ryan," she said simply, staring right into his eyes.

"Who's Ryan?" Her father had noticed that something was going on between the two of them, and he was now interested in finding out what it was.

"Just a friend of mine from school," Jamie replied after Jack hit his next shot — a powerful slice that landed on the third fairway.

"A guy?" Jim asked hesitantly, thinking that perhaps this was an issue with the young couple.

"Only partially," Jack answered his question as he stalked off to find his ball.

Jim and Jamie watched Jack stomping his way across the fairway with shock registering on both of their faces. "What in the heck is wrong with him?" Jim finally asked her.

"He's just been in a mood for a while," Jamie replied neutrally. "I think he's got too much stress with law review and his class work."

"What did he mean by that comment?" Jim persisted, refusing to let the issue drop.

Jamie pulled her five iron from her bag and hit her second shot — watching it land softly on the green. Turning to her father she said, "Ryan's a friend from school that Jack doesn't like."

"What did he mean when he said she was partially a guy?" he asked.

"Ryan's a lesbian. And for some reason Jack feels threatened by that," she finally admitted.

"Hmm," Jim replied. "That does seem strange."

At least he's on my side, Jamie thought as Jack finally reached the green.

They holed out in silence, and not another word was said until they finished up on eighteen. Jim looked at them both and said, "Let's go into the grill. I don't want you two to leave like this."

Jack looked a little guilty about his belligerent attitude, and Jamie had no reason to refuse, so they agreed. After they were settled with drinks, Jim finally broke the silence again. "Do you mind talking about what's bothering you two?"

"It's not a big deal, Daddy," Jamie said. "Jack has been unhappy about my friendship with Ryan, but I'm sure he'll feel better about it when he gets to know her a little." She could have gone on, but she really didn't want her father to know how childish Jack was being.

"I don't want to get to know her, Jamie," Jack said through gritted teeth. "If you really respected my opinion, you would stop spending all of your free time with her."

"I don't spend all of my free time with her, Jack," she defended.

"How many times did you see her this week?" he asked, bearing down on her like a prosecutor.

She cleared her throat and fidgeted in her seat. "Well, we played golf on Monday, as Daddy mentioned. I saw her in class twice; we had to volunteer together on Tuesday and Thursday night; she trained me at the gym twice; and then I made her dinner on Friday."

"Is that all?" he asked, staring at her intently.

Swallowing audibly, she shook her head briefly. "I went to her house yesterday. You were going to be gone all day, so I went to her family birthday party."

Jack didn't say a word in response to her statement. He merely raised one dark blonde eyebrow and narrowed his eyes a bit in obvious triumph.

Her voice rising, she said, "I don't see her that much all of the time. This week was an anomaly."

"That's not what Cassie says," he said with a touch of drama.

Jamie's face had been relatively composed, but now it grew bright pink with anger. "Do you have any others spies keeping track of me, or only Cassie?" she ground out.

"Jack, Jamie," her father finally said, trying to calm them down. "It's obvious that this is a big issue between you two." Jamie continued to glare at Jack who was glaring right back at her. "Jamie," he said as he turned to her, "I think the solution is rather obvious."

"I don't know if I can wait for Jack to grow up, Daddy," she sniffed, turning to look at her father.

"No, honey," he said firmly. "You can't put your friendships ahead of your commitment to Jack. Friends will come and go, but your spouse is with you for life."

Jamie felt all of the color drain from her face. She turned from her father to Jack and then back again, feeling absolutely betrayed by both of them. "So, that's what makes a good marriage? Giving in to every irrational request that your partner makes? Or is it only the woman who has to give in?" she added, her voice dripping with sarcasm.

The looks she was regarded with were identical. Neither man had ever seen her stand her ground so forcefully, and neither liked it. Rather than cause a bigger scene, she stood and gazed at them both for a moment then shook her head and fought to control the tears that desperately wanted to come as she turned and left the room.

After a half hour in the Jacuzzi, she was feeling more like herself, and she got dressed and left the locker room. Jack was waiting right outside the door, his anxious expression testament to his worry. He got to his feet and approached her, saying quietly, "Let's go to your house and talk about this. Things are really starting to get out of hand."

⌘

They had taken separate cars to the club, and Jamie arrived at the house first. She spent a few minutes making a snack and opening a bottle of wine, and when Jack came in he couldn't help his fond smile. "You're the only girl I know who would prepare hors d'oeuvres for an argument."

She gazed at him for a moment and said, "I don't want to fight, Jack. I want to work on the issues that keep causing conflict between us. Fighting isn't the answer."

"Okay," he said, nodding briefly. He took the tray and started to carry it up to her room, but she indicated that she'd rather sit in the living room.

"Neither Cassie nor Mia should be home for a while. I like it better down here."

They sat next to each other, their bodies on the verge of touching. Jack looked at her and asked, "Mind if I start?"

"No. Please do."

He picked up his glass and took a long sip of the crisp, fruity wine. "First, I want to apologize for being a baby today. Making snarky comments to you isn't how I want to act, Jamie. You deserve better than that." She nodded and gave him an encouraging smile, and he continued. "And though I didn't handle myself well, I still believe in what I was trying to say. I thought your dad had a very good point — and I think it's one we both have to try to follow."

"And that is?" she asked slowly, her eyes narrowing slightly.

"Please don't give me that look," he sighed. "If you'd let me talk without making a face, I could get this out."

She shook her head briskly. "Sorry. Go on."

"Okay." He took in a deep breath and said, "We each have to try harder to make the other the most important person in our lives." His gaze sharpened as he stared deeply into her eyes. "You're the most important person in my life, Jamie. I'll do anything to make this relationship work. I swear that to you."

His hope-filled expression demanded that she respond in kind, and she did so without hesitation. "You're the most important person in my life, too, Jack. I love you very, very much." She buried her face in his neck, filling her lungs with his musky, masculine scent. With each deep breath, some of the stress left her body until she was resting limply in his embrace.

Jack leaned back against the sofa and pulled her onto his lap. With a relaxed sigh, she put her head on his shoulder and snuggled up against him. He ran his fingers through her hair, bending to kiss the crown of her head repeatedly. "I love you, Jamie," he soothed gently, continuing to stroke and caress her until she nodded off. His gaze traveled up and down her body, marveling at how close to her he felt when they were together like this. Sipping his wine, he cuddled her tightly, wishing that it could always be like this.

⌘

When she woke from her short nap, Jack was gazing right into her eyes. "You're so incredibly beautiful," he whispered. "Watching you sleep makes me feel closer to you than I've ever felt to anyone else in my life." She was still blinking her eyes open when he pulled her to his chest and started to kiss her. Her surprise at the immediacy of his need stopped her from protesting, but when she felt him begin to get aroused, she called a halt to the fervid embrace.

"Jack, please," she said softly, pushing him away gently. "We haven't resolved anything yet, sweetheart. Just agreeing that we'll try to make each other most important is just one of the things we have to settle."

"Huh?" he asked, his passion slowly dimming.

"I said I'd try my best to remember that I have to take your feelings into consideration — that I'd try to include you in my decisions and my plans. But that's just the big picture, Jack. How do we do that? How do we respect each other's individual needs while satisfying our own needs?" She saw that he was beginning to understand her, and she mentioned the continuing point of contention. "How can I continue to be friends with Ryan without driving you nuts?"

Sitting up fully, he pushed a hand through his hair and straightened the collar of his shirt, a pair of oft-seen nervous habits. "I … uhm … thought that might be one of those making me the most important person things."

She blinked at him in shock. "Do you honestly think that the way to make our relationship better is for me to stop seeing someone that I'm very fond of?"

His cheeks colored slightly as he said, "She takes away from our time together! You saw her on Friday and on Saturday!"

Fixing him with a glare, she snapped, "Nothing, I repeat, nothing takes away from our time together more than law school."

"That's hardly the same thing, Jamie —"

"Of course it is! Let's get real, Jack. Once we're married, you don't even have to work if you don't want to. You certainly don't have to work at such a demanding job!"

"But it's what interests me," he protested. "You would never respect me, and I'd never respect myself, if I let my wife support me!"

"And I'd never respect myself if I let you dictate who my friends are!"

He pursed his lips so tightly that they whitened at the corners. "God damn it, Jamie! I am so jealous of that woman, I can't see straight!"

Her mouth gaped open in shock at this stunning admission. "Jack, what on earth do you have to be jealous about?"

Struggling to control his temper, he took in a few deep breaths. "Jamie, how would you feel if my law review partner were a gorgeous woman with a reputation for seducing every guy she could get her hands on?" He cut her off with a raised hand when she tried to interrupt. "And what if I spent a lot of my free time with her, not doing school work, just hanging out?" He cocked his head at her. "Wouldn't that bother you?"

"That's not a good analogy, Jack," she explained patiently. "A better one would be if your partner were a very good-looking gay guy who had a reputation for dating lots of other gay men." He began to scowl at this analogy. "It would not bother me one bit if you became friends with a gay man," she added.

"That's not the same thing," he replied confidently, concurrently trying to figure out why it wasn't.

"Tell me why it isn't," she said sweetly, knowing he could not.

"I don't know, but it's not," he said firmly, his features worked into a scowl befitting a three-year-old.

"Okay, let's start over. Tell me exactly why you're jealous of her."

"I'm afraid she's just being friends with you to seduce you," he admitted quietly.

"Well, I'm not sure who that insults more, but go on," she encouraged, trying to hide her pique.

"I don't see how hanging out with her is any different than hanging out with a guy who's after you," he finished.

"Well, it's simple, really. One — she's not after me. Two — she is not a guy; she is a woman. Three — I'm committed to be married to you, and I wouldn't cheat on you with a man or a woman, no matter how much they wanted me." Looking up at him she added, "I do have some amount of self-control and an abundance of fidelity."

Looking at her with his eyes slightly narrowed, he asked, "How do you know she isn't after you?"

"Because I asked her," she said simply.

"You what!"

"I had heard the rumors about her, and I had seen her flirting with the other women in class, so I asked her if she was interested in me," she patiently explained. "I had no interest in developing a friendship with her if she was going to be flirting with me the whole time, and I wanted to get it out of the way right from the start."

"What did she say?" he asked, astounded by this development.

"She said she knew I was straight and that she didn't like to date straight women. I've since learned that she has a firm policy against seeking out anyone who's seriously dating someone — and I am extremely serious about dating you," she said, touching one of the buttons on his shirt as she batted her eyelashes at him. "She also said that she thought I was cute and that she had been interested, but that she didn't like to date her friends."

"And you believed her?" he asked, his tone indicating that Jamie was more than a little gullible.

"Yes, I did then, and I do now. We spend a lot of time together, Jack. She tells me all about her life and the women she sees. I know her family. I know what kind of a person she is."

"What kind of person is she?" he asked, his head cocked in question.

Thinking for a moment, she said, "She's loyal and honest and very forthright. I trust her completely, Jack." Just to tweak him a bit she added, "She's got three older brothers and about a dozen cousins who are just as good-looking as she is. And the best-looking one of the bunch is always flirting with me. That's who you should be jealous of," she added, a teasing smirk on her face.

"Oh, now I feel better," he grumbled good-naturedly. He put his arm around her shoulders and drew her close once again. Placing a kiss on her head, he said, "I don't want to question your judgment, honey, but let's face it. You don't have a lot of experience in this area. Guys will tell girls anything to get them into bed. Hell, I spent seventh and eighth grades being best friends with this dim-witted cheerleader in the hopes of one day sleeping with her."

She nodded, sparing a smile at his revelation. "Would you have done that if you could have been sleeping with nearly every other girl in your class?"

"Well …"

"Of course you wouldn't have," she insisted. "The same is true for Ryan. She can have her pick of women at school. Believe me, honey, they practically throw themselves at her. She certainly wouldn't be wasting her time trying to turn me into a lesbian when she has so many to choose from. That just doesn't make sense."

"So, you're saying that she treats you just the same as your other friends do, right?"

She thought about this for a long while. Desperately wanting not to prolong this, she was equally determined not to lie. "No, that's not true," she admitted. "The dynamic is different with her. She's very comfortable touching other women, and that makes her a bit more physically close than my other friends." She gathered her courage. "And she's very comfortable in her own body. She's a massage therapist as well as a trainer, and she's very comfortable with physical contact."

"Like what?" he inquired suspiciously.

"Like rubbing my legs after a workout or giving me a hug when I've had a bad day," she replied.

"And you truly don't think that she gets aroused when she touches you?" he asked warily.

"I'm certain that she doesn't," she replied firmly. "I'm certain of that." He was quiet for a moment, eying her thoughtfully. Then he nodded his head, seemingly satisfied with her answer. *Thank you; thank you for not asking the inverse question,* she shuddered.

"Okay. I'm going to trust that you know what you're doing here," he said. "I believe that you won't put yourself in a position that would undermine our relationship." He focused intently on her, and she felt herself shrink back under his penetrating gaze.

He wrapped his arms around her tightly, and she nuzzled her face into his neck. *God, I hope I'm worthy of that trust*, she worried inwardly. *I trust Ryan completely, but I'm not sure if I can trust myself!*

Pulling back from the hug, he once again settled his intent stare upon her, finally allowing a smile to form on his lips. His eyes shone with love for her, and when he bent to kiss her, she found herself responding with rare enthusiasm. Her feelings were still a little bruised, but the emotion of the day propelled her to show him exactly how she felt about him. Within minutes she was half-naked on the couch, tugging his shirt from his slacks. His good sense prevailed, and he carried her to her room where they coupled in a frenzy of desire, expressing all of their pent-up emotion through their bodies.

Later, their need slaked, his head rested on her breast as she rubbed his back and rocked him gently. "I love you, Jack," she murmured. "I love you."

⌘

After class the next day, the classmates adjourned to their usual spot for a glass of juice. Ryan was expansive and relaxed, sitting casually on the bench, with one knee drawn up to her chin.

"You seem in a good mood," Jamie smiled, getting a word in after Ryan's chattering during their walk.

"I am. Had a good weekend."

"Wanna share?"

"Well, you were with me through most of it," she smiled. "But I was left to my own devices yesterday. I went on a screamin' hot ride up on Mt. Tam in the morning, then I hooked up with an old friend." She pointedly looked at her watch and added, "Our little date lasted until two hours ago when I raced through the house like a wildfire, trying to get my stuff together so I wasn't late for class." She gave Jamie a very self-satisfied smile. "Good weekend all around. How about you?"

"Well, I'm sure yours had more sustained excitement," she said, giving her a playfully disapproving smile, "but mine had a few fireworks."

"Give," Ryan demanded, cocking her head.

"I found out yesterday that my good friend, Cassie Martin, has been fanning the flames with Jack again. He basically said that she had told him that I spent every free minute of my time with you."

"I should be so lucky," Ryan scoffed.

Shaking her head slightly, Jamie smiled, "You sure do know how to make a girl feel good."

193

"That comes in handy in my line of work," Ryan decided, easily ducking a forcefully thrown bottle cap.

Her eyebrows twitching together in a small frown, Jamie looked at Ryan pensively. "Would you mind if I wanted to talk about Jack for a bit?"

"Not at all. Go for it."

"Do you think I'm crazy to be getting married so soon?" *Where did that come from?* she wondered, not having any idea those words would pop out of her mouth.

"Thanks for starting with a nice, simple question," Ryan smiled sardonically. After a moment she answered, "I wasn't ready to make that kind of commitment when I was your age, but you're a lot more mature in many ways than I was three years ago. Actually, you're more mature than I am now," she grinned.

"But you know me, Ryan. Do you think I'm ready to be married?"

Ryan took the question as seriously as Jamie had posed it. "Can I ask you a few questions?"

"Ask away."

"What does marriage mean to you?"

Giving her a smirk, Jamie replied, "You started with a toughie, too, pal." Ryan smiled warmly, and Jamie let her mind work on the question for a long time. "I think of it as a lifetime commitment to share all of the joys and sorrows of life with one special person. I pledge to share my deepest thoughts and feelings with him. I promise to share my body with him alone. And I promise to do everything I can to make his life more complete."

"Damn good answer," Ryan responded after a moment to reflect on her words. "Do you feel able to honor all of those pledges to him?"

"I do," Jamie started to reply, but she caught herself. "I did," she corrected. "Well, I think I do … but now I'm less sure. I'm not unsure of my feelings for him," she said decisively. "I just worry that we have too many unresolved issues between us. I mean, we're still arguing about how much time I spend with you — and that's such a silly thing to fight about."

"What else?" Ryan inquired.

"Well, we had a good discussion about this yesterday, but I don't think he can change as quickly as he thinks he can. He seems to feel entitled to tell me how to spend my time, and I don't know that he'll be able to stop doing that just because I tell him to. Also, I'm really into my prep for the AIDS Ride. And it disappoints me that he doesn't seem to support me at all. He doesn't ask about my training or anything." After a moment she added, "Although he has been complimenting me on my body."

"Well, at least he's not blind," Ryan teased. "Did he used to be interested in your life?"

"I think so, but I'm not really sure. I mean, I have changed since I've known you Ryan. I do want more from him than I used to want."

"Why is that, Jamie? What have I done?" she asked, a bit confused.

"You're interested in me. You make me feel like I'm important. You ask me about what I do and what I like. It's made me wish for that from him. I shouldn't have to get that from my girlfriends. My lover should care more about me than my friends," she explained logically.

"You might be right, Jamie, but I'm not sure. It's a rare man that can make you feel connected like a woman can, and believe me, I'm not knocking men. I just think there are things you can get from women that are hard for men to give."

"I suppose you are right. Like when we fight, he doesn't want to talk about it or work it out. He just wants to, uhm ... be intimate. But that doesn't settle things for me. I don't get over my emotional pains through sex," she said pensively.

"I know that a lot of men express their feelings through sex. Maybe you just need to spend more time explaining what your needs are. There's a good chance he'll try to meet your needs once he knows what they are."

"I suppose that's true. I haven't been very forceful in making him realize what my needs are." She sighed and said, "I just wish he knew without my having to tell him."

"That doesn't seem fair to him," Ryan said, shaking her head. "I know from dealing with my brothers that they're often clueless about emotional issues. They really need to be guided."

"You seem to know a lot about men. I guess being raised with all those brothers really gave you an advantage," Jamie said.

"All I know is that it's really different being in a relationship with a man versus a woman. With a woman I feel like I can use shorthand, and she'll be able to understand. You need to be much clearer with men."

"It sounds like it's so much easier being with a woman," Jamie lamented.

Ryan looked at her thoughtfully for a long time. "In a way it is, but there's a tendency for women to identify with each other too much and become too interdependent. In an opposite-sex couple, there is a push-pull, yin-yang kind of thing that creates a lot of tension. And tension can make for really hot sex," she said with a showy smile.

Jamie nodded thoughtfully. "I guess you're right," she mused. "Our best sex is after a fight or when the emotion is really high. I'd really prefer to be able to generate some of that heat when we're not angry with each other, though," she added.

"You'll work it out," Ryan soothed. "As long as you're both fully committed, you should be able to get off on the right foot."

That does become the question, doesn't it? Jamie mused, letting her eyes wander up and down Ryan's long body when the taller woman got up to throw their bottles away.

⌘ CHAPTER NINE

ONE TUESDAY IN EARLY NOVEMBER, JAMIE SHOWED UP AT THE GYM, hoping to get a little cardiovascular work in. She looked around for her friend and found her in a rear corner of the gym, chatting with a woman. Trying to be unobtrusive, she hopped on a StairClimber to get warmed up, but being on the slightly elevated machine gave her an even clearer view of the action, and she could not help but watch.

Ryan was leaning up against one of the chest press machines. The woman was seated on the integrated stool of the machine, and she gazed up at Ryan with a very flirtatious look. Jamie was pretty sure that she was not one of her friend's personal clients, and as she looked more closely, she noticed that the woman was considerably older than Ryan. *She's old enough to be my mother!* she thought in alarm. The woman looked to be about forty-five or so, but she was in great shape. About five foot six inches, she was very fit, with short dark hair. The woman was obviously well-heeled, and the thought occurred to Jamie that this could be any one of her mother's friends.

Ryan had adopted a very casual pose. She had one of her long arms extended above her head to hang over the top bar of the machine, and she was leaning against the bulk of it so that the woman had to crane her neck to make eye contact. Though her pose was casual, there was that barely-concealed force that just begged to be released from her body. Jamie had often seen her friend look completely relaxed and casual. But every time Ryan was sizing someone up, she adopted this predatory posture. Jamie had to admit that it was very appealing, and for one brief instant she felt the sting of jealousy. But she quickly brushed that troublesome thought from her brain as she tried to watch, while appearing not to.

After a few minutes the woman tried to stand, but Ryan was directly in her way. She did not budge one inch, and the woman was forced to alter her path a bit. Since Ryan had a good six inches on her, the woman still had to look up to meet her gaze, and she seemed unable to look away from Ryan's penetrating stare. They were standing terribly close to one another, and Ryan was clearly not going to move. To get past her the woman placed her hands on Ryan's waist and gently moved her out of the way. *Gotcha!* Jamie thought. *Once you touch her there's no escape!*

Ryan leaned over to hear a question, and when she lifted her head again she had the confident smirk that she so often wore when she was hitting on someone. She nodded her head slowly and leaned back on her heels to watch the woman make her way to the locker room. Jamie watched her walk over to another trainer; the pair spoke for a moment or two, and then Ryan went to the front desk and chatted with the woman on duty. After another moment she walked over to the coat hooks, picked up her leather jacket, then walked out the front door with a definite swagger.

A minute or two later her prey emerged from the locker room. She left quickly, and Jamie spent a moment wondering if they were meeting up in the parking lot. *Knowing Ryan, they don't even have to leave the lot if that woman has a big enough sports utility vehicle,* she thought as a shudder rolled down her body.

⌘

After class the next day, Jamie took notice of the strangely lethargic mood her friend seemed to be in. They were sitting in a small café on Telegraph, since the day was cold and windy. Speaking up over the background noise, Jamie asked, "You doing okay? You look kinda down."

"I'm fine," she said, forcing a smile. "No biggie."

"Hey." Jamie gazed at her until she turned to meet the surprisingly serious look that Jamie was sending her way. "If something is bothering you, I'd like to hear it if it might help you feel better. It doesn't have to be a biggie for me to care, Ryan."

Jamie felt her heart skip a beat when Ryan gave her a high wattage smile. "Thanks. I know that ... I just ... I'm a little embarrassed."

"You don't have to be embarrassed around me," Jamie assured her. "You can tell me anything, Ryan."

The larger woman stared into her glass of juice for a few minutes, a deeply contemplative look on her face. "I, uhm ... did something yesterday that's really bothering me," she began.

Jamie nodded, saying nothing.

"I hooked up with a woman from the gym," the dark woman continued. "I've seen her around, and I've flirted with her a little bit, and yesterday I was finished for the day and she was still there. It didn't take long," she smirked. "Before I knew it, we were at the Mark Hopkins." She shrugged her shoulders and gave Jamie an adorably helpless look.

"Nice place," Jamie said, adding her own shrug.

"We had a good time together," Ryan continued. "At some point she asked me how much I charged, and I assumed she meant how much I charged to train someone." She looked down at the table, obviously shamed. "She must have thought I was a hooker, 'cause she left me $250 in cash."

Jamie couldn't pull the gasp that slipped from her lips back in, and she felt even worse when Ryan flinched noticeably at the sound. "Oh, Ryan, maybe she was just paying you for the time that you were away from work. Maybe she thought you gave up a couple of clients to be with her."

With a heartbreakingly sad smile, Ryan shook her head. "No, that's not it. She rented me for the afternoon. I gave her all the sex she could handle, took a little in return, then she left. I don't know her last name, and for all I know, she made up her first name."

Jamie reached across the table and clasped her hand over Ryan's, not caring who saw her make the gesture. "You're not a prostitute, Ryan. She was wrong about you."

"Was she?" Ryan asked softly. "She was older than I am," she said. "Nearly as old as my mother would have been. I was actually lying in bed while she showered, feeling pretty smug about being able to snare someone so worldly and sophisticated," she muttered. "We had a suite, and she'd obviously paid for the night, so after she left, I had Conor come over. He was just teasing me, but he made some comment about Da finding out." Her dark head shook, her hair cascading down to obscure her face. "I thought of my father ... and my mother."

Jamie couldn't see her eyes, but she could tell by her voice that she was crying softly.

"She'd be ashamed of me," Ryan finished in a raspy whisper.

"She would not be ashamed of you!" Jamie's voice was far too loud for the venue, and Ryan's head shot up in surprise. The dark woman wiped at her eyes with a napkin, fixing her watery blue orbs on Jamie's face. Ryan's expression was that of a small child waiting to be reassured, and Jamie did her best to fill that need.

"Your mother would be so very proud of you, Ryan," she said fiercely. "She'd see how loving and generous and selfless you are. How you give so much of your time and energy to helping others. The fact that you're intimate with a number of women doesn't diminish any of your wonderful attributes." She gripped her shoulder firmly and gazed deeply into her eyes. "I think the person you are is absolutely fantastic. If you could see yourself through my eyes, you wouldn't have any doubts about the person that you've become."

Ryan's face curled up into a crooked grin and she reached out and returned the pressure on Jamie's shoulder. "That was a very generous thing to say. Thanks for the vote of confidence."

"I'd vote early and often for you," Jamie vowed said as she beamed up at her friend. "Feeling a little better?"

"Yeah," Ryan nodded. "I'll feel better still when I return the money." She shrugged and said, "I'm not looking forward to that encounter, but I just can't keep it."

"Are you afraid of offending her?"

"A little. I mean, there is a small chance that she didn't intend to pay me for sex. I guess my bigger problem is that I don't want to see her again, and I'd rather not have to discuss this. I might just leave it in an envelope for her at the front desk."

Saying nothing, Jamie raised an eyebrow in question and Ryan rolled her eyes. "Yeah, I know, that's a pretty cold way to do it."

"It is a little harsh, Ryan."

Ryan's chin tilted downward and she sat quietly for a few moments. "What's harsh is that I let her touch me and taste every part of my body just yesterday, and today I don't want to make eye contact with her. That's fucked-up, Jamie." She met her friend's eyes and said, "I've got to step back and take a good look at how I'm living my life."

Jamie reached across the table and gripped her folded hands. "I'm here if you ever want to talk."

"I know," Ryan smiled warmly. "That helps a lot."

⌘

The classmates finally agreed on the destination for their "gay for a day" outing. Ryan had suggested so many possibilities without Jamie's taking her up on any of them that she'd begun to think that Jamie was just dodging. But to her surprise, Jamie came up with a suggestion that was bolder than any she had offered. "Why don't we go have tea at the Peninsula Tearoom?" she asked.

"Well, I'm an Irish lass," Ryan said in her brogue. "I love a good cuppa. But why's that appropriate to our class?"

"It's just outside of Atherton," Jamie said, "and populated exclusively by moneyed matrons, who love nothing more than to spend the afternoon gossiping about each other. It's so stuffy, my mother won't even go there — and she's as stuffy as they come!"

"Works for me," Ryan agreed. "But to make an impact, we're gonna have to act gay."

Jamie gave her a wry smile and said, "Just follow my lead, baby."

⌘

They settled on the second Saturday of November. Jack was frantically working on his law review article — so intent on his work that he barely looked up when Jamie told him she was leaving for the day. She arrived at Ryan's, carrying her dressy clothes in a garment bag and was surprised to find that her friend was wearing a pair of sweat pants and a T-shirt. "I thought you wanted to get dressed up?"

"I do, I do," she nodded. "I just can't force myself into my clothes. I have one acceptable outfit to wear. And I don't wanna wear it."

Jamie claimed the bathroom, since Ryan was nowhere near ready to get dressed. She emerged a few minutes later, looking every bit the young Hillsborough debutante, wearing a short, dark tan skirt in silk. Atop the skirt she wore a long, silk jacket in a tan, black and cream paisley. The jacket was made to be worn without a blouse, as the stand-up collar buttoned all the way up to her throat. Large gold knots graced her earlobes, and a heavy gold chain hung from her neck, resting atop her collarbones.

Jamie gasped in surprise as she took her friend in. Ryan might not have liked her outfit, but it liked her very, very much. A pastel pink cashmere sweater set covered a simple, short black shirt. A black velvet headband held her bangs off her forehead, and a string of pearls nestled against the hollow of her throat. Plain stockings and simple black pumps combined to make her legs look tantalizingly long, and her smoothly curved calves were very attractively displayed.

"Why on earth do you not like this outfit?" Jamie marveled. "You look absolutely beautiful."

"I hate, loathe and despise skirts," she said with disdain. "Next to skirts, I hate heels." She held up her foot to display the offending footwear. "They both change the way you walk and the way you sit. I'm not much of a conspiracy theorist, but I'm sure they're both an evil plot to subjugate women and render us unable to protect ourselves." After a pause she continued with a smile, "But thank you for the compliment."

She prowled around Jamie slowly, examining her wardrobe. "This kind of thing looks like it was made for you," she said, pulling the jacket up to look for a label at the neck. "And knowing your family, it might have been," she said teasingly.

"No, I bought this off the rack with the rest of you mortals," she replied haughtily. "But I did buy it in Milan, if that makes you feel better."

"Well, I can't match Milan, but my Aunt Maeve gave me this outfit five years ago for Christmas. This is only the second time I've worn it," she said proudly.

As they walked back upstairs, they met Conor coming down from his room. "Wow! Where are you two going?"

"We're going to the Peninsula for tea," Ryan replied with studied elegance.

"I don't know how you did it, Jamie, but keep up the good work," he teased as he eyed his sister's legs and unsuccessfully tried to tickle her waist. "I forgot she was a girl."

⌘

As they drove along 101, Ryan did her best to prepare Jamie for the encounter. "The only way you'll get a taste of what being gay is like is if we really act like girlfriends. But I want to be sure that's not going to bother you."

"I guess that depends on what you're planning on doing to show that we're together," Jamie replied, using her humor to stem her nervousness.

"Nothing graphic, Jamie," Ryan laughed, slapping at her arm.

"I was afraid you were going to act like you did that night I saw you at the bookstore with, uhm … Robin?"

"Good memory," Ryan smiled. She gave her a speculative look and decided, "I think that course of action is a little advanced for you. I was thinking more along the lines of handholding. Maybe a few deep kisses … a little tongue dueling." She barked out a laugh at the expression on her friend's face. "Kidding," she assured her.

"Good thing," Jamie smiled nervously. "I think it's illegal for straight people to do that in Atherton."

⌘

They arrived just before noon. Since the shop was located on the main business street, parking was always a problem, and Jamie and Ryan found themselves forced to park several blocks away. Jamie lagged behind to feed the meter, and when she gazed up ahead, she found herself truly amazed at the physical transformation that had come over Ryan. The long–legged woman acted completely comfortable and natural in her outfit. Her gait was shorter, and her hips moved more as Jamie was all too happy to observe, walking slightly behind her. Somehow her posture was significantly less aggressive, giving off an almost-demure aura. Remarkably, she looked physically smaller and more feminine, and Jamie was unable to stop herself from staring. Turning unexpectedly, Ryan noted her stare and teased, "I like to keep 'em guessing. I think I do a pretty good straight girl imitation, don't I?"

"It's … it's amazing," Jamie stuttered. "How do you do that?"

"I just try to look a little less imposing. I try to look less like a jock, too," she added with a grin. "Wearing a skirt and heels helps because they really don't let you take your normal gait."

"But your demeanor is so different."

"I'd have to be painfully unaware not to know how society expects women to look, Jamie. I don't follow the norm, but I'm able to copy it."

"Truly remarkable," Jamie remarked. "I don't think I've ever noticed before, but you really are different from my straight friends."

"Well, aren't you observant?" Ryan smirked. "What was your first clue?"

Jamie gave her a pretty good elbow, right in the ribs. "Not that difference, silly. It just dawned on me what's different about you. You don't look like you're trying to please or appeal to men. You just look like yourself."

"Exactly!" Ryan cried. "It's not that I don't like men, I just don't go out of my way to appeal to them."

"Right," Jamie agreed. "It's like you relate to men as an equal. I noticed that when you met Jack. But when I see Cassie around him, she's always batting her eyes at him or acting kind of helpless. And I do that, too. I always let him do things for me that I could easily do for myself, because he seems to enjoy showing that he's stronger than I am."

"I think a lot of that's very unconscious, almost like it's hard-wired into people. I don't consciously try to intimidate men, but I do a really good job of it. Guys flirt with me all the time, but it usually only lasts for a few seconds. Once they interact with me for any time at all, they invariably back off. Funny, huh?"

"Yeah, you just give off a vibe that says, 'Not interested.' But when I see you flirting with a woman, the energy coming off you is almost visible."

"Really?" she asked, blinking in surprise. "I don't think I realized that."

"Oh, yeah," Jamie drawled. "Every ounce of your considerable charisma comes right to the surface. It's fascinating to watch."

"I've got to be more discreet," she moaned as Jamie laughed at her obvious discomfort.

⌘

When they walked into the tiny shop, Ryan noticed that the room was rather stuffy and proper, just as she'd expected. They were greeted at the door by an elegantly dressed woman who graciously showed them to a center table. After they were handed menus, Ryan asked Jamie if she had noticed the admiring glances from the other diners when they had entered. "No, I didn't notice anything."

"Pay closer attention," Ryan instructed. "People are definitely looking at us."

Jamie casually glanced around the room and noticed that people were still looking at them with approval. She looked back at Ryan and said, "I agree that people have noticed us, but I get that a lot. Don't you?"

"Why do you think people do that?" Ryan asked, ignoring the question.

"I guess because we're attractive and we're dressed well. We look like we fit in, I suppose. I guess it's also because we look especially nice for people our age. That always gets a round of approval down here."

"Precisely," Ryan agreed. "Now, continue to pay attention to the other diners." Jamie watched in fascination as the real Ryan returned. She slid her hand across the table and gently grasped Jamie's. Her eyes softened, and she stared intently at Jamie, silently expressing a very loving emotion. After a moment she tenderly lifted Jamie's hand and kissed her palm, closing her eyes in pleasure, then softly placed Jamie's hand on her cheek, cradling it there for a moment. As she released her, she kissed the inside of her wrist, letting her lips linger for a moment. She whispered, "Still paying attention?"

"Huh?" Jamie mumbled vacantly. After a moment, she mentally slapped herself back into consciousness and looked around the room again. The formerly friendly faces had uniformly grown dark and disapproving, with some of the bolder women discreetly pointing them out to others who had not noticed them. Jamie nodded her head to show that she was still doing her job.

"Want to make it worse?" Ryan asked, a challenge in her tone. A small nod caused Ryan to pick up her chair and move very close. She took a roll from the basket on the table, broke it apart, and put a little butter on one of the pieces. She held up the morsel in front of Jamie and raised an eyebrow seductively. Jamie nodded mutely as her mouth practically fell open. Ryan placed the bread in her mouth, tipping it in with her index finger. She gave Jamie an extremely sexy smile as the smaller woman tried to summon enough saliva to swallow.

When she was in control of her muscles, Jamie looked around again. Now no one was looking at them. Every other diner had tried to render them invisible. They continued to chat and observe the other patrons, but as time passed, Jamie began to grow impatient. They had been at the restaurant for a good fifteen minutes, but no one had come to take their order. After another few minutes passed, Jamie signaled to the hostess, but she blithely ignored her. So she got up from her chair and stormed over to the woman, ready for a fight. "Why haven't we been served?" she demanded rather loudly.

"We're very busy today," was the arch reply as the woman turned and headed for the kitchen.

Jamie raised her voice even louder, speaking to the woman's retreating back. "Every table that entered after we did has been served. I'm asking you again, why haven't we been waited on?"

"Why can't you people stay in the city?" she asked with an aggrieved sigh as she continued into the kitchen.

Jamie stood in shocked silence for several moments. Every other diner in the restaurant was looking at her, either blatantly or surreptitiously. She finally walked back over to Ryan with a very angry look on her face. "For two cents I'd throw you right down on this table and ravish you in front of these idiots!" she said fiercely.

As Ryan trotted out the door after her, she said somberly, "That's why I hate to wear skirts."

Jamie turned to look at her with a puzzled look on her face. "What?"

"No pockets for change. I don't have two cents."

Jamie backhanded her right in her firm belly. "Wiseass," she muttered as they walked to the car laughing.

⌘

Ryan patiently listened as Jamie vented her anger all the way back to Noe Valley. She was just about out of steam as they neared the house. "Ryan, why aren't you angry?" she finally asked out of frustration.

After considering the question for a long while, Ryan finally replied, "I don't find anger that productive. I figure that if people are put off by me, it's only because they're not used to seeing lesbians be authentic with each other." With a little shrug she added, "I try not to take it too personally."

"But how can you not?" Jamie insisted.

"Look, Jamie, I get my feelings hurt just like everyone else does. I wish that everyone could just get over it and stop making gayness such a big deal. But that's not going to happen very soon. I just can't afford to waste my energies caring what strangers think of me."

"Does it ever bother you?" she inquired, a little annoyed that Ryan seemed so unaffected.

"Of course it does. Every once in a while if I'm feeling vulnerable or I have PMS, I'm tempted to really lash out when it happens. You saw how it bothered me when Cassie was giving me a hard time. But I still try not to get angry. Anger is just not an emotion that works well for me."

Jamie looked at her friend thoughtfully, "You are incredibly well-adjusted you know."

"Some of my former dates wouldn't agree with that, but thank you anyway," she grinned.

⌘

When she dropped Ryan off, Jamie smiled and said, "Back to the Peninsula for me. Time to make dinner for my man."

Ryan nodded and gave her a kiss on the cheek. "I had a fantastic day, Jamie. Thanks for making it so much fun, and thanks for going out of your way to give me a ride. Roaring up on my Harley would have been a little much — even for me."

"I'm the one who should be thanking you, Ryan. It was really cool to be let into the inner sanctum," she said with a laugh.

"Well, you didn't really see the inner sanctum," she admitted. "You have to take the oath before we let you in there. More importantly, you have to learn the secret handshake." With a lascivious wink, she got out of the car, laughing over her shoulder as she swished her hips — knowing that Jamie was watching her.

⌘

Jack finished his dinner and stretched for a few minutes, trying to get the kinks out after a long day of concentrated effort. "Damn, it feels like I don't have time for anything that I like," he sighed. "It's just class, studying and working on my article." He gave Jamie a long look and said, "Are you feeling horribly ignored?"

"Not horribly," she smiled. "This is just a rough patch, honey. Do you have to work tonight?"

"I should," he nodded. "But I'm just wasted. My back and neck are so stiff, I'm about ready to find a chiropractor."

"Come with me," she urged, standing to take his hand. He followed her compliantly, and she led him to the bedroom. "Take off your shirt and jeans, honey, and lie down on your tummy. I'll give you a nice, long massage."

His eyes were wide with surprise, but his mouth was already curling into an appreciative smile. "Best offer I've had all ... well, I'm not sure how long."

She fetched some of her body lotion and began to work on him, tsking when her fingers hit a particularly stiff spot. "Honey, you can't let yourself get this wound up. It's not healthy."

"I know," he sighed. "But this feels so wonderful, I might get a few cramps in my back just to get the attention."

She leaned over so that the top of her head rested on the mattress, right next to his face. "You don't have to hurt yourself to have me care for you," she reminded him. "It's my job to take care of you, Jack."

"No one I'd rather have care for me," he said, a very satisfied smile on his face.

⌘

She awoke at around 10:00. Jack was lying behind her with his arms wrapped tightly around her naked body. His head was snuggled against her back, and she felt content for the first time in a long while. A few stray thoughts fought for attention, but she pushed them down, refusing to consider the fact that her orgasm came on the heels of the image of Ryan kissing her palm.

⌘ CHAPTER TEN

ON THANKSGIVING MORNING JAMIE AND HER FATHER SAT IN THE sunny library of their Hillsborough home, enjoying a cup of coffee. "You've been on my mind recently, Jamie," he said, giving her a contemplative look. "I've actually been worried about you a little bit. Is everything okay between you and Jack?"

She shrugged and said, "Things are pretty good. I guess we're just going through what every couple has to, to work things out."

With a slight scowl, he stared at her intently. "I really got a bad feeling that day at the golf course, Jamie. Correct me if I'm wrong, but I got the impression that things had been difficult for a while. Do you want to talk about it?"

"No, not really. I think we're just going through a phase. He had some issues with some of the changes I've been making, but we've talked it out, and I think we're both re-committed to being there for each other."

"I must admit that I was concerned when Jack mentioned that your new friend was a lesbian," he stated thoughtfully. Jamie felt her hackles start to rise as she looked at him carefully, hoping he would drop the matter. When she didn't respond, he persisted, "Well?"

"Well what, Daddy?" she asked blankly.

"Why are you spending your time with a lesbian, Jamie? That hardly seems appropriate for a young woman like you."

"What do you mean by 'a young woman like you'?" she asked, her eyes narrowing. "Ryan is a perfectly lovely young woman, too."

"She's not a young woman who's engaged to be married," he said clearly. "Don't you think it's wiser to spend your time cultivating friendships that can carry over into your married life? You two need to build some relationships with other couples," he explained.

"Ryan's my friend, and I enjoy her company immensely, Daddy. The fact that she's a lesbian is an inconsequential element of our relationship. Yes, I think it would be nice to have some friends who were in a couple, but since we never leave Jack's apartment, that's a little hard to do."

"Well, Jack certainly didn't seem to think that it was inconsequential, and as he made clear, neither does Cassie." He paused for a moment as he

208

regarded her carefully. "Is your new friend more important than Jack's feelings?"

Eyes flashing with anger, she snapped, "Yes, she most certainly is more important than his feelings, if his feelings are based on preconceived, stereotypical notions of what a lesbian is." Shaking her head in ill-concealed disgust, she mumbled, "I really thought you were more open-minded than this."

"I am completely open-minded, Jamie. And I don't appreciate being referred to as otherwise," he said with a good deal of pique.

The doorbell rang, and after someone on the staff answered, Jack poked his head into the library, his smile freezing when he saw two sets of angry green eyes looking at him. "Uhm ... am I disturbing something?"

Jim composed his expression and smiled at his future son-in-law. "Not at all. Come in, Jack."

He strode into the room, bent and gave Jamie a kiss on the cheek. "Hi," he said quietly.

She stood and slid an arm around his waist. "Hi. Let's go take a walk." Casting a look over her shoulder, she gave her father an insincere smile and said, "We're finished here, aren't we, Daddy." There wasn't a hint of a question in her tone, and with a smile put on only for Jack's benefit, Jim nodded.

"Sure. Check with Marta to see when we're going to eat."

They wound up in the garden, the farthest point from the house on the property. "What was going on with you and your dad?" Jack asked when they settled down onto a bench.

"God knows," she sighed. "He says he's worried that you and I aren't getting along well." Shaking her head in puzzlement, she said, "It's just not like him to get involved in my life. I just don't know what the big deal is."

"What's he worried about — specifically?"

Giving him a weary look, she rolled her eyes and said, "He doesn't think I should be friends with a lesbian ... a common theme."

Bristling, he said, "I'm trying, Jamie."

"I know you are," she soothed, gently patting his thigh. "He tried to make it not sound like the homophobic comment that it was by saying I should concentrate on making friends that I can sustain when we're married."

Jack was quiet for a moment, then suggested, "That's not a bad idea."

Raising an eyebrow, she fixed him with a look and said, "Meaning?"

"Well, it would be nice to have some couples we can do things with."

Using her most sarcastic tone, she asked, "Oh ... so we're waiting for another couple to do things with. Is there some law in Palo Alto against a couple going out alone?"

"That's not fair," he snapped. "You know weekends are the only time I can catch up on things."

"Oh, so you're free on weeknights? Why don't you come up to Berkeley so we can go out?"

His head tilted, and he gazed at her with a question in his eyes. "This has been our pattern for three years now. Have you been pissed off the whole time, or is that a recent development, too?"

"What do you mean by the too?" she asked, anger flickering in her eyes once again.

"You know very well what I mean," he snapped. "Everything was just fine until she came along. You didn't mind just being with me on the weekends, and you weren't off riding your bike for hours every Saturday and Sunday. Damn it, Jamie! We used to want the same things!"

She stood up and glared at him, her face contorted into a mask of outrage. "Yeah. We used to want me to sit down, shut up and not ask for anything! Well, I've changed, Jack! I have my own goals and my own friends! And if you think I'm going to sit on your couch and watch you study all weekend, I've got a newsflash for you. It's not gonna happen, buddy!" She was gone before he could get another word in. He followed her into the house and heard the door to her room slam — as did everyone else in the vicinity. He shuffled into the living room and sat down with Jim and Catherine, all three of them managing to act as though Jamie were not upstairs throwing things around her room.

⌘

As she had so often during her youth, Jamie sat alone in her room, wishing that at least one member of the family would try to understand her. She sat down at her desk to try to put her thoughts into words, brightening a little when she realized that her grandfather would arrive soon.

Charles Evans, Jim's father, had always been the one person she could rely on to listen to every problem and never, ever judge her.

Luckily for Jamie, Reverend Evans had sensed that the child needed special attention, so he'd made it a point to at least speak to her on the phone once or twice a week all through her youth. Once she'd learned how to drive, she spent even more time with him, traveling to San Francisco every week or two to have dinner with him and share the details of her life.

She still sought his advice, though she wasn't able to see him nearly as often as she did when she was young, since he was the rector of a small Episcopal church just off Nob Hill in the city. After Sunday services, he would usually accompany the family to the club for brunch, but since the whole family attended, there was little time for private conversation.

She knew that her grandfather would always be her biggest supporter, but for some reason, she hadn't been very forthright with him about the problems she and Jack had been having. Somehow she felt that she needed to deal with these very adult issues as an adult and not run to him to help her figure things out — but as she stewed in her room she began to doubt the wisdom of that instinct. As she mulled the situation over, the doorbell rang, so she splashed some water on her face, straightened her clothing and went down to say hello to the one person she actually wanted to spend Thanksgiving with.

⌘

Regrettably, not even Reverend Evans could improve the tension-suffused atmosphere. As soon as the torturous hour was over, Jack and Jamie got ready to go to his family's gathering for dessert. She wanted to go to her room and not emerge until Monday, but she didn't have the nerve to put Jack in the position of explaining her absence, so they set off after a very strained goodbye.

Something had occurred to Jamie when she was alone in her room, and now that she had the opportunity, she asked, "Did you ever talk to my father about our problems, or about how you feel about Ryan?"

He shot her a very perturbed glance, replying, "No, Jamie, I have not. Frankly, I'd be embarrassed to admit how little you respect my opinions."

"Pull the car over, Jack," she said in a tone that did not allow for discussion. He pulled over onto a street on the outskirts of Hillsborough, killed the engine and rolled down his window to let some of the crisp fall air into the tension-filled car. Turning as much as he could in his small Honda, he faced Jamie with a look of quiet resignation on his face.

"Yes?" he asked wearily.

"It's obvious that both you and Daddy are unhappy with the changes that I've been making," she said slowly. "Even though I love both of you very much, neither of you is going to control me." She took a deep breath as she continued. "We can have a good life together, Jack, but it has to be a life where each of us gets to be who we really are."

He sat in silence for a bit, his shoulders a little slumped. Finally, he took a deep breath and slowly let it out. "Look, Jamie, I know you're used to getting everything you want. I know you've been terribly spoiled — both with material things and by always having things done your way." He ignored her look of outrage and blithely continued. "That's part of you, and I'm willing to accept that most of the time. But you've got to learn that there are some things that you're going to have to give in on. It can't be me who has to give in all of the time," he explained as patiently as he could.

She was silent for a long time as she dropped her head back against the vinyl seat. Shaking her head slowly, she asked in a voice filled with sorrow, "Is that really how you think of me? As a spoiled, little rich girl who gets everything she demands?"

"Well, yes," he said, hesitating just a bit. "I feel like I'm supposed to make most of the sacrifices in our relationship, and I've got to admit that I'm growing a little tired of it."

Her anger had been bubbling up throughout his explanation, and when he finished, she felt the words begin to fly from her mouth. "What sacrifices have you made, Jack? I'm dying to hear them," she said bitterly. "Tell me about how you have to leave your house in rush hour traffic every Friday night. Tell me how you no sooner arrive than you have to start dinner, alone, while I sit in the living room and read. Tell me how you feel when I barely comment on what you've made. Tell me how you do the dishes alone, while I continue to read. Tell me about how you sit in the living room and watch me study every Friday, Saturday and Sunday. Tell me about how you feel when the only time I pay attention to you is when we have sex. Tell me how you lie in bed and get so damn frus —" She yanked herself back from the abyss just before she told him exactly how unhappy she was with their sex life. The tension in the car was so thick that it was nearly visible, and she was afraid to look at him. Long minutes passed before he finally spoke.

"I didn't realize you were so miserable," he got out as a tear escaped down his face.

"I'm not miserable!" she said fervently. "I'm not!" She lifted her hand to his face and softly stroked his cheek. "I'm not," she whispered as her own tears started to flow. "Are you miserable, Jack?" she asked softly.

"No," he said shakily through his tears. "But I was so much happier before. You seemed happy, too," he said. "Now you just seem tense around me. I know you're not happy, Jamie, and it's driving me crazy!" he choked out as he began to sob. She continued to stroke his cheek and run her fingers through his hair for a long time. As he got control of his voice he added, "I know you're not crazy about what we do in bed, but sometimes I just don't know how to please you. I swear I've never had this problem with any other woman. I just don't know what to do," he moaned.

"It's okay, Jack. I swear I'm not unhappy with you. It's just that I'm changing and growing up a little bit. I love to come down here on the weekends, and I love to cook for you. But when you give me such a hard time about what I do when we're not together, it just drives me insane! I think that's why it's been hard for me in bed," she admitted. "I need to feel totally connected with you to be able to enjoy sex. When we have this ongoing tension I just can't relax. But that's all it is, honey, I'm sure of it."

He looked over at her with an expression that was equal parts fear and trust. The sadness in his blue eyes nearly broke her heart. "Can we get out for a moment?" she finally asked.

He looked a little suspicious, but he complied, coming around to stand on the sidewalk next to the car. She got out and stood right next to him as she put her arms around his waist. He slid his arms around her back and held her close for a long time. Bending his head, he breathed in her reassuring scent as he felt some of the tension ebbing away. Jamie felt the same way, and she looked up into his eyes and said, "I feel so good when you hold me. It just feels so right to be close to you."

He squeezed her tightly as he felt the emotion build up in his chest. "I'll try harder, Jamie. I swear I will."

⌘

The evening spent with the Townsends was, thankfully, more jovial than the tension-filled afternoon at the Evanses. Jack came from a fairly large extended family, and a raft of aunts, uncles, cousins and their children were in attendance. Jamie spent some time playing with the assorted children, and that lifted her spirits substantially. She took a little break to go into the kitchen and offer to help, noting that every adult woman was there chatting about her kids and her husband. The conversation was fairly interesting, but it seemed a bit alien to her. After her offer of help was rebuffed, she went into the living room to watch a bit of the Dallas-Philadelphia game on TV. She paid close attention to the conversation and noted that not one man mentioned his spouse or his kids. They talked exclusively about the game, politics and their jobs. *Are we really so different? How can we ever expect to get along for fifty years if we just aren't interested in the same things?*

She was not really included in the conversation, and she realized that Jack didn't even seem that happy to have her in with the men. Even though she knew more about football than half of them, she felt like her comments wouldn't be appreciated, so she eventually went back to play with the kids.

It's odd how I feel so out of place here. When I'm at the O'Flaherty's, I never feel like a woman; I just feel like me. The boys treat me like one of them, not like I'm different. But here it feels like there are two different camps, and I'm not in either one. The women don't accept me because I'm not a member of their club yet, since I'm neither married nor a mother, and the men never will. Where do I belong?

Jack's cousin, Stephanie, had a six-month-old boy named Ethan whom Jamie was drawn to. She cuddled the infant to her chest, speaking into his ear, while she wished the little boy were Caitlin and that Ryan was right there with her, making her feel like she belonged. "You can get one of these for yourself," Stephanie teased as she came up from behind.

"Not for a long while," Jamie said confidently. "I'm sure I won't have a child before I'm thirty." She hadn't noticed, but Jack was standing next to Stephanie, and as Jamie turned, she caught the shadow that passed over his face. *Now what did I do?*

"So, you want to keep her all to yourself for a while, huh, Jack?" Stephanie asked playfully.

"Jamie's the boss," he said with a thin smile as he turned to head back to the safety of the football game.

Well, that answers that question, she thought with a disgusted sigh.

⌘

Jamie was staying at her parents' house for the break, and on the way back there, she decided to bring up the topic that had been niggling at her brain all evening. "I know you heard what I told Stephanie about having children," she said quietly.

"Yeah?"

"Yeah. I also know that my answer upset you. Can I tell you why I answered her like I did?"

"Sure. Better late than never," he grumbled.

Placing her hand on his leg, she said, "She asked if I wanted kids right away. I don't, Jack. I'd prefer to wait ten years or so." He shrugged his shoulders resignedly, and she continued, "But that's just what I want. That doesn't mean that's what we'll do."

He gave her a doubtful glance, but she insisted, "I mean that. If you want to start our family the day we get married, and I want to wait ten years, we'll just have to work out a compromise or figure out some way that we can both get what we need." Squeezing his thigh, she said, "This is our biggest problem, Jack. We both just make assumptions and then get mad over them. We don't spend nearly enough time discussing how we feel."

Giving her a wry look, he admitted, "Nothing makes a guy quake in his boots more than the words, 'We have to talk.'" Looking rather helpless, he added, "Talking isn't something I'm very good at, Jamie."

She smiled at him and said, "God knows I talk a lot, but I have trouble talking about things that are upsetting, or that I know will upset you. I think we have to try harder to get some of these things out, Jack. You should have pulled me aside or brought it up when we were alone — rather than just getting angry because I want to wait to get pregnant."

They were on El Camino Real, and when he pulled up to one of the near-continuous stoplights, he gazed at her for the full three minutes. "You do want to have children with me, don't you, Jamie?"

Her eyes fluttered closed as she said, "I do. Nothing would make me happier than having a family with you, Jack."

Placing his hand on her flat belly, he teased, "You won't mind losing this perfectly toned tummy?"

"To have your child? I wouldn't give it a second thought," she assured him, beaming.

His return smile was relaxed and full of affection. Looking into his eyes, she wanted nothing more than to kiss him, and as soon as they pulled into the drive of her family's home, she did exactly that.

Their gentle exploration of each other quickly escalated, and within minutes he was panting, "Can't we go inside?"

"No, no," she gasped. "I've never asked my parents if we could sleep together here. We just can't, Jack. I wouldn't be able to relax."

He grunted with frustration, but didn't let the bad news deter him. Maneuvering in the small car, he pinned her to the seat and kissed her senseless, his warm, wet lips making her wild with desire. His determination, and refusal to let the physical constraints deter him, sparked her passion in a way that was very unusual, and she was soon begging him for release. It wasn't easy, but he managed, thankful that she'd had the foresight to wear a dress. When his hand slipped between her legs, she wrapped her arms so tightly around his neck that she practically strangled him — but this was a quest he was willing to die for at that moment, and he didn't murmur a word of protest.

With her hips, she gently guided him and soon was calling out lustily, pushing against the seat so firmly that the seatback popped out of the track, and she flopped onto her back as it gave way. Giggling helplessly, she said, "I'll pay to fix it if it's broken. That's the least I can do for that little present."

"Little?" he asked, gazing at her in a teasing challenge.

"Gargantuan … stupendous … colossal," she smiled. "I would go on, but I'm about to have a brain cramp."

He pulled her into a sitting position and cradled her in his arms. "That was fun," he said, with a touch of wonder in his voice. "I don't remember the last time we just played with each other."

"You can play that little game any time you want, big boy," she smiled, slipping her hand behind his head to pull him down for another torrid kiss.

⌘

Gazing at herself in the bathroom mirror, Jamie smirked at her image and mused, *Well, that was a first. I fought off every guy that tried that in high school, and now that I'm in love, engaged and on the pill, I start groping in cars in my parents' drive. What's wrong with this picture?*

She got into bed, emotionally wrung out from the endless day, and was almost asleep when a startling thought came to her, unbidden. *That's the hottest I've been since the day we had that big fight! Jesus! Not only do I need emotional upheaval to get hot — now I have to wrestle around in a car!* Her mind started to race, her raw emotions jumping to outlandish conclusions. *What am I going to do? Start a big fight and then lure Jack to a car every time I want to have decent sex?*

A thought came to her that she tried to push down, but she was so emotionally unguarded that she was completely unsuccessful. *It wasn't hot because you were in the car,* her mind cruelly informed her. *It was hot because you knew he couldn't manage to enter you.* She sat bolt upright in bed, her heart beating so wildly that she grew dizzy. Gripping the sheet with her fists, she tried to slow her racing heart, taking deep breaths that only made her dizzier. Slowly, she sank back onto the mattress, her body covered in a fine sheen of perspiration. *Oh, my God,* she moaned over and over. *That's it … that's really it. I knew that we couldn't have intercourse, and that simple fact freed me up enough to let myself go! Oh, shit!* she sighed heavily, her stomach gripping in pain. *Now what do I do?*

⌘

As soon as it was polite to do so, she called the Christopher household and asked to speak to Mia. Her friend picked up, sounding like she'd been woken. "H'lo?"

"Mia? Jamie. I need to talk to you. Can I come over?"

"Huh? Uhm … sure. Can I stay in bed while we talk?"

"Yes. I'll be over in a few."

She ran downstairs, not bothering to leave a note, and drove the short distance, her heart once again beating wildly at the mere thought of exploring this distressing issue. Mrs. Christopher answered the door, and she blinked at Jamie in surprise. "I think Mia's still in bed, Jamie."

"I spoke with her a little while ago," she smiled thinly. "She's expecting me."

"Would you like some coffee, honey? Or maybe some juice?"

"No thanks, Mrs. Christopher. I had breakfast already."

"I wish your schedule would rub off on my baby," the older woman smiled. "She comes home for Thanksgiving break, and we never see her. I swear she's part vampire!"

Jamie just smiled at her, not willing to share with Mrs. Christopher that her early rising was equal parts habit and gut-churning anxiety. She dashed up the stairs of the home, knocking lightly on Mia's door. "Yeah," the brunette mumbled, her pillow half covering her face.

Sitting down on the edge of the bed, Jamie started to scratch the mostly-bare back that was exposed by Mia's T-shirt having crept up to her shoulder blades during the night.

"Nice," the curly-haired woman sighed. "Keep that up and you can stay."

Smiling at her friend, Jamie kicked off her shoes and climbed onto the bed, sitting up against the headboard. Mia sensed her position and shifted so that her head rested in Jamie's lap, her back still exposed. Jamie began to stroke her bare skin once again, the gentle rhythmic touch soothing some of her own anxiety. The touch was just enough to prevent Mia from falling asleep again, and after a few minutes she was lucid enough to ask, "What's up, babe? Must be something bad to tempt my early-morning wrath."

"Oh, you're not so bad," Jamie smiled. "You only bite when you're woken too abruptly."

"Avoiding the question," she mumbled. "Bad sign." One dark brown eye popped open, and she focused on her friend. "You don't look so good, either. Did you sleep last night?"

"Not much," Jamie admitted. "Last night I had a massively unpleasant thought that I haven't been able to shake ever since."

Mia opened both eyes and gazed up at her. "You gonna tell me, or do I have to guess?"

"I'll tell you," she said nervously. "I uhm ... I realized that I don't like to have intercourse."

"What!" Mia's eyes were both fully open now, and they grew round as

217

she repeated, "What did you say?"

"You obviously heard me," Jamie grumbled. "It just dawned on me last night. It's not because of his technique or how much foreplay we have or what position we use. I just don't like it." She stared at the wall for a moment, then added quietly, "I don't think I ever will."

"Jamie," Mia sighed, sitting up and tugging her T-shirt into place. "How can you be so sure? I mean, maybe it *is* the position you use. Uhm … maybe he's too big for you, or maybe he's not big enough. There must be something that you can change."

"No," she said, a resigned look on her face. "It's not the technicalities. I don't like it, and I never really have. The only times I've really enjoyed it are the times I've been so worked up that I didn't have time to think about it. That's been less than a handful of times," she added quietly.

"Oh, Jamie," Mia said, gazing into her eyes. "Maybe it's Jack. Maybe he just doesn't know how to please you."

"It's not about pleasing me, Mia. I don't like the position; I don't like to feel him on top of me. I don't like feeling that he's in control, and that we're just going to do it until he comes — no matter what."

"That could be because you need to be on top," Mia soothed. "I really like to be on top, too."

She shook her head slowly. "That's a tiny part of it, but it's clearly not all of it." Looking at Mia for a moment, she related, "Once, at the park, I saw a young female dog get pinned by a much bigger male. She was apparently in heat because he entered her and started to hump her. It went on forever, and I just couldn't look away. I felt so much empathy for that poor female. She looked like she would rather have been anywhere else in the world — but the male dog looked like he was in doggie heaven." She looked at Mia with a disgusted glance and said, "That's how it is with us most of the time. I just want him to finish and get off of me."

Mia scooted up until she was sitting against the headboard, then looked at her friend somberly. "I've never asked you this, and you don't have to answer, but were you sexually molested when you were younger?"

"No," she said, shaking her head roughly. "Nothing — nothing like that ever happened to me. I'm certain of that, Mia. Believe me," she sighed, "I clearly don't wish that I had been, but at least that would explain some things."

"Maybe it's Jack," Mia tried one more time. "Maybe you're just not in love with him, Jamie."

She shook her head and said, "I do love him, Mia. And I do have desire for him. When we're just kissing and touching each other, I feel totally turned on. Especially if we're not in the bedroom. We'll be on the sofa, and I know that if he just touches me with his hand, I'll be able to orgasm, but he invariably leads me to the bedroom and I can feel myself tense up with every step. By the time he enters me, I've lost the feeling and I just want it to be over." When she finished speaking a few hot tears slipped down her cheeks, and she brushed them away with an irritated gesture. "It's driving me crazy, Mia! I want to love him, I want to please him, but I need to please myself, too!"

"Jamie," Mia soothed, pulling her to her chest. She rubbed her back and reassured her, "This is not that big a deal, honey. It's just a technical thing — really. You just need to talk about this and figure out a way around it."

"Oh, right, I'm supposed to say, 'Hand jobs for the rest of your life, Jack. Is that okay?'"

"I'm not suggesting that," Mia scoffed. "He'd have a mistress by the time your wedding reception was over."

"Gee, I feel so much better," Jamie grumbled.

"Let me finish. This just sounds like you got off on the wrong foot and haven't gotten into a good rhythm yet. Maybe you need to be on top all of the time; maybe you need to touch yourself while he's inside. There are a thousand positions and ways to do it, Jamie, and it doesn't sound like you've tried to experiment with them."

"No," she admitted, "we really haven't. We both like to ignore problems and hope they go away."

"Well, this one won't," Mia predicted, "and if you get into these bad habits, it's just gonna get harder to change later. You've got to talk about it, and you've got to insist that you get your pleasure, Jamie. I know that Jack loves you, and I know that he wants to please you. Let him!"

"I … I think he does," Jamie said, a note of uncertainty in her voice. "I guess that's another thing I have to be sure of." She scooted down until she was lying flat on her back. "I'm so depressed I can't bear the thought of going home. Can we take a nap together?"

"Only if we can cuddle," Mia smiled, seeing how much her friend needed some physical affection.

Jamie rolled onto her side and grasped Mia's arm, tucking it around her waist. "Wake me for class on Monday," Jamie sighed, feeling strangely relieved to feel her friend snuggle up to her back.

In moments Jamie was breathing evenly, her fatigue rendering her nearly unconscious. Mia patted her gently, mulling over the dilemma. *I think there's a darned good reason that you were drawn to take Lesbianism 101 — I*

219

just hope you figure it out before you make the mistake of getting married, 'cause if you don't, I'm gonna have to be the one to tell you, and I'm sure not looking forward to that.

⌘

Jamie didn't return from Mia's until lunchtime. Her father was waiting for her, obviously a little irritated with her because of her unexplained absence. "Where've you been? I stayed home today to spend a little time with you. I finally had Marta go check your room, and I find out you've taken off without a word."

"I needed a little time to myself," she said, only partially lying. "I had a tough day, Daddy, and I'm really not up to being scolded. If it's going to be like this, I'll just go back to Berkeley right now."

He blinked at her, amazed to hear her talking to him like this. "What in the hell has gotten into you?" he asked, his mouth gaping open a little.

"Nothing has gotten into me!" she said, her anger rising. "Have you ever heard of the concept of growing up? I'm supposed to start making my own decisions as I mature, aren't I? Isn't that the whole point?"

He nodded, his head bobbing up and down slowly. "I guess it is," he admitted. "I just ... I'm not used to you snapping at me like this, Jamie."

She stared at the floor and quietly said, "I'm sorry, Daddy, I'm just on my last nerve. I came home to get some peace and quiet and some support, and I feel worse than I did when I got here. I think I'm going to go back to Berkeley, turn off the phone and just get into bed and pull the covers over my head until it's time to return to class."

He reached for her and enveloped her in a hug, holding on to her tightly even when she tried to move away. "Shh," he soothed. "It's all right, honey. I'm sorry for jumping on you yesterday. I can tell things aren't going well for you, and I tried to tell you what to do to make things better. I'm sorry, Jamie. I was trying to run your life for you, and you're right — that's not something I can do any longer. You're an adult, and you have to make your own decisions."

"It's hard sometimes," she sniffed, feeling very young and very vulnerable.

"I know, sweetheart." He tightened his hug and kissed her head. "Let's do something fun this afternoon," he suggested. "Just you and me."

She gazed up at him and allowed herself to feel the old pull, the thrill of excitement that came with getting a block of time alone with her always-overextended father. "I would love nothing more than to go to the marina and rent the fastest damn speedboat they've got."

He smiled warmly at her and said, "I've got the answer to your prayer, honey. I know a guy with a beautiful Cigarette — the kind the DEA uses to catch drug runners — fastest craft on the water. This guy definitely owes me a favor — I'll call him right now."

She sat in the living room, patiently waiting for her father to return from his study. He came back in just a few minutes, a smile affixed to his face. "Put on your thermals, Jamie. It's gonna be a wild, wet ride in this weather."

"My favorite kind," she smiled, some of the fire returning to her eyes.

⌘

That evening, after dinner with her parents, she decided to go spend the night with Jack. He was glad to see her and patiently listened to her enraptured recollection of a day spent bouncing over the whitecaps, but within an hour he was engrossed in his schoolwork. Jamie pulled out her own books and spent the evening reading, while sitting on the couch with her legs in Jack's lap.

Before bed she went into the kitchen to get a drink. He came into the kitchen just as she closed the refrigerator and sat down at the kitchen table. "I love having you here, Jamie," he said with a smile as he took her hand and pulled her onto his lap. "It just doesn't feel like home when you're not around."

Warning bells were sounding in her head, knowing that Jack's strong suit wasn't analyzing their relationship, but she ignored them and asked the question that had been buzzing around the back of her mind ever since she had spoken to Mia that morning. "Why do you love me, Jack?"

He looked completely dumbfounded. "You know why I love you, Jamie," he said defensively.

"No, I really don't," she disagreed. "I know that you tell me you love me, but you never tell me why." She grasped his hand and looked at him with pleading eyes. "Please tell me."

He stared at her for a long time before he finally answered. "I guess I love how I feel when I'm with you," he said thoughtfully. "You make me feel whole."

Is that all? She continued to stare at him without saying a word. Silently, she prayed that he would continue with something — anything — about her.

"I'm really attracted to you," he continued, sensing that she needed more from him. "I love the way you look, and I love the way I feel when I touch you." He smiled warmly as he began to do just that.

She concentrated mightily and finally found the strength to shut down the voice that was screaming for her attention. She repeated the mantra, *He does love you, he just doesn't know how to express it. He does love you, he does.*

⌘

On Monday Jamie got to the gym just as Mia was finishing her training session with Ryan.

Ryan's mood was ebullient when she greeted her friend. "Hiya," she said with a big grin as she gave Jamie a quick hug.

"You certainly look happy," Jamie said, catching some of the infectious mood.

"What's not to be happy about?" she asked lightly.

"Good point," Jamie replied, feeling lighter and freer than she had since she left Berkeley.

⌘

Mia was still at the gym, working on the StairClimber when Ryan and Jamie had finished their session. Jamie approached her and asked, "Would you like to go grab a bite with Ryan and me?"

"Sure," she said. "Thai?"

"Works for me," Jamie agreed. They settled on a Thai restaurant within walking distance. During dinner Jamie grew pensive and asked, "Do you guys think it's odd that Jack can't tell me why he loves me?"

Mia looked at Ryan who returned the gaze. They mouthed "Uh-oh" in unison and then laughed. Mia spoke first, "I guess that doesn't really surprise me," she replied. "Guys aren't great at that kind of thing." She paused for a moment, "Let me guess; his answer was either, 'Gee, I don't know; I just do' or it was about how you make him feel," she said presciently.

"Ding, ding, ding, we have a winner," Jamie replied. "His answer, and I quote, was 'I love how you make me feel when we're together.' " She let out an aggrieved sigh. "It makes me feel like I have to guess how he feels and then assume I'm right."

"Well, that is the safest course," Mia agreed with a slight chuckle.

Jamie noticed that Ryan had not responded and was, in fact, gazing down at her meal, deep in thought. She decided to drop the subject, and they began to discuss their workouts and the AIDS Ride and other topics of mutual interest. At about 7:30 Mia announced that she was meeting some friends for a movie. Both Ryan and Jamie declined the invitation to join the crowd, and Mia took off, hugging both of them goodbye.

After they had settled the bill, they began to walk down Telegraph. The street was still filled with the merchants who set up tables along the sidewalk, and they browsed for a long time. After they had turned down a quieter street, Jamie suggested they stop for a coffee. They found themselves at Hallowed Grounds, Jamie's favorite spot, and were soon seated at a table near the window.

Jamie noticed that Ryan was still a little reserved, so she finally asked, "What's bothering you? You were so up before dinner, and now you seem a little sad."

Ryan looked down at her coffee and shrugged her shoulders a little. "I don't know if I should talk about it," she finally replied.

"Should or want to?" Jamie asked. "If something is bothering you, I want to know about it, unless you don't want to talk about it, of course."

Ryan looked up and stared at her intently for a long minute. "It's about what you said about Jack," she finally revealed. "It hurts me that he isn't able to talk to you like you need. I want you to have a great relationship. I really want you to be happy and fulfilled, Jamie," she said sincerely as their eyes locked again.

"I appreciate that more than I can say, Ryan," she said as she patted her friend's folded hands. She sighed heavily and brushed her hair from her eyes. "I know I expect an awful lot from him. Maybe I just didn't give him time to think."

Ryan shook her head a little. "That's what I was doing in the restaurant. It only took me a moment to think of what I love about you," she said with smile that bore signs of mild embarrassment.

"Tell me," Jamie said simply as she grasped her hands, and they continued to stare into each other's eyes.

"Okay," she began hesitantly. "I love how you treat other people. You have a ton of empathy for others, and it's very genuine, not just token. You're thoughtful and kind and very considerate. I've never heard you make a derogatory comment about anyone. Not even Cassie, who certainly deserves a few," she laughed. "I love your intelligence and your sense of humor. You have a really quick mind, and I love to see you work on a problem. I appreciate how much you love language and literature, and how deep your knowledge is on the topic. You make me laugh more than anyone I know, and that's saying a lot," she smiled. "I love how interested you are in other people and topics that you aren't familiar with.

You have a real love of life, and you're really open to new experiences." She thought for a minute as she continued, "The bottom line, though, is your heart. Your compassion and love for other people constantly impresses me. It's what I love the most about you." As she finished she looked up to see tears forming in Jamie's eyes. She pulled one of her hands from Jamie's grasp and laid it on top of hers as she smiled tenderly at her.

"That was the most amazing thing anyone has ever said to me," she finally choked out. "But do you know what the funny thing is?"

Ryan shook her head a little as she cocked it in a question.

"As you spoke I was thinking that every trait you ascribed to me was exactly how I would describe you," she said sincerely. "I've never met anyone who is as connected to her feelings as you are, Ryan. That is such a gift. I hope you find someone who really appreciates it."

Ryan looked a little surprised but finally replied, "That's part of the reason I'm so happy tonight."

"What do you mean?" Jamie asked, a bit confused.

"I've been thinking a lot about love and relationships lately. My interaction with that older woman has been haunting me," she said quietly, staring at the table contemplatively. "I've been mulling over some of the things you've said to me, and I've finally come to the conclusion that you're absolutely right — I have been avoiding real intimacy. I'm not sure why I avoid it, and I'm not sure I want to know," she chuckled. "I'm intimate with you and my family, and I'm physically intimate with women I sleep with. But that's really not enough. I'm worried that if I keep avoiding it with lovers, I won't be able to be intimate when I feel I'm ready. So, I'm going to try to find a real girlfriend and stop my serial dating."

"Do you think you'll be able to do that?" Jamie asked, realizing what a sea change this was for Ryan.

She smiled warmly. "I'm pretty determined, Jamie. When I make up my mind, I don't tend to waver. Having the realization that my mother would be ashamed of my behavior really woke me up." Her expression grew even more determined as she gazed at Jamie. "I will never run the risk of embarrassing my family again."

"What does your vow entail?" Jamie asked carefully. "No sex until you're — what — committed to someone?"

Ryan grew thoughtful and said, "What I'm giving up is the quick pick-up — the have-sex-before-I-know-her-name kinda dates that I've been having. I'm certainly not going to be celibate," she smirked. "I don't think there's anything wrong with sex per se, so I'll still see Ally or Alisa if the opportunity arises. Those are women I know well and have a relationship with — even though it's based primarily on sex. That doesn't feel exploitative to me. But what I really want is to find someone who wants to have a relationship — and hold off from having sex until we're both sure we're right for each other." She looked up at Jamie with a painfully hopeful expression on her face. "I want to make it special again. I want it to be more than just scratching an itch."

"Anyone in mind?" Jamie inquired.

"Yeah, as a matter of fact. It's someone you know," she revealed.

"Who?" Jamie asked, unable to think of anyone they both knew.

"Tracy Stuart, from class," she explained. "You know her, right?"

"Yeah, I know her." *Boy, do I ever know her.* From the first day of class Jamie had been impressed with the tall, lean brunette. It was a tossup between Ryan and Tracy for who was more beautiful, and Tracy had a sleek, smooth feminine grace that was mesmerizing. Jamie had often thought that Ryan and Tracy would make a knock out couple, but the woman had never seemed interested in Ryan. "How did you make a connection with her?" Jamie finally asked.

"Well, I tried to talk to her one day just after school started, but she shot me down fast," she said with an embarrassed grin. "She was dating another woman, so I didn't approach her again. A couple of weeks ago, I heard that they had broken up, and I tried to talk to her again." Smirking, she revealed, "She told me that she had no intention of being just a stop on the O'Flaherty Express."

"Ooo, cold," Jamie chuckled.

"Yeah. Not many women call me on my game. I liked that she had gumption, even though I didn't like the result. I was gonna just blow her off, but after this soul-searching that I've been doing, I decided to call her."

"So what happened?" Jamie asked.

"We talked for a long time. I confessed that she really had my number." She paused for a moment. "But then I asked her if she would go out with me if I promised not to see anyone else, and I promised to remain open to having a real relationship." She looked up at Jamie. "I had no idea that I was going to offer that, but she really is something, Jamie. I don't remember the last time I was this attracted to a woman," she revealed.

"So, did she agree right then?"

"Nope," she said happily. "She made me wait until today. She called me this afternoon and agreed to go out with me tomorrow evening." She laughed a little. "She also told me in no uncertain terms that when she said 'go out,' she meant 'go out.'" Chuckling mildly, she admitted, "I don't think I'm going to have my way with this one for quite a while."

"Are you okay with that?" Jamie asked with a laugh. "I know you have needs that you're used to having filled, and I can't imagine that she'd appreciate it if you're having sex with your other friends while you're dating."

"I won't see other people if Tracy and I decide to be exclusive. It will be a little weird for me, but I think my overactive libido could use a rest," she reflected.

"This could give you a chance to get to know yourself and discover what's really important to you in a relationship," Jamie said thoughtfully.

"Oh, believe me, I'm going to continue to know myself," she chuckled. "A girl's gotta have an outlet!"

⌘

On the first Friday after Thanksgiving break, Jamie walked into Jack's apartment and was astounded to find him setting the table for dinner. She smelled something cooking, but she was too shocked to even try to guess what it was. "Hi," he said brightly when he saw her.

"Uh, hi," she managed to get out. "What's up?"

He walked over to her and wrapped his arms around her tightly. "I've been giving a lot of thought to what you said on Thanksgiving, and I've really resolved to do something about it. I don't want to have a marriage like my parents, Jamie, but I have been falling into their patterns. I'm sorry that you got so frustrated before you told me, but I'm glad you told me eventually."

"I had no idea that you even took me seriously," she said in wonder. "I can't tell you how good it makes me feel to know that you care enough to try to change."

"Jamie," he said softly as he lifted her chin with his fingers, "your opinion of me matters tremendously. You're the most important person in my life. Don't you know that?"

She rested her head on his chest and let herself just sink into his embrace. His strong arms completely enveloped her, and she felt warm and loved for the first time in weeks. "Thank you," she said softly. "Thank you for everything."

⌘

The following Monday morning, Ryan walked up to Jamie after class and asked, "Juice?"

"Sure," Jamie agreed, very thankful that Ryan did not seem to want to stop their little breaks together, even though she was getting close to Tracy. Out of the corner of her eye, Jamie saw the good-looking brunette talking to a group of women. "Would you like to ask Tracy to join us?" she asked with just a moment of hesitation.

"Uhm … I guess I could, but I like having time alone with you," she demurred. "So, I wouldn't mind asking her once in a while, but I don't want to make a habit of it."

Jamie smiled sweetly up at her friend as she shook her head. "You are such a sensitive woman, Ryan O'Flaherty. I really like having time with just you also, but I'd like to get to know her a little. Is it okay?"

"Sure. I'll ask her," she said with a winning smile. She sauntered over and gently placed her hand on Tracy's back. The dark head turned to regard her, and Jamie watched as Tracy's face broke into a big smile. Seconds later both women were walking her way. "Ms. Stuart has accepted our invitation," Ryan said with mock formality. "Our usual?"

"Perfect," Jamie said with a smile.

⌘

After a few minutes of topical conversation, Jamie hopped up from the table to buy another round of juice for her always-thirsty friend. Ryan had whipped through her two bottles and was eyeing Jamie's rather hungrily, so since it was her turn to buy, Jamie strolled over to purchase another cranberry juice. *I am amazed by how natural Ryan seems with her*, she mused during her short walk. *I thought she'd have on the predator persona, but she doesn't at all. Hmm, maybe she puts that on only when she has a woman alone.* She considered this idea but reminded herself, *No, she was very predatory with the women she picked up during class. Having an audience sure didn't seem to stop her then.* A smile crossed her lips as she watched Ryan gently flirting with Tracy. She wasn't up to her usual tricks, however. She was just smiling shyly at something the gorgeous brunette had said. Her eyes were half lidded and reflected incongruously innocent shyness. Tracy obviously appreciated this new attitude as she playfully touched the tip of Ryan's nose. But Jamie realized that there was still a little predator left as she watched a feral grin appear on her friend's face just before her mouth

S.X. MEAGHER

opened to grab Tracy's index finger between her perfect white teeth.

Jamie set the bottle down on the table, admonishing her friend, "I've brought more calories. You don't have to resort to cannibalism."

Ryan just gave her a rakish look as she tamely released her prey. Tracy leaned over and patted her gently on the cheek, murmuring, "Good girl."

Tracy turned to Jamie and twitched her head in Ryan's direction, asking, "How long have you and blue eyes here known each other?"

"Mmm, just since class started," Jamie informed her.

Tracy blinked a little at that bit of information. "Gosh, I thought you'd known each other for years. You just seem so close."

"We are," Ryan said, locking her eyes onto Jamie's. "Jamie's the best friend I've ever had."

Jamie did not waiver as she echoed Ryan's thoughts. "Best class I've ever taken," she said with a small smile. "I've learned a lot and got a best friend in the bargain."

Tracy gave each woman a long, appraising look as they grinned at each other, oblivious of her presence.

CHAPTER ELEVEN

SHE'S TURNED YOU DOWN TWICE, JAMIE. TWICE IN A WEEK. OF ALL the times you've asked her to do things, she's refused you just twice. Don't be such a baby! She has a girlfriend now, and she can't be sitting by the phone just waiting for your call. Tracy is everything that you say you want for her. She's smart, she's sweet, she's very funny and Ryan is adorable with her. Do you want her to be happy or not?

"Hey," Ryan said as she responded to Jamie's page on the following Tuesday. "What's up?"

"My father offered me four tickets to the Warriors tonight. Wanna go and bring a couple of brothers?"

"Ooo, I'd love to," she said quickly. "But I've got a date."

"That's okay," Jamie said quickly, trying to hide her disappointment.

"I could ask Tracy to go, too, if it's important to you," Ryan offered.

The thought of sharing Ryan's attention made the evening seem much less attractive. "No, she doesn't seem like a basketball kind of girl," Jamie admitted.

"No, she kinda doesn't, does she?" Ryan agreed. "Tennis maybe, or even the LPGA, but probably not basketball."

"That's okay. Maybe I'll call Conor and see if he'd like all four."

"He'd love to have you go, too, Jamie," Ryan reminded her. "He thinks you're fine."

"Yeah," she laughed. "I think he thinks I'm too fine," she admitted with a little chuckle. "I'm having a hard enough time with Jack. Going to a game with Conor probably isn't in my best interests."

"Well, let me give you his pager. I'm sure he'd be happy to take the tickets if you don't want to use them."

"Okay," she said when Ryan had given her the number. She knew she should hang up, but she just didn't want to. "Where are you going tonight?"

"Tracy's having me over for dinner," she replied with a laugh. "But I have a feeling that someone else is doing the cooking. She's not very domestic."

"Where does she live?" Jamie asked, just trying to prolong the contact.

"Marina. She has a nice little apartment — and no roommates," she added with a deep chuckle.

"The perfect woman," Jamie laughed gently, trying to get the image of

Ryan and Tracy locked in a passionate embrace out of her mind.

"Yeah, so far so good," she conceded. "It's still too early to tell, but she's pretty special."

"She'd better be. You deserve the best."

"Thanks, Jamie. I've got to run, but thanks again for the offer. Ask me again, okay?"

"Count on it," she promised.

⌘

Two days later Jamie went to the gym to get in a little cardio work. Ryan was just finishing up her last client of the day. "Hey," she said by way of greeting when she spotted Jamie on the treadmill.

"What's up?"

"Not much. I just finished for the day."

"Wanna hang around for a few? I could make you dinner."

"Oh, no can do. I'm going to the opera," she said as she rolled her eyes rather dramatically.

"The opera? I didn't figure you for the type."

"I'm not, but apparently Tracy is. The things we do for love," she said with a shudder as she considered how long the evening would probably be. "I'd rather be eating your delicious food, but I've got to make some sacrifices I suppose."

"Well, have fun," Jamie said lightly, her tone not revealing her disappointment at being turned down.

"You okay?" Ryan asked as she came closer and gave her a penetrating gaze.

"Fine. Just trying to keep up a conversation when I'm laboring on this machine," she said, slightly out of breath.

"Okay, take it easy," Ryan said as she gave her a sweet smile and took off for her date.

"I liked her better when she was a slut," Jamie grumbled to no one in particular.

⌘

At least Tracy is going home to visit her parents for a couple of weeks during winter break, she thought as she watched her friend leave the building. *That's nice, Jamie, very generous of you. Do you think Ryan would wish the same for you? She's been entirely supportive of your relationship, and now it's your turn to do the same for her.*

Jamie knew that her conscience was correct, but she really did not want to share Ryan with another woman. That honest reaction made her feel quite ashamed of herself. *Do you really want Ryan to be fulfilled, or do you just want her to be available to you when you call? You can't have it both ways. Either be her friend, or admit that you're just using her to satisfy your own needs!*

⌘

After class on Friday, Ryan popped over to Jamie and asked, "What's the earliest you're free today?"

"Ahh, I'm free after 2:00. Why?"

"Let's have some fun before you have to go down to Palo Alto," she suggested. "I thought we could take our workout outdoors for a change of pace."

"Okay," Jamie said cautiously. "Where should we go?"

"Let's meet at the football stadium at 2:15. But first let's get some juice. I've gotta tell you all about this opera thing!" She turned and caught Tracy's eye, blew her a kiss, then slung her arm around Jamie's shoulder, guiding her from the classroom.

⌘

At 2:15 sharp, Ryan climbed out of the small set of bleachers set up next to the track and jogged over to meet her friend. "Been waiting long?" Jamie asked as she trotted over to meet her halfway.

"Nope. Just got here," she smiled. Slung over her shoulder was a small nylon gym bag, which Jamie eyed suspiciously.

"We're gonna duplicate our workout with the things you have in that little bag?" she asked as she pointed at the Kelly green bag that read, "Lady Dons." "And what in the heck is a Lady Don?"

"Oh," Ryan said rather absently, "That's my old school, U.S.F. And to answer your question, yes, we can duplicate your workout with even less than I have in here. I'm gonna work out, too, and I bet I use less of this stuff than you do," she challenged.

"Okay, Ms. Magic, let's see what you've got."

"Well, first, let's just do some warm-ups. Since it's cool out, we need to make sure we get loose before we try anything strenuous." Ryan guided her through the exercises, watching her carefully to make sure she didn't overstress herself.

When she was satisfied that Jamie was loose and flexible, Ryan

231

produced several lengths of rubber tubing in various colors. "What are these?" Jamie asked as she examined one length.

"These are your weights," Ryan said.

"These little things?" Jamie scoffed. "How can they duplicate what we do at the gym?"

"Oh, you'd be surprised," she assured her. "I believe this is leg day?" she inquired.

"Yep."

"Okay. On your back," she ordered as she produced a very thin foam pad for Jamie to lie on. Once she was down, Ryan showed her how to use the bands to provide resistance for her quads. She had her using the strongest band, and after ten reps of the exercise, her legs dropped to the ground and she moaned, "Enough!"

"Not so easy, is it?" Ryan laughed. "I'll knock you down one level for your next set."

"You'd better if you want me to do more than four reps. That was killer!"

"Well, it isn't just the tension in the band. When you use these, you don't have the machine guiding you at all. Every bit of force and energy has to come solely from you, and that takes a lot more effort."

"I'll say," she agreed as she started her next set with the lighter tubing.

The next exercise called for her to tie one of the ends around each ankle, and slowly pull one leg away while balancing on one foot. This motion also had her calling for mercy after only nine reps. "Jeez!" she complained. "Am I that weak?"

"Not at all," Ryan assured her. "This is much harder than what you're used to. This makes you use your legs to keep your balance at the same time, and that makes it very tough. But it's important that your balance be very good, especially for a long bike ride. I work on my balance all the time," she conceded.

"With these?" Jamie asked.

"Sometimes, but I've got lots of things I do to keep myself entertained."

"Show me some of them if you can," she urged.

"Happy to," Ryan obliged.

⌘

Ryan proceeded to delight her friend with an exhibition of her upper body strength, performing feats that she claimed to have learned in gymnastics. Jamie was only mildly surprised when her friend informed her that she'd taken gymnastics for years — but that she'd always been in the boys' class. Jamie was still smiling at her friend's recounting the tale of how Brendan practically had to come to blows with the instructor to get Ryan admitted.

Something caught Ryan's attention as they walked along the track, and she darted into a tunnel, calling out to Jamie to join her. With a smirk and a small shake of her head, the blonde trotted over to the underside of the bleachers where Ryan stood waiting. Near the end zone of the football field, the school had erected relatively modern bleachers to make the stadium homier for the normally small crowds that Cal drew for football. The underside of the bleachers was a series of interconnecting metal supports running through it like a maze. Ryan was staring at the interlocking braces with a very studious look on her face. "Doesn't this remind you of a great big jungle gym?" she asked thoughtfully.

"Ahh, yeah, I guess it does," Jamie agreed. "Boy, I used to like the one we had at a park near our house. But they decided that too many kids got hurt on it, so they removed it and the slide and the swings and replaced them with a really lame bunch of horses on springs. I never wanted to go again," she said somewhat wistfully.

"Well, you've got to admit that they can be a little dangerous," Ryan said with a gleam in her eye. "Especially when they're really, really tall." Her words were accompanied by a small grunt as she leapt to her full reach and grabbed one of the supports with both of her hands. She was only about eighteen inches off the ground, but she looked pretty comical, nonetheless.

"Okay, Tarzana, let's go," Jamie said, giving her a fond smile.

"Go? You want to go?" Ryan said, the challenge in her voice very clear. "Race you to the other end!" she cried as she started to propel herself along the underside of the structure. Jamie not only did not race her, she was stuck in place as she stared at her daredevil friend. Ryan was motoring along at a quick clip, but she had to follow the supports to get where she was going, forcing her to climb higher and higher, until she was at the very top of the very tall structure, dangling like a chimp. A wildly laughing chimp, that is, who was having the time of her life.

Jamie started to jog just to keep up, but Ryan was moving much too fast for her, her momentum carrying her rapidly across the space. She truly looked like some breed of beautiful simian as she swung up and down the supports, gracefully propelling herself along with ease. She was standing on the ground, looking rather bored, when her panting friend caught up to her moments later. "Are you insane?" Jamie shrieked as she ran up and slapped Ryan hard on the chest with both of her open hands.

"You said you wanted to go," she said innocently as she blinked down at her. "I assumed you wanted to go fast."

"I can't imagine what I would say to your father if you had fallen!" Jamie chided her.

"You could have said, 'You were right, Martin. She did finally fall and break her neck!'"

⌘

They walked the rest of the way in silence, with Jamie reflecting on all that she had seen. "Do you know that you can do things like that?" she finally asked with a very thoughtful look on her face.

"What do you mean?"

"I guess I want to know if you're certain that you can do something dangerous before you try it," she said.

"Oh, heck, no," Ryan admitted. "Where's the fun in that?"

"Ryan!" she said as she stopped and grabbed onto the back of her tank top. "You mean to tell me that you might not have been able to do that, but you tried it anyway?"

"Well, yeah," she explained slowly. "That's what makes it fun. I mean, I know I'm strong and that my grip is really good. I know I'm flexible and that I have good balance. There's no reason to assume I can't do something like that, so I try it. Once I get into a situation, I'm certainly not going to back out, so I have to figure out a way to finish without breaking my neck."

Jamie's mouth moved for a second before sound came out. "You really have never done something like that before? You just did it and hoped for the best?"

"Right," she smiled. "I only tried it because I've never done it before. Heck, if I had I probably wouldn't be interested in trying it again. Once I've done something, it loses its allure," she admitted with a toothy grin.

Like your women, Jamie thought with an internal smirk as she stole another glance at the grinning, sweaty, gorgeous hunk of woman who blithely strolled along beside her.

⌘

When they reached their gear, Ryan checked the position of the sun and regretfully announced, "Time to go, pal."

"I don't wanna go," Jamie pouted. "I'm having too much fun."

"Come on," Ryan urged as she bent to pick up her keys and her gym bag.

Her smaller friend was too quick for her; Jamie's hand snaked out and grabbed the keys at the last instant. "You can't leave without your bike!" she declared, defiantly dangling the keys in front of the brunette's darting eyes.

One quick swipe with her hand left Ryan grasping nothing but air as Jamie laughed wildly and took off. Ryan joined her laugh and doggedly began to pursue her. In reality, she could have caught the smaller, slower woman within three strides. But Ryan felt a little guilty about turning down her last two invitations, and she was loath to cut the session short when Jamie was obviously having so much fun. *Jamie seems so childlike and free today,* she thought with a smile. *She hasn't been this way very often lately. We've got to get outside and play more,* she decided immediately.

Ryan calmly assessed the path that Jamie had chosen and quickly tried to cut off some of her options to trap her into making a mistake.

The blonde darted around the infield, using various track paraphernalia as shields to keep Ryan away. She scurried around hurdles, the long jump pit, even the huge cushion that the pole vaulters landed on. But Ryan was dangerously close, never more than two body lengths away, no matter what she tried. She saw what she hoped would be her salvation. A large, bright blue, square cushion that protected the high jumpers was beckoning to her. She latched onto an idea and scampered aboard, crawling frantically on all fours just before Ryan grabbed her feet. The cushion stood about four feet high, clearly no barrier for her chimp-like pursuer. But as Jamie coyly reminded her, "Wherever you start to climb, I can run to the other side and jump down before you get up!"

Ryan pursed her lips and reviewed the situation. Jamie did have a point, her analytical mind agreed. It would not do to just try to climb aboard. She needed to get up there, but not by going up the side. A sly smile crossed her lips, and Jamie looked around suspiciously, recognizing the look on her friend's face. "There's more than one way to skin a cat," Ryan declared as she walked back to her gym bag at a leisurely pace and sat down to put on a pair of track spikes. When she was finished, she walked back to the cushion and turned her back to it as she appeared to be measuring off a distance in her head. She was obviously satisfied because she turned back towards Jamie and started to run, gaining speed as she approached the bag. Jamie didn't try to flee because she still didn't know what Ryan was going to do — she just stood stock still and watched in amazement as Ryan continued to barrel towards her.

As she approached she actually slowed down appreciably and turned her back just as she flexed her knees deeply. She propelled herself into the air, landing rather forcefully and inelegantly on the cushion. Her momentum carried her, on her back, quite a few feet across the surface, but she eventually skidded to a halt right at Jamie's feet. She looked up at her with a wicked gleam in her eye and put on her sexiest smile as she drawled, "Hi there."

"Yikes!" Jamie cried as she tried to run. But Ryan's cat-like reflexes halted her progress abruptly as an ankle was captured in an iron grip. She crashed into the cushion face-first and quickly rolled onto her back just as Ryan began to crawl up her body like a panther — first her right hand, then her left knee, left hand, right knee. She hovered over the supine woman, staring at her intently as she asked, "I believe you have something of mine?"

"Can't have it!" Jamie insisted, still not willing to give up. In an impetuous move, she took the keys and shoved them into her cleavage, safe within her tight, navy blue sports bra.

"That isn't much of a barrier," Ryan purred, locking her eyes on her prey. She was panting a little from the exertion of her leap.

"No, but I fight dirty," the smaller woman promised. "When you reach for the keys, I've got two hands free to cause all sorts of mayhem." Her eyes had grown fiery in the last rays of sunlight, and Ryan mused that she could see flecks of gold and amber and even a bit of orange in the shining orbs.

"Hmm, I have an idea," Ryan mused aloud. "When my brothers had me pinned, they would invariably spit in my face to gross me out enough to give up whatever prize I had. I bet that would work with you, too."

Jamie gave her a slightly suspicious look, but she didn't think Ryan had the nerve to spit on her.

"Nah, that's too easy," the dark woman decided, causing Jamie to let out the breath she didn't know she had been holding. "But this might work," she said as she quickly spread her hands out and clamped vise-like grips on each of her captive's wrists. "That'll keep you docile," she mused, still surveying her options.

Jamie felt the deep sigh leave her chest as she looked up at the gorgeous woman holding her prisoner. *I've been in worse situations,* she mused as she watched Ryan's eyes dart around in thought. "How does it help you to have both of my hands if you have to use both of yours to hold them?" she smirked. But as soon as the words were out of her mouth, she knew she had made a fatal tactical error. Almost before the end of the sentence, Ryan pushed her hands together, placing one atop the other. Her much larger and stronger left hand easily grasped both of

Jamie's wrists, pinning them firmly above her head.

"Got any more bright ideas?" Ryan growled, wiggling the fingers on her free right hand directly in front of Jamie's face. That determined hand moved slowly towards the target, a fiendish look in her eyes that showed she was not afraid to claim her prize.

"You wouldn't dare," Jamie croaked out nervously.

Ryan leaned down until their noses were touching. Her damp skin smelled like the earth — like rich, warm soil, just turned over after the spring rains. Jamie had never smelled anything like it on another person, and she decided that she'd be happy to lie there beneath the weight of her friend and breathe in that heady aroma for a very long time. Ryan's voice startled her back into her senses. "I've never … ever … ever refused a dare," she purred with a determined look in her eyes. Her right hand was less than an inch from Jamie's heaving chest, and the captive knew that she had to put a stop to the game. But something deep inside wanted Ryan's hand to snake inside her bra and stay there for as long as it wished.

Her conscience finally woke up and forced her to utter the only appropriate response. "Uncle!"

⌘

A few minutes later they were standing in the deep dusk, once again clad in their sweats. "I had a fantastic time today, Ryan," Jamie said gratefully.

"I had a great time, myself," Ryan said with a grin. "But that's not a surprise when I'm with you." She raised her left hand and touched Jamie lightly on the nose, giving her an affectionate smile to go with it. "You bring out my wild side," she added with a chuckle.

"I think you do all right bringing it out on your own," the blonde scoffed, but secretly she hoped that Ryan's statement was true.

She leaned in for a hug, but Ryan complained, "I'm all sweaty. I must smell terrible."

Jamie didn't argue with her, but she nonetheless ignored the warning. She held her in a fierce embrace for a few moments, wishing to imprint that distinctive scent onto her memory forever.

"See you on Christmas Eve," Ryan said softly as she pulled away. She looked at Jamie for a full minute, a smile blooming on her lips as she took her in. "I'll miss seeing you almost every day."

"I'll miss you, too," Jamie sighed, letting her arms slip around Ryan's waist for another hug. She didn't let go for a long time, just listening to the slow, steady beat of her friend's heart.

Ryan dropped a soft kiss onto the crown of her head and said, "You know you can call me any time, right? Day or night, if things start to bother you — you just call, and we'll talk."

"I know," she sighed into the damp cotton of Ryan's sweatshirt. "Thanks for being such a good friend."

That warm, deep voice resonated through her entire body. "The pleasure is all mine, Jamie."

⌘

After getting into her car, Jamie rolled the windows down and eased her seat back. She sat in the quiet parking lot for a long time, trying to focus her mind enough to drive to her parents' home. She mused that going from an afternoon with Ryan to a visit with her parents was a huge culture shock, and she tried very hard to hold on to the feeling of total acceptance that she always felt when she was with her friend. As she started the car, she glumly acknowledged that she rarely received that reaction from her family, and given the difficult time they'd had at Thanksgiving, she doubted that things would be much better during this long visit.

Upon arriving, she was cheered to learn that Marta had prepared a lovely meal for her homecoming. Jamie sat in the kitchen with the cook for a long while, talking about school and the training she was doing for the ride. Marta was fascinated by the changes in her body, and she teased her about her new muscles and asked if she could now pick Jack up.

They ate dinner after her parents arrived home from an event. It was late, around 8:15, and dinner was a bit overdone from resting in the warming oven, but the meal was still pleasant.

Jim was in a very good mood, having just come from an office party for partners and their spouses.

During dinner, Jim talked about the little party and how enjoyable it was to get to know some of the younger partners. "I did have to stop and wonder at one point, though," he reflected. "One of those young men brought another man to the party. What on earth do you think came over him?" he directed his question at his wife.

"I'm sure I don't know, dear," was her flat reply as she failed to look up from her plate.

"They just seem to have taken leave of their senses," he continued. "Why can't they realize how uncomfortable that makes everyone else at a party?"

Jamie knew that her color was rising, but this was the first evening of a thirty-two-day stay, and she couldn't afford to blow up now. She fought with every bit of her self-control to refrain from speaking, breathing out a sigh of relief when she felt the urge pass.

For some reason, the lack of response from the Evans women didn't stop Jim from continuing. "I guess you're used to that type of thing at Berkeley, Jamie," he said as he regarded his daughter. "But it just isn't done in the business world."

Jamie stared at her soup until she could see the individual molecules bumping into one another. She fought for composure before she finally replied, "I need some more spice in my soup. Does anyone else?" as she rose from the table, soup bowl held by a shaking hand.

She leaned against the door to the kitchen, willing her knees to stop shaking. Marta came over to see what was wrong, but Jamie just shook her head and went to the sink for a glass of water. "Marta, could you please get me a small glass of Scotch?" she finally asked. When Marta returned, Jamie thanked her and downed the two fingers of amber liquid in one burning gulp. "Thank you," she politely replied as she stepped back into the dining room, leaving the cook staring at her in disbelief.

⌘

Jamie spent most of Christmas eve day with Jack. He had studied through most of the day, but he did take an hour break to convince her to make love. As she got in the shower after their break, she devised her plan. She had called Ryan earlier and been issued a blanket invitation to come any time and stay as long as she liked.

Jamie put her casual clothes back on and announced, "I'm going to Berkeley to take care of a few things. Would you mind just meeting me at church before the service?"

"Gee, Jamie, that's awfully late."

"I know, but there are a couple of little things that didn't arrive before I left. I want to go to my house and wrap them. Then I need to go shopping for one teeny thing for my outfit. Rather than come back here, I thought I could just go home and take a nap before Mass. I want to be rested for the service tonight," she batted her eyes sweetly. *Or: I'm leaving now so I can spend as much time with Ryan as possible, and I like her family so much better than mine. One of these two stories is the truth. Oops, wrong choice,* she thought when he gamely agreed.

Well, things are really going well. I have to drink Scotch to get through dinner with my parents, and I'm making up baldfaced lies to avoid being with Jack all day. Have yourself a merry fucking Christmas!

Despite her gloomy mood, she raced to Berkeley and dressed carefully. She donned a pure white, heavy, silk jacquard blouse, embroidered with an Asian-inspired design, banded collar held together by a tiny, black pearl button. A trim, black velvet, square-cut vest just brushed the waistband of her black velvet pleated slacks, and black velvet slippers covered her feet. She stood in front of the mirror and fluffed her hair a little, then added a small touch of perfume and was on her way. She called Ryan from her car to inquire if she needed anything, laughing at her friend's response. "Yeah, a bigger house or fewer relatives."

Ryan answered the door, looking lovelier than Jamie had ever seen her. Her black hair was combed straight back, held off her face by a black velvet headband. She wore a crimson-colored, angora turtleneck sweater that gently hugged her smooth curves. Simple pearl earrings graced her ears, and a single strand of pearls hung just above the swell of her breasts. Black silk pants covered her long, shapely legs, and simple, black leather shoes completed the ensemble. "Wow!" was all that Jamie could get out.

"Wow, yourself," Ryan said, looking up and down Jamie's small form. "You look positively lovely," she said sincerely. "C'mon in and let the men pretend not to stare at you," she teased. When she saw Conor making a beeline for them, she whispered, "All except one who has no shame, of course."

Conor complimented Jamie until she blushed to the roots of her hair. He looked fabulous also, however, wearing a well-made, navy blue double-breasted suit with a crisp, white shirt and a green and red rep tie. His hair looked jet black and very shiny, and it was neatly combed for a change. "Are you going to stay and go to Mass with us?" he asked hopefully.

"No, I can't. I'm meeting my fiancé for services at my grandfather's church," she replied.

"Your grandfather is a minister?"

"Actually, he's a priest." When she saw the shocked look on his face, she added, "Episcopal."

"Oh, I thought maybe I'd been away from church too long, and I missed something important," he laughed.

Maeve came up behind him at that moment and stated, "You have been away from church too long, sweetheart. The last time I saw you there was Easter," she gently chided.

Ryan took Jamie by the arm and whispered, "Let's get out of here before she starts on me." They squeezed through the mass of relatives until Ryan spied her prize. She snatched Caitlin from her Aunt Peggy and eventually blazed a trail to her room.

Duffy followed them down the stairs, eagerly sniffing at the bundle in Ryan's arms. When they got downstairs, she sat down on the bed and allowed Duffy to lick the baby's giggling face clean.

"Duffy sure is good with her," Jamie observed. "He seems to know he has to be very gentle."

"Yeah, he loves kids more than I do. Luckily, Caitlin is crazy about him, too," she replied as the big dog started to clean the tiny hands one at a time. "Okay, Duff, you've had enough baby kissing," she said as she scooped her off her lap and over her shoulder. She went to her dresser and took out a clean T-shirt, which she placed over her shoulder and chest. "Can't be too careful," she said from experience. "She just had dinner, and there's always a chance of rejection."

They all sat on the bed as Ryan propped the baby up against her legs. "So, what have you been up to this week?" Jamie asked.

"Ooo … I had a great week."

"What did you do?"

"Conor has a friend with a condo up near Tahoe, and everyone who could manage some time off went up to ski and snowboard for a few days. I think seven of us made it, and it was absolutely fantastic," she said with a very happy grin covering her lovely face. "Just skiing, boarding, take-out pizzas and more skiing. My idea of bliss."

"I can't imagine what a hellion you must be on the slopes," she mused. "Do you ski a lot?"

"Every chance I get," Ryan admitted. "If I had just a little less of a work ethic, I could really be a ski bum."

"That would be a pretty sweet job for you," her smirking friend admitted. "You could live in Aspen or St. Moritz and have the wealthy women support you in the style you deserve."

"Hmm, maybe this work ethic thing isn't such a good idea," she purred as she considered the suggestion. "Well, that's enough about me. I really want to know how it's going for you so far." Ryan said.

Jamie considered how much to reveal, finally deciding that she needed to talk. "I had to chug a glass of Scotch to get through dinner one night, and I told Jack a blatant lie today." She grimaced as she continued, "All in all, not great."

Ryan thought about this for a moment. "Did you enjoy being with your family in the past? Or is this a new development?"

Jamie knew the answer, but was a bit embarrassed to admit it. "I didn't mind before because I thought that was what families were supposed to be like. But after spending time with you and your family, I see how stilted and formal my family is. I swear, Ryan, your family shows much more interest in me than my own does."

Ryan smiled at her sympathetically. "We love having you here, Jamie. I think of you as a part of my family. You're always welcome." She shook her head briefly. "I feel sorry for your parents. They don't know what a treasure they have in you."

As she blushed shyly at the compliment, Jamie replied, "In their defense, it's me who has changed. I want more from them, and I want more from Jack. In a way it's a bit unfair of me; I'm the one who has changed the rules."

"It's never unfair to expect the people closest to you to love and honor and cherish you, Jamie." She got up from the bed and went to her dresser. "I certainly do," she said as she handed her friend a small package.

Jamie looked up, a wide smile lighting up her whole face. "I really love getting presents, you know. But I feel the time I spend with you is a gift. I don't need anything tangible to know how you feel about our friendship." After a pause she added with a giggle, "But I still love presents."

She carefully removed the red and green striped paper from the little box. Inside was a small, black leather book about the size of a paperback. She opened it to find a little map of each of the major bike routes in the Bay Area. The maps had obviously been meticulously removed from another book, each one carefully glued to a strong piece of heavy white paper. Underneath each map was a legend in Ryan's hand, detailing the options for each route and the difficulty of each. On the page opposite each map was a space for Jamie to mark the date she completed the ride, what the weather was like and how she felt during the ride. Every fourth or fifth page carried a small handwritten message meant to inspire or motivate. Some were funny, some spiritual and some just practical. Jamie was touched beyond words at the time and effort that Ryan had obviously expended in making this journal. She fought back a tear as she wrapped her arms around her friend in silence. After a moment she simply whispered, "Thank you."

After Jamie pulled back, Ryan gave her a luminous grin. "I'm glad you like it." Then she added, "You know, I don't think I tell you enough how much it means to me that you're doing this ride. I know that AIDS hasn't had a big impact on your life, and I appreciate how willing you were to take on this challenge. I think part of the reason that you agreed was because you knew it was important to me. I really thank you for that."

"That is the biggest reason I agreed to do it," she replied honestly. "I knew that you wouldn't give so much of your time to something that wasn't really worthwhile." Jamie looked at her friend for a moment before revealing, "I had another reason, though."

"What's that?"

"I'm tired of just giving money to worthwhile causes. I don't want to be that way anymore, Ryan. If a charity is important enough for me to give money to, it should be important enough for me to give my time and my efforts to. Seeing how much satisfaction you get from being involved in the ride made me want that for myself." She gripped her friend's hand and said, "You've made me want to challenge myself."

Grinning shyly, Ryan just ducked her head and said, "Thanks."

Just then Caitlin expressed her displeasure at lying still, so Jamie placed the shirt over her shoulder and picked her up. She carried her around the room, letting her short attention span be captured briefly by all the books and the small items on the shelves. She pointed out the pictures of Ryan and the rest of the family and explained who each person was, even though Caitlin had no idea what she was talking about. Ryan lay back on the bed and watched her friend charm her little cousin. After a while Jamie announced, "I have a gift for you, too, Ryan. It's in my purse. Would you mind getting it out?"

Ryan gamely retrieved Jamie's purse and began looking through it. She found a card with her name on it and held it up questioningly. "Yes, that's it," Jamie replied.

Ryan sat back down on the bed with a look of anticipation on her face. "I like presents, too," she admitted. She tore open the card, and several pieces of paper fell out onto her lap. She began to gather them up as she pulled the card fully out of the envelope. After she had organized all of the paper, she began to look at them carefully. Her face lit up with childlike glee as she read off each ticket. "Oh, wow, the Exploratorium! The Children's Museum, Marineland!" she shouted with delight. She came over to Jamie and held up the tickets, "There are two adults and one child for each of these. Where will we ever get a child?" She dangled the tickets in front of the baby and said, "We're going to play, sweetie!"

Jamie laughed at Ryan's obvious delight. "There are a few more in there." Ryan grabbed the envelope and found, after a thorough audit, that Jamie had purchased tickets for them to do nearly every baby-friendly thing in the Bay Area. Finally, she read the card, "Thank you for giving me a second chance at a happy childhood," read the note.

Ryan hugged her friend soundly, catching the baby in the embrace for good measure. "This was a fabulously thoughtful gift," she said sincerely. "Caitlin and I thank you very much. She's a little young to know where she is most of the time, but by summer I think she'll be ready for everything."

"I figured it would take most of the year to do all of these things," Jamie admitted, not mentioning that was part of her reason for choosing so many events. "I've just never seen you happier than you are with her. Being around you two is so healing for me. It allows me to experience some of those childhood pleasures that I didn't get to have," she admitted.

"It really surprises me that you didn't do these things as a child. I mean," she struggled a bit, uncomfortable to say what was on her mind. "I thought that people with money did all these things, especially for an only child." She blushed a bit. "I just assumed you were spoiled."

"I was spoiled with things," Jamie admitted. "I had every toy and stuffed animal known to mankind. But my father didn't have time to do kid stuff, and my mother had no interest. She took me to the symphony and to plays and the opera when I was three and four years old. So, it's not that I didn't go places, I just didn't go to kid places."

"Did you enjoy going to those places?" Ryan asked gently.

Jamie gave her a sardonic look, "You're kidding, right?"

"Didn't you have friends or cousins to do things with?" Ryan continued to probe, unable to believe that Jamie's life had been so barren.

"I don't have very many cousins that we socialize with. My father's sister has two kids, but she lives in Chicago, so they weren't very convenient. My mother is an only child, and the maternal side of her extended family just gets together in Rhode Island in the summer. We're not a real close group," she said, stating the obvious. "I didn't start making friends until I was in Montessori school when I was four, and I was never encouraged to have those kids over. I basically played with Marta, our cook, or the maids."

"So you've been a little adult your whole life, haven't you?" Ryan said sympathetically.

"Yeah, I guess I have," she replied.

"Well, Caitlin and I are going to change that pretty darn quick. You'll have regressed to infancy when we get through with you," she said confidently as she put her arm around her friend.

"I have one more thing to give you, but it's not a gift," Jamie said tentatively.

Ryan cocked her head in question, and waited for her friend to continue.

She walked back over to her purse and extracted another envelope as she braced the baby against her hip. This one was not marked, and she withdrew a white form and a check. "I was sending in my check for the

AIDS Ride because I wanted to make some charitable donations before year end. I decided to donate $25,000, and it dawned on me that I should make a donation in your name of at least that much. I wouldn't be doing this ride without your support, Ryan. It's become much more to me than an athletic goal. It's helping me to change my life in a fundamental manner. And it's all because of you," she said sincerely. "I know you like to secure your own pledges, but I also know how busy you've been. I just want you to know that if you are running short, you don't have to worry."

Ryan closed her eyes tightly as she struggled to hold back the tears. She bit her lip to control her shaking chin and took in a few deep breaths. Finally, she was able to open her eyes. She gazed at Jamie unwaveringly and opened her arms. Jamie walked right into the embrace, cuddling Caitlin between them. Ryan didn't say a word, but she leaned over and kissed each of Jamie's cheeks. She had so much emotion threatening to spill out that she didn't trust herself to say a thing, but she maintained the hug for a very long while, kissing Jamie's head and cheek repeatedly.

⌘

The rest of the evening was spent laughing and eating and joking with the whole O'Flaherty clan. Small gifts were given to Caitlin by everyone in attendance, and by the time Jamie was ready to leave, the baby was once again fast asleep in Ryan's arms.

The two friends walked to Jamie's car together. "I think this was the best Christmas I've ever had, Ryan," she said softly when they reached the little car.

"You made it more special for me than I'll ever be able to say," Ryan replied as she gave her friend a one-armed hug, being careful of the sleeping infant. "If your family gets to be too much, I want you to call me. I've got a lot of free time before school starts, so don't be shy."

"I won't and thanks again for everything," Jamie said as she pulled the Boxster onto the small, quiet street for the short ride to Nob Hill.

⌘

On the Wednesday after Christmas, Jamie had to get away for a while. Jack was obviously trying hard, but his attempts at being closer were driving her absolutely crazy. The message that he had gotten was that she didn't like to make meals and clean up alone. So he gamely hung around in the kitchen while she tried to work. But he really was inept; whether through design or inability, she wasn't sure. He was in her way so badly that she finally released him to go back to his work. So the pattern returned to their previous one. He studied, she read. He studied, she cooked. He studied, she watched a movie. The routine was getting so monotonous that she wanted to scream. *We never **do** anything,* she whined to herself. *We don't go out for dinner; we don't even go for walks any more. I know he has a lot on his mind, but I feel like we're setting up a schedule that might never vary. He'll replace school with work and be just as unavailable to me.*

She realized that the main outside activity they had was brunch and golf at the club. *But I've been doing that since I was born. I want some excitement in my life!*

She dialed Ryan's pager and waited just a few minutes for her call. "Hi, what's up?" her friend asked cheerfully.

"What's your schedule today?"

"I'm at the gym right now. I've got clients until 11:00, then I don't have much scheduled for the rest of the day. Why, do you want to play?"

"I need to do something fun," Jamie moaned pathetically. "I feel like my life is so routine! If I don't get my blood pumping a little bit, I swear I'll go mad!"

"When do you have to be back home?"

"I don't care if I ever go home," she sulked.

"Okay, meet me at my house at 11:30. Dress warmly and wear boots if you have them. We'll go burn the carbon off your sparkplugs."

"You want to take a drive in my car?"

"Nope. Just be there."

At 11:30 on the dot, Ryan was sitting on her front steps. When Jamie pulled up, Ryan walked over to the Porsche and inspected her outfit. Jamie was wearing a distressed, brown leather, fleece-lined bomber jacket, a taupe-colored turtleneck and faded jeans. As she got out of the car, Ryan nodded her approval at her ankle length brown boots.

Ryan was wearing her usual jeans, a crew neck, sky blue sweater and her black leather jacket along with her low heeled black boots. She gave Jamie a sly look as she said, "I know just the prescription for boredom. Come with me, little girl."

She led Jamie over to the Harley, handed her the spare helmet and they climbed on. Jamie immediately slid her arms around Ryan's waist and got ready to take off.

Moments later they were heading over to Route 1. Even though she had been on the bike several times, they had never gone very far or very fast, and she found that she loved the excitement of the higher speed.

Ryan drove the bike just like she drove a car. She went as fast as possible, while being as careful as she could be. When traffic slowed, she would straddle the line between the number one and two lanes and slide right between the stalled cars.

Jamie knew that she should feel some level of fear or trepidation to be so thoroughly exposed at such a high rate of speed, but she had never felt calmer or safer. Every bit of anxiety left her body as they flew down the highway. She forgot all about her fights with Jack and the unhappiness with her parents. All she felt was warm and protected and safe. The wind was really quite intense, and she found herself tucking her head down and nestling it against Ryan's broad back. From her little cocoon, she truly felt impervious to harm. Her world was just Ryan's protective body, the bike thrumming between her legs and the freedom of the open road.

She wasn't at all sure where they were going, but eventually she saw the Golden Gate bridge looming in the distance. They crossed the structure and continued, staying on Highway 1 the whole while. The scenery was absolutely beautiful at this time of year. There were very few cars on the road as they passed the forested acres around Muir Woods. They kept going, and eventually the road wound down to Stinson Beach. Ryan pulled the bike into the deserted parking lot and hopped off. "Let's go for a walk," she said as she held out her hand to Jamie.

After Ryan had secured their helmets, they began to walk along on the hard-packed sand. Even though the day was beautiful, there was not another soul on the beach. The sun was bright, although the wind was stiff and cold as it blew in from the ocean. "I'm glad you told me to dress warmly," Jamie said as a chill shot down her spine.

Of course, Ryan noticed this and held her arm out in an inviting gesture. Jamie shot her a shy grin, but snuggled up against her anyway. They walked along in companionable silence for at least a mile, before Ryan turned around and guided her back. *I would feel odd talking so little with anyone else. But with Ryan, the silence is never uncomfortable. Even when we don't speak, I feel like we're communicating. Like now, she just wants me to feel free. She brought me here so I could feel how huge the world is, and she probably realized that would make me feel less confined.*

They neared the bike, and Ryan grabbed a thermos that she had stashed there. Leading Jamie to a picnic table, she sat down on the tabletop and urged Jamie onto the seat in front of her, so her body would block the wind.

Jamie looked up into her eyes and smiled at her, feeling calmer than she had in days. "Thanks for this," she sighed. "I really needed a break."

With a contemplative look on her face, Ryan busied herself for a minute, pouring a steaming cup of hot chocolate, which she offered to Jamie. "I'm not happy," she said, gazing at her friend.

"What? You're not happy? Why?"

"I'm not happy," Ryan said, "because there's something that's really bothering my best friend, and I'm not sure what it is or how to help her."

She maintained her steady gaze, not even blinking until Jamie nodded and said, "You know what's bothering me. I'm trying to find my own way, and neither my fiancé, nor my family are being very supportive."

Ryan's dark head shook, her long braid flying over her shoulder from the stiff breeze. "No, Jamie, I don't really know. You're always pretty vague about what the problem is. I don't want to pry, but it hurts me to see how restless and unsatisfied you seem. I really want to help you, but I don't know how to, since I don't know specifics."

Reaching up, Jamie patted the hand that rested on her shoulder. "I don't know that you can help," she admitted. "It's ... it's my problem."

"My problems always feel like they're less of a burden when I share them with someone," Ryan said. "I just want you to know that I'm interested and very willing to listen if you want to talk."

Jamie nodded again and was set to refuse the offer, when she looked into her friend's eyes and heard herself say, "I hate to admit it, but a very big part of the problem is sex."

"I have a lot of experience in that area," Ryan smiled. "Give it a go."

Looking down at the ground, Jamie fidgeted for a moment, trying to think of how to even frame her problem. "I, uhm ... I can't believe I'm admitting this to another person, but I don't like Jack's penis." She snuck a look up at Ryan, surprised to see a composed, open expression. "Is it really okay to talk about this?"

"Yes," Ryan insisted. "I worked on the teen talk line for years, Jamie. I've talked to as many young guys as girls. I know a lot about penises." She gave her a warm smile and added, "My knowledge is academic, but it's still valid."

"I'm just horribly embarrassed to admit this," Jamie grumbled. "It just doesn't make sense!"

"Is there something in particular that bothers you? Is it too big? Too small? Uncircumcised?"

The blonde head shook rapidly, hair flying in every direction. "No, no, nothing like that. It's fine, as penises go," she decided. "I just wish he didn't have one."

Ryan did her very best not to let her eyes go wide as they so very much wanted to. "You, uhm ... wish he didn't have one ... because?"

"Because I don't really like having intercourse," she grumbled. "I'm not sure why I don't like it, but I just don't care for the entire act. Not surprisingly, Jack's rather fond of it," she said, giving Ryan a wry look.

"Did you like it with other guys?" Ryan asked gently.

"Don't know. Never did it with any other guys," Jamie admitted.

"Oh." Ryan was beginning to regret her offer, feeling quite out of her depth at this point.

"Look," Jamie said. "I never had much desire before I met Jack. I certainly wasn't going to sleep with someone just because he wanted to."

"No, of course not," Ryan agreed. "But things were different with Jack?"

"Yes," she said firmly. "They really were. Before we were engaged, we'd spend hours just kissing." She sighed heavily. "That's what I really love."

"Mmm ..." Ryan smiled. "Kissing's my favorite thing. I've been known to climax from kissing alone."

Jamie's eyes widened as she said, "Now that would be nice. My problems would be over if I could do that."

Ryan looked at her for a moment and asked, "Do you think it's the way you have intercourse? I mean, maybe the position you use doesn't work for your physiology. Maybe the angles are wrong."

Shrugging her shoulders, Jamie admitted, "That's probably part of it. We're not really very experimental."

"Why don't you suggest a few things?" Ryan asked. "I'd be happy to tell you some of my favorite positions."

Jamie blinked at her, not having any idea of why Ryan would have favorite positions for intercourse. Afraid to find out, she shook her head. "It's more basic than that," she admitted. "I've got to own up to something here. We're not experimental because of me."

Ryan just cocked her head, forcing Jamie to continue.

"He's been really patient with me," she admitted. "He's had a lot of experience, and I think he's probably a pretty good lover. But I'm shy about things, and I'm pretty uptight. I think he's afraid to push me too far, to be honest. He's a patient guy — I mean, he had to be patient to wait for sex as long as he did. The problem is that neither of us is very good at talking about sex. Instead of talking about our needs, we try to manipulate each other. He tries to just push me a little bit, and I try to avoid it as much as possible. It's just not working, Ryan, and I'm about at the end of my rope."

"How about other kinds of sex?" Ryan asked. "Do you have oral sex?"

Jamie's head shook forcefully. "I can't," she gulped. "I just can't."

"Because ...?" Ryan asked, obviously determined to get a complete answer.

"I can't imagine anything more disgusting," she said with a shiver. "The thought of putting that thing in my mouth ..." She looked like she was about to be ill, making Ryan scratch her head in amazement.

"Does he go down on you?" she asked hesitantly.

"No. He's tried, plenty of times, but it seems unfair to let him try, since I'm not gonna reciprocate."

Ryan's brow furrowed, and she looked completely puzzled. "Did your parents do a number on you about sex? I mean, did they convince you that sex was evil or something?"

"No. They're both pretty relaxed. My nanny did most of the damage," she admitted.

Feeling entirely perplexed, Ryan said, "You know, a therapist can help you work out some of your fears about this. You actually sound a little phobic about penises."

"That's it!" Jamie cried, looking amazingly pleased. "I feel phobic about it. I know I'm not going to like it, so I start to tense up. When I tense up it feels a little painful, and when sex is painful ..."

"That makes perfect sense," Ryan agreed. "You really should consider talking to someone about this, Jamie. I'm sure you can get over your fears if you can talk about them."

The smaller woman nodded. "I suppose you're right, and if I felt better about sex and agreed to have sex more frequently, Jack would feel a lot better."

Ryan put a hand on her shoulder and asked, "Is that your biggest issue?"

"Sort of," she said. She paused a second and corrected herself, "Not really. We have a lot of issues — none of which we talk about much. He's a workaholic — just like my father," she admitted, "and I know it will only get worse as time goes on."

Ryan nodded her agreement. "Most people don't stop that habit unless they're forced to."

"He's not happy with the changes I'm making. Of course, neither is my father," she added.

Giving Jamie a very thoughtful look, Ryan commented, "There are a lot of similarities between your dad and Jack, aren't there?"

Jamie nodded. "Yeah. Too many. My dad's not a great husband, to be honest. You'd think I'd choose a guy that promised a more fulfilling life than my mother has."

"It's pretty common to choose someone that reminds you of your parent," Ryan agreed.

"I don't wanna be a cliché," Jamie grumbled.

Smiling warmly, Ryan assured her, "You don't have to be a cliché, Jamie. If you can find someone to talk to, you can make some changes here that both you and Jack will benefit from."

The smaller woman stood and handed Ryan the top from the thermos. "I guess you're right. I'll look into finding someone when I get back to Berkeley."

They walked back to the bike, and Ryan gazed at her and asked, "Are you ready?"

"To leave?" she replied with a wistful look on her face. "I guess so," she said, even though that was the last thing in the world she wanted to do.

"No," Ryan said, smiling broadly. "Are you ready to get started?"

"Get started doing what?"

"Having your first lesson, of course," she explained patiently.

"In what?"

"Your first lesson on how to drive a motorcycle," she said as though it were obvious.

"What?"

"I don't know of a better way to get your blood pumping than to put eighty cubic inches of power between your legs," she purred.

"Uhm … uhm …" Jamie stuttered as she tried to decide what was more stimulating: the thought of driving the bike or considering the clear sexual tone of Ryan's invitation.

"Come on," she urged as Jamie's feet seemed unable to propel her forward. "Once you've driven a Fat Boy, you'll never be the same."

"Fat Boy?" she gulped as she thought, *Is there a sexual allusion to every part of motorcycle riding?*

"That's the style of bike I have; it's a Harley Fat Boy."

"And you want me to drive it," she finally got out.

"Yep. Your blood is going to pump so hard, you might have to open a vein," she teased.

"Or several," Jamie squeaked out as she pictured her broken body strewn across the pavement.

"I guarantee you'll enjoy this," Ryan reassured her. "And I've never lost a student."

With her usual patient, thorough style, Ryan explained the bike and the process of riding it in great detail. Jamie listened patiently, interrupting with questions whenever one occurred to her. After a while, she got on the bike and went through the motions of shifting, braking and accelerating. After a half hour of constant detail, Ryan smiled and said, "Well, let's give it a try. I'll sit behind you, and we can give it a go."

Placing her hands on the hand grips, Jamie shifted around on the seat until she felt comfortable. It was particularly comforting to have Ryan nestled up against her back, and she realized that she felt really good sitting in front.

"Okay, I'm going to stand up a little and let you feel what it's like to hold her up. I'll be right here if you have any trouble. I promise," Ryan vowed as she began to stand.

Jamie's heart began to thump in her chest, but she concentrated and held on tight. She found, to her amazement, that it wasn't really that hard to balance such a huge weight if you stayed centered. "I feel okay," she said slowly.

"Great! Now I'll show you how to shift." Ryan provided a basic lesson in shifting and let her practice a few times, going through all of the gears one at a time. "Why don't we go for a little spin? I'll keep my hands on yours and guide you up and down the hill. All you have to do is shift when I tell you."

"That's all? You're sure?"

"Yep. Believe me, Jamie. I will not trick you into doing something you're uncomfortable with. I'll tell you what you need to do, and I swear I won't expect you to do one thing more than that. Okay?" she asked as she leaned over to make eye contact.

"Okay," she agreed, now completely reassured.

Ryan brought the bike to life and sat back while Jamie got comfortable. "Are you ready?" she asked as she glued herself to her back. A small nod was her answer. "Okay, put her into first gear," she instructed. As Jamie did so, Ryan's large hands covered hers, gripping the brakes firmly. "Now I'm going to let the brakes off, so the bike might move a little. I'm going to give it a little gas. Just relax and let me guide you," she said confidently.

Her stomach leapt to her throat, but she did her best to stay relaxed as the bike began to move. Ryan really was driving, but sitting in the front was a very heady experience. And the experience was made even headier by having her friend covering her body almost totally. Ryan's chin was hanging over Jamie's shoulder, and her chest was pressed tight against her back. Her warm pelvis was snuggled up against her butt, sending jolts of feeling down and between her legs. *Oh, I hope I don't have to walk anytime soon. I know my legs are completely useless.*

As they slowly climbed the small grade, Ryan called out when she wanted her to shift. By the time they reached the turnaround point, she was up in third gear, and she felt proud of her small accomplishment. Ryan was very enthusiastic in her praise, and Jamie was excited about the trip back down. She paid rapt attention to how Ryan's hands worked the throttle and the brakes, and by the time they reached the bottom, she was ready to go up again. They made the little one-mile loop three more times.

Jamie was having a ball and was more than happy to keep her knowledge right at this level. But Ryan raised the stakes when she said, "I think you're ready to move on."

"What do you mean?" she asked suspiciously.

"This time, you take the throttle and the brakes. I'll scoot up and shift for you, so you don't have too many things to think of."

"I don't know, Ryan," she demurred.

"I have total confidence in you, Jamie. I know you can do this easily," she insisted.

Somehow, Ryan's confidence was enough to bolster her own, and she finally agreed. Ryan had to scoot even closer to comfortably reach the shifter, but Jamie was not about to complain. She rested her hands on the grips and prepared herself mentally, and then she nodded to show her readiness. Ryan kept her feet on the ground until the last moment, to help balance the big bike. Jamie slowly turned the throttle, and the bike began to roll. Ryan kept her promise and kept her own hands down on the grips by her butt — letting Jamie have complete control. Jamie could feel her warm body pressed against hers, and she was reassured by the relaxed posture that her friend maintained. *If she's relaxed, I should be*, she thought. Within seconds they were at the turnaround, and she performed her next little test very well, slowly squeezing the brakes to bring the bike to a smooth halt.

Ryan's arms circled her waist for a quick hug as Jamié turned and beamed at her. "More!" she demanded as Ryan laughed heartily.

"It's addictive, isn't it?" she teased.

An enthusiastic nod was her clear reply. Ryan took the controls to negotiate the sharp turn, but quickly turned it over to her happy friend. They made a half-dozen circuits before Ryan's deep voice rumbled through her back, "Wanna go all the way?"

God, how does any woman refuse her? Oh, that's right, no one does refuse her! she thought wryly.

"O … o … okay," she stuttered. Ryan sat back an inch or two and let Jamie have full control. She put the bike into first and let her go one more time. The increase in sensation was small but significant. Now she was really in charge. If she hit the accelerator too hard or grabbed the front brake alone, they could easily be on the ground. But the responsibility didn't frighten her at this point. The slow buildup had reassured her at every step of the way, and now she just felt confident. They did three more circuits just the same way, but before they began the fourth, Ryan said, "This time, you negotiate the turn on your own."

Jamie gulped noticeably, but she nodded slightly and started up again. Her heart was pounding when she neared the top, but she downshifted smoothly, just like she had seen Ryan do. When the bike was going nice and slow, she turned the wheel and leaned over just a tiny bit, turning the bike perfectly. When they reached the bottom, Ryan squeezed her until she had trouble getting a breath. "I'm so proud of you!" she said, leaning over to show a high-wattage grin. "That was so awesome, Jamie!" she yelled. "You are a total natural!"

Jamie could not help but catch the enthusiasm of her friend. She jumped off as Ryan tipped the bike a bit to give her better egress, then threw her arms straight into the air as she ran around like a two-year-old. "I am *so* pumped!" she shouted.

Ryan had secured the bike on its stand, and she threw her arms around Jamie's small waist and picked her up as she began to twirl her in a tight circle. "Wasn't that the most wonderful feeling?" Ryan demanded as the world flew by.

It took all of Jamie's willpower not to shout, *No, this is!*

⌘

It was nearly 9:00 when they reached the city after stopping in Larkspur for dinner. As they approached the Marina district, Ryan pulled over and turned in her seat. "Do you mind if I stop by Tracy's apartment for a second? She's supposed to fly in this afternoon, and I told her I might come by tonight."

"Jeez, Ryan, we didn't have to stay at the restaurant that long! I don't want to interfere with your relationship."

As she turned even more fully in her seat, Ryan locked her eyes onto Jamie's. "There's not one minute of this day that I would cut out. Don't demean our relationship like that," she said emphatically. "My friendships are just as important to me as my relationship with Tracy."

"Ryan, I'm sorry," Jamie said quickly. "Our relationship is incredibly important to me."

"I just can't stand people who immediately drop their friends when they get into a serious relationship," Ryan admitted. "I like to nurture my friendships just as much as I do a sexual relationship." She allowed her face to curve into a crooked grin as she started over. "Do you mind if I stop by Tracy's for a second?"

"Not at all," Jamie smiled.

A few moments later, Ryan was buzzing the apartment. They walked up to the third floor unit together, even though Jamie felt a bit uncomfortable. Tracy was a little surprised to see Jamie, but she greeted her warmly. "Well, well," she said as she looked them over. "What do we have here?" she asked as she wrapped her arms around Ryan for a very friendly kiss. "You've already had dinner," she said as she narrowed her eyes a bit. She leaned in for another kiss, which they held for a bit longer than Jamie was comfortable with. "And dessert," she added.

If she starts looking for what kind of toothpaste she uses, I'm out of here!

"So, where were you little scamps all day?" she asked. "I called your house and your pager, Ms. O'Flaherty," she said as she placed her hands on her hips.

"Did you really?" Ryan asked as she pulled the device from her waistband to check it. "I didn't get a page, Tracy. Did you need something?"

"No, I didn't, really. I called to tell you I wouldn't be home until about 9:00. I actually got in right before you got here."

"Good. I hate to inconvenience you," she said apologetically. "But the answer to your previous question is that we were up in Marin by Stinson Beach. I taught Jamie how to ride my bike," she said proudly. "And she was an excellent student," she added.

"Ooo, tell me all about it," she demanded as she pushed Ryan down onto a chair. "Let me get you both a drink first. Do you want a beer or some wine?"

"I'll have some wine," Jamie said.

"Water for me," Ryan added.

A few moments later, Tracy came back to the living room with wine for her and Jamie, along with Ryan's water. There was seating for seven in the spacious, well-decorated apartment, but Tracy chose to sit on Ryan's lap. "I've missed you," she said quietly as she placed another kiss on Ryan's lips.

Ryan gazed up at her with a sweet, shy smile. "I missed you, too," she replied as she sat up a little bit for another warm kiss. They were obviously used to sitting in this position because Ryan looked completely comfortable. She was sitting on a deep, overstuffed, upholstered chair, and Tracy was leaning against her chest with her legs draped over the arm. She had her arm behind Ryan's neck, and Ryan's arm cradled her back. All in all, they looked very comfortable and relaxed with each other. It didn't seem to bother either of them that Jamie was there, even though she was still a little uncomfortable.

They had just been dating for a little over a month, but they were already finishing each other's sentences and other cute little girlfriend things. Tracy would occasionally brush Ryan's bangs from her forehead or push a lock of hair behind her ear. Ryan teased her quite a bit and seemed to know exactly where each of her most ticklish spots was. She seemed to delight in holding her down with her strong right arm while her left hand got in under her ribs or just behind her knee to make her squeal.

When Tracy spoke, Ryan would look up at her with barely disguised fascination. She would cock her head and focus intently on her as though she had some vitally important information to impart. *They really are cute together*, Jamie thought. *If I really care for her as much as I think I do, I'll be happy for her. Even though Tracy takes her away from me sometimes, it's important for Ryan to have this. I get my needs fulfilled by Jack. Or at least I should,* she thought disparagingly. *Ryan has needs, too, and her needs aren't limited to sex. She needs intimacy and romance and tenderness, and it looks like she's getting that from Tracy.*

At around 10:00, Ryan decided that it was time to go. Jamie wanted them to have a few moments alone, so she excused herself to use the restroom. She was gone as long as she thought was polite, but when she walked into the hallway, it was clear that they were a long way from completing their goodnights. Ryan had the brunette backed up against the wall, and Tracy's arms were draped languidly around her neck. Neither of Ryan's hands was visible, and Jamie could only guess that they were palming Tracy's firm butt. It was obvious that Ryan was pulling her forward by the hips, and equally obvious that Tracy did not mind one little bit. Both of them were uttering soft moans as they frantically devoured each other's mouths.

Oh, boy, now what? I guess I can go back into the bathroom, but other than shaving my legs, I can't think of anything else to do in there. But just as she was beginning to turn to go back in, Ryan pulled away with a few loud, wet kisses. "Gotta go, baby," she whispered. Jamie was afraid that Tracy was going to collapse right where she stood. Her legs looked a bit rubbery, and her eyes remained closed. She pulled Ryan towards her and whispered something into her ear that caused Ryan to say, "I know; I'm sure I will, too." She then grasped her head and placed several more searing kisses on her lips before she let her go. Ryan leaned her forehead against her girlfriend's and murmured, "Now I know I will," as she gave her one last tender kiss. "See you tomorrow, baby," she said as she patted her cheek in a loving fashion.

"Bye, Jamie," Tracy breathed as the wide-eyed woman followed Ryan out.

"See you, Tracy. Thanks for the wine."

"Anytime," she replied as she weakly waved a hand.

⌘

Ryan slid her arm around Jamie's shoulders as they walked back down the stairs. "Are you okay?" the smaller woman asked tentatively.

"Yeah, why wouldn't I be?"

"I thought you might need to … uhm … stay over," she hesitantly suggested. "I could easily grab a cab back to your house."

"Nope. I want to go home," she replied easily.

God, I'm so turned on I ache, and all I did was watch for a moment!

When they got to the bike Ryan teasingly asked, "Wanna drive?"

"I think I'll stick to less-populated areas if you don't mind," she replied as she gave her a little pat.

Fifteen minutes later, they pulled up in front of Ryan's house. As they both got off, Jamie gave her a big hug and a kiss on both cheeks. "I had one of the most delightful days of my life, Ryan. Thank you so much for sharing it with me."

"You're welcome, Jamie. I had a great time, myself. Do you want to come in for some cocoa before your drive?"

"No, I'm sure you need to get to bed."

"Well, I do have a date," she admitted with a rakish grin.

"A date!"

"Yeah," she replied as she held up her left hand and wiggled her fingers. "I'm so turned on, I could scream!"

That makes two of us, buddy, she thought.

⌘

Lying in bed just a few minutes later, Ryan's left hand got busy, driving her arousal until she was near orgasm. Thoughts of Tracy's warm mouth and searching tongue filled her mind, and she abandoned herself to them, letting the images combine with the scent of the woman she could still smell on her skin. She was seconds from climax when the memory changed to the sensation she had when her thighs were wrapped around Jamie's legs just a few hours earlier. As she crested, she could feel the softness of those pink lips where they had just kissed her cheek. "Oh, God," she moaned throatily, as much from dismay as pleasure. She pulled her hand from herself and slapped it to the bed, grumbling, *Don't start with this again! She's engaged! She's in love! She's straight!*

Her brain heard all of her reasons, just as she'd heard them each time before, but her body just wanted to enjoy the afterglow of the sense memories of that toned body, those warm lips and the delightful scent that was Jamie's alone.

Face it, Ryan. You couldn't pick a worse person to have a crush on. She's a straight girl who's just having some trouble getting used to being in a relationship. You're in deep with Tracy, and that's where you've got to focus.

Just a straight girl, she repeated, in a familiar mantra. *A straight girl who hates penises. A straight girl who hates penises?*

⌘ Chapter Twelve

DAVIS & GRAY TRADITIONALLY HELD A VERY LARGE, VERY ELEGANT New Year's Eve party for partners and their spouses. Jamie had never been invited, and she had never regretted the oversight. But this year her father had broached the subject just after Thanksgiving. After the disagreement they'd had, she was more amenable to doing small things to please him, but she was very leery of attending this party. She rather doubted that Jack would want to go, since he seemed almost agoraphobic lately, but she decided to ask him anyway, just so she could tell her father that she had brought it up.

She was as surprised as she had ever been when Jack's reaction turned out to be not only favorable, but downright enthusiastic. "I think that would be a lot of fun," he said with more enthusiasm than she had heard all year. "It'll give us a chance to get dressed up for a change. I would love to be able to dance with you when you're all sexy looking," he said wistfully. *Dance*, she thought with surprise. *He dances?*

As the day approached, Jamie spent a fairly enjoyable afternoon with her mother, shopping for new dresses. Catherine had enough formalwear to clothe a small, fashion-deprived country, but she hated to wear the same dress twice, so she needed something, too. At her current weight, Jamie could easily have worn one of her mother's dresses, but Catherine would not hear of it. "My things are far too mature for you, dear. You need something that fits your age and your style." And so they descended on the small, elegant shops of the South Bay, both finding selections that suited their individual tastes.

On the day of the party, she waited until she was alone in the house to page Ryan. She had just spoken to her the day before, but she hadn't remembered to ask her about her plans for the night.

Minutes later her phone chirped. "You rang?" Ryan's cheerful voice asked.

"I forgot to wish you a happy New Year," she said. "I couldn't let that oversight ruin my evening."

"Your evening? Ha! What about my evening? I would have been the one without your good wishes. You could've ruined a whole year for me,

Jamie," she teased. "I hope you're more careful in the future!"

"Maybe I should just call you every day and give you my good wishes."

"Now, that's the best idea you've had in weeks," Ryan said happily. "I'll expect your call from here on in. So, what are you up to tonight?"

"We're going to a big, formal party at the Fairmont Hotel," she said with much less enthusiasm than Ryan thought normal.

"Well, that sounds pretty cool. Do you have a new dress?" she asked, knowing Jamie's penchant for shopping.

"Yep. Navy blue velvet. I look pretty good in it if I do say so myself," she said with a light chuckle.

"I've known you since August, and I've yet to see you look anything but fabulous," Ryan said. "But I would bet navy blue velvet is just perfect for you, given your hair color and skin tone. Jack will be the envy of every guy there."

"So what are you two up to?" Jamie asked, momentarily nonplussed that Ryan had obviously spent some time assessing her physical attributes.

"We're going to a big party at the Mark Hopkins," Ryan said.

"Really? That surprises me a bit. I thought you didn't like large gatherings."

"I don't. But you have to make some sacrifices for a relationship," she said wisely.

Tell that to Jack, she thought, but decided to keep her gripes to herself. "Is this for girls only?"

"Yep. It's put on by some promoters who host big weekend parties in the city. I told Tracy I'd take her anywhere she wanted to go, and this is what she chose."

"Do *you* have a new dress?" Jamie taunted.

"I have my version of a new dress," she conceded with a little laugh.

"And what might that be? Did you find formal jeans?"

"No, but that does sound appealing. Maybe I should have spent more than ten minutes shopping."

"Come on, tell me what you bought. I'm not familiar with formal lesbian attire."

"Well, the dress code is pretty darned flexible. I guarantee the diversity of my group will surpass yours," she teased.

"Spill it, O'Flaherty."

"Okay, I bought some black leather pants and a white pleated shirt — kind of a woman's tuxedo shirt. It's got little, bitty, black studs rather than buttons." She paused for a moment and said, "Jamie, are you still there?"

Jamie slapped her head to make her brain start to work again. "My cell phone must have blanked out for a second," she said hurriedly. "Your outfit sounds cute. I'd like to see it someday." *Yeah, like tonight,* she thought dejectedly. *I'd rather tag along on Ryan's date than hang out with a bunch of lawyers. And I sure can't imagine a person who would look better in leather pants.*

"I hope you have a very good time tonight, Jamie. I send you every good wish for the new year, but you'll have to wait for your kiss," she promised.

"Happy New Year, Ryan. I hope you and Tracy have a wonderful evening. Make sure you pay attention, so you can tell me all about the unique outfits."

"Will do, buddy. I'll call you tomorrow."

⌘

Later that night, Jamie came down the stairs to the appreciative gazes of both her father and Jack. "Wow," was all that Jack could get out.

"You look wonderful, honey," Jim gushed as he walked to the stairs to kiss her cheek.

"Thank you both. You look pretty wonderful yourself," she said softly as she leaned in for Jack's kiss. He had purchased a tuxedo for himself, figuring that he would need one once he started his full-time job. He asked his law review partner to help him pick it out, and Jamie had to admit that Natalie's taste was exquisite. The suit was quite traditional with a shawl collar, which set his broad shoulders off quite attractively. It was impeccably tailored, and Jamie knew that it had cost more than he could comfortably afford, but she had to admit that it looked fabulous on him. His wing collar, white shirt and black tie completed the traditional look, but he looked anything but stodgy. She thought that he had never looked more handsome, and she began to feel a little better about attending the party. *If he cares enough to dress this carefully, he must really want to attend,* she thought. *Maybe he really does want to cut loose for a change.*

Catherine made her entrance a short time later and gracefully accepted the compliments of the small crowd. She also looked particularly lovely in a deep emerald green, silk cocktail dress which showed off both her figure and her pale blonde hair to good advantage.

"Shall we?" Jim asked as he took Catherine's arm to lead her to the waiting limo.

⌘

The evening started off well enough. They sat at a table with the other senior members of the firm, but the ambient noise forced them to speak mostly to each other. As soon as dinner was finished, Jim invited Jack to join him and the other senior partners down in the bar to have a cigar. Jamie watched in horror as Jack immediately agreed. *He doesn't smoke!* she thought in alarm. *That is such a disgusting habit! And he'll reek of the smell all night long,* she groused to herself.

She was in quite a little funk when Catherine leaned over and said, "You may as well get used to it, honey. These events are not made for us. It's just an extension of the office. Our job is to look good and not get drunk enough to cause a scene," she laughed wryly at her own joke, but Jamie caught the bitter edge to her voice. "I'm having vodka tonight. How about you?"

"I think I'll stick with champagne," she said since she had already had a glass.

Catherine called the waiter over and signaled for him to come closer, "I'd like an Absolut on the rocks and a bottle of decent champagne."

"We're serving ..."

"I know what you're serving, but that's not what we're drinking," she said, giving him a pleasant but determined look. "I'd like a bottle of Cristal, 1994 if you have it. I can sign for it separately," she added.

"Yes, ma'am," he said as he snapped to it. A few minutes later, Jamie was sipping the excellent champagne, while various partners and their spouses paid homage to her mother.

When they were alone for a moment, Jamie asked, "Do you really know all of these people?"

"I know quite a few of them. We've been friends with some of these people since we were your age," she laughed. "But many of them are complete strangers. I have no idea why they insist on talking to me. It's not like your father quizzes me at the end of the evening, 'So, Catherine, did all of the partners kiss your ring?'"

Jamie laughed at her mother's wry sense of humor. *She's so much more fun when Daddy's not around,* she thought to herself.

After a while, a well-dressed woman who looked a little older than Catherine came up and asked, "Could I have a word with you in private, dear?"

Catherine looked like she wanted to refuse, but she got up and followed the woman to the side of the room.

It was almost 10:00 when the men returned. They reeked of cigar smoke, and Jamie felt a little nauseous when Jack sat next to her and spoke in her direction. But she had no interest in making a big deal about it, so she tried to ignore the strong odor. After a few minutes, he asked her to dance, and she accepted mostly to see if he really knew how. They had never been in a situation that required they dance, and she hoped that he had some idea of what to do, since she didn't think it would be wise to lead.

Her chin nearly hit her chest as he gracefully placed one hand behind her back and grasped her other hand in his. As the music started, he led her around the floor as though he had been dancing for years. He seemed so self-assured and elegant that she had to question her long-held perceptions of him. They didn't speak as they danced, but that didn't bother her one bit. She just let him lead her with his calm but determined manner.

They remained on the dance floor for a several more songs, and when they returned to their table, he looked at her with his normal, boyish face and whispered, "How'd I do?"

She sat back in her chair to regard him for a moment. He looked exactly like a young boy seeking approval from his teacher for a well-written essay. "You dance beautifully, Jack," she said sincerely. "I had no idea that you knew how."

"I didn't," he said rather proudly.

"But how ...?"

"When you invited me, I knew I couldn't stumble around looking stupid, so I signed up for lessons," he said with a big, boyish grin.

"You ... you took dance lessons?"

"Yeah. It's important to look like you belong, Jamie," he explained patiently.

"I think I get that," she said, trying to keep the edge from her voice. "But when did you have time to take lessons?"

"Natalie and I took a course together. She didn't know how, either, so it seemed like a good way to learn," he explained.

"You took dance lessons?" she asked for the second time, still unable to get her mind around the concept.

"Yes, Jamie, this evening is important to me," he said as he gave her a little squeeze.

She had never considered herself slow. As a matter of fact, she usually thought that she caught on rather quickly. That's why this revelation hit her with such force. *How stupid am I? I honestly believed he wanted to come to this party to be with me!* She silently berated herself for a few minutes, and shortly thereafter her father whisked Jack away for "face time" with some of the other important people at the party.

Sitting alone at the table with the boisterous crowd around her, she suddenly felt more alone than she could ever remember feeling. The walls of the huge banquet room seemed to be closing in on her, and she fervently wished that she were at home alone just to get away from the noise and the emptiness. Catherine returned, slipping into her chair soundlessly. Turning to her mother, she caught a look of unguarded despair on the older woman's normally placid face. The look was so heart-rending that Jamie had to turn away. "You'll never survive a lifetime of these events if you don't learn how to drink, Jamie," her mother's voice floated past her ear a few minutes later. "You've barely had a full glass."

Just then the waiter ambled past. He caught Jamie's eye, and she mumbled, "Morphine and soda, please."

⌘

Ryan was dressed and ready to roll at nine o'clock. Martin had insisted that she take his truck for the evening, since he would be at work and would have no need for it. "It's not wise to be gallivanting around on New Year's Eve on a motorcycle," he decreed. Rather than risk worrying him, Ryan had accepted his offer and dropped him off at work in the afternoon.

Waiting for Tracy to buzz her up, she gazed at the gleaming shine of her boots, pleased that she had taken the time to polish them.

As the door to the apartment opened, Tracy pulled her in and spent a moment looking her up and down. Ryan patiently waited for her to finish and was rewarded with a low whistle. "You look so totally hot," she purred as she pulled Ryan in for her first kiss of the night.

When she broke free, Ryan stood back and regarded her date. Tracy looked more beautiful than Ryan had ever seen her, and that was saying a lot. She wore a heavy, white, silk tank top, and a very short, very tight, black velvet skirt. Shimmery black stockings showed off every inch of her long legs, and her two-inch heels brought her up much closer to Ryan's hungry mouth. Her shoulder-length, chestnut hair was swept up off her face in a tight chignon, and the attractive style highlighted the delicate planes of her lovely face. "You look so beautiful," Ryan murmured softly as they came together in another series of passionate kisses. Ryan wasn't sure if it was Tracy's luminous beauty or her mesmerizing perfume, but something was ratcheting her desire out of control. She knew that if they did not leave soon, they would see the new year in from a horizontal position. "We'd better go," she said softly as she finally pulled her mouth from Tracy's voracious one.

"Maybe we should just watch the countdown on TV," the brunette suggested. "It's very dangerous to be out on New Year's, you know."

"It's more dangerous in here," Ryan smirked. "Let's go, babe," she said as she held out a matching, collarless, black velvet jacket for Tracy to slip into.

⌘

By the time Jack returned to ask for another dance, Jamie could hardly feel her feet, but she was not in the mood for a lecture, so she sucked it up and gamely followed him out to the dance floor. She was a bit surprised to see her mother being led out seconds later, and she thought, *Now being displayed for your viewing pleasure, Catherine and Jamie Evans. They walk, they talk, they dance!*

⌘

Ryan had been to many lesbian dances and parties, but this was by far the most elegant event that she had ever attended. The room was decorated beautifully, and the music was not ear-splittingly loud.

Almost as soon as they entered the room, Tracy led her to the dance floor, and they spent a good half hour moving against each other so sensually that Ryan knew her resolve didn't have much of a chance of holding out tonight.

They had both agreed to hold off on having sex until they were sure of their feelings for each other, but Ryan was getting clear signals that Tracy was changing the rules. At first she wasn't sure if she was reading her signals correctly, but the sultry glances were a good first clue. Even if she had not noticed the glances, the torrid kisses would have been another indication. But no matter how oblivious Ryan was, she could not ignore the stocking-covered thigh that kept sliding between her legs. Tracy grabbed onto her hips and pulled her in close, twitching her hips in time to the music, while that insistent thigh kept pressing into Ryan's groin. By the third song, Ryan's head was throbbing from her unquenched desire, and her will was way past weak.

Just to clear her head, Ryan suggested they have a drink. Tracy agreed and immediately used the opportunity to push Ryan against the rear wall and latch onto her mouth again. By the time Ryan came up for breath, she was all in favor of seeing if she could snag a room upstairs.

But just when she was about to suggest that they head home, Tracy pulled her back onto the dance floor and began the delicious torture once again. "Give me strength," Ryan moaned to whatever saint was in the neighborhood.

⌘

At 11:50 Jamie focused on the slightly blurred vision of her mother. "Will they come back at midnight, or do we kiss each other?"

"Oh, they'll be back," Catherine replied knowingly. "It wouldn't look right to leave us alone then."

Even from her fog, Jamie could tell that her mother really didn't look very drunk at all. *How in the hell does she do that?* she marveled. *She's had as many as I've had, and she's drinking vodka. That's three times as much alcohol as champagne.* As she regarded her for a moment, she really let herself see the vacant, almost despondent look in her mother's eyes. *Why is she so unhappy?* she wondered. *Is it her life or her self, or is it just her biology?*

Jack and Jim flew up with three minutes to spare. "Miss me?" he whispered into Jamie's ear as he pulled her to the dance floor to join with all the other couples as they welcomed in the new year.

"Desperately," she replied in the same flat monotone her mother used with her father.

"Good," he smiled as he wrapped her in his arms and kissed her with enough intensity to shock her out of her fog.

Oh, right, she said to herself as she caught her breath. *He has to look like he's passionate.*

⌘

The stroke of midnight found Tracy looking up into Ryan's eyes and murmuring in a soft voice, "Happy New Year, Ryan," as she pulled her head down for a tender, emotion-filled kiss.

Ryan lost herself in the kiss, which seemed to go on for hours. Letting Tracy explore her mouth, her mind wandered to consider her feelings for the lovely woman. She had to admit that Tracy was exactly what she had been seeking. She was a lot of fun, smart, sexy, very passionate and probably great in bed. As Ryan's mouth was sensually invaded by Tracy's searching tongue, she rethought that statement. *No, she's definitely gonna be great in bed.*

⌘

266

By 12:30 the Davis & Gray party was winding down. The younger partners and their spouses were still on the dance floor, but the more senior members of the firm were starting to depart. Jim approached and asked, "A few of the managing committee members want to have a nightcap over at the Top of the Mark. Will you two join us, or would you rather stay here and dance?"

Jamie knew the answer before the question was fully out of her father's mouth. "We'd love to join you," Jack answered without even looking at her.

⌘

As they waited for the elevator to the top floor of the Mark Hopkins, Jamie turned to scan the sign that listed the location of every event. She perked up when she saw the event that most interested her. *Hmm, Ryan's party is on the lower level.* "I'm going to use the rest room down here, Jack. I'll be up in a few minutes. Will you just order me some sparkling water?" He looked like he knew he should wait with her, but all of the big kids were going to play, and he didn't want to be left out. "Go on," she urged. "I'll be up in a few minutes." His smile of relief was actually mildly funny, and she patted his cheek and stood on her tiptoes for a kiss. "See you soon," she promised as she started off in the direction of the rest rooms.

After a quick stop to check her makeup, she made her way down to the lower level. It didn't take long to figure out which party was Ryan's. Women of every shape, size and color were streaming in and out of the largest room on the floor. Jamie noted with relief that no one was checking tickets, so she slid right in and looked around for a few minutes.

She was just about to give up when she felt a warm presence behind her. A deep voice floated past her ear, "Are you here to learn the secret handshake?"

Jamie's entire face broke into a delighted grin as she turned to greet her friend. Ryan's arms enveloped her in a hug, and she relaxed into the embrace, feeling all of the tension leave her body. "Mmm, you smell good," Jamie said as she pulled away. "And you look fabulous," she enthused, standing back to get a good look.

"Actually, it's Tracy who smells good. I just smell like her," she said with a lascivious grin. "Boy, Jack must be unconscious somewhere to let you get away tonight," Ryan mused. "You look as good as your lasagna tastes."

Jamie playfully slapped her on the shoulder as she looked around. "Speaking of dates, where's yours?"

"I just left her in a ridiculously long line for the restroom. Where is Jack, by the way?"

"He's with the other fascinating conversationalists from Davis & Gray. They're having a drink while they try to bore each other to death."

"Uh-oh," Ryan said playfully. "Is somebody grouchy?"

"I shouldn't be," she said with an embarrassed smirk. "But I had the crazy notion that Jack wanted to be with me tonight."

"And he doesn't?"

"Nope. It's just business."

"I'm sorry, Jamie," she said as she squeezed her shoulder. "I wish you were having more fun."

"That's okay. I need to get used to this, since it will be my life for the next several hundred years."

Ryan gripped her shoulders and, without allowing herself time to censor her words, said, "It doesn't have to be that way, Jamie. You don't have to do anything that you don't want to do." Her grip increased as the fire burned in her eyes, "You deserve so much more."

Jamie fell into her arms, letting Ryan's strong embrace soothe her raw nerves. They held each other for a long time, not speaking, just relishing the closeness.

As Ryan released her, Jamie looked up with a painfully sad look in her eyes. "I've got to get back. Within an hour or two, they'll miss me."

"Only a fool would treat you so casually," Ryan murmured, pulling her in for another hug.

"Thank you," Jamie whispered as she drew away. "It really helps to know that someone thinks I'm special."

"I do, and I always will," Ryan pledged, tilting Jamie's head up with her fingers. "Happy New Year," she said as she bent and placed a soft kiss on her lips.

Jamie felt as though a spike had been driven into her heart. Every instinct cried out, telling her to wrap her arms around Ryan and never let her go. But she knew that wouldn't — couldn't — happen, then or ever. She was engaged and would be married in a little more than a year, and Ryan was committed to building a relationship with Tracy.

She stifled the tears than threatened to flow, her sadness overwhelming. Patting Ryan gently on the cheek, she whispered, "Happy New Year to you, too. I hope you and Tracy have a wonderful year together." Another quick hug and she was gone.

⌘

Minutes later Tracy was back. As she wrapped her arms around Ryan for another deep kiss, the taller woman could feel the passion flare up again.

"Why don't we get a room?" Tracy purred.

Ryan looked down into her sultry, dark eyes and wrestled with her conscience. Tracy was definitely a little drunk, but Ryan thought that she was still able to make thoughtful decisions. Ryan's body urged her to take her upstairs and ravage her all night long, but a nagging voice kept trying to be heard.

Leading her to the bar, Ryan ordered her first real drink of the night. Sipping her whiskey, Ryan looked at her date and lightly grasped Tracy's hand. "Are you really ready to be intimate?"

A slow nod accompanied by a sly grin was ample evidence of her readiness. "Are you?" she asked as she squeezed Ryan's hand.

"I want to," she murmured. "I really, really want to." Tracy leaned forward and took Ryan's lower lip between her teeth, nibbling seductively on the tender flesh. Shaking her head, Ryan managed to say, "I made you a promise when we started to date, and I want to be sure we're both aware of where we stand."

"I'm not very interested in standing tonight — or tomorrow for that matter," Tracy replied with a leer. "I want to take you to bed and not let you out until school starts."

"But that's two weeks!" Ryan squeaked.

"I know," she whispered. "It'll take me that long to love you thoroughly."

Amazed to hear the words come from her mouth, Ryan said, "I don't think I'm ready yet, Tracy. I made a promise, and until I'm ready to commit to you, I don't feel right about it."

Tracy's hand was wandering up her thigh in the most alluring manner that Ryan had ever felt. "I release you from your promise," she purred. "Turn your vigilant little conscience off and follow your desire. It's okay if you don't love me yet — or ever for that matter. I just want you to take me home and love every little inch of me — slowly."

"Oh, God," Ryan moaned weakly as she felt her resolve float away in a cloud of erotic thoughts.

⌘

The last drink was obviously the kicker, since Tracy was sound asleep with her face pressed against the window of the truck by the time they reached the Marina. She woke when they reached her apartment, and as soon as they hit the door, she was on Ryan like a hungry dog on a bone. But the drive and Tracy's obvious intoxication allowed Ryan to step back and assess the situation, and the erotic temptation was quite a bit less than it had been at the dance. She lovingly undressed her friend with only a momentary desire to jump on top of her. After waiting for Tracy to finish in the bathroom, Ryan guided her back to the bed. "Aren't you going to undress?" the smaller woman asked hazily.

"I think these leather pants will feel really good against your skin," Ryan said softly. "Let's try it and see."

Tracy was obviously in the mood for a little experiment, since she dropped face forward onto the bed. Ryan climbed on top of her thighs and forced herself to concentrate when Tracy let out a sexy, low moan. *God, she has a gorgeous body,* she thought as she fought to keep her desire at a manageable level. Ryan began to massage that gorgeous naked body, starting at her shoulders and slowly working her way down. By the time she reached her waist, she heard the soft, deep breathing that signaled sleep. Leaning over Tracy's prone body, she kissed her cheek and slid off her hips. She covered her with the sheet and duvet and carefully removed all of the pins that held her hair up. When she finished, she ran her fingers through the silky tresses and thought, *I would love to have that hair trailing over my breasts right about now, but a promise is a promise!*

⌘

Tracy had been even more inebriated than Ryan had guessed, and when they spoke on the phone the following day, she confessed to a near-complete blackout of the events of the evening before. She was embarrassed to admit that she didn't even know if they'd had sex, and Ryan hastened to assure her that all she'd done was put her to bed.

The O'Flaherty's were having their usual New Year's Day celebration, and Ryan was only a little miffed when Tracy begged off the invitation to join them. Ryan assumed she must be horribly hung over, but a bit of doubt remained when she considered that Tracy always had a convenient excuse to avoid doing things with the entire family. *Oh, well, maybe she's just shy,* she decided.

⌘

As the days of winter break crawled by, Jamie felt close to leaving so many times that she lost count. The most frustrating thing was that her parents were absolutely no different than they had ever been. She felt like a blind person who has been given the gift of sight: seeing things that annoyed her in the interactions between her parents, in the way they treated her, even in the way they treated the staff. The insight was driving her crazy, and she yearned to go back home to Berkeley.

Things were no better with Jack. She felt absolutely trapped – and seeing him work the room at the New Year's party simply confirmed that he was merely a young clone of her father. Her stomach clenched painfully when she pictured herself at forty, imagining the same deadness in her soul that she saw so clearly in her mother's eyes.

The only thing helping her to maintain her sanity was Ryan. They started working out three times a week, and after her session, Ryan took her over to the big, empty parking lot of the local high school and patiently explained more of the intricacies of the motorcycle, allowing Jamie to ride the big bike for at least an hour each time. A week before break was over, she surprised her completely by driving her over to the Department of Motor Vehicles and announcing that Jamie had an appointment to take her driver's test for her motorcycle license.

To Jamie's shock, she passed the test easily, and after breezing through the written test, she proudly displayed the temporary license to her beaming friend. "I'm proud of you," Ryan said fondly as she enveloped her in a generous hug.

"This was a wonderful gift, Ryan," Jamie said sincerely. "Spending your time with me and being so patient has really made me feel special."

"You are special," she insisted, leaning over to kiss her lightly on her cheek.

Jamie looked up at her, seeing the affection written on Ryan's face and knowing that their relationship was the best one in her life.

⌘

As she got ready for a bike ride on the Thursday before she was to leave Hillsborough, she heard a knock on the door. Before she could reply, her mother opened the door and popped her head into the room. Jamie was only wearing her underwear, and her mother's jaw dropped in pure shock. "My God, Jamie what have you done to your body?" she asked in alarm.

"What do you mean?" she replied defensively, grabbing her jersey to yank it over her head.

"You know perfectly well what I mean," her mother replied in an uncharacteristically stern tone.

"I've lost some weight, but I'll put it back on soon," she replied, feeling very uncomfortable at this invasion of her privacy.

"That's not what I mean. Your weight is fine, Jamie, it's those muscles. You've done this intentionally, and I want to know why."

Jamie was baffled at her mother's behavior. *Now she's interested in me?* "I've been working out quite a bit, Mother. I'm going to participate in a big, charity bike ride, and I need to get in shape to complete it."

"That makes no sense at all, Jamie. What does riding a bike have to do with looking like this?" she accused as she pointed at Jamie's sinewy body.

"I need to be in good shape overall to be strong enough to ride five hundred miles. I look a lot more muscular than normal because of the weight that I've lost," she said meekly.

"Do you mean to tell me that you plan on riding that bicycle of yours over five hundred miles?" she nearly shouted. "I'll not have it, Jamie. That is a ridiculous feat to even attempt. There is no reason on earth for you to do that, and I forbid you to even try."

Jamie was absolutely dumbfounded. She stared at her mother for a few long moments. Neither woman spoke as the gulf between them widened perceptibly. Jamie simply turned and removed her jersey, then folded it and put on a T-shirt. She then began to pack up her clothes in silence.

Her mother stared at her back for a few minutes. "Jamie, I want your word that you will stop this nonsense right now."

"I can't do that, Mother. I refuse to lie to you just to ease your mind. I make my own choices in life, and this is a choice I have made that I intend to pursue. I would prefer that you support me, but I don't require it."

"Don't forget that we do support you, Jamie — quite well if I do say so myself. I believe we do have a right to express our opinions about your choices so long as you are our dependent."

She picked up her heavy suitcase and dragged it towards the door. "Mother, I appreciate your financial support, but we both know that I don't need it." She continued down the stairs, leaving her mother to stare at her in shocked silence from the doorway of her bedroom.

As soon as she was in her car, she dialed Ryan's pager. Moments later she heard the reassuring tones over her cell phone. "Hi, are you going to be at home for a while?" Jamie inquired.

"Yeah, until 6:00 or so. I'm having dinner with Tracy. Why, do you want to come over?"

"Yeah, if you don't mind. I just had a really bad fight with my mother, and I need to talk about it," she replied shakily.

"I'll be waiting for you."

⌘

When Jamie arrived an hour later, she saw Ryan rollerblading down the street at breakneck speed. *I can't believe she can blade up these hills. I have trouble walking up them! Damn, I bet my mother would love her body.*

"I think I understand why your father had to take you to the emergency room all the time if this is the kind of stuff you used to do," she chided her sweating friend.

"Actually, most of my injuries were from skateboarding," she related. "I used to go down to the financial district and zoom down all those cool plazas and walkways. He would have to come get me from the security guard's office and take me straight to the E.R."

"Did you hurt yourself badly?" she inquired.

"Nah. Mostly broken bones."

Jamie shook her head at her cavalier friend. "And my parents think I'm tough to handle."

When they went downstairs, Ryan took a quick shower, while Jamie just looked at the pictures on the walls. She particularly loved the pictures of Ryan when she was a little girl. There were at least a dozen framed shots of her taken at various stages of her youth. Her favorite was one of her as a toddler, no more than two years old. She had the cutest little round face, and with that shock of black hair and those crystal blue eyes, she looked like a beautiful little china doll.

When Ryan came out, wearing a long-sleeved, red T-shirt and faded, navy blue sweats, Jamie crossed the room and asked for a hug. Ryan responded quickly, and Jamie just stood in the embrace for a very long time. "You're the only person I feel safe with anymore," she mumbled into the strong chest.

"Come over here and relax," Ryan said as she tugged her over to the bed. Ryan lay down first, scooting to the middle of the big bed. She pulled a couple of pillows behind her back to elevate herself, and then she held out her arm in invitation. Jamie gratefully accepted the offer and climbed right up next to her. Ryan wrapped her arm around Jamie's back, resting her hand on her hip.

"Tell me what happened," she urged.

"She came into my room and saw me in my underwear," Jamie said as though that explained everything.

"I didn't convert you to boxers like I wear, did I?" Ryan asked with a hint of levity in her voice.

Jamie's head rotated, her eyes blinking slowly. "Boxers?"

"Calvin Klein," Ryan smirked. "They're made for women. I don't wear my brothers' or anything."

Trying to erase that mental image, Jamie muttered, "It wasn't the underwear — it was my body."

Ryan nodded her understanding. "I remember we talked about this at the beginning. We talked about how Jack would feel, but we didn't discuss your parents," Ryan reminded her.

"She was unbelievably proprietary about how I looked. She forbade me to participate in the AIDS Ride, and she threatened to cut off my support," Jamie muttered, still shocked by the events of the afternoon.

"Can you survive if they cut you off financially?" Ryan asked.

"Yeah, I've got a good chunk of money in my personal account, and I get a part of my inheritance on my birthday. I'm certain they can't do anything about that ... unless they try to have me declared incompetent," she said with disgust.

"Is it enough to live on?" Ryan inquired delicately.

"Yeah," Jamie finally smiled. "It's enough for your extended family to live on, including the ones still in Ireland."

"Does that mean you're finally gonna start paying me to be your best friend?" she asked as she began to tickle Jamie's waist.

The smaller woman began to giggle uncontrollably at the attack. "How did you know I was ticklish?" she howled.

"You just look like the sort that would be," Ryan replied with a devious smile as she began another round of the assault.

After Jamie recovered her breath, Ryan got serious again. "What can I do to help you, Jamie? You know I'll do anything I can."

"Just knowing you're here and that I can count on you is an immeasurable blessing," she said softly, cuddling up until she could feel her slow, steady heartbeat.

⌘

When she returned to Berkeley, there were four messages from her father and two from Jack.

I wonder who will be less supportive? she thought glumly. She decided to call Jack first. He was very upset that she had left the Peninsula without calling him, and he didn't understand why she would upset her parents like this. "Jamie, don't you care enough about their feelings to give up this ride?" he finally asked out of exasperation. "Does it really mean more to you than their happiness?"

"Why does no one ever suggest that they give up what they desire to please me?" she asked plaintively. "Why is it assumed that in every one of my relationships, I have to be the one to give in?"

"I assume that we're talking about us now, Jamie. I certainly think I've been more than understanding about all of your changes and your new friends. Your mother told me why she was upset, and I have to admit that I agree with her. You're hardly looking like a woman, anymore," he grumbled. "Are you trying to look like Ryan and her kind?"

"Call me when you're ready to apologize," she snapped, hanging up with finality.

The conversation with her father went just as well as the one with Jack. Jim was truly perplexed, and he commented that her new friends were likely responsible for these changes. He suggested that perhaps she should live at home for a while and commute until she was thinking more like herself again. Struggling mightily for control, she thanked him for his concern and said she would think about it. *February eleventh cannot come soon enough. I'll be twenty-one then and legally responsible for myself in every way.*

⌘

As was so often the case, Jamie didn't hear from Jack at all during the week. She knew he was angry, and he had to know that she was angry as well, but neither would take the first step to break the impasse.

She knew that Ryan was right, and that she had to seek some professional help to be able to figure out her life. But she had a remarkably resilient streak of pure denial mixed in with a healthy dose of raw fear that kept her from taking the step. Deep inside, she knew that shining a bright light on her inner desires would force her to take actions that she was unwilling to take at this point — so she put it off and tried to make small changes have a big impact.

One of her ideas was to read as many self-help books as she could get her hands on. One book suggested that women should not be afraid of their secret desires and fantasies. The author suggested that many, if not most, women occasionally had a fantasy or a desire that they didn't really wish to live out. She suggested that giving in to the fantasy completely was the best means of dealing with it, and Jamie decided to give it a try.

She called Jack before he left for school on Friday morning, trying to ascertain if she was welcome or not. "Jack? It's me," she said.

"Hi," he responded, not adding another syllable.

"Do you want me to come down tonight? Or do you need a break?"

"A break?" he asked softly. "Jamie, I love you. I don't ever need a break from you." He sighed and added, "I would like a break from fighting, though. I can't take much more conflict."

"I can't, either," she agreed. "I'll come down tonight, and I promise not to start a fight. Let's just spend some time together and try to heal some of our wounds, okay?"

"I'd like that." He paused for a second, then added, "I really do love you, Jamie. Let's try to keep focused on how we feel about each other, okay?"

"I'll do my best, Jack," she vowed.

⌘

Friday night went surprisingly well. Jack didn't even try to crack open a book, and they went for a long walk after dinner, while he told her all about the interviewing process for his dream job as a clerk for the U.S. Court of Appeals. When they got home, they spent a long time sitting on the couch, just slowly kissing and touching each other. When they did retire to the bedroom, she was pleased by her response, trying her best to avoid the pangs of guilt over the images of Ryan that kept flitting through her mind. *They're fantasies because you don't act them out,* she patiently explained to her conscience.

On Saturday evening, they went out for a walk to the bookstore so he could pick up some notebooks. The evening was surprisingly warm, and as they walked along holding hands, she started to feel more like herself. They decided to stop for a latte and sat outside watching the constant traffic on University Avenue for a few minutes.

"You're not moving around as easily as usual, honey," Jamie commented as she gently ran her fingers down his back. "Is your neck stiff?"

"Yeah, you know how it tightens up when I'm concentrating for too long. I wish I could remind myself to get up and move every half hour or so, but I just get too absorbed."

She moved her chair over behind his and worked on his tense neck and shoulder muscles for a few minutes. His head was hanging loosely by the time she was finished, and he let out a deep, relaxed sigh as her fingers left his body. He turned his chair around to face her, moving as close as he could. Smiling gently, he lifted his hand and tenderly traced the planes of her face. "It makes me feel so good to have you notice when a little something is wrong with me. It really shows me how much you love me," he said softly, gazing steadily into her eyes.

"I do love you, Jack," she whispered. Turning her head slightly, she placed a kiss on his large, warm palm. "Even when we're fighting, I still love you."

He leaned over even closer and placed a gentle kiss on her lips, staring into her eyes for a few moments. She slid her arms around his neck as she felt her desire for him begin to stir. As she lifted her head, his dropped a bit until their mouths met for several slow kisses. "Make love to me," she said softly as he began to pull away.

He didn't reply with words, but he immediately stood up and took her hand again. As they walked home, she mused that even though she did not like to have to resort to fantasies to reach orgasm, she had to admit that those few seconds of pleasure cut the tension between them dramatically. He was more playful and lighthearted, and his playfulness made her feel more relaxed. When she was relaxed, she was able to be more physically affectionate, which led to better sex. It was all terribly interconnected, but she was glad for the increase in affection.

As soon as they got into the apartment, he began to strip her clothing off. She allowed him to undress her in the leisurely style that always enhanced his desire, smiling warmly at him while he worked.

One of her self-help books urged that women should try to cast off their sexual hang-ups, and she was determined to give the suggestion a good try. Once Jack had her undressed, he removed his own clothing and started to kiss her, slowly working his way down her body. When he reached her thighs, he lingered a bit, nuzzling at her, seeking permission. Letting out a breath, she tried to relax her body and let him love her exactly as he wished.

He looked up at her with a hint of surprise on his face, and she patted his cheek gently, saying, "This makes me anxious, but I'll try it if you want to."

Moving quickly, before she could change her mind, he smiled up at her and lowered his head, kissing her softly until she began to relax and move against him. This time her mind didn't flit to an occasional image of Ryan — she lost herself in the fantasy — letting her body feel Ryan's loving touch. In seconds, she was moaning throatily and pushing her body against Jack's determined caress. It took just moments before she was in the throes of a shuddering climax, and she was just able to wipe the disappointment from her expression when she pulled at her lover's shoulders, expecting to find the wide smile and dancing blue eyes that soothed her soul.

⌘

She was remarkably receptive to Jack's continued attentions, finding intercourse much more enjoyable after she'd had an orgasm. They made love for a very long time, and while she hadn't been able to have another climax, she didn't mind a bit. Jack seemed very satisfied as he collapsed against her chest, and she soothed his damp head, kissing his sandy hair repeatedly. "I love you," she whispered, and her soul echoed her words. She fell asleep feeling truly content, hopeful that a little experimentation could help put their sex life back on track.

⌘

Lying on her back in her Berkeley bed, Jamie spread her legs wide, tugging Ryan's bare shoulders to ease her into position. "That's it," she purred when the incredibly soft tongue delved between her wet folds. "Oh, Ryan, you're *so* good." Her hips were thrusting gently, urging her talented lover to increase the pace. "Oh, yes," she cried, panting roughly. "Oh, yes! Oh, Ryan!" Her orgasm raced through her body, leaving her moaning and writhing as the sensations swept over her.

Suddenly, the image changed, and Ryan's beautiful face disappeared. Jamie reached down, patting the bed, but she was alone. The door opened, and her mother stood in the open doorway, staring at her in shock. Struggling to cover her nakedness, Jamie's flustered exclamation made her mother start, and the older woman closed the door quickly — just after Jamie saw the look of unmitigated disgust on her face.

Image after image floated through her mind, each one making less sense than the last. Finally, her mind quieted, and she sank into a deeper sleep, her dreams abandoned for the rest of the night.

⌘

She woke late, rolling over onto her belly while she stretched and growled. Jamie felt amazingly well-rested and very sated, finally assured that she and Jack could make some progress on their sexual incompatibility. "Jack?" she called, needing to connect with him.

When there was no answer, she rolled over and languidly stroked her body, trying to wake up fully. She was feeling more sexual than she could ever recall, and as she lay there, just feeling her skin, a brief image of her dream came to her. *Oh, my God,* she moaned internally. *That dream was so vivid!* She giggled softly, thinking, *Not even you're that good, O'Flaherty. I practically came before you even touched me!* With another short laugh, she mused, *This can really work out. I can marry Jack and express my genuine love for him, and have great sex with Ryan — who doesn't even have to know about it! Everybody's happy!*

Smiling broadly, she rolled to her feet and grabbed Jack's T-shirt from the night before. Padding around the apartment, she was surprised to find that he wasn't at home. A more thorough look revealed no note — not even a clue as to his whereabouts. She dialed his cell, but it was obviously turned off, so she left a voice mail message asking him to call.

After a shower and a quick breakfast, she went downstairs and looked around the neighborhood for his car. Finding it two blocks down the street, she scratched her head and continued walking, stopping at their favorite coffee shop for a latte and a copy of the *New York Times*. Every half hour she called home, never leaving a message, since it was clear he hadn't returned. Finally, paper read and coffee drunk, she walked back home and sat down to study.

By lunchtime, she was getting anxious, but she didn't really know what to do. He didn't own a pager, and with his cell turned off, she had no choice but to sit and wait.

Her anxiety grew with each passing hour, and by 7:00 she had called everyone in the contacts list on his computer. No one claimed to have seen him, and she finally couldn't stand the inactivity any longer. She left him a note, asking him to call her cell phone if he returned, then took off on her bike. He lived just five blocks from the main entrance to Stanford's campus, and she investigated every possible spot between the two points. Once she was sure he wasn't in any of his favorite restaurants or bookstores, she continued on to the campus and locked her bike up near the main quad. Methodically, she went to every library that was open, investigated every carrel and poked her head into every possible nook and cranny.

Thoroughly stumped and increasingly sick to her stomach, she went to the law school, finding every door locked. She knew he had a key to the building for law review business, but that didn't help her a bit. Banging on the main door in frustration, she decided to fetch her bike and return home.

Flopping down on the couch, she eventually fell asleep in the same position that she had collapsed in, exhausted and thoroughly anxious. Around midnight, she woke with a start to the sound of his key in the lock. She dashed to the door before he was even in the room and tried to speak to him, but he brushed her aside as he placed his book bag on the floor and walked into the bathroom.

She banged on the door with all of her might. "Where in the hell have you been?"

He not only didn't answer, but when the door opened, he walked past her like he didn't know she was in the room. He stripped down to his boxers and got into bed, turning his back to the door as he turned off the bedside light. "Aren't you even going to speak to me?" she asked, rooted in place. "I've spent the entire day looking for you, Jack! You didn't leave a note … no one knew where you were! Are you trying to drive me insane?"

Silence was his reply. She ran around to his side of the bed and leapt for him, grabbing him by the shoulders and giving him a rough shake. "What is wrong with you?" she shouted, her rage incendiary.

With cold, lifeless eyes, he glared at her while he peeled her fingers from his shoulders. "Leave my house," he spat, turning over to avoid having to even look at her.

"I will not!" She was standing now, her hands balled into fists. "Tell me what's going on!"

Slowly, he rolled over, staring at her for a full minute. "Go to her," he demanded. "She's the one you want — so go to her! I'm the one who's being driven insane, and I won't stand for it!" His voice had risen with each word, and by the time his statement was complete, he was shouting at full voice — a tone Jamie had never heard from him.

She shrank back in fear, certain for a moment that he had snapped from the pressure he put upon himself. He saw the fear in her eyes and cruelly exploited it, leaping from the bed to tower over her. "I told you to leave," he whispered harshly, menace dripping from his words.

Somehow, she knew that he would not hurt her, and she summoned all of her courage and stayed right where she was. "No," she said quietly. "I won't leave until I know what's wrong."

He was panting from the effort to contain his rage, and she could see drops of sweat form on his brow. His entire body shook, and she began to doubt her assessment of whether he would strike her. Just when she was ready to run, he sank to the bed heavily. "Did you always do it, or did you just do it the times you had an orgasm?" he asked, his voice filled with defeat.

"What? What in the holy hell are you talking about?"

"Ryan," he spat, her name sounding like a curse. "Have you always fantasized about her, or do you just pull her out on special occasions?"

Before she could blink, she was on her ass, her rubbery legs unable to hold her up. The stunned, guilty look on her face told him everything he needed to know. "Now get out." He walked into his office and turned the lock, leaving her sitting on the floor, unable to process a complete thought.

It took a while, but she finally collected herself enough to go to his office door and beg him to come out. All he had in the room was a desk chair and a side chair, clearly not the kind of furniture he could sleep on. Reassured by that thought, she sat down in front of the door, determined to stay until he eventually came out. The entire time he was locked inside the room, she quietly spoke to him, keeping her voice just loud enough for him to hear. She told him how much she loved him, how much she wanted their relationship to work. Professing her devotion to him, she began to cry quietly, her voice growing more ragged by the minute.

His compassion eventually overtook his anger, and he opened the door, squatting down so they were at eye level. His eyes bore into her, seemingly penetrating her very soul. "Did you ever love me?" he asked, his voice catching.

"I do love you," she whispered. "I've loved you since that first summer when we started to date." Tears were streaming down her face, and she wiped at them ineffectively. "I want to marry you, Jack, and raise a family with you."

He sat down opposite her, not touching. His back was propped against one side of the doorframe, hers against the other. "Then why do you call out her name while you're touching yourself in your sleep?" Her mouth opened and shut several times, her mind too shocked to form a response.

"I don't do that!" she gaped, her mouth dropping open.

"You did. Last night," he flatly stated. "You were bouncing the bed so hard, it woke me up, and when I turned over, you had your hand between your legs and you were moaning something. I leaned over and distinctly heard the word 'Ryan.'"

Her eyes nearly popped from her head. "Is that all? You tortured me for an entire day because I said her name in my sleep!" She got to her feet, feeling a little dizzy from the altitude change. Holding onto the doorframe, her face contorted into an expression filled with anger. "I said her fucking name! Now you don't only want to control my waking hours — you want to control my subconscious!" Pacing in a wobbly line, she growled, "Have you ever had a fucking dream? You have an erection every time I get up during the night. What's that about? Tell me what you think about every time you get hard, Jack!"

"You're being ridiculous," he grumbled defensively.

"I am not! I don't know what I mumble in my sleep. I don't have complete control over what I dream. But I know my feelings, and up until this moment, I was in love with you!" Storming back into the bedroom, she started to throw her clothes into her overnight bag. He followed right on her heels, placing his hands upon her shoulders. She shrugged them off, stomping into the bath to get her toiletries. "I won't have you policing my every thought, Jack. I've been entirely faithful to you, and I won't tolerate an inference that I haven't been."

He reached for her again, but she pushed him away roughly. "What you did today was unspeakably cruel. With all of the problems we've had, I was always sure that you were a kind, caring person. I don't have that confidence any more."

Slinging the bag over her shoulder, she stalked out, leaving him frustrated and more confused than ever.

⌘

Jamie struggled to her early class, having not slept a wink. To her surprise, Ryan was standing outside of her classroom, smiling broadly at her. "Hi. I had a little free time, and I couldn't think of a person I'd rather spend it with."

Her heart fluttered in her chest as, once again, the urge to wrap herself up in Ryan's embrace grew to astounding proportions. "You must be psychic," she said. "I could really use a hug."

Without question or hesitation, Ryan dropped her book bag and pulled the smaller woman to her, holding her close until Jamie finally grew uncomfortable from the curious looks they were getting. Placing a warm hand on Jamie's cheek, Ryan looked deep into her eyes and said, "Tell me what's wrong. You look like you haven't slept in days."

"Just one," she admitted. Looking up at the woman, she realized that she couldn't really explain what happened, since Ryan was so inextricably involved. "We just had another nonsensical fight. But this time, he disappeared for about sixteen hours — making me frantic. It just felt cruel," she muttered.

Ryan tucked an arm around her waist and led her from the building, guiding her to their favorite bank of vending machines. "I'll buy," she offered once Jamie was sitting on a bench.

Her cell phone rang, and seeing Jack's name on the LCD readout, Jamie decided to answer, not willing to shut him out the way he had done to her. Ryan returned with the juice, and Jamie told her that Jack was on the phone. She started to walk away, but Jamie grabbed her sleeve and pulled her back down, patting her hand gently. Ryan sat and gazed at her friend, listening patiently as Jamie took the call.

"Hi," she said, her tone rather flat.

"I want to apologize," he said immediately. "I spent all night thinking about this, Jamie, and I really handled this poorly."

"That's one thing we can agree on," she said, very little color to her voice.

"Look, we're both really raw from this weekend. Why don't we just take a little time to ourselves, and get together on Friday?"

"You can't manage a few hours together on my birthday?" Her tone didn't betray much surprise, and Ryan just shook her head, wondering at the quality of this relationship.

"I have a law review editors meeting from six o'clock on," he explained. "They usually run for four to six hours, honey. If you have some time around lunch, I have two hours free then."

"No. I have a one o'clock class." She sighed and said, "Fine. I'll come down on Friday. See you then, Jack."

As Ryan regarded Jamie's lifeless eyes, she thought, *Thank God she never uses that flat monotone on me. What in the hell is going on with these two, anyway?*

⌘   CHAPTER THIRTEEN

RYAN HAD BEEN PESTERING JAMIE FOR DAYS, TRYING TO GET HER TO decide what she wanted to do to celebrate her birthday. Once she knew that she would be the only one to commemorate the day at the appropriate time, it became even more important to make sure that Jamie had a great evening.

On Wednesday Jamie finally decided that she wanted to go to a bar to have a legal drink. This was fine with Ryan, but the next problem was finding an acceptable bar. "Where do you normally go?" Jamie inquired.

"I don't go to a lot of bars, to be honest," Ryan said. "I don't drink much, and I'm not crazy about crowded places. But when I do go to one in the East Bay, I usually choose a lesbian bar right on Telegraph. I don't think that's what you had in mind, though. Maybe we should ask Mia; I'm sure she knows every hot spot in the Bay Area."

"I don't really care about the atmosphere, Ryan. I just want to have a drink without fake ID's."

"Would you be comfortable in a lesbian bar?"

"Yeah, I would if I were with you. Besides, we'd be bothered less at a gay place."

"Hey, speak for yourself," Ryan said haughtily as she ineffectively hid a grin.

"You know what I mean, silly. The men there won't want us, and you've said that women aren't as aggressive, so I thought we would be left alone."

"That's probably true" she replied. "It's fine with me if that's what you want to do. How about dinner first?"

"Sure. You pick where we go. Why don't you come over at 6:00 or so, to pick me up?"

⌘

As promised, Ryan showed up slightly before six o'clock, dressed in her black silk T-shirt and a new pair of black, lightweight wool slacks with deep pleats. The pants were held up by a thin, black belt, and they draped

284

attractively over her long legs. Her black leather jacket was draped casually over her shoulder, and she grinned at Jamie with obvious excitement in her eyes. "Hey there, birthday girl." She leaned in to kiss each of Jamie's cheeks and offer a warm hug.

"Nice outfit," Jamie murmured, tugging her into the house. "New slacks?"

"Yep. I've finally found the key — Macy's men's department. If I can find slacks made in Italy or France, they're usually cut narrowly enough for me so long as they have pleats."

"You must get a look when the tailor comes in to hem them," Jamie teased.

"Nah. They see everything in San Francisco. I swear, I thank God every day that I was born here. People barely raise an eyebrow at me, and I know that wouldn't be the case in much of the country."

"I've seen more than a few eyebrows rise when you walk into a room, Ryan O'Flaherty, and they're not expressing shock."

"Yet another good thing about San Francisco," she smiled. Looking at her watch, she said, "We need to get going. I made reservations for dinner at 6:00 sharp."

"Reservations? We're going somewhere that you need reservations?" she asked in surprise.

"It's your birthday, knucklehead. I thought it would be nice to take you somewhere where the biggest question isn't 'You want fries with that.'"

"You wait right here; I'm going to change," she said as she looked down at her jeans and golf shirt. "I need to keep up with my escort. You look so ... so ..."

"Evil?" Ryan supplied helpfully, her face breaking into a crooked grin.

"No, I'd say you look sleek," she decided.

"Sleek; I think I like that," Ryan mused.

⌘

Five minutes later, Jamie came down the stairs in an outfit that clearly rivaled her escort's in terms of sleekness. She had changed into a little, black, crepe tube dress that followed every curve of her slim body. The dress was covered by a supple, black leather, bolero jacket that gleamed dully in the light of the staircase. Small black flats finished the look. "I've decided that we should both be PIB's," Jamie announced.

"PIB's?" Ryan inquired as she slowly walked around her friend, looking at her outfit with open appreciation.

"People in black," she replied. "It's very L.A."

"If this is how they look in L.A., I'm moving tomorrow," Ryan said decisively.

"You are such a tease," Jamie chuckled.

"Oh, I'm not teasing," she said with mock sobriety. "You just look so ... so ... so ..." Ryan fumbled.

"Sleek?" Jamie inquired.

"Yes, but more than that." She pondered her image again. "Sophisticated, glamorous, sexy — somewhere in there," she finally decided as she waved her hands in the air in a gesture of futility.

"That's probably because my mother bought this for me. We attended an art exhibit down in SoMa recently, and she insisted that all of my clothes were either too 'mainstream' or 'juvenile.'"

"Well," Ryan reflected, "I would agree that that is one of the least juvenile outfits I've ever seen."

Ryan drove, of course, and they pulled up to the valet at Chez Panisse at 6:00 sharp.

"Ryan, you are so sweet! I told you I liked this place months ago. It's adorable that you remembered," she enthused.

Ryan gave her a curious look as she replied, "If it's important enough for you to tell me, it's important enough for me to remember." As she held the door for her, she related, "I couldn't get reservations downstairs, but I thought we'd be more comfortable upstairs, anyway. It's a lot more casual," she said knowledgeably.

"I actually prefer the upstairs. It's not filled with stuffy businessmen trying to impress clients. Normal people from the neighborhood eat upstairs."

Jamie ordered her favorite meal: a small steak with french fries. Ryan had rack of lamb with some delectable oil-roasted, rosemary potatoes. She insisted on ordering a bottle of wine, but made Jamie pick out the vintage, since she was wholly ignorant of the subject. Jamie was just a bit disappointed that the server did not ask for her ID, but she had to admit that she was glad that she looked over twenty-one for a change.

Jamie was impressed that Ryan seemed very comfortable in this atmosphere, even though she was certain that she did not dine out much. After they had savored cups of cappuccino and a delightful piece of chocolate silk cake, they headed home. The bar was very close to Jamie's house, so rather than trying to park near it, they had planned on walking. After they left the car, Ryan dashed out to her bike and removed something large that had been lashed to the seat. She carried the big box into the house with a wide grin on her face.

Jamie tried to wrest the box from her hands, but Ryan held it securely, finally holding it above the laughing woman's head. "What makes you think this is for you, anyway?" she teased.

"Because it's my birthday, and you're too sweet not to give me a present, even though you don't need to," she replied logically.

"Well, you've got me there. This is for you," she said, presenting the box to Jamie with a flourish.

Jamie proceeded to rip off the wrapping paper and tear the heavy cardboard in a matter of seconds. She was delighted to pull out a brand new, bright yellow motorcycle helmet. "Ryan, this is so cool!" she said gleefully. "I absolutely love it!"

"I've been worried about your wearing my spare," Ryan admitted. "It's fairly large so that anyone can wear it. I wanted to get you one that would fit properly. Your head is mighty important to me, you know," she said as she began to adjust the helmet properly. The fit was perfect, and now Jamie wanted to take the bike to the bar. Ryan agreed, but she suggested that Jamie might want to change first. "Have you ever ridden a motorcycle in a short, tight skirt?" she asked helpfully.

"Oh, good point," the blonde agreed, eyes wide. "Should I change, or should we drive my car?"

"I'm very content to have you remain in that outfit," she said, eyeing Jamie's clothing. "But you get to choose. It's your birthday."

"Can I drive?" she begged as her face scrunched into an adorable little pout.

Ryan pursed her lips as though deep in thought. Her face quickly slid into a grin as she admitted, "You know I'm powerless against that puppy dog face. Of course you can."

"Be right back," Jamie called out as she ran up the stairs to change.

⌘

In a surprisingly short time, Jamie came trotting back downstairs, still looking lovely, but much more equipped to drive a motorcycle. The short black leather jacket remained, but now it covered a white turtleneck. Neat black jeans topped shiny black boots, now firmly placing Jamie into the sleek category. "Do you often have to warn your dates not to wear skirts?" she teased as they made their way to the driveway.

"Well, no," Ryan admitted with a leer. "I encourage my dates to wear short skirts."

Jamie was concentrating on getting onto the bike, and she hadn't noticed Ryan's leering grin. "Why would you ..." she started to say, but the obvious answer came to her quickly. "Ryan!" she cried as she slapped her friend in the stomach. "You are such a ..."

"Letch?" she once again helpfully supplied.

"At least!" her giggling companion agreed.

⌘

Moments later, they pulled up to a rare legal parking space near the bar. It was still early, and there were not many people in the establishment yet. It was dark and smelled of smoke, even with the ordinance that banned smoking in bars. Jamie figured that years of smoke smell had just permeated the walls.

"Well, well, well," smiled the bartender. "The class factor in here just went up one hundred per cent." The woman reached across the bar and shook Ryan's hand. "Haven't seen you for a while, Ryan. I would ask what you've been up to, but it's pretty obvious." Her dark eyes rotated in Jamie's direction, giving her a long, pointed look.

"You are incorrigible, Sandy," Ryan grinned, shaking her head. "This is Jamie. Tonight's her twenty-first birthday, so treat her right."

"You certainly look like you're used to being treated right, Jamie," she said as she leaned over the bar a bit and moved her head close. "I guarantee that I'll continue that tradition."

Jamie unconsciously moved closer to Ryan and meekly ordered a white wine spritzer. Ryan asked for the same, instructing Sandy to hold the wine. After Sandy had placed their drinks before them, Jamie whispered with a laugh, "I thought you said women didn't come on so strong."

"Sandy would be the most surprised person in the world if anyone ever took her up on one of her propositions. She's been in a committed relationship for years, but she loves to joke around," Ryan informed her.

They found two stools near the rear of the bar. The jukebox was on, and the volume was a little higher than Jamie would have liked, but they could hear each other if they leaned close. "So, what do you think?" Ryan asked. "Is it what you expected?"

"Well," she said as she looked around, "I haven't been to a lot of neighborhood bars, but from the few I've seen, this one looks pretty typical. If you looked in quickly you wouldn't notice it was a gay place at all. Are most gay bars like this?"

"No, this is more like your typical, middle class, lesbian place. Some of the weekend clubs are very glitzy and appeal more to the 'lipstick lesbians.' I don't know why, but I feel more comfortable here. There are tons of good-looking women at the weekend places, but they're always really noisy. I think I just like the more laid back atmosphere of this place."

"Why do you call them weekend places?"

"Some promoters have a traveling club that's only open one night a month or one night a week. You'll see signs up advertising where the party will be. It's a lot cheaper to just rent a place for one night. Then they don't have the expense of keeping a place open on the slow nights."

"But you don't like them?"

"No, it's not that. Sometimes they're a lot of fun. But they're real high energy and, uhm … well, let's just say that I wouldn't take a date to one."

"Why not?"

"It's hard to, uhm ... well, I tend to, uhm …"

"You get hit on a lot, don't you?" Jamie asked with a big grin.

Ryan's chagrined look was a clearly affirmative answer. "There are usually a lot of people I know who go to those, and it gets kind of embarrassing," she admitted.

"You can't help it that you're irresistible," the blonde teased.

"It's hardly that, Jamie. I've just dated so darned many women that it seems like half of the city knows me when I go to one of those big parties."

"Well, I think it's because you're so darned cute," she said, tweaking her nose. "I've got to use the restroom. Is it right there?" she asked as she pointed.

"Yep. It's just behind that wall. I'll keep your seat warm."

There were about five women in line, and she waited patiently while watching a spirited game of pool. When she emerged from behind the partition, she was surprised and a bit peeved to see someone on her stool. *Hitting on her when I go to the bathroom? Unacceptable!*

She marched right over and slid in between Ryan and the stranger. Ryan's legs were splayed wide apart, and she nestled herself right between them as she leaned back against her. When she received a rather wide-eyed look from the stranger, she smiled sweetly and said, "Hi, I'm Jamie, Ryan's date. Who are you?"

"Just leaving," the woman said quickly, doing just that.

Ryan's head moved forward just a bit to rest on Jamie's shoulder. Her deep chuckle rumbled across Jamie's back as she said, "I guess I could take you to one of those weekend clubs. You'd just open a can of whoop-ass on anyone who got near me."

"It's all about respect," she said easily. "You've got to let them know they can't mess with you."

⌘

After Jamie had reclaimed her stool, they sat and chatted amiably while they people watched. After a while, Jamie ordered another drink, which surprised Ryan a bit. "Are you sure you're up to another?" she gently inquired.

"Yes, Mom. I may have just turned twenty-one, but I've been drinking for years. I've spent a lot of time in Europe, and wine is part of every dinner there."

"I just want you to be careful. Alcohol will hit you harder because of your weight loss. You won't be insulted if I drive home, will you?"

"Nope. I'm a big fan of the designated driver. But since you're driving, it won't kill me to get buzzed on my birthday," she decided.

⌘

Around ten o'clock, Jamie decided that she needed to dance. The small dance floor was nearly filled as she pulled Ryan to her feet and led her to a spot near the jukebox. A current song that Jamie particularly liked was playing as they began to move to the beat. *My God, I assumed that she could dance, but this is ridiculous!* she thought as Ryan became one with the music. Every part of her body reflected the strong beat of the thrumming bass. She moved her hips and her shoulders in a teasingly seductive way that had every pair of eyes on her. *I'm sure she's not conscious of how sexy she is. Every woman in this bar wants her,* she marveled. They continued to dance as three more good songs came on. Jamie was no slouch as a dancer herself, and by the time they finished, most of the women in the bar were deciding which one of them they would choose if given a chance. But most spectators knew they wouldn't have that chance this night, given the incredible chemistry the pair exhibited.

The exertion of their dancing and the closeness of the room made Jamie feel a bit tipsier than she normally would have after her two drinks. Ryan actually felt a little light-headed herself, due to the lingering effects of the wine they'd had at dinner. They went back to the bar for a few minutes, and Jamie signaled Sandy for another round. When her spritzer was delivered, she drank it quickly, mostly to rehydrate. She knew she was getting buzzed, but she was having such a good time that she just let herself go for a change, ignoring the inner voice that normally kept a tight watch on her actions and her emotions. It was her birthday; she was going to have fun.

It was too loud to talk now, so they just sat back on their stools and watched people dance for a few minutes. After a while, Jamie felt cool again, and as soon as another favorite came on, she rose and took Ryan's hand. The song was very slow and sensual, and Ryan cocked her head as she gazed down at her. She leaned over a little and asked, "Are you sure?" Jamie's answer was to guide her to the dance floor without a word. As she slipped her arms around Ryan's waist, she felt her partner's strong arms slide around behind her shoulders and drape loosely behind her neck.

As they moved to the slow, insistent beat of the music, Jamie drew imperceptibly closer to her friend. There was still a respectable distance between them, but she could occasionally feel Ryan's thigh brush against hers. A warm tingle passed through her body when Ryan's breasts touched hers slightly, but she didn't pull back from the incidental contact, letting it caress her body gently.

The song changed, with the tempo remaining slow and sensual. There may have been other people on the dance floor, but only one person existed for Jamie at that moment. The connection between them was both soothing and electric. Each small touch, each warm breath that went past her ear made her feel more and more deeply bonded. The next song was considerably faster, but neither woman made a move to break the connection. They continued to hold one another as they moved at half time to the quick beat.

When the next song began, Jamie found herself drawn inexorably closer to Ryan's body. The slow love song played in the background, but Jamie felt so connected that she swore they were moving to the merged beat of their hearts. The song was over much too soon, and as it wound down, they stood back slightly, still gently holding each other, and silently regarded each other for a few long moments. Ryan leaned down just slightly to speak, but Jamie misinterpreted her movement. She slowly closed her eyes as she slid her hands up the powerful back to rest behind Ryan's neck, gently pulling her forward. She placed her lips softly on Ryan's and let the warmth just wash over her like a warm summer rain. The kiss was gentle and tender and relatively chaste, but it lasted considerably longer than she had intended. Ryan didn't make any move to separate, so they continued the tender touch — with Jamie savoring the scent and the touch and the feel of Ryan's body so close to hers. Finally, Jamie pulled back, but Ryan's eyes locked onto hers, freezing her in place for a moment. There was a hint of a question in those eyes, but Jamie simply wrapped her arms around her neck and held her in a tender embrace for a few seconds. Ryan returned the affection, and when they broke apart, Jamie found that she held Ryan's hand in hers.

Her eyes had gentled as Ryan looked down at her and asked, "Are you ready to leave? It's getting a little late." Her face broke into a sweet smile when she added, "I think we're both a little drunk."

"Yes, we probably should go," Jamie said as she leaned against the taller woman for another full body hug. "It's nearly midnight, so my special day's almost over."

"That's where you're wrong," Ryan said as she slid her arm around Jamie's waist. "The day doesn't make you special. It's the other way around."

Jamie dropped her head against Ryan's shoulder as she mused, *How does she do that? She just makes me feel so precious.*

When they emerged from the bar, they stuck to their previous agreement to have Ryan drive. It was just a few short blocks to the house, but as Jamie hopped off, the skies opened up as a heavy rain began to pelt them. They both made a mad dash for the door, making the front porch relatively unscathed. Both Cassie and Mia were obviously at home, but the house was quiet. Jamie beckoned Ryan to follow her into the kitchen where they could speak normally without waking anyone.

"I don't want you to ride home in this weather, Ryan," she said.

"This is one of those nights I told you about," Ryan admitted. "You know, fifty degrees and raining like heck."

"Take my car home tonight. You can return it tomorrow," she offered.

"I don't really feel comfortable driving your car alone, especially in the rain, since my motorcycle insurance wouldn't cover me if I wrecked it. I'm a careful driver, but not everyone else is. I don't want you to have to explain an accident to your father," she stated firmly.

"Then call home and tell them you're staying here," she insisted. "I won't be able to sleep if you drive home in this."

"Okay, you win," Ryan finally agreed. "I can ride in the rain, but it isn't the safest thing to do." She looked a bit shy as she asked, "Where should I sleep?"

"It looks like everyone is home, so you're stuck with me," she said with a crooked grin. "Unless you want to sneak into Cassie's room and make a woman out of her," she teased.

"I think that's beyond even my abilities," she replied with a return grin.

⌘

Jamie took her clothes into the bathroom to change, while Ryan called home to tell her father she was taking refuge from the rain. A few minutes later, Jamie emerged in glen plaid flannel pajamas with her face scrubbed and her teeth brushed. She offered Ryan a new toothbrush and showed her where the clean towels were. Finally, she asked, "What do you normally sleep in?"

"Uhm, my normal outfit is a little casual for a sleepover," she admitted.

"It's okay if you like to sleep in your underwear," Jamie reassured her. "If you wear boxers, your underwear covers a lot more than mine does."

"My normal attire is quite a bit more casual than that," she grinned.

"Ooo," Jamie replied. "That would be a touch casual. I'll find something for you." Jamie rummaged through her dresser, finally coming up with an old pair of sweats and a T-shirt that Jack had left with her during the summer. "Jack's a little bigger than you are, but these should fit," she said as she handed the bundle to her friend.

Ryan followed Jamie's lead and went into the bathroom to change. As she brushed her teeth, she reflected on the events of the evening. *God, I don't know what happened at the bar, but it felt altogether too good. I know the alcohol got to her a little bit, but there was more to it than that.*

Gazing at herself in the mirror, Ryan let her face break into a smile. *Damn, it felt good to kiss her.* She closed her eyes and let herself remember the softness and warmth of the caress. *Jack is such a damned fool!*

As she slipped into Jack's clothes she thought, *I don't know if it's a good idea to sleep in her bed tonight. I wish there were another place to crash, but it would really be insulting to curl up on that little loveseat when she has a king-sized bed. I just have to remind myself that she's a wonderful, attractive, sexy* **straight** *woman, who's engaged to be married.*

Taking another long look at herself in the mirror, her gaze sharpened and she thought, *How long are you going to continue to play this game? She says she's straight, you say she's straight ... everybody agrees that Jamie Evans is the straightest fucking woman on the planet. But straight women don't look at you like she does ... straight women don't dance with you like she did tonight ... and straight women don't kiss you with so much feeling. You know damned well that if you had encouraged her in the least, her tongue would have been in your mouth!*

She sighed deeply and shook her head. *If she were any other woman, you'd be in that bed showing her just how straight she isn't. But she isn't any other woman.* Looking at herself and seeing the deep longing in her eyes, she forced herself to admit another truth. *If she were any other woman, you'd stop seeing her. An ostensibly straight woman who kisses you with such feeling is nothing but trouble, and you know that better than most.*

Sternly lecturing herself, she stared into her own eyes and thought, *She might be in denial, but you can't afford to be. You keep your hands to your damned self tonight, no matter what!*

Properly chided, she emerged with her hair in a simple braid and Jack's clothes covering her body. Jamie marveled at her appearance for a moment, "You and Jack could not look more different, but those are exactly your size," she said.

"Yeah, we just fill them out in different places," she grinned.

I'll say, thought Jamie. She climbed into bed and turned the covers down for both of them.

Ryan looked at the bed and hesitated. After Jamie was settled, she attempted to pull the covers back up on her side and lie down on top of them. "What are you doing?" asked Jamie with a confused look on her face.

"I just thought I should sleep outside the covers," she offered.

"Afraid I'll bite?" Jamie replied, a bit cross at the insinuation.

"No, not at all," she replied, although that was exactly what she was afraid of. "I just don't want to put you in a bad position. I know Jack isn't wild about me, and I don't want you to have to explain anything that might make him mad."

"It'll make me mad if I'm trapped by these covers all night. Get in here," she ordered.

Ryan complied, despite her reservations. "I do kind of hate to sleep on top," she admitted. "It's lots cozier inside."

They kept a respectful distance as they shifted and adjusted their positions for a few moments. As they both settled down, Ryan quietly said, "Happy birthday, Jamie."

Jamie smiled at her friend in the dark and replied, "You made it happy, Ryan. Thank you."

⌘

The alarm sounded at 6:30 a.m. Jamie stuck an arm out of the covers and slapped it with her hand. She groaned as she opened her eyes and saw the time, then turned and saw Ryan gazing over at her with a big smile on her alert face. "You're not a morning person, are you?" the dark woman observed happily.

Jamie's only response was to cover her head with the pillow. She felt Ryan hop out of bed and found herself falling asleep again when she heard the shower running. When Ryan was finished in the bathroom, she came over and perched on the side of the bed. She was wrapped in a huge bath sheet, and she debated whether to put her nice clothes back on or try to get away with wearing Jack's sweats. While she debated her wardrobe choices, she decided to wake Jamie. She looked down at her friend, so peaceful and serene in sleep. She contemplated a gentle way to wake her, finally letting her evil side win. Throwing the covers back, she climbed onto the bed and began to tickle her mercilessly. Jamie giggled and thrashed about on the bed as Ryan refused to let her go. They were making so much noise that neither heard the very brief knock on the door that occurred almost simultaneously with its being opened.

Cassie opened the door a bit and stuck her head in. Ryan was mostly covered by the bath sheet, but she was straddling a wildly twitching Jamie. A long expanse of bare thigh peeked out at Cassie, and her eyes went from the half-naked woman to the hands locked together playfully. Both women caught the expression on Cassie's face, which was a mixture of glee and revulsion. "Jack's on the phone," she said as she ignored Ryan's presence and their very compromising position. "He said he called you yesterday to wish you a happy birthday, but you were obviously … out. Do you want to speak to him … or are you too … busy?" she said, batting her eyes innocently.

"Of course I'll speak to him," Jamie snapped, wishing she could spare a moment to strangle her snide roommate. She grabbed the phone in her room and panted out, "Hi."

"Hi, Jamie," he said, his voice sounding a little distant. "I just called to wish you a happy birthday."

"Thanks, honey," she said, desperately searching his voice for signs that Cassie had told him of Ryan's presence.

"Are you coming down tonight?" he asked, his calm affect giving no clues as to his mental state.

"Yes, of course I am. I can't wait to see you, Jack."

"Fine. See you then," he said, then quietly hung up.

⌘

Sitting in class later that morning, Jamie's mind kept drifting to Jack. She had somehow lost the ability to read him — and now she felt like she was going down to Palo Alto blind. And even though she knew that she should be concentrating on him, she could not help thinking about Ryan. *I cannot believe that I kissed her like that! God, I can't believe how incredibly soft her lips were. So very different than kissing a man. It was just like melting into the softest thing I can imagine. And what in the hell must she have been thinking? She wasn't as buzzed as I was, and she's always in such control. Did she enjoy it, too? I know I should bring it up or apologize or something, but I don't think I can. She acted perfectly normal this morning — so maybe she didn't think much of it. But I did,* she forced herself to admit.

⌘

When Jack arrived home that night, Jamie was already making dinner. He offered a rather perfunctory kiss, but that wasn't odd, considering that they hadn't seen each other since their huge fight. She finally gave up trying to read him and decided to just go with the flow.

When they went to bed, he made love to her, but she could tell that he was not very emotionally connected. Normally, he spent a lot of time looking into her eyes while they made love. But this time, he broke off eye contact just a few moments after he entered her. He buried his head in her shoulder and just pumped away, almost like he was forcing himself to finish. She didn't have an orgasm, and for the first time that she could remember, he wasn't concerned about that fact. When he was finished, he merely kissed her on the cheek and rolled over. He was asleep in moments, but she was awake for hours, feeling partially aroused and desperately lonely even lying next to him.

⌘

On Saturday night they went to her parents' home for her belated birthday celebration. Jack looked very handsome in a navy blue, double-breasted blazer, over a white, long-sleeved golf shirt. Gray flannel, pleated slacks finished his preppy look, and Jamie only spent a moment wondering if the slacks would fit Ryan. Jamie was dressed in a short, sleek, silk dress in a deep burnt umber. The deep earth color complimented her golden hair and showed off the tan she had obtained from her frequent bike rides.

Catherine greeted them at the door. She was obviously over her pique at Jamie as she kissed each cheek and gave her a firm hug. Jim came down the stairs moments later, giving Jamie a hug and a kiss as well.

They chatted about law review and Jack's recently completed finals. Jim was working on a case that had been in the news, and he and Jack discussed it in detail. After a while, Catherine asked what Jamie had done on her actual birthday. She casually replied that she had gone out for a drink with friends, noticing Jack's discomfort at the topic. She did not elaborate, and, as expected, no one pursued the topic.

After a delicious dinner, Catherine brought out several small boxes as Marta presented a lovely white cake with coconut frosting — Jamie's favorite. Her mother had purchased a beautiful pair of emerald earrings, the stones fashioned in a brilliant cut, nestled in simple gold collars. The earrings were exquisite, and they looked fantastic when Jamie put them on.

Her father gave her the thinnest watch that she had ever seen, its solid gold case gleaming in the warm light. It was waterproof and shock resistant, which made her happy as she thought about wearing it while working out and riding. It had a woven gold bracelet that hung a little loosely on her small wrist, looking very elegant on her. Engraved on the back was "Happy 21st. Love, Daddy."

Jamie was enormously pleased with the gifts, and she thanked both of her parents profusely. They told her of the various choices available to them in deciding on the gifts, and after a little while, Catherine handed Jamie an envelope. Inside was a first class ticket to Florence via Milan on Alitalia . "I want to take you to a wonderful new exhibit at the Uffizi," Catherine said with excitement in her voice. "Then I thought we could take the train back to Milan and stay at my apartment for a few days. We haven't done any serious shopping all year, Jamie. I've seen so little of you recently, I thought it would be a great way to reconnect a little bit."

Jamie's pleasure turned to dismay when she noted the departure and return dates. "Oh, Mother, this is so thoughtful, but I'm not free during these weeks," she lamented.

"Of course you can be free, Jamie. School will be out by then; I checked myself."

"Mother, I told you about the bike ride I'm participating in," she explained. "My ride is right in the middle of this trip."

"Jamie, I thought I made it clear that I didn't want you to do that ride," Catherine said slowly.

At this point, Jim interrupted. "I don't know anything about a bike ride," he said with a confused look on his face.

"As I told Mother, I've committed to riding in the California AIDS Ride this year, Daddy. It begins on June 6th and ends on the twelfth."

"Where are you riding to, New York?" he asked in surprise.

"No, no, it's from San Francisco to Los Angeles. This year almost three thousand people are going to participate," she explained.

Catherine interrupted, "Jim, have you ever heard of anything more dangerous or foolhardy? You know what Highway 1 is like. I'm afraid she'll be killed!"

Jim regarded his daughter for a long while. He cast a glance at Jack, who seemed to be studying the pattern of the Oriental rug. "Is this something you're preparing for properly, Jamie?" he asked.

"Yes, Daddy. I bought the right kind of bike, I've been working out in a gym with a trainer and I'm riding about one hundred miles a week now," she stated confidently.

"What do you think of this, Jack?" he asked.

"Jamie makes her own decisions, Jim," he said without much enthusiasm.

"Catherine, I think that Jamie is old enough now that she can make her own decisions in matters such as these. I trust her judgment, and this seems like a good character-building experience." He smiled at his now grinning daughter, "How does this benefit people with AIDS?"

"Every rider pledges to raise at least $2500. The money I raise will go to the San Francisco AIDS Foundation. People who live in southern California donate their pledges to the Los Angeles Gay and Lesbian Community Center. Both of those groups give direct care to people living with AIDS," she said knowledgeably.

"Catherine, I think you should allow Jamie to decide if she wants to go to Europe with you this summer. If she chooses not to go, perhaps she can turn that ticket in and donate the money to her ride," he suggested.

Jamie jumped off her chair and went to her father, wrapping her arms around his neck and whispering into his ear, "I knew you would understand. Thank you, Daddy."

As she pulled back, he laid his hand on her cheek and smiled up at her with admiration. "I'm proud of you, cupcake," he said as he used a favorite childhood nickname. He turned to Jack and beamed, "This girl has a ton of determination, doesn't she, Jack?"

"Yes, sir, she certainly does," he replied somewhat stiffly.

Catherine finally relented and agreed that Jamie could use the ticket however she chose. She was firm in her resolve to worry as much as she wanted, however. "I still think of you as my little girl, Jamie. I'm having a hard time letting go, I guess."

Jamie walked over to her mother and kissed her cheek. "I don't want you to let me go completely," she smiled. "Just let me make my own choices."

"It is so hard for me to believe that you'll be married in a little over a year. But I suppose you can decide to ride a bike if you can decide to get married," Catherine laughed.

Jack had been nearly silent during this whole interchange. He finally spoke up to tell Jamie that he had a present for her back at his apartment. She found that a bit odd and tentatively nodded her assent.

⌘

At around ten o'clock, the young couple was on the way back to Palo Alto. Jack was silent on the ride home. Jamie noticed that he looked very tired and that his movements were not as smooth and graceful as usual.

When they arrived at the apartment, Jamie was surprised that Jack did not immediately change into his sleepwear. He sat down on the couch and looked at her with a blank expression on his face. She was very uncomfortable with his attitude, and she sat next to him on the couch as she took his limp hand in hers. "Honey, are you all right?" she asked hesitantly.

In a flat voice, he responded "Don't you want your gift?"

"Uhm, sure, if you want to give it to me," she said unsteadily as her heart started to pound strongly in her chest.

"I'm giving you what you most want, Jamie. I'm giving you your freedom," he said as he stared at her with emotionless eyes.

"H ... h ... how are you giving me freedom?" she asked, already knowing the answer.

"I'm giving you the freedom to live your life exactly as you wish. You no longer have to answer to me. You no longer have to be concerned with my feelings. You are officially a free woman, Jamie. Congratulations."

"Jack, please don't do this," she begged in a quavering voice. "It doesn't have to be like this, sweetheart."

"Yes, it does, Jamie. I just don't feel the way I used to feel about you. You've become a different person." He slowly looked directly into her eyes as he delivered the knock out punch, enunciating clearly. "I don't like that person."

Jamie rose on shaking legs to stare at him as she backed away from the couch. "Is there anything I can do to make you change your mind?" she finally choked out.

"No. It's one thing to call her name out and quite another to sleep with her. I tried to get past it, but I realized last night when we had sex that I just can't do it. I'm not in love with you anymore ," he flatly stated.

She could feel her ire rise as her eyes narrowed dangerously. "Did you realize that before, during or after we had sex, Jack?" she spat out in anger.

"During," he said through gritted teeth. "I tried to connect with you, Jamie. But as usual, you looked like you would just as soon have been riding your bike as making love."

Jamie used every bit of control she had left in her shaking body to refrain from hurling an insult back at him. She knew from the look in his eyes that his love for her was gone, and she slowly, sadly and thoughtfully removed his grandmother's engagement ring from her left hand and handed it to him. "You're right, Jack," she said slowly. "You do deserve someone who can be what you need. I'm just sorry that it couldn't be me." With that, she turned and went to the bedroom to pack her bag.

When she returned to the living room, he was sitting right where she had left him with silent tears running down his cheeks, his eyes staring at the floor, unfocused. She stood by the couch and looked down on his face as she touched his cheek with her palm. After a moment, she leaned over and kissed him one last time, whispering as she rose, "I'm sorry, Jack. I'm truly sorry."

⌘

She didn't want to do it, she really didn't, but she just didn't have any other option. It was nearly midnight, but it was Saturday night, and there was a good chance that Ryan was still out. She just had to call her. She dialed the pager number from memory.

Minutes later, the smooth, deep voice came through the little phone, "What's wrong?" It was more of a statement than a question.

"Are you busy right now?" was the hesitant reply.

"No, I'm just trying to get to sleep after a very frustrating evening with Tracy," Ryan replied.

"Did you have a fight?"

"Not that kind of frustrating," Ryan's voice rumbled out a full octave lower.

"Oh, I'm sorry. I ... I ... I didn't mean to disturb you," Jamie muttered.

"Jamie, I'm teasing you. Now, please tell me what's wrong," she said, the concern evident in her voice.

"Jack just ... broke up with me," she sobbed in reply.

"Oh, God, I'm so sorry to hear that," she soothed. "Where are you?"

"I'm in Palo Alto, sitting in my car."

"Jamie, it's not a good idea to drive when you're upset. I can come get you, wherever you are."

"No, I can drive," she said as she continued to sob. "It just hurts so much," she wailed as she had to pull over to the curb. She was overcome by wracking, deep sobs that felt like they were being forcibly pulled from her body. She continued to cry without pause for several minutes with Ryan jumping to her feet to pace across her bedroom floor.

"Jamie, Jamie," she said loudly to be heard over her crying. "Where are you?"

"I'm just about to get on the freeway," she said weakly.

"I'm going to come get you," Ryan declared. "I don't want you to drive in this condition."

"I'll be okay. I don't want to just sit here and wait for you."

"Could you go to your parents?"

"No, that's the last place I want to be tonight. I just want to go home," she said as the sobs began again.

"Please, let me come get you," Ryan begged. "I'll be crazy with worry if you drive home."

"How about if I drive but stay on the phone. Would you feel better then?"

"Call me back in five minutes. I want to get dressed in case you can't make it," she said as she hung up. *Damn him — damn him to hell! He breaks up with her at midnight and then lets her get into her car and drive all the way home!*

Ryan was sitting on the front stairs of her house when Jamie pulled up thirty minutes later. She was exhausted emotionally from trying to keep her friend focused on the long drive, and her constant pacing made her feel like she had made the trip by foot. She approached the car as Jamie killed the engine, then squatted down by the driver's door. "You can stay here tonight, or I'll drive you home. I want you to think about where you'd feel most comfortable," she soothed.

"Can I stay here with you?" the blonde uttered through her tears.

"Absolutely," Ryan replied firmly. "For as long as you'd like." She stood, opened the door and offered her hand to Jamie. When her friend was firmly on her feet, Ryan slipped her arms around her and hugged her close. They stood like that on the street for many long minutes, then Ryan pulled back and guided the distraught woman up the stairs.

"I'm going to make us some cocoa," Ryan said. "Why don't you go downstairs and change into your pajamas? Then we can talk, okay?"

"Okay," Jamie sighed and picked up her bag lethargically.

Ryan carried two big mugs with her as she settled herself on the bed. Minutes later, Jamie emerged from the bathroom still in her dress, crying inconsolably. "I only have one of Jack's T-shirts," she held up the light blue garment. "I can't bear to smell him," she sobbed violently as she bent over, wrapping her arms around her stomach.

Ryan had learned this early warning signal, and she jumped up to steady her friend. "Are you going to be sick?"

A silently bobbing head was her answer. She came up behind Jamie and quickly unzipped her dress, then slid it down her slim body and helped her step out of it. She guided her over to the toilet and supported her as she fell to her knees and began to retch violently. Ryan knelt down right next to her with her reassuring hands around her friend's heaving waist. When all of the contents of her stomach had been expelled, Jamie was stark white and sweating. Ryan dropped the lid and maneuvered her so she was sitting on the seat, then she grabbed a washcloth to tenderly wipe the sweat from her friend's clammy face and neck. When she was fairly certain that the nausea had subsided, she guided her over to the bed and sat her down.

Ryan made an executive decision, pulled a T-shirt from her dresser and quickly managed to put it on the still-shaky woman.

When she was dressed, Jamie looked a bit better. Her color was returning, and Ryan was relieved at the thought that she would probably not pass out. She held the mug up in front of Jamie's eyes. "What do you think?" she inquired.

Jamie reached for the still-steaming mug and gingerly sipped a little. "I think it'll be okay," she said as she savored the concoction. They sat in companionable silence as they sipped their drinks. Ryan didn't want to rush her, so she allowed her friend to go at her own pace. After a good half-hour of reflective silence, Jamie was ready.

"You know, I'm mostly sad, but there's a small part of me that's so angry at him, I can hardly see straight. I think that's the part that's making my stomach hurt," she pondered.

"Why are you angry?" Ryan inquired.

"I think he said something just to hurt me," Jamie sighed heavily. "I've never known him to do that, and it just made me question what kind of a man he is."

"Do you want to tell me about it?" Ryan asked gently.

"Yeah, I guess so," she replied. "He told me that he realized he didn't love me anymore while we were having sex on Friday night." Her cheeks colored at revealing this intimacy, but she forced herself to continue. "I asked him at what point he had arrived at this conclusion — before, during or after sex." With a shudder, she gasped out, "He said during!"

Ryan wrapped her arms around her friend and began to rock her gently. After long minutes, she was able to continue. "It just made me feel so violated!" she cried. "I thought we were making love, while he was planning on breaking up with me." She heaved a few more deep sighs, "Could you continue having sex if you had that realization, Ryan?"

Fuck, no! she wanted to scream. *I would never have sex just to satisfy myself!* But instead she soothed, "I don't know that I can answer that, Jamie. Except for Sara, I've never had sex with someone I love. It's impossible for me to be able to put myself in his place, but I can empathize with how that made you feel." She continued to rock her. "I'm certainly not on Jack's side here, but you might feel better if you don't try to understand his motivations and just let yourself feel the hurt," she said tenderly.

Jamie nodded her agreement as she tried to let go of her anger. But she quickly realized that the anger was helping her stay afloat. As she felt it ebb, she was overcome with sadness. She rested her head on Ryan's chest and let herself reflect on the three years she and Jack had shared. Images of their life together flooded her mind: his smile, the way he cocked his head when he was interested in something, his quick mind, his long, lean body, the way he smiled at her in pleasure after she climaxed. There were so many sweet and loving things he had done for her, it became impossible to focus on this one betrayal. But the sorrow was so overpowering that she felt too weak to bear it. Only Ryan's strong arms and powerful body kept her grounded.

It was nearly 3:00 a.m. when she began to feel a little more in control. For the past ten minutes or so, Ryan had been softly humming into her ear. The melody was gentle and smooth as the vibrations rumbled through her body. Finally, she asked, "What are you humming?"

Ryan paused for so long that Jamie was unsure if she was going to answer. "A song that my mother used to sing to me," she finally said in just above a whisper.

"And you remember it after so long?" Jamie inquired gently.

"Yeah, it's the only one I really remember," she sadly admitted. "She sang it as a lullaby. I'm sure I heard it hundreds of times." After a very long pause, she finally asked, "Would you like me to sing it for you? It always worked to make me feel better."

"I would love it," Jamie replied. "I've never had anyone sing me to sleep," she admitted.

"Then we're even because I've never sung this for anyone," Ryan revealed.

Ryan pulled down the covers and got Jamie all snuggled in, then slipped off her own sweats and nestled close. When Jamie was in her favorite sleep position, lying on her left side, Ryan snuggled up against her back as she wrapped an arm around her and began to sing the tune.

Her deep, melodious voice enveloped Jamie like a warm blanket, and after just a few verses, the blonde was soothed into slumber. Her last conscious thought as she drifted off was of the bone deep connection she felt with this woman. *There is no safer place on earth than in her arms.*

⌘

She felt Ryan slip out of bed just after the sun came up. Not one molecule in her body wanted to follow her friend, so she slipped back into sleep easily. At around 9:00 a.m., her body demanded that she answer its call, and she slowly stirred. She heard a soft chuckle from behind, and she sleepily turned and saw a smiling Ryan, sitting at her desk in her underwear, pouring over her books. "I didn't wake you, did I?" she asked.

"No, I didn't hear a thing. How long have you been up?" she asked through a yawn.

"About three hours," Ryan replied after checking her watch. "Duffy and I went on a run, then I made breakfast for the boys, and I've been studying for about an hour," she said.

"What time is it?" Jamie inquired after shaking the fog from her brain.

"It's just after 9:00. What can I make you for breakfast? You name it."

"Something bland would be good. I'm still a little queasy," she admitted. "I think I'm going to go to Mass at 10:30." She stretched languidly and asked, "Do you want to go with me?"

"Uhm … I will if you need me to," Ryan replied after a brief hesitation. "I have plans to have brunch with Tracy, but I'm sure she wouldn't mind if we shifted it to a late lunch. Actually," she said as she rose and went to the phone, "let me call her and cancel. I think I need to stay close to you today."

"No, Ryan, really. I'm fine going alone. I'll call my grandfather and see if he can spend some time with me after the service. You go meet your girlfriend," she said as she climbed out of bed and patted Ryan on the shoulder. She walked a step or two before she turned back and wrapped her arms around Ryan's neck and gave her a strong squeeze. "I can't thank you enough for last night. I honestly don't know what I would have done without you."

Ryan leaned her head down to rest on Jamie's entwined arms and gave her a gentle pat. "I'm sorry you needed to, but entirely glad that you called, Jamie. Now, go get ready while I get your breakfast."

⌘

As Jamie was leaving, Ryan inquired, "What are you doing after you speak with your grandfather?"

"I guess I'll just go home," was her sad reply. "I've got some reading to do for school."

Ryan moved around so that she was facing her friend. She squatted down a tiny bit so that she could look directly into her sorrow-filled eyes. "I'd feel better if you came back here," she insisted. "You've got your books with you, don't you?"

When Jamie admitted that she did indeed have them, Ryan persisted. "I want to see you again today. My date will be over by 3:00 at the latest. Why don't you come back here and study?"

"I don't know, Ryan. I might feel a little uncomfortable with you not here," she replied with a tiny bit of hesitation.

"Let me ask Conor if he'll be home. If you're lonely, he can keep you company, or you can go to my room and read." When Jamie hesitated Ryan played her trump card, "Will you do it as a favor to me? If you won't come over, I'll have to come to your house to check on you. It will save me a lot of driving."

"Like I could refuse to do you a favor, huh? Very sneaky, Ms. O'Flaherty, very sneaky indeed," Jamie teased her as she easily saw through the ruse.

⌘

As they had arranged, Rev. Evans waited for Jamie in the sacristy after Mass. He was in very good spirits and was happy to see his granddaughter, but one look at her forlorn face immediately alerted him to the fact that something major was amiss. "Do you want to tell me what's wrong now or over lunch?" he asked as he gave her a hug.

"Over lunch I think," she replied. "It's gonna take a while." They walked next-door to the small house that the church provided. The housekeeper had made them a nice lunch before she left for the day, and as they sat down at the kitchen table, Rev. Evans placed his hand on Jamie's and said, "Tell me what's wrong, sweetheart."

Before she could even attempt to stop them, the tears started to flow. Jamie could not remember crying like this in front of her grandfather, but he patiently waited until she was able to speak. Finally, she was able to say, "Jack broke off our engagement, Poppa."

His expression reflected his shock. "Oh, Jamie, I'm so sorry. What a sad thing for both of you," he soothed. "Tell me what happened."

"Well, we haven't been getting along very well since the school year started. We'd just fight about little things, and we had never done that before," she related.

"I must admit, that surprises me. I honestly never saw any tension between you two."

"Maybe that's part of the problem," she ventured. "Neither one of us is very good at showing how we feel," she reflected. "Anyway, it's been getting worse lately. He's gotten very jealous, and he really doesn't like one of my friends."

When Rev. Evans looked confused, Jamie explained, "Remember Ryan who is training me for the ride?" At his nod she continued, "Jack doesn't like me to see her, and it had become a big issue. I don't think the issue is really Ryan, though. I just don't think he liked the fact that I did something against his wishes."

"Do you really think he called off your marriage just because he didn't like your friend? That doesn't seem like Jack."

"Part of it is that, but another part is that I was spending lots of time with Ryan, even though it didn't interfere with our time together. He didn't like the fact that I was doing this ride, and he didn't like the changes in my body," she hesitantly admitted.

"Still, Jamie, that is a drastic action over some minor issues. Is this really everything? What specifically doesn't he like about Ryan?"

"I think it's mostly that she's a lesbian," she revealed. "He thinks that hanging out with a lesbian is exactly like hanging out with another man. I've got to admit, I've been disappointed in his attitudes about gay people, Poppa."

"As you know, that's not an uncommon reaction, Jamie." He paused to look at her carefully. "Do your parents know your friend?"

"Uhm ... no, I've never taken her home."

"But you've been at her home," he said with a tiny frown. "Quite often if I recall."

"Yes," she said, smiling softly. "Her family has just about adopted me."

"Why haven't you introduced her to your family?"

"Mainly because Daddy agrees that I should stop seeing Ryan because Jack doesn't like her. He doesn't understand why I would make Jack unhappy over a friend," she replied.

He leaned back in his chair and nodded briefly. "Do your friends like Ryan?" he persisted.

"Well, Cassie hates her. She's part of the reason this got so bad with Jack. She's been trying to get him upset about Ryan, and she's been very successful," she admitted disgustedly. "But Mia likes her a lot. She's even hired her to train with."

"I want you to think about the next question carefully, Jamie. You tell me that your fiancé has broken up with you over her, your father agrees with him and one of your closest friends hates this woman. Is there something about her to create this emotion, or are they all just narrow-minded?"

Jamie did as he suggested, letting her mind reflect for several minutes. Finally, she replied, "I think Ryan is the sweetest, most thoughtful, kindest person I've ever met. I swear there is nothing about her that isn't a positive force on my life. I really think they've just jumped to conclusions because she's gay, Poppa."

He let out a breath and rubbed the bridge of his nose in a frustrated gesture. "Well, it wouldn't be the first time that people had an irrational reaction to a lesbian." He shook his head a little and turned to gaze thoughtfully at his granddaughter. "How do you feel about her, Jamie?"

Shifting nervously in her seat, Jamie realized that she had to tell everything. "I feel safe with her. She's my best friend, and I treasure every moment we share. Honestly, Poppa, she's the most extraordinary person I've ever met."

Rev. Evans leaned over and gently grasped Jamie's hand. He gave her a small smile as he said, "Seeing how your face lights up when you talk about her could be part of the issue. Perhaps Jack felt that he had to compete against her — and maybe he thought that he would lose."

"What do you mean, Poppa?" she gasped in surprise.

"Describing her as the most extraordinary person you've ever met doesn't leave much room at the top for Jack, does it, honey?" he asked gently.

A deep sigh preceded her answer. "No, I suppose not," she replied glumly. "But she really is remarkable, Poppa. She's helped me change and grow in so many ways. And I just couldn't give her up. Not for Jack — not for anyone!"

After a moment spent gazing at her face, he asked, "Do you have romantic feelings for her, sweetheart?"

The blush that flew to every exposed inch of her skin was a dead giveaway. "Uhm, I ... I ... I guess the thought has crossed my mind," she admitted rather weakly. "She is incredibly attractive, and I ... I think about her sometimes and ... well, let's just say that she's on my mind a lot." She shook her head as the words left her mouth, adding, "But all of that is really recent. I haven't had any thought about leaving Jack for her, I swear! I love her, Poppa, but just because I love her it doesn't mean I'm *in* love with her, does it?"

"Of course not. It's entirely possible to form a very close and loving attachment to a friend. But you say that you have recently been thinking about her in a different manner," he reminded her. "Tell me more about that."

"I guess it's just snuck up on me," she said slowly. "I ... I actually kissed her on my birthday," she admitted quietly. "But it was just one kiss, and we didn't even talk about it afterwards. We've slept in the same bed twice since then, and nothing has happened, so I think it was just kind of a fluke."

"Do you think it is within the realm of possibility that Jack could have picked up on your changing feelings?" he asked.

"What? That I kissed her?"

"No, honey," he said. "Could he have picked up on the fact that your feelings are beginning to deepen?"

"I'm not sure that they have deepened, Poppa. I'm just so confused," she moaned. "I suppose it's possible that Jack noticed something. But he disliked her from the very beginning, long before I knew her well at all."

"Besides this thing with Ryan, how are you getting along with your parents?" he asked.

"Not great. Mother is very unhappy about my involvement with the AIDS Ride. Daddy actually defended me last night, and that made me feel better, but I just don't think the issue is dead. And I'm worried about their reaction to Jack's breaking up with me. I'm sure they'll blame me."

"Anything else?" he persisted.

"I just feel like I'm growing up all at once, Poppa. I'm making decisions for myself, and no one is supporting me. They still think of me as a child, and I think Jack did, too," she added.

"How have you been feeling, honey? Is this all bothering you a lot?"

"Yeah, it really has. My sleep has been way off, and I can't seem to keep my weight up. You know how I get my nervous stomach? It's been a lot more nervous than normal, and that contributes to the weight loss," she admitted. "I'm down to less than I weighed when I entered high school."

"Have you ever considered seeing a counselor, Jamie? I think this would be a great time to get some professional help with these issues," he opined.

"Can't you help me? You always have before," she said with a look that reflected both fear and surprise.

"No, I'm too involved. I don't think you have any terrible secrets just waiting to jump out at you, Jamie. But I do think you're going through a tough time dealing with some very adult matters, and I think you could use some help. What do you think?"

"I guess that's a good idea," she replied a bit hesitantly. "Can you help me find someone?"

"I don't know anyone who practices in the East Bay ..."

"That's okay, Poppa. I'm sure I can find someone on my own."

"I really think it will help to speak to a professional about your feelings, Jamie. Give it a little time, and I guarantee you'll feel better. Now, lets try to get some of this lunch into you," he said affectionately.

CHAPTER FOURTEEN

JAMIE APPROACHED THE HOUSE IN NOE VALLEY AND HESITATED before knocking. She felt a little uncomfortable to be at the O'Flaherty home without Ryan, especially since she knew that the boys and Martin probably knew about her breakup, and she was loath to talk about it. But she swallowed her discomfort and knocked.

Conor and Duffy answered, and to her surprise, Conor wrapped her in a hug, then leaned over to kiss her head. He didn't say a word, and Jamie realized that his response was just perfect — letting her know that he cared, without making her go into the gory details. When he released her, he said, "Ryan just got home. Go on down."

She started down the stairs, but stopped abruptly when she reached the open door. To her astonishment, Ryan was lying half on the bed, feet on the floor with her new pants around her ankles. Her legs were spread wide, revealing white, knit boxers that shone in the afternoon sun. Tracy was straddling her waist and had pinned Ryan's wrists to the bed with her own hands. Both women were moving against one another — Tracy, in a stunningly erotic grind against Ryan's pelvis, and Ryan, who seemed, oddly, to be struggling against her.

While Jamie watched, transfixed, Tracy bent over and pressed her mouth to Ryan's, kissing her hard. Finding the strength to move, Jamie turned to go back upstairs and heard her friend utter a long, low moan that turned her knees to rubber. She had to place her hand on the wall to steady herself, but with effort, she was able to climb the stairs and reach the safety of the living room. Unsure of how she got there, she found herself standing in the kitchen when she heard Martin come in the front door.

Doing her best to compose her face, she went out to greet him. "Hi, Martin," she said lightly.

"Ah, Jamie. I hoped that was your little car I spotted out in front," he said as he came over to give her a hug. "What are you girls up to today?" he inquired.

"Nothing much. I just got here. I've been at church, and Ryan went to brunch with Tracy. I think she's downstairs changing or something," she said, lying just a little.

"Does she know you're here?" he inquired. "Go on down if you like."

"No, no," she responded immediately. "I'll just wait until she's finished."

"Let me get you a drink or a little something to eat, Jamie," he said as he regarded her thoughtfully. "Is everything all right, sweetheart?"

Forcing a nervous laugh, she said, "Actually, no, everything's pretty bad today. My fiancé broke off our engagement last night." It still sounded unbelievable to her ears, and she found herself blinking back tears once again.

"You poor little lass," he said soothingly as he wrapped her in his arms. For reasons she could not understand, Jamie felt completely comfortable resting her head on his chest and letting out her feelings. "That man must be daft to let a prize like you get away."

"Thanks, Martin," she said softly while pulling away. "That really does make me feel better." She sighed, running a hand through her hair. "I just thank God that I have Ryan in my life. She's been so wonderful these past few months. I honestly don't know how I could get through this without her."

He smiled warmly at her and said, "That doesn't surprise me in the least. There's no woman with a bigger heart than my Siobhán."

"You know how special she is, don't you?" she finally asked softly, looking up into the eyes so similar to her friend's.

"Jamie, there is no man on earth who's more proud of his daughter than I am," he said sincerely. "She's been an extraordinary person since the day she was born."

Suddenly, for reasons that were unclear to her, she needed to know Martin's feelings on a very personal matter. "Was it hard for you when she told you she was gay?" she delicately asked.

"I can't say that it would have been my choice for her, but it certainly didn't upset me," he said reflectively. "I do wish she would find a nice woman that she could really love, but that will come in time, I suppose."

"Maybe it'll be Tracy," she commented.

"Perhaps," he said shortly and without elaboration.

"How would her mother feel about it?" she ventured to ask.

"You know, Fionnuala was a very insightful woman. When Maeve told her about Michael, she claimed she'd always known the lad was gay. She really made her sister see that it was the same Michael we had always known and loved. We didn't find out about his illness until my poor Fionnuala was just about gone, but she summoned every ounce of strength she had to stick up for that boy." He grew quiet for a while but finally continued. "She couldn't make a dent in old Charlie, though. His rejection of Michael weighed very heavily on her heart. About six months before she died, we were just talking one night, and she made me promise that if any of our brood turned out to be gay that I would love them just the same. I looked at her and made that promise without hesitation." His eyes filled with tears as he acknowledged, "I think she knew that Siobhán would be the one. There was something about her that was just different from the other little girls," he reflected. "And I don't mean her activity or her athleticism. It's hard to describe, but there was something different about her spirit. And she has that same confident spirit today, Jamie." After a long pause, he continued with a quavering voice, "When I think of making that promise to my Fionnuala, I realize that I've never made a promise that was easier to keep."

"She's a very lucky woman to have a father like you," she said, catching a tear escaping from her eye.

"We're the lucky ones, Jamie. I think it was our love for her that kept us all so close. She was such a small child when her mother died that we all had to join together to make sure we could do our best for her."

"You've done a marvelous job, Martin. And I know your wife would be proud of you all."

At that moment, Ryan and Tracy came into the kitchen, hand in hand. Martin greeted them both as Jamie struggled to compose herself.

Ryan looked at her quizzically as she asked, "Have you been here long?"

"No, just a few minutes," she fibbed. "I was just chatting with Martin here," she said as she smiled at him.

He smiled back and replied, "I'm going to go change out of my uniform." Addressing Ryan, he added, "Try to get this one to eat a bite or two, will you, darlin'? There's more meat on a butcher's apron."

"I try, Da. I really do," she said as she grinned at her friend.

Tracy walked over to Jamie as Martin left the room and placed her hand on her shoulder while looking directly into her eyes. "I'm really sorry to hear about your breakup, Jamie. I really feel for you."

"Thanks, Tracy," she replied, still a little shaky.

Tracy went back to Ryan's side and smiled sweetly at her, while slipping an arm around her waist. "I've got to go study. I had a very nice time at brunch."

Ryan placed two of her fingers on Tracy's chin, then slowly lifted her head and gently touched her lips with her own. Both kept their eyes open, and Tracy's mouth broke into a grin as Ryan pulled away. The kiss was completely chaste, no more than a light touch. But Jamie knew she had witnessed a terribly private moment, more private than the bumping and grinding that had been going on in Ryan's room. It was the depth of the tenderness that moved her, and she felt her chest fill with an ache that she slowly realized was longing. And right at that moment, she knew. She was as sure as she had ever been about anything in her life. No qualms, no doubts. She wanted Ryan. She wanted to be with her, to touch her, to love her. She wanted to partner with her — to declare her love to the whole world. Her eyes landed on those incredibly soft lips, and she felt her whole body pulse with yearning — needing to press her mouth to Ryan's and feel the energy surge through her.

Tracy's voice pulled her from her fantasy, and she felt herself mutter some sort of goodbye. Then Ryan walked her date to the door, leaving Jamie shaken and weak.

Moments later, she was alone with Ryan. She wasn't sure who moved first, but in seconds, she was wrapped in Ryan's arms, holding on tight. But this hug felt different from all the other hugs she had received from her friend. This time she forced her barriers down and allowed herself to really feel the woman who held her so gently. She inhaled deeply to imprint her delightful scent upon her brain. She luxuriated in the warm, moist breath that tickled the side of her face. She let her fingers wander over the smoothly defined muscles carved into Ryan's perfect back, and finally, she reveled in the supple firmness of breasts that pressed against her own, sending tingles down her spine. *This is what I want! This is what I need! This is my home!*

⌘

On this breezy, cold day in February, the San Francisco skyline was blessedly clear of fog. From Jamie's perspective, however, the fog had merely retreated into her own brain. She could never recall being as disoriented as she was then, and after a time, she just decided to go along with the flow and not even try to think. They all ate dinner together, but she was fairly sure she didn't speak. At one point Ryan leaned over and placed a forkful of potatoes into her mouth, so she surmised she wasn't doing a very good job at feeding herself, either, but the family politely didn't make mention of her incapacity.

They spent the evening in Ryan's room, studying. Rather, Ryan studied as Jamie tried to force herself to look at her books instead of daydreaming about the beautiful creature sitting mere feet from her, clad only in her underwear.

As the evening wore on, Jamie watched Ryan repeatedly shove her dark hair behind her ears in an irritated gesture. Since her entire focus was on her lovely friend, Jamie found herself standing behind her and gently pulling the dark tresses back into a ponytail. The silky hair felt so fabulous in her hands that she unconsciously began to run her fingers through it, starting at the scalp and extending all along the length. A deeply contented murmur of satisfaction answered her ministrations, which only served to encourage her. She continued her stroking until Ryan sleepily mumbled, "Two more minutes and I'm out."

Her eyes flew open as she stared down at her hands in amazement. She was fully conscious, but she had no memory of getting off the bed and beginning to rub her friend's head. She stood there with her fingers entwined in the dark hair, not able to reply in any fashion. Slowly, Ryan turned her head, and Jamie felt the silky threads fall from her hands, one lock at a time. Ryan gave her a gentle smile and asked, "Are you having a tough time concentrating tonight?"

Jamie tried to control the blush that was rapidly traveling up her neck. "Yeah, I guess I am. I just have so much on my mind that it's really hard to focus."

"Is there a lot you need to do for class?" she inquired.

"No, I'm actually pretty caught up. I studied a lot on Friday night, so I'm just trying to stay ahead."

"Why don't we go for a walk? I'm about to go cross-eyed from looking at these chem problems. If you feel up to it, we could walk over to Castro and get some ice cream."

"How far is that?" Jamie asked suspiciously, knowing that Ryan's athletic capacity far exceeded hers.

"It's about a twenty-minute walk, at a leisurely pace, " she replied. "I guarantee it's not too far for you."

They got their shoes and sweatshirts on and stepped out into the crisp, cold evening. There was not another person in sight, and the streets were devoid of traffic. The silence made Jamie feel like they were all alone, even though they were in the middle of a very large city. Ryan slipped her arm around her shoulders and said, "I'm so sorry that things are hard for you right now."

Jamie just smiled up at her friend, happy for the closeness. She reached up with her right hand and held onto Ryan's dangling hand, pressing it into her shoulder. They walked for another few minutes before Jamie commented, "Things seem to be going well with Tracy, don't you think?" She was asking partly for Ryan's sake and partly to determine if she had a ghost of a chance to ever be with Ryan.

Ryan's eyebrows gathered in concentration. After a moment, she cocked her head slightly and said, "I'm not sure, to tell you the truth. I thought a long walk might actually clear my mind a little."

"Wanna talk about it?"

"Oh, I don't know. You've got so much on your mind, Jamie, I don't want to add my issues."

"I'd rather think about yours than mine," the blonde commented wryly.

"Okay," Ryan agreed. "As I've told you, I made a conscious decision to stop having sex with people that I'm not in some form of relationship with."

"Yes, you have, and I've been very impressed with your fidelity," Jamie smiled. "You've only been with Tracy since November now, right?"

Ryan smiled at her and said, "Well, after a fashion, yes." Cocking her head, she admitted, "We haven't had sex yet, and I don't think we're going to."

"What!" Jamie was aghast. Ryan was the most sexual person she knew, and for the libido-charged woman to be celibate for three months was stunning news.

"I promised myself that I wouldn't have sex indiscriminately, and I promised Tracy that we wouldn't have sex until we were ready to commit to each other," she explained. "I've kept my end of the bargain, but she's obviously changing the rules, and it's beginning to irritate me."

"Irritate you?"

"Yeah. This is really hard for me, Jamie. I really want to have sex with her, and she knows it. Lately, she's been telling me that she doesn't care if we're committed — she just wants to do me," she muttered with a surprisingly embarrassed look on her face.

"Okay," Jamie said slowly. "You want to have sex; she doesn't hold you to your promise — why not just do it?"

Her forehead furrowing, Ryan cocked her head and said, "I told you that I made a promise to her — but I also made one to myself. That one is just as important as the other."

Jamie gripped the hand she held and slowed to a stop. Looking into her eyes, she said, "You did say that. And knowing you, I can understand how important your word is. I understand now."

"Thanks," Ryan said, giving her a charmingly adolescent smile. "I just wish Tracy understood." A pair of lines formed between her eyebrows as Ryan said, "A part of me thinks she's almost made a game out of it, and that really pisses me off."

"I'd feel the same," Jamie assured her. "I've had more than my share of experience with people trying to get me to have sex when I'd decided I wasn't ready, so I know how you feel."

Ryan removed her arm from Jamie's shoulders, reaching down to grasp her hand. She gave it a squeeze, then held it gently. "I don't have much … well, any … experience in saying no. It kinda sucks," she admitted, grinning shyly.

"What do you think you'll do?" Jamie asked.

"Well, I don't think it's gonna work out, to be honest. I've really tried, Jamie, but we have some issues that just don't seem fixable."

"Like what?" she asked curiously.

"She's not very willing to do things with my family, for one thing — and that's a fatal flaw as you can imagine."

Jamie blinked up at her and said, "Maybe she's insane! You'd have to be crazy not to love your family."

Ryan dropped her hand and draped her arm around Jamie's shoulders again. "You're my kinda girl," she smiled, placing a kiss on her head. "She also doesn't seem all that interested in having kids, and since I'm definitely going to …"

"Wow, those are two pretty good reasons," Jamie agreed.

Ryan nodded. "It's funny, but this last reason really surprised me. I didn't know this would be important to me, but I'm finding that it really is."

"What is it?" Jamie asked, hoping that she possessed whatever the quality was.

"She doesn't believe in God," she said quietly.

"Do you mean she's agnostic?" Jamie inquired.

"Nope. She's a card-carrying atheist. I don't think I ever considered that I would require a girlfriend to have some spiritual belief, but I think I do." She added thoughtfully, "It wouldn't even bother me if she were agnostic, you know, like she didn't believe in God, but she allowed that there was a possibility of a God. But we've talked about this several times. She believes in nothing. No God, no creator, no karma, no afterlife. She thinks we're here by some cosmic accident, and she thinks every bit of our energy dies and is put in a box. She has actually referred to spirituality as a 'fairy tale.'"

They were approaching the crest of the hill that led them down into Castro, and Jamie stood quietly for a moment, looking down at the bright lights, the pause letting her collect her thoughts. "I think I know what you mean, Ryan. My faith is so much a part of my life that I would hate not to be able to share it with someone I loved."

"Exactly!" Ryan replied. "I mean, it's clear that I have issues — big issues — with the Catholic Church. I go back and forth between being really connected and really disconnected. I'm in a disconnected period right now, as a matter of fact. But my belief in God as the source of love

315

and goodness and peace is unwavering. I just don't know if I can love someone who doesn't believe in what I trust to be the source of love," she said with conviction.

"I get it, Ryan, I really do. I mean, I love to go to church. It's often the highlight of my week. And I could love someone who didn't go. I could love someone with an entirely different view of the world, like a Buddhist or a Hindu. But I would hate to have my lover think I was wasting my time or doing something foolish."

"That's precisely the problem with Tracy. It's not just that she doesn't believe, I think she equates my faith with believing in the Easter Bunny or Santa Claus. She seems to think it's kind of a cute little phase that I'll grow out of when I mature. I mean, I like her very much, but if I'm going to be committed to her, we have to have a similar moral framework. My faith and my family are so integral to me, it's almost like she can't know me if she can't understand and respect that."

"It sounds to me like you've already made up your mind, Ryan," Jamie observed quietly.

"I have," she sighed. "At this point, I'm playing a game as well." She gave Jamie a glum look. "I just hate to waste three months for nothing. No relationship and no sex!"

"Those are the breaks," Jamie smiled wanly. "I just wasted three years. I even gave him back his ring."

Ryan tucked her arm tightly around her friend. "I didn't mean to equate my situation with yours. Mine's a slight disappointment. Yours is —"

"Hey," Jamie said, gripping her hand. "You have a right to have your feelings, too. I understand that you're disappointed. You just have to give it another try."

"Not for a while," Ryan decided. "This relationship stuff takes a lot out of you."

Jamie smiled up at her and agreed. "It sure does."

⌘

As they started to descend the steep hill, Jamie commented, "I've never been to Castro you know."

Ryan stopped short and stared at her. "You haven't? I thought they brought bus loads of straight children up here to observe the natives in their habitat!"

Jamie laughed at her exaggeration. "Nope. I missed this on the cultural tour. I guess I just never had a reason to come here. There's no museum, gallery, symphony or outstanding restaurant here, is there?"

"Nope. Although I think Hot 'n' Hunky Hamburgers is worth a trip."

"Right," she said, drawing out the word. "Sounds just like my mother's kind of place. No, for living so close to the city, we didn't come up for anything other than restaurants, sporting events or culture. We actually didn't do a lot of investigating in the Bay Area. I've spent much more time sniffing around Tuscany than I have San Francisco."

"Well, stick with me, and I'll introduce you to every dark alley in this town."

"Did your family do a lot of things together in the city?"

"No, not really," she admitted. "Because there's a six year difference between Brendan and me, he was involved in sports and school things by the time I was old enough to go out in civilized society. So, it was hard to do things that appealed to all of us. We stuck pretty close to home as a family. Our lives centered around our extended family, our parish and our sports teams."

"Then how do you know so much about the back alleys?"

"'Cause as soon as I was old enough to ride my skateboard over these hills, I was gone," she said with satisfaction. "I still remember the first time I had the guts — or the stupidity — to ride down Castro."

Through the encroaching fog, Jamie saw the steep terrain that they had to descend to reach the main business area of said street. "You … you rode down this?"

"Yep. I strapped my little helmet on as tight as I could and let 'er rip! My heart was in my throat the whole time, and my legs were shaking so badly I almost fell off, but I did it. When I got to the bottom, I actually spent a minute feeling my body to make sure I was still in one piece. I was tingling so much that I couldn't really tell!"

"So, once you crossed the Rubicon, there was no stopping you, huh?"

"Nope. I had some buddies from the neighborhood, boys of course, who had to do it since I could. Once we all had our 'wings,' we just started ranging farther and farther from home. We had passes that let us take Muni for free, so we'd go over to Castro and Market and just jump on the first train. We'd ride until we got tired of it, then get off and skate around until we got bored. Then we'd get back on and head home."

"My God!" she cried. "I had to get advance permission to go to a friend's house, and she lived three doors down!"

"Well, Da didn't know a tenth of what I did, and it's better that way. But I remember the first time I got pinched for trespassing down in the Embarcadero."

317

"The Embarcadero! That's miles and miles from here. How old were you?"

"Probably ten or so," she mused. "Anyway, we were skateboarding down some really cool handicapped ramps some of the big buildings have. The big-clothes trend had just barely started, and we were all dressed up in our big skateboarding pants and those huge parkas. It was winter and really cold, so I had on a stocking cap, too. Da would not buy me the big pants of course, so I would swipe Rory's pants when Da was at work and roll them up so I didn't break my neck. Anyway, the pants were too big, even for my purposes, and they started to fall down just when the guards started running. My buddies blew out of there, but I caught the rolled up hem in a wheel and took a header. One of the guards caught me and started treating me pretty roughly, just to teach me a lesson."

"Did he hit you?" she asked in horror.

"No, he was just dragging me by my coat and screaming at me. Anyway, he dragged me into the security office, and they started to give me the third degree. Of course, I clammed up and refused to talk. I figured they'd let me go after scaring me, but no dice. They searched me and found my Muni pass. It was in my name, but they still hadn't figured out I was a girl yet, and the pass didn't help! I had to sit in that office with these goons threatening me for hours! They left a message on the machine at home, since the number was on my pass, and Da finally called at around six o'clock. Listening to their end of the conversation was pretty funny," she recalled. "I heard them say, 'Mr. O'Flaherty, we caught your son illegally skateboarding, and we're holding him prior to sending him to the Youth Authority.'"

Jamie was horrified at the rough treatment that her friend had been subjected to. "Weren't you terrified?" she cried.

"Not of them or the Youth Authority," Ryan admitted. "Actually the Youth Authority sounded pretty good compared to facing my father. The guy on the phone started insisting that I was Da's son, and I could just imagine him telling the boys to line up and count off," she laughed. "But then the guard's eyes got big, and he turned to me and yanked off my stocking cap. He about croaked when he saw that I was a little girl. They got real nice to me after that — brought me a soda and some cookies. That really pissed me off," she grumbled.

"What? It pissed you off that he was nice to you?"

"Yeah, since it was only because I was a girl. If he was going to be a jerk 'cause I was a boy, he should have been a jerk when I turned out to be a girl!"

"You're something else, Ryan," she laughed. "So then what happened?"

"Oh, I had to sit there until Da came to get me."

"Was he mad?"

"He was more mad about the parking fee than anything else," she laughed. "I had to pay him back for that out of my allowance. Since I only got $2 a week it took me a month!"

"Was that your only punishment?" she asked, not imagining that Martin would ever hit a child.

"Yeah, plus a very long lecture that I really deserved about using a handicapped ramp for play. We learned our lesson that day, though," she admitted. "From then on, we always kept one kid near the ramp to warn us if a handicapped person was coming."

"You are incorrigible, Ryan O'Flaherty."

"Yeah, well, hanging out on my skateboard was nothing compared to the trouble I got into down here," she smirked as they entered the business district of Castro Street.

"It looks so … ordinary," Jamie remarked as she looked around.

"You expected what? Dungeons, transvestites in every window?"

"No … I don't know what I expected, but it hardly looks gay at all," she mused as she turned in a complete circle.

"Yeah, it's pretty hard to tell," Ryan dryly remarked as they stopped in front of a small housewares store. "Do you like those towel bars?"

Jamie squinted at the very small towel racks that were displayed right near the front window. The bars were actually cast concrete replicas of massively engorged penises, all extra large. The towels were embroidered as was usual for guest towels, both reading "His." The blonde's eyes closed, and she shook her head slowly. "I've never been to a neighborhood that should have an NC-17 rating!"

But Ryan wasn't finished with the tour, taking great delight in shocking her friend. A nearby video store had a display up celebrating the upcoming Academy Awards with Oscar replicas lining the display window, each Oscar sporting a massive, gold erection. Jamie gazed up at her smirking friend and asked, "Is the other side of the street all vaginas?"

"No," Ryan laughed. "It's pretty much all about the penis in Castro."

Now Jamie's sense of equality was insulted. "That hardly seems fair," she demanded with hands on her hips. "Lesbians need love, too!"

"I couldn't agree more," Ryan soothed as she wrapped her arm around her feisty friend to continue their walk.

⌘

When they reached the ice cream store, Ryan insisted that Jamie get two scoops of the double chocolate flavor. Because it was a little cold out, they ate in the small shop. Ryan had ordered a hot fudge sundae, and Jamie watched her eat with obvious pleasure.

"Are you sure you like kissing better than eating?" she teased.

"I'm positive," Ryan replied with a saucy grin.

"Then you must really like kissing," Jamie drawled. "'Cause you sure like to eat."

"You have no idea," Ryan intoned solemnly, tilting her head to place a wet kiss on a fudge-covered scoop of vanilla ice cream. Her pink tongue emerged from her lips and sensually licked the ice cream and chocolate from her mouth, with Jamie offering up a prayer of thanks that she was already sitting down — since her legs would surely not hold her.

⌘

Back on the street, they decided to return via the opposite side, just in case there were hidden vaginas that Ryan hadn't previously noticed. "It really seems unfair to me, Ryan," Jamie insisted as they confirmed that the street was clearly focused on gay men and their equipment. "I mean, Castro is supposed to be this big gay Mecca, but it's all about men. I mean, lesbians are the least interested group in the world when it comes to penises."

"Well," Ryan drawled, "ones with feeling in them at least."

"Huh?" she asked, turning to face her friend, cocking her head slightly as she did so.

"Sorry," Ryan said quickly. "I was just making a joke. I was referring to lesbians' interest in non-human penises."

Jamie gazed down at the ground for a moment, and Ryan thought she had offended her by the little joke. But she was obviously considering the matter, because she finally looked up and said, "Is that really a *thing*? I mean, I thought that was a bad joke that guys always make."

Ryan's color rose dramatically as she pursed her lips and tried to decide how much to reveal. "Uhm … well, it's kind of a … do you really … uhm … should I give you my personal response, or do you want a lesbian-wide answer?" she finally got out.

Jamie immediately grasped her arm as she assured her, "I'm sorry, Ryan, I don't mean to make you uncomfortable. I've just heard snide little comments about lesbians and their fake penises for years. I just wanted to know if there's any truth to it."

"Uhm ... well ... I guess it depends on the, uhm ... person ..." she stammered.

"You don't have to answer, Ryan," she assured her. "I just ... I guess I'm surprised this embarrasses you, since nothing else has seemed to."

Ryan considered this as they started to walk again. "Hmm, you are right about that," she mused. "Maybe it's because I know you a lot better now. I don't know, Jamie," she said slowly. "Maybe I don't want you to think badly of me ... your opinion has come to mean an awful lot."

"Why would something like this change my opinion of you?"

"I don't know," she mumbled, looking young and unsure of herself. "You've been pretty conservative with your sexual expression, and I guess I worry that you'll think my experiences make me kinda ... I don't know ... uhm, maybe slutty?" She gazed down at Jamie through the long bangs that had fallen into her eyes, adding to her child-like demeanor.

"Ryan!" she nearly shouted. "You are a totally honorable woman! I would never think any such thing about you! But I also have no desire to make you uncomfortable. Let's just drop the whole topic, okay?" she asked gently.

"'Kay," she agreed, happy that Jamie respected her privacy. She slung her arm around her friend's shoulders, and they walked on in silence.

"We're back already?" Jamie asked when they neared the house. "That seemed so fast."

"Yeah, it did," Ryan agreed. "But time always flies when I'm with you."

Jamie looked over at her grinning friend's guileless face, and gave her hand a gentle squeeze. "You can say that again."

Ryan let her smaller friend precede her as they climbed the short flight of stairs up to the front door. When they were nearly at the top, she leaned in close and whispered, "Just for the record, I've been on both ends of artificial penises. As Martha Stewart would say, 'It's a good thing!'"

⌘

When they went back downstairs, Jamie had to admit that she felt a lot better about her breakup, but now she had a whole new topic setting her teeth on edge. *Both ends? What in the hell does she mean by that?* she mused, unable to get the images of Ryan and artificial penises out of her mind.

Ryan walked over to her bookshelf and pulled out a neatly labeled photo album. Idly turning the pages, she found the photo she was looking for and called Jamie over. Turning the book and handing it to her, she pointed at the photo in the center of the page without comment. Jamie barked out a laugh, slapping her hand over her mouth and staring up at Ryan in shock. There, memorialized for all to see, was the little street urchin that Ryan had described earlier in the evening. "My God!" she finally got out, now able to control her laughter. "Is this really you?"

Ryan walked around to stand next to her friend. Taking the book in her hands, she smiled fondly at the image of her young self and nodded briefly. The photo showed five little ragamuffins, all of a similar age. They were posing on Maeve's front steps, and each child tried to appear older and tougher for the camera. The other four were boys, but they were all dressed nearly identically. Ryan was in the front, standing on the ground in front of the stairs. She was so extraordinarily tall that she was the same height as the two boys standing on the step behind her. Jamie guessed that she was rail thin, but it was very difficult to tell for sure because of her laughably large clothes.

She had on a canvas barn jacket, tan in color, with a darker brown corduroy collar. The hood of a dark green sweatshirt peeked out past the collar, but the jacket was so huge she could have easily fit another sweatshirt on and still have had room. Stiff-looking dark blue jeans covered her long legs, the cuffs rolled up at least five inches. The pants were so large it was impossible to see where one leg started and the other stopped — it just looked like a big mass of fabric. She also sported flat, black, thick-soled tennis shoes that looked to be about size eight. A black baseball cap rested on her long, black hair in its usual backwards position, and her trusty skateboard was resting on its tail, held upright by her long, slender fingers.

Every child bore a scowl with varying degrees of success. Ryan was probably the least successful of all, her vivid blue eyes and microscopic smile giving her away.

Jamie stared at the picture for so long that her eyes became dry. "I don't think I've ever seen anything more precious," she finally said, looking up into Ryan's bemused eyes.

"Precious?" she squawked. "I look like a ... I don't even know what I look like!"

"You look just like a tiny little seed of who you've become," she said with a voice full of wonder. "Look at yourself!" she urged excitedly. "You look so confident and strong! Those boys weren't leading that little group — you were! That's completely obvious," she announced. "And even though you were trying to look tough, you still have that terribly gentle spirit just oozing out of those blue eyes. See it?" she demanded.

Ryan gazed at the picture and then turned back to her friend. "Are we looking at the same picture? I just look like a little hoodlum!"

"Not at all!" Jamie cried. "I would have killed to be able to hang out with you for just a day! I bet you guys had more fun in an afternoon than I did in a year! This is what being a kid should be, Ryan," she cried. "Testing your own capabilities, learning to interact with other kids, trying to look outrageous! That's the essence of youth!"

"I guess I see your point," she said slowly. "Da let me test myself constantly when I was little. I don't think I ever got in trouble for trying something stupid. He only got mad when I did something that could hurt someone else, like taking over those handicapped ramps. He really let me be who I was, even though I'm sure he was constantly worried about me. That really was a gift," she reflected soberly. "I hope I can do the same for my kids."

Jamie wrapped her arm around her friend's sturdy waist. "You'll probably be completely overprotective," she teased.

"Hmm, maybe," she allowed reflectively. "But I don't think so. I want my kids to experience the freedom that I had. It's what allowed me to dream," she added with a small smile.

As she closed the book and replaced it on the shelf, she turned to her friend and announced, "Now it's time for you to dream. To bed wit' ya."

The walk, or the climb, as Jamie referred to it, had really relaxed her, and she felt ready to sleep. She went to the bathroom to put on her pajamas, and when she returned, she was pleasantly surprised to see a grinning Ryan, sitting on the bed, holding a bottle of massage lotion.

Jamie flung herself onto the bed, pulling her shirt up as she fell.

"I don't want to force you ..." Ryan teased.

As the strong, cool hands began to work their magic, Jamie closed her eyes and silently wished that one day those hands would know her completely.

⌘

On Monday night Jamie summoned her courage and made the announcement of her break-up to her roommates. Both of them were sitting in the kitchen when she returned from school, and she did her best to sound as if it were a mutual decision based on some incompatibilities. She would not, under any circumstances, allow Cassie to know how great a role the devious blonde had played, nor would she let her know how truly devastated she was.

After Cassie had made some sincere-sounding comments expressing sympathy for Jamie, she left to go to her boyfriend's apartment for the night. As soon as the door closed, Jamie let out a sigh and said, "Thank God she's gone. Now I can tell you the truth!"

⌘

Now that her roommates were out of the way, Jamie had to talk to her parents, and she decided to do so in person. On Tuesday afternoon, she drove down to the Peninsula, arriving just after her father had returned home. She had never come down on a weekday, and when she thought about it, she realized she had never come down unannounced. Her parents were obviously quite surprised to see her, and they both seemed a little anxious over the unexpected visit, so she immediately launched into the reason for it. She told them most of the story, omitting, of course, the role that Ryan had played, focusing instead on the difficulty of being apart during the week, of Jack's intense schedule and of her own doubts about her commitment.

To her amazement, her parents were completely sympathetic. It was obvious that her father was saddened by the news, since he had grown quite fond of Jack. But she had tried her best to remove any animus towards Jack when she described the reasons for the breakup. Both of the Evanses seemed to agree that even though he was a wonderful young man, Jamie was probably not really ready to make a permanent commitment, and Catherine in particular seemed relieved that Jamie would not be tied down at so young an age.

As she was leaving, her father walked her to the car. "Was part of this because of your friend, Jamie?" he inquired with a touch of hesitation.

"Yes, Daddy, it was partly that," she admitted.

"It seems odd to me that Jack would be so bothered by that, but maybe that was just a sign that he wasn't ready, either," he reflected.

"I am so happy that you and mother are so supportive of me, Daddy. I can't thank you enough," she said sincerely.

"I love you very much, Jamie. I've always been proud of you, and the way you've handled this makes me that much prouder," he said with a smile.

"I want you to promise me that you won't treat Jack any differently, Daddy. I don't want this to interfere with his job opportunities."

"I don't mix business with emotions, honey. Jack will be a good lawyer, and we'll be lucky to land him. Don't worry about that," he said as he kissed her cheek.

⌘

On Wednesday morning, Jamie sat in a long hallway waiting for Linda Levy's office hours to begin. The professor came strolling down the hall and waved a friendly greeting. "Hi, Jamie," she said. "Sorry I couldn't see you earlier in the week. Come on in and tell me what's on your mind."

"I need a referral for a therapist, and I thought you might be able to refer me to someone good," she related, a bit hesitantly.

"Sure, I know a lot of therapists in the area. Would you feel comfortable telling me what types of issues you need to deal with?" she asked.

"I'm just having some general growing up issues. I'm having a little trouble with my parents," she said as she stalled for time. "And I think I might have some issues with my sexual orientation," she finally got out.

"Okay, I know a lot of people that could probably help you. Is cost a factor?"

"No, not really," she admitted.

"Do you have a preference for any particular type of therapist, like a psychiatrist or a psychologist?"

"No. I just want someone I can relate to," she said.

"Do you care if it's a man or a woman?" Linda continued.

"I think I'd like a woman," she blushed as she heard her double entendre.

Linda grinned back at her and looked through her address book, finally jotting down three different names. "I'm going to refer you to a psychiatrist, a psychologist and a clinical social worker. They're all good, and I think you'd like each of them. You can set up an appointment with each if you'd like to interview them, or you can just pick one. Do whatever feels comfortable, Jamie."

"Is there one of these women whom you would recommend more highly than the others?"

"I know the psychologist pretty well. So, I would say I know her style the best. I suppose she would be my pick," Linda replied.

"Thanks a lot, Linda. I really appreciate your input."

"Any time, Jamie. If you ever need to chat on a non-therapeutic basis, I'd be happy to. I hope things work out well for you." Jamie reached for the note, but Linda held onto it tightly, drawing Jamie's eyes to hers. "One piece of advice," she said quietly. "You can never make a mistake by being who you really are, no matter how scary the truth might seem."

Jamie nodded briefly and took the names from the professor. They shared a quick smile as Jamie left the office.

That evening, Ryan finished preparing the simple dinner that she and Conor were going to share. He finished setting the table and came back into the kitchen to help carry their plates to the dining room. "Boy, Tracy sure looked good on Sunday," he said appreciatively. "She looks fabulous in that dark brown color. You should have her wear it more often."

"I don't think I get to have input any more," she said as she carried the last of the dishes into the room. "We broke up this afternoon."

"What? I thought you were serious about her?" He had stopped in the center of the room, a big plate of pasta held in one strong hand.

"I was. But I finally realized that she wasn't 'the one.' So, rather than waste her time, I told her the truth."

"How did she take it?" he asked, remembering some of his more disastrous breakups.

"Fine. Actually, a little too fine," she admitted with a smirk. "She took it like a trooper."

"That's kind of weird," he decided. "But why did you break up with her? She was pretty, smart, funny and very sexy. Well, she looked sexy," he grinned. "But you'd know better than I."

"She was all that," Ryan agreed. "But she didn't really like the amount of time I spent with the family. She preferred to do things with just the two of us — exclusively."

"What is she, some kind of psycho?" he teased. "What's not to love?"

"That's how I feel," she agreed with a smile. "But she was pretty reserved. I think we were a little overpowering for her when we were all together. I noticed that she doesn't like to be teased, and as you know, you can't get through a dinner here without being teased ten times!"

"Gee, Ryan, did we contribute to your breakup? If you had told us, we would have laid off the teasing."

"Nope. That's not the kind of woman I want. I can't be with someone that I have to be so careful with. If she had told me that she wanted to work on being more comfortable around you guys, I would have made some concessions. But she just wanted to maneuver me into spending less time at home. And that was just not going to happen," she said firmly.

Conor looked at her for a moment and said, "It's too bad Jamie's straight. She would be perfect for you."

"Really? I thought she was perfect for you," she dryly observed.

"Yeah, but I've never gotten any vibes from her. She treats me like an older brother. How about you? Any vibes?" he asked, mostly because he was interested, but partly to protect his $50 bet with Rory.

"Uhm ..." A decided flush bloomed upon her cheeks.

"I thought so," he said slowly. "You two have been sending off some serious sparks. So, what are you gonna do about it?"

"Well, she did a little something about it last week. But it was nothing huge," she said defensively. "She got a little tipsy on her birthday, and she kissed me, but we both just acted like it didn't happen."

"Again, what are you going to do about it?"

"Nothing," she said quickly. "I have a firm policy not to date good friends, and Jamie is the best friend I have. I couldn't stand to lose her companionship."

"You know, Ryan, I'm certainly not the best person to give relationship advice, but maybe you should change that policy."

"Why do you say that?"

"Well, you claim you're ready to find a real girlfriend. Why not get rid of six months of work and date someone you already know? You were with Tracy for more than three months before you found out she didn't have some vital requirements. If you tried to make it work with a friend, you could concentrate on the love and sex parts, instead of having to get to know one another."

"That might be a good idea in theory, but given my record, all I would succeed in doing is losing her as a friend as well as a lover."

"That's not being fair to yourself," he admonished her. "You haven't tried to have many steady girlfriends."

"That's true, but I just don't think it's wise to even consider Jamie. She's ostensibly straight, she just broke up with her fiancé and she's my best friend. That's an awful lot to overcome."

"But you do find her attractive, don't you?"

"I'm not blind, Conor," she laughed. "She's way beyond attractive in my book."

"So, you would try to date her if you weren't friends, right?"

"I'd be on her like green on grass," she said with a sly grin.

"Well, I still think you should consider what I said," he urged.

"I'll give that some thought, Conor, but I think I have to keep her safely in my fantasies." Her eyes grew wide as she realized that she was being way too frank. She ladled another helping of penne onto her brother's plate. "I've got a perfectly available woman on tap for tonight, and I don't want to keep this one waiting."

⌘

"Hi, Ally," she purred an hour later.

"Hey, gorgeous. Long time no see. Come on in. Did you come prepared?" she asked, giving Ryan the once-over.

"You told me to bring a hearty appetite," Ryan grinned, "and I'm practically starving to death."

⌘

The next morning, Jamie was waiting for Ryan after her eight o'clock class. "I was going to ask you if you wanted to go get coffee, but I can see I'm too late," she said as she pointed at the empty twenty-four ounce cup in her friend's hand.

"I could use more," she said as she shook her head.

"Are you okay? I know you were planning on speaking to Tracy, and I was concerned that it might have been hard for you."

"No, actually we had lunch yesterday, and we talked it all out. She admitted that she didn't really have an interest in being part of my extended family. She said that she wanted to have a relationship with me, but that she wasn't really ready for a big commitment thing. She said she probably doesn't want kids, either, so my suspicions were correct."

"So, how did you leave it?"

"Well," she blushed a little, "she was more than willing to have a little fling, but I stood my ground and turned her down flat."

"Really?" she said happily. *Maybe she's getting this serial dating out of her system. Oh, please, oh, please.* "Maybe you've really changed how you feel about sex. Maybe you won't be satisfied without some substance in your encounters."

"I think that's a rush to judgment," Ryan admitted wryly.

"Why? Are you already planning for your next victim?"

"Uhm ... I had a date last night," she admitted.

"Jeez, Ryan! You didn't break up with her until noon. How did you find someone to go out with in an afternoon?"

"I didn't really go out," she revealed. "I called my friend, Ally, and she, uhm ... helped me ... make up for lost time."

"God, I bet Tracy would love to hear that!"

"She was really okay with breaking up, Jamie. As a matter of fact, I got the impression that she was mainly interested in me to see if she could get me to be faithful. She was hardly broken up about it. It made me realize that I can't just look at a checklist of what I want in a woman. There has to be some chemistry there, and I don't think Tracy and I ever had that.

We really wanted different things from a relationship."

"I'm sorry if I sound judgmental, Ryan. I think I'm projecting how I'd feel if Jack had had a date on Sunday."

"I understand, Jamie. It's hard not to apply other situations to your own. But believe me, Tracy didn't cry herself to sleep last night."

"And you obviously didn't, either," she said as she gave her a mock scowl.

"Oh, I cried," she teased. "I cried for mercy. I'm seriously out of sex shape!"

⌘

After her first visit with her therapist, Anna, Jamie told Ryan about her decision to finally seek some counseling. Ryan was supportive and offered a blanket invitation to listen to anything Jamie had to say about the experience, but she commented that she understood if Jamie wanted to keep everything private.

Jamie had been seeing Anna for three weeks when she finally had the nerve to bring up her sexuality. Since cost was not an issue, they had decided that twice-a-week sessions were a good idea, at least until Jamie felt some relief. After only four sessions she actually felt significantly better, but she had spent nearly all of those sessions talking about Jack and her distress over the breakup. Now it was time to open up fully.

During her seventh session she finally broached the subject. "There's something else that's bothering me, Anna," she said hesitantly.

"Tell me, Jamie," she replied neutrally.

"I think that I might be gay," she replied as she stared at the pattern on the rug, hearing the words come from her lips for the first time.

To her surprise the world didn't stop turning. Anna just gazed at her, her normal empathic expression on her face. "What makes you think so?"

Feeling emboldened by Anna's neutral reaction, Jamie revealed, "I'm incredibly attracted to my closest friend, Ryan. I ... I haven't really told you the whole story about why Jack and I broke up," she admitted.

After going through the entire story Anna asked, "Have you ever acted on any of your feelings for Ryan?"

"Sort of. On my birthday I gave her a kiss on the lips," she replied.

"How did she react?"

"We both acted like everything was normal, but right after that, she said she thought we should leave because we were both a little drunk." After a moment she added, "She wasn't drunk, though. Maybe it made her uncomfortable, and she used that as an excuse."

"Did she act any differently towards you after the incident?"

"No, not really. She's pretty much the same."

"So, it must not have bothered her too much," she observed. "Do you want to pursue her, Jamie?"

"I really think I do, Anna. But I just feel so overwhelmed by everything that's happened. I'm afraid of what I'll do if she isn't interested."

"Do?" the older woman asked, tilting her head.

Jamie's head dropped back against her chair, and she let out a long breath. "I know I said that I think I might be gay, but that isn't really true. I feel like I'm gay for Ryan, if that makes any sense. I'm not interested in being with women as a group — it's just Ryan that attracts me. If she's not interested in me, I don't know what I'll do next! I sure didn't do well with a man, and I don't think there are any Episcopalian nunneries," she groused.

Anna smiled at her attempt at humor. "Is there any reason that you feel compelled to do something right now? Or could you wait a while until you feel more grounded?" she queried.

"I guess I'm not in a rush," she said, considering the suggestion for the first time. "She just broke up with someone, and I don't think she wants to get into another relationship right away. You know, it makes me feel better to think that I don't have to hurry."

"You might feel better if you resolve some of your feelings about Jack before you put all of your energies into connecting with another person, Jamie. And I think you would be more clear on what to do about Ryan if we spend some time really exploring your feelings."

"So you would recommend that I not tell her about how I feel right now?" she asked.

"My recommendation is that you keep your life as simple as possible until you're sleeping better and able to eat. If expressing your feelings to Ryan would cause more stress, I would advise against it for the time being," she replied.

"Well, given that I feel one hundred percent better already, I guess that's good advice," she smiled.

⌘

On Friday afternoon Ryan was waiting for Jamie when the blonde emerged from her final class. "What are you doing tomorrow?" she asked without preamble.

"Uh … nothing. Why?"

"It's Saint Patrick's Day, lassie!" she announced in her lilting Irish accent.

"Okay ... what are you doing?"

"I'm the barmaid at The Celtic Knot, of course!"

"Since when do you work in a bar?"

"I do it every St. Patrick's day," she explained in her normal voice. "If you're free, come over and have a pint. Conor and some of the cousins will be there to harass me, of course, so it should be fun."

"Is that the place right on 24th Street?"

"Yeah, and if you come, be prepared for a huge crowd. It's quite a zoo." She draped her arm around Jamie's shoulders. "Now, let's go work out. We've got to make sure your drinking arm is in tip-top shape."

⌘

Jamie didn't want to be at the bar alone, so she waited until 8:00 to head over. She had to park so far away from the bar that she wound up a block past Ryan's house. *My God, it's never been this congested over here,* she marveled. *I guess everyone is out celebrating St. Patrick's Day.*

Her suspicions were confirmed when she tried to wedge into the bar. The rowdy patrons were packed in so tightly, she knew they were violating several city ordinances, but she assumed the local police turned a blind eye on St. Paddy's Day. It took a great deal of patience and a few well placed elbows, but she finally made her way near to the large wooden bar. She lucked out and found that the crowd had deposited her right next to a happy little group that included Brendan, Conor, Niall, Kieran and Frank. "Jamie!" they cried, nearly as one.

The overly exuberant tone of their call indicated the advanced level of their inebriation, but she gamely allowed each of the men to offer a hug and didn't even complain about Conor's rather sloppy kiss on her cheek. "How long have you boys been here?" she shouted over the din.

"We walked Ryan over at 5:00," Brendan supplied. "What time is it now?"

"Almost 9:00," she yelled in reply.

"No wonder I can't feel me feet!" he marveled in his own Irish accent.

Just then Jamie spotted her favorite barmaid. Ryan looked extremely attractive this evening, not that that occurrence was odd. But there was something about her that looked very different. It took Jamie a moment to realize what it was — Ryan looked straight! It wasn't just that her hair was held back with a braided green and white ribbon. It wasn't that she was dressed in a form-fitting, emerald green knit vest sans blouse. It wasn't even the fact that she wore a touch of makeup. No, it was the fact that she was *acting* straight and that, most decidedly in Jamie's experience, was a rarity. Ryan spotted her and gave a demure little wave along with a toss of her jet-black hair. Jamie grinned and shook her head at the display, but when Ryan approached the man to her left, she nearly fell from the stool that Brendan had insisted she occupy.

"Evenin', darlin'," she announced in a rather dramatic, thick Irish accent, as she graced him with her most winning smile and a girlish batting of her eyes. "How can I help ya?"

The tongue-tied man seemed as flabbergasted by the raven-haired beauty as Jamie was, but he managed to choke out, "Are you new around here?"

"Indeed!" she cried. "Just over from Killala in Mayo!" She said this with such joy, that it appeared she expected the man to be a relative from the old sod or at least a fellow Kilallan.

"Welcome to America," he said dreamily. "Can I have a pint of Guinness and your phone number?"

"Aw, go on wit' ya!" she cried. "You lads are all so friendly! I've had more good wishes and offers to show me around than I can count. Such a friendly place!" she said as she turned to draw his pint. Jamie noticed that her friend bent over just enough to show her best assets as she drew his stout, smiling that unnerving smile the entire time. She placed the pint in front of him and said coyly, "I'm not sure how long I'll be stayin', love. It costs a pretty penny to stay in your lovely city."

He nodded as if in a trance, pulling out a five-dollar bill for the $3 pint and thanking Ryan profusely as he walked back to his mates, happy to leave the gorgeous woman a sixty-six percent tip. Ryan dashed to the register and rang up the $3, sticking two singles into her bulging back pocket. Jogging back down the long bar, she signaled to Jamie and said, "Meet me at the end of the bar!"

It was a tough trip, but she made the short distance not too much after her grinning friend. Ryan dug into her straining pocket and handed the gob of slightly damp bills to her friend. "Keep my tips, will you?" she said right into Jamie's ear in order to be heard. "It doesn't look right to look like I'm doing too well."

"Jeez Ryan!" she cried. "How did you make all this?"

"An Irish accent, a tight sweater and a Wonderbra!" she laughed. "How else?"

"So you put on this act just to make money?" she asked, slightly incredulous.

"Mighty!" she agreed as she pinched Jamie's cheek and trotted back to her post.

⌘

By the time Jamie made it back, Conor had procured a perfectly poured pint of Guinness for her as well as another round for his drinking buddies. She had never seen any of the boys in their cups — had never, in fact, seen them drink at all, and she had to admit that they were a fun group of drunks. Conor especially was twice as charming if a little sloppy. He tossed an arm around Jamie and held on to her for the duration of the evening. But after a while it became clear that he did so to maintain his balance as much as to show his affection.

The boys had been teasing and taunting each other mercilessly all night, and Jamie found herself on the end of a few pointed barbs herself. But she didn't mind a bit — in fact it made her feel like one of the group, and she did her best to give as good as she got. She limited herself to two pints, but that was more than enough to give her a very pleasant buzz. Her mind reeled at the thought of how the boys must be feeling, since she had personally seen them each have three in the two hours she had occupied her stool.

When one patron got a little too enamored of Ryan, she watched all of the boys give him a long, stern look, but they didn't make an obvious move to deter him. Ryan took the man's wandering hands in stride, stepping quickly out of the way when he tried to grab a handful of her shapely butt. "I'm amazed you didn't flatten him," Jamie chuckled into Conor's ear.

"Aw, you can't blame them, Jamie," he explained rather expansively. "She looks like she wants them to grab her; she flirts with them constantly … hell, *I'm* half-tempted to make a play for her!" He laughed at his own joke and nearly passed out in hysterics when he caught the look on Jamie's stunned face. "I'm kidding, Jamie!" he howled. She slapped him lightly on the side, and rolled her eyes in exasperation at his antics. But he leaned over as he pulled her tightly against his side. "How about you?" he purred rather seductively.

Her mouth grew bone dry as she stammered, "M … m … me what?"

"Do you have an interest in my baby sister?" he asked in the same seductive growl.

"W … w … why would I have an interest?" she stuttered weakly.

"I asked first," he reminded her. "Come on now, you can tell Uncle Conor," he crooned. "I promise I won't tell."

"I … I … I, uhm …" she muttered, annoyed at her own inarticulateness.

"Uh-huh," he murmured, "Just as I thought." Her rapidly blushing face and weakening knees caused him to pat her shoulder comfortingly and hold on a bit tighter. "There, there," he assured her. "You could do worse than to fall for my sister, you know. And personally, I think she'd be a fool to let you get away." He tilted his dark head down and rested it against Jamie's for a moment. "You're quite a woman, Jamie."

She closed her eyes tightly and tacitly acknowledged her attraction, but then a relatively soft object hurled at her head at close range broke the moment. Turning faster than her slightly blurry eyes appreciated, she whirled around to find a grinning Ryan tossing peanuts at her head from a dish on the bar. "Don't encourage him, Jamie," she warned. "He'll follow you home like a lost puppy."

"No problem," she replied, managing a grin of her own. "I've always wanted a puppy," she said affectionately as she teasingly petted Conor's dark head.

"Well, don't blame me if he starts humpin' your leg," she warned, accent firmly in place as she dashed down the bar to pour another pint.

⌘

Even though she had tried valiantly to leave several times, Jamie found herself still in place as Ryan called out, "Last call, lads! Final pints!"

She lifted her arm to gaze in amazement at her watch, which did, in fact, read 1:45 a.m. "My God," she muttered. "How did it get to be so late?"

"And how did I get to be so drunk?" Brendan moaned, dropping his head into his hands.

"You are drunk," Frank agreed, shaking his head and clucking in distain.

"Can't hold his liquor," agreed Kieran, who was clearly as drunk as the rest of the boys.

"I've only had two, and I can hardly talk!" Jamie moaned. "How will I get home?"

"Yer comin' wit' us," Conor insisted in his own Irish accent. "As soon as we help da wee one wit her chores."

Jamie watched in awe as the drunken O'Flahertys got to their wobbly feet and gamely bussed the small tables around the still-crowded bar. "Drink up, drink up," Niall insisted as he walked from patron to patron, trying to retrieve their nearly-full glasses.

She hopped to her feet and went behind the bar to aid Ryan and the other two women in their daunting task of washing each glass that was returned. But many hands made short work of it, and by the time Frank and Brendan rather forcibly ushered the last patron out at 2:30, the bar was clean enough for the professional cleaning crew that arrived every morning to clean the floors and the bathrooms.

Ryan walked, and the others stumbled the few short blocks, first to Frank's home, then another few to Kieran and Niall's. They arrived at the O'Flaherty house at 2:45, grateful for the fact that Martin was at work. Ryan guided Brendan to her father's room and gave him a kiss on the cheek as he fell to the bed. Conor was able to make it all the way up to his room, but he accomplished the feat by holding on to the banister for dear life.

Ryan tossed an arm around Jamie and guided her down to her bedroom. "So, did ya have fun?" she asked, back in her Gaelic persona.

"Yeah, very much so," she admitted. "Your family is really a blast to hang out with, Ryan. And it was worth the trip to see you playing the coquettish straight girl," she teased as she playfully backhanded her in the belly.

Ryan looked thoughtful as they reached the lower floor. "It's fun for me to act like that once in a while," she mused. "But I can't imagine having to do that every day. I don't know how some straight women keep that act up!" She held out her hands as Jamie started unburdening her pockets of the plethora of bills she carried. "Like you," Ryan said as she started to sort the money. "You're a straight girl, and you hardly ever seem like you're putting on that 'Oh, you're so cool, and I'm such a helpless creature' routine." She looked up at Jamie who was choosing a T-shirt from the massive selection in Ryan's neatly labeled drawers.

"Hardly ever?" Jamie asked.

"Well, I saw you do it with Jack that time I was in Palo Alto," she mused. "But that's the only time."

"Hmm, I guess I don't do it much," she admitted. "But Cassie does it constantly," she observed as she considered her circle of friends. "She acts like she's got a brain stem injury when her boyfriend is around."

"Well, it's nice that you don't do it much," Ryan observed. "It must be demeaning."

"Well, you do some manipulative things to get women, too, Ryan. Don't act like you don't."

Ryan looked up at her with a completely guileless look on her handsome face. "I don't think I do," she said. "Oh, I flirt and act a little more forceful than normal, but I don't think I try to alter who I am, or what my capabilities are," she mused. "I just try to show my assets to the best of my ability," she said with a wicked glare as she shook her shoulders and jiggled her breasts in an entirely provocative manner. "That kind of stuff is too easy," she muttered disdainfully. "Women just don't go for it."

Some women do, Jamie thought as she quickly scrambled to the bed to avoid falling down.

⌘

After Ryan had methodically counted her booty, they got ready for bed and hopped in together. "What's up?" Jamie finally asked after she felt Ryan toss and turn for long minutes.

"I don't know. I guess I'm just a little worked up after tonight. I'm having a hard time relaxing," she admitted.

"Let me help you out for a change," Jamie said as she sat up and patted her lap. "Let me give you a nice head rub."

Ryan smiled in the darkness and willingly rolled over onto her side, laying her head onto Jamie's thigh. "Nice," she chuckled, patting the smooth skin. "Your leg makes a nice pillow."

Jamie started to trail her fingers through the inky strands, the faint moonlight making the glossy hair appear midnight blue. Soon, she was lost in the moment, feeling deeply connected to the beautiful woman lying next to her. As Ryan got more comfortable, she relaxed her posture, eventually nestling her body all along Jamie's length.

Not minding the invasion of her personal space in the least, Jamie continued to work, focusing intently on the sense of deep inner peace she felt when Ryan was close to her.

Eventually, the larger woman fell asleep, her soft, even breathing signaling the depth of her slumber. Her incredibly luscious breasts were pressed against Jamie's thigh, and if the smaller woman concentrated, she could feel her heartbeat thrumming strongly.

Not wanting Ryan to move a muscle, Jamie scooted down just enough to be able to curl slightly around her sleeping body, rendering a human model of the yin-yang symbol. Letting Ryan's scent fill her senses, Jamie drifted off, her dreams peaceful, gentle and filled with love.

⌘

Ryan woke just before 7:00, puzzled by a few sensations. One was that she and Jamie were wrapped around each other like a pair of snakes seeking warmth on a cold day. The other was how totally marvelous it felt to touch her friend so intimately. *God, this is a pleasant way to wake up.* She wanted to just lie there and feel the connection, but she knew she should move away. *Why does it feel so good to have her touch me in such an innocent way? Damn! I don't think I can keep my wits about me this morning.*

Regarding her friend's sleeping face in the morning light, Ryan watched the advance of the sun, which was just beginning to touch the pillow where Jamie's head rested. Her golden hair was mussed from sleep and tumbled in an attractive fashion around her face. The tips of her long, dark-blonde eyelashes were lightly brushed by the sun's rays, and her smooth skin was beginning to take on a golden tone from all of the outdoor activity. Ryan grew fascinated by the few freckles that dusted her nose, and it was all she could do not to lean over and kiss each of those cute little dots.

God, I wish she were a lesbian! It's so frustrating to feel this way about her, and not be able to do anything about it. But she knew that she could never do anything about it. It was one thing to take a lesbian friend and try to make her into a lover. But it was quite another to take a straight friend — even a friend who was admittedly acting contrary to that designation — and try to turn her into a lesbian. *Thanks, Conor, thanks a lot! I'd never seriously thought of the possibility, but you had to put the idea in my head!* She shifted a bit in frustration as she gazed at the peaceful face resting so close to her. *God, I would love to kiss her. She just looks so delectable lying there, all soft and smooth. And she smells so good. It can't hurt to take a little sniff can it?* she thought as she leaned in to inhale.

As she drew near, she gasped as Jamie's eyes opened, and the corners of her mouth curled up, giving her friend a lazy, sweet smile. "Is it time to get up?" she asked through a yawn as she stretched slowly and thoroughly.

Ryan was having a hard time ordering her thoughts, but she finally replied, "Only if you want to. We're not in a rush today."

Purring with delight, Jamie looked up at her friend and asked, "Are you comfortable?"

"Uhm ... yeah ... I'm comfortable," she said, taking a gulp.

"Me, too," Jamie smiled, cuddling even closer as she once again fell asleep.

After staring at her with her mouth agape, Ryan tried to get her mind around this startling development. *She's doing this consciously! This isn't just a little inadvertent cuddling because she's lying next to a warm body. But do I want this?*

She once again regarded the unlined, innocent-looking face and felt herself draw even nearer. *Yes, I do,* she sighed. *I just don't know if I can do this and not want more!*

Letting herself luxuriate in the sensual feel of Jamie's body, she allowed her hand to travel up and rest on her hip, tugging her just a little closer. Immediately, Jamie responded, leaning against her heavily. *Damn! I want more*, Ryan admitted. *But I'll never ask for what I want. Jamie has to make the decision to be more than friends.* She tilted her head and kissed her friend on the forehead. *Want me as much as I want you*, she silently begged. *We could be so good together.*

The lure of her friend's rhythmic breathing slowly calmed her, and soon she fell asleep, holding Jamie in her arms .

⌘

They remained in bed until ten o'clock, neither woman moving a muscle. The boys woke and stumbled around the kitchen, then decided to go out for breakfast. "Is Ryan up?" Conor asked.

"She must be," Brendan said, looking at his watch. "She's never been in bed this late."

"I'll go see if she wants to join us," Conor decided. "Maybe Jamie's still here, too." He walked down the stairs quietly, mostly so he didn't have to hear his own footfalls. His sister's door was wide open — which meant she didn't mind visitors. He got to the doorway and watched in stunned surprise as Jamie shifted a little in her sleep, nestling her golden head against Ryan's breasts. The smile on Ryan's face was unmistakable, and he smirked at her previous denials. *This is gonna cost me $50, Ryan, but I'll gladly pay it to see that smile on your face.*

CHAPTER FIFTEEN

ON A FRIDAY NIGHT IN MARCH, RYAN DROVE MARTIN'S TRUCK UP A fire road on Mt. Tam and parked, then she and Jamie hopped out and began to unload their mountain bikes.

Jamie felt more than a little apprehensive about the ride. The regular Friday night riders were a very proficient group, and she was essentially a novice. She and Ryan had discussed going on the ride months before, and to properly prepare her, Ryan had spent long hours showing her how to shift her weight to climb curbs and small rocks and tree stumps. She had spent quite some time learning how to position herself in the saddle to go down a steep incline and was beginning to feel pretty confident. But she knew her experience didn't amount to much compared to the experience of these women.

Since it still got dark early, they each had halogen lamps on their bikes. As an extra precaution, Ryan had insisted that she wear a light on her helmet also. Ryan's bike was a serious off road machine. She had switched tires on the bike, opting for a very aggressive tread pattern, made just for dirt.

They didn't have to wait long before the other riders drove up in their trucks, Jeeps and sport utility vehicles. When they were a group of about twenty, they took off. It was a fairly normal ride until they reached a small plateau. Ryan turned around and said, "Don't follow me," with a wild grin on her face. She and another woman took off, pedaling furiously until they stood on the top of a set of very large boulders. Each rock was at least twenty feet tall, and they sat atop one another to form an outcropping almost one hundred feet high.

When they reached the peak, she and her partner gave each other demonic smiles just as Jamie wondered what on earth they were going to do. She found out a split second later as Ryan hurled her bike straight down the rock face. Jamie was too shocked to scream, or she surely would have done so. Ryan and her friend catapulted down the sheer face at incredible speeds, then crossed paths as they came down in a zigzag pattern, much the way a skier descends a steep slope.

When they reached the bottom, Ryan threw her head back and howled like a wild dog. She slapped hands in the air with her friend, and as they rode back to the group, they were laughing uproariously. When Ryan pulled up next to Jamie, she smiled an enormous grin and proclaimed, "Sweet Jesus, that rocked!"

Jamie caught her infectious happiness as they sped along down the trail. They came to a small, rocky creek that still had a decent amount of water flowing after the winter rains. The descent at this point was not too steep, but some of the rocks were rather large. Another woman came up to Ryan and slapped her hard on the butt. "Tag!" she shouted as she pedaled away right down the middle of the creek.

Within a heartbeat Ryan was on her tail. The creek curved down the mountain in such a way that it was possible to stand at the top and see the path of the water for a good half-mile, so Jamie scrambled over to the edge to watch the pursuit. Ryan flew down the hill, seemingly without regard for her safety. Jamie's heart nearly stopped beating when Ryan slipped dangerously at one point, but her incredible athleticism kept her from flying over the handlebars. She caught her assailant near the bottom of the creek, slapping her equally hard on the butt as she yanked her bike one hundred eighty degrees and began to climb back up the creek bed. The woman tried to keep up, but Ryan had a good ten yards on her by the time they reached the top of the hill.

Jamie was shocked when she saw her. She was dripping wet from head to toe with mud covering her legs and halfway up her back. But she wore the most blissful smile that Jamie had ever seen on a human being. "I won," she said proudly.

⌘

The rest of the ride was a bit more sedate. Since it was now fully dark, they stayed on the trail, although the dust from the dry earth stuck to Ryan's wet body like glue. The ride was entirely uphill, and by the time they made it back to the car, they were all sweating heavily. Jamie had never felt so grimy, and she could only imagine how Ryan felt.

One of the riders called Ryan over, and Jamie surreptitiously watched them speak. Jamie wasn't sure which of the riders this was, since it was so dark, but as some of the other cars turned their headlights on, the pair was illuminated for a few seconds. The woman was a particularly striking Latina that Jamie had noticed immediately upon their arrival. She was very dark-skinned and had gorgeous jet-black hair that went halfway down her back. She had put it into a loose braid for the ride, but shaken it loose while they spoke, and it now framed her beautiful face. They were obviously well-acquainted, and they stood very close to one another, speaking softly. The woman put her hand on Ryan's cheek, and Ryan turned her head slightly and kissed her palm. It was unclear what the woman was asking, but Ryan was gently shaking her head no. She reached into the woman's SUV and pulled out a couple of wet wipes, quickly wiped her own face and then delicately cleaned all around the woman's mouth, trying to remove the caked on mud and dirt. When she was satisfied, she leaned in for a few very friendly kisses. As she pulled away, she started to turn, but whirled around for another more passionate kiss. She reached up and gently touched the woman's cheek, then she turned and crossed back over the road to the truck where Jamie waited.

Most of the women were going out for a few beers. Ryan was tempted, but she finally decided that she needed dry clothes more than a cold beer. "I can't believe I forgot to bring a change of clothes," she said as she drove away .

"Who were you speaking with?" Jamie inquired as casually as she could muster.

"One of my friends. I should have introduced you," Ryan smiled.

"That's okay."

When Ryan didn't elaborate, Jamie persisted. "Are you close friends?"

"Pretty close," she said noncommittally.

Jamie couldn't take any more of this cat and mouse game, so she blurted out, "Who the hell was that?"

Ryan let out a deep laugh that rumbled through the cab of the truck. "I'm sorry, Jamie. I'm just playing with you. That was Alisa Guerra. She's an assistant district attorney in the city. I've known her for about three years."

"Were you an item?" she asked delicately.

"We still are," Ryan grinned. "Or at least as much of an item as we ever have been. She's one of my long term buddies," she explained.

"Oh, well, I'm not stopping you from seeing her, am I? I can easily head on home if you want to go out."

"Nope. She wanted me to come over, but I'm not in the mood. I'm really too tired for anything other than a warm shower and a soft bed."

"Well, I should think so," she agreed. Jamie studied her filthy form for a few minutes. Ryan still had an energized glow about her that Jamie found mesmerizing. "I don't think I've ever seen you be that wild," she finally said.

"I don't do it very often, but every once in a while, I just need to blow off some steam. Riding up here is the easiest way I know to really clean out the pipes."

"You just seem so full of joy when you're doing something crazy like that sprint down that huge hill," she said with a shake of her head. "Aren't you afraid to try something like that?"

"That's the whole point, Jamie," she replied with a confused look on her mud-spattered face. "It's the fear that makes it hot. If you knew you were safe, you wouldn't get off on it."

"Get off on it ..." she mused, unconvinced of the sentiment. "Do you need that kind of excitement?"

"Yeah, I guess I do. I've always been an adrenaline junkie. I was just like this almost every day when I was a kid. If some other kid dared me to do something, I did it, no matter the consequences."

"Is that what you mean by blowing off steam? Is it a real release?"

"Yeah, I guess it is. If I don't have some excitement in my life, I get kind of anxious and I have to find an outlet," she admitted. "It's almost like a sexual release. As a matter of fact, this is the first time I've been on a ride that I didn't go home with Alisa. We don't see each other a lot, but we both get kind of hot after a really good ride."

"Do you think your need for excitement is why you like to, uhm ... date lots of different women?" she asked, just a bit afraid of the answer.

"I guess that's part of it. I get bored easily, and I need to have a different kind of stimulation, if you'll excuse the double entendre," she grinned.

Looking over at Ryan with a concerned look on her face, Jamie asked, "Do I ever bore you?"

Abruptly, Ryan pulled the truck over to the side of the road. She turned fully on the big bench seat and looked directly into Jamie's eyes. "Never," she said firmly. "I don't know what it is about you, Jamie, but every time I'm with you, it feels fresh. Sara was the only other person I've ever felt that way about. It's funny, but I was with Ally for a few days a couple of weeks ago. She is the most amazing lover," she said appreciatively. "I mean truly amazing," she repeated just in case Jamie missed it the first time. "But after being with her for three days in one week, I'd had enough. It's not that I don't like her; I really do. And she is so totally hot in bed!"

"You mentioned that," Jamie said dryly.

"Oh, right," she said with a smirk. "Anyway, I was thinking about that since I had just broken up with Tracy. I thought maybe I could make it work with Ally. Conor had just given me this big talk about how he thought I should date a friend rather than a stranger, and I mulled that over when we were together. But I had just seen enough of her after those three days." She turned again to fully face Jamie. "That has never happened with you. Never. Other than my family, you're the only person I don't get tired of."

Jamie was outrageously pleased to hear this information. She gave her friend a luminous smile and simply patted her leg as she said, "I've never gotten bored with you around, either, you wild woman."

⌘

When they arrived home, Martin came out to the front porch to greet them. He laughed at the sight of Ryan and told Jamie, "She's just lucky you're here, Jamie. I usually take her out in the back yard and hit her with the garden hose to clean her off before I let her in the house."

After a short lecture about contracting pneumonia, Martin ordered them to enter the house through the door next to the garage to avoid tracking mud through the living room. Jamie was so exhausted that she gladly accepted Ryan's invitation to sleep over, and after two long showers, they relaxed on the bed.

As they settled down, Jamie heard a sharp grunt when Ryan rolled onto her side. "What's wrong?" she asked with concern.

"When I was going down that creek, I almost lost it," Ryan admitted. "I yanked it out at the last second, but I felt something pop in my leg. It pulls a little when I roll over."

"Let me massage it for you," her friend offered as she switched the bedside light on. Ryan was fully dressed for a change, wearing thin, Royal Stewart plaid flannel pajama bottoms and a dark blue T-shirt, instead of her usual T-shirt and boxer ensemble.

Turning her face to gaze at her friend for a moment, she gently demurred. "I think it'll be okay; you don't have to do anything."

Jamie leaned over just a bit until she was able to face Ryan fully. She placed her hand on her shoulder and asked, "Why won't you let me help if I can? You're always so solicitous of me, and I've got to tell you, it feels great to be pampered a little."

"I know it does," she admitted as she obviously found it difficult to maintain eye contact. "It's just that you might be uncomfortable with the location of the problem." She quirked her mouth into a lopsided grin and rolled her eyes just a bit when Jamie looked a little stumped.

Ryan was lying on her side facing her friend, who was lying in a mirror pose. She reached over and gently took the blonde's hand, bringing it behind herself to place it on the abrupt swell of her right buttock. "It's my hamstring," she muttered. "And it's really high, almost in my glute."

Smacking her lips together to increase the flow of saliva, the smaller woman took a deep breath and found the courage to say, "The offer still holds. A sore muscle is a sore muscle, no matter where it is. If it would help, I'd be glad to work on it for you."

With a dubious tilt of her head Ryan decided to take her friend at her word. She rolled over until she was fully on her belly. "It's right around here," she said, indicating the general area, then stretching her arms out above her head.

Grateful that Ryan couldn't see her face, Jamie sucked it up and allowed her hand to explore the area. As she probed gently, she heard a sharp intake of air pass Ryan's lips when she touched the spot. "Does it hurt a lot?" she asked as she gingerly palpated the swollen muscle.

"It's just tweaked a bit. I'm sure it's nothing serious," she assured her. "Start a few inches below the swelling and slowly work up to actually touching the muscle."

"Okay, I can do that," Jamie replied firmly as she tried to figure out how to position herself. Making a quick decision, she moved Ryan's legs apart a bit and straddled the injured leg. From there she could work on the injury from a good position.

The pants were going to be an impediment, but Ryan made no move to remove them — to Jamie's concurrent relief and disappointment.

She decided to draw an imaginary circle around the injury and attack it from all sides before actually touching the sore spot. Regrettably, this called for a large amount of actually rubbing her friend's smoothly muscled buttock. But she had made the offer, and she felt obligated to perform the task without allowing herself to become sexually excited.

Working as gently as possible, she began to knead all around the injury, never drawing closer to the actual spot. In order to reach the surrounding muscles she had to exert a lot of pressure, and after a few minutes Ryan mumbled, "You're rubbing my skin raw." She lifted up onto her elbows and reassured Jamie once again, "It's okay. It's just a tough one to reach."

"We can do this," Jamie insisted as she placed a hand on the small of Ryan's back to hold her in place. "Lotion would help." But when she thought of applying lotion to that bare skin, she began to regret her idea.

Ryan sensed her hesitation, and she turned her head to gaze at her friend for a moment. "You sure?" she asked again.

Now feeling trapped, Jamie felt her head move slowly up and down. But it was obvious to Ryan that she was struggling with the concept. Jamie just stared at her, waiting for Ryan to take her pants down.

Suddenly, the dark head bobbed up and down briefly as she scrambled off the bed. "I think an equipment change is in order." She was standing in front of her underwear drawer as she made this declaration, and after rummaging through the neat stacks for a moment, she found what she was looking for and held out a tiny, black piece of material. "Better access," she grinned, going into the bathroom to change.

Jamie could feel her heart thumping through her chest so audibly that she feared Ryan could hear it in the bath. *Please, God, don't let that be a thong!* When Ryan emerged, revealing a high-cut, black thong in a satiny material, an explosion of sensation traveled from Jamie's spine and slammed straight into her groin. The look of terror mixed with lust must have been evident, because Ryan stopped in her tracks and asked, "Is this okay? Uhm ... it's really all right if you don't want to do this, Jamie."

"*No!* No, really," she insisted. "I, uhm, just didn't want to get anything on those," she fumbled. "They look really ... uhm ... nice."

"Oh," Ryan said as she looked down at herself, relieved that Jamie was only concerned with the state of her clothing. "Thanks. I never wear them for long," she laughed. "They're more of a prop than anything."

"A prop?"

"Yeah," she said with a chuckle. "My friend Ally likes things like this — although she never lets me leave them on for long." Ryan found this fact quite humorous, but Jamie couldn't loosen up enough to find humor in anything right then. She needed every bit of her strength and concentration just to stop her hands from shaking.

Ryan climbed back onto the bed, once again face down. Unfortunately, this position did nothing to alleviate Jamie's discomfort. She hadn't realized it until just that moment, but she discovered with a gut-clenching jolt that she was inordinately fond of Ryan's butt: Ryan's rounded, incredibly firm, finely muscled, smooth, creamy white butt, that is. And to have that perfectly shaped derriere placed right in front of her eyes for her shaking hands to massage was too much for her racing heart.

She nearly stumbled as she got to her feet, but she managed to right herself as she declared, "That ride really dehydrated me. I'm going upstairs for a drink. Need anything?" One foot was on the bottom step by the time Ryan could reply, but she managed to respond, "Uh, sure, a little water or Gatorade would be good. You sure you don't want me to go?"

"No, no, I know my way around," she assured her as she scampered up the stairs. Luckily, she was modestly dressed in the roomy top to Ryan's pajamas along with her own panties because she ran into Conor sitting on a stool in the kitchen, reading the paper.

"Hello there," he rumbled, looking her up and down briefly. "Nice outfit," he added with more than a passing interest showing in his bright eyes. "You should wear that type of thing more often."

"Thanks," she blushed, suddenly feeling very exposed even though the top covered her body to mid-thigh. "It's your sister's," she explained. "We went on a big bike ride up on Mt. Tam, and I was too tired and dirty to go home. I guess I should keep some pajamas here, since I'm always staying over unexpectedly."

"Oh, riding with the big girls, were you?" he chuckled.

"Yeah, and I did pretty well, if I do say so myself. Of course, I could never keep up with Ryan. She's amazing." She walked over to the refrigerator and peeked at the contents. "What are you doing down here?"

"Oh, I had a long meeting with some thick-headed clients. Ruined my whole evening. So, I thought I'd at least have a beer and read the paper before I went to bed."

She turned and eyed his dark, creamy-looking beer. "What is that? It looks delicious."

"Murphy's stout," he proclaimed as he held the glass out. "Have a sip."

All of a sudden, the thought of alcohol was very, very attractive. She reached for the heavy glass and took a long gulp. Wiping her mouth with the back of her hand, she pronounced, "Now, that's a beer!"

"Have one with me," he urged. "Ryan won't miss you."

"I'd like to," she prevaricated. "But Ryan hurt her leg, and I promised I'd give her a massage after I got something to drink."

"Well, if you had a wee one with me, you would be getting something to drink," he said in his most seductive voice.

"You know, a little alcohol might make her leg relax. Would you pour one for us to share?"

He graced her with a big smile, and a gentle, one-armed hug. Then he took another beer from the refrigerator and poured it expertly, handing her the glass. "Go take care of your patient," he ordered. But as she started from the room he asked, "She's not hurt badly, is she?"

Looking over her shoulder, she gave him a grin and reminded him, "It takes more than old Mt. Tam to get the best of your little sister."

⌘

She was a good bit more relaxed as she made the turn to descend the stairs, but just for good measure she slugged down at least a quarter of the pint on the short trip. Ryan was just where she had left her, lying on her tummy with her arms extended. She was obviously very relaxed, but Jamie could still see the muscular tension in her powerful thighs and butt. "Where've you been?" the dark woman mumbled. "I was about to come looking for you."

"Oh, Conor was upstairs, and he talked me into having a short one with him," she commented. "I brought a pint down for us to share. I thought a little alcohol might help relax your leg."

"Hmm," she speculated, rolling onto her side and supporting her head with her hand. "That might be the key to increasing my massage business. 'Have a pint and a rub.'"

"I think they already have that in the Tenderloin," Jamie laughed, mentioning the city's notorious sin district.

Ryan held out her free hand and took the glass, giving first it, then Jamie, a speculative look. But she didn't comment further about the large missing portion, easily matching the amount Jamie had siphoned off with one enthusiastic gulp. "Ah, that's smooth," she murmured.

Jamie got up on the bed and took another hearty swallow, and they passed the glass back and forth, drinking quickly and in silence until it was drained. "I guess we were thirsty," Jamie observed as she eyed the empty glass. "Care for another?"

"Nope." Ryan rolled over onto her belly and turned her head to maintain eye contact. "Still interested?"

"Yep," Jamie bravely agreed as she resumed her former position. The stout had helped a bit, she was pleased to note, and her hands were hardly shaking as she poured a generous amount of massage lotion onto them. Swallowing audibly, she steeled her nerves and set to work, delicately beginning to implement her former plan, again working around the perimeter of the obviously swollen muscle. Once again Ryan relaxed into the touch, controlling her breathing with deep, steady breaths, evidently to manage the pain.

Jamie imagined that the distended muscle must be terribly painful, but Ryan stoically allowed her to work, never even flinching at her touch.

As she got into the endeavor, Jamie carelessly allowed her mind to wander. She soon realized that she was straddling her friend's firm thigh with only her own satiny panties between them. Further, she acknowledged that the movement that she needed to press deep into the muscle caused that firm thigh to rub in a most delicious fashion against her throbbing vulva. At this point her only option was to distract herself, and to her credit, she tried everything. She thought of car crashes, world hunger, tornadoes, pestilence and earthquakes, but nothing helped.

Finally, she remembered one of Ryan's tricks, and she focused her mind totally on Ryan's leg and the sore muscle — ignoring every sensation and visual stimulus that attended the affected area. She rubbed, kneaded, stroked, tapped, fondled and petted that sinewy muscle all the way to the middle of Ryan's buttock, never allowing her mind to recognize the alluring charms of the surrounding flesh.

Enormously pleased with herself, and emboldened by her laser-like focus, she spent a few minutes working on the hamstring's twin. Small, satisfied grunts greeted her touch, but she was so focused that she did not need oral feedback. All of the information she needed came from Ryan's body, and the clear message she received was that the body was very happy indeed.

When both hamstrings were loose, she slid off and instructed, "Roll over for me." Ryan did not question her plan, meekly complying with the edict. With new territory to focus on, Jamie began to work on the stressed quads, making both legs as pliable as possible. After a very long time spent in very loving connection, she began to emerge from her focused fog and realized that she had not heard a sound out of Ryan for a long while. She abruptly lifted her head, and she saw it: the image that she longed for and dreaded — an unguarded look of pure desire on Ryan's beautiful face.

Ryan knew from the look on Jamie's face that she had been caught. Nonetheless, she tried her best to adopt a neutral expression as Jamie slid off her leg and lay down next to her. Without allowing herself to form a conscious thought, Jamie placed her hand on Ryan's soft cheek and turned her head until they were breathing the same charged air. As though guided by a magnetic force, she dipped her head and closed her eyes as she began to place delicate kisses on her friend's forehead, across her cheeks, her chin and even the tip of her nose. Nothing existed for her except the sensation of her lips caressing the softest, smoothest skin imaginable.

She pulled back for a moment to gather her thoughts, and to her horror, she saw not the desire of moments before, but confusion, laced with wide-eyed fear, clouding that beautiful face. She shot bolt upright and leapt to her feet. "Oh, God, Ryan," she cried, shifting from foot to foot in a near panic. "I'm sorry, I'm so sorry. I thought ..."

In the next instant Ryan was on her feet, wrapping Jamie in a strong embrace, cooing into her ear, "It's okay, Jamie, it's all right." She rubbed her back and ran a hand through her hair as she continued to reassure her shaken friend.

Jamie was crying softly against her chest. "I'm so ashamed," she whimpered. "I don't know why I did that. I promised myself I wouldn't ..."

Ryan pulled back and stared at her for a long minute, "What do you mean, you promised yourself that you wouldn't?"

This brought on a new flood of tears as Jamie shook from head to toe. Ryan guided her back to the bed, urging her to lie down. She wrapped her arms around the quivering body, murmuring comforting words the entire time. After a few minutes, Jamie finally had the ability to speak. "I am so sorry, Ryan. I just assumed that you might feel the same way," she murmured, her voice filled with grief.

"Is this something that you've felt before tonight?" Ryan asked softly.

"Yeah," she admitted, sending Ryan's heart soaring. "It's one of the reasons that I started seeing Anna. I was so confused about how I felt about you that I just needed to talk to someone about it. She told me I wasn't ready to act on my feelings," she said glumly. "I guess I should have listened, huh?"

Ryan pulled away just enough to be able to fully focus on Jamie's face. She gazed at her for so long that the smaller woman began to shift nervously under the intense scrutiny. Finally, the low, warm voice asked, "You're attracted to me?"

Jamie just nodded, her embarrassment precluding speech.

"Do you want to know how I feel about you?" Ryan asked, her voice so filled with warmth that Jamie found herself nodding, even though she was terrified of the answer.

Placing a hand on the small of Jamie's back, Ryan pulled her closer, letting their bodies touch all along their lengths. Her eyes were filled with affection as she whispered, "I'm very, very attracted to you, too. I have been for a very long time." Her eyes fluttered closed, and she could feel her lips magnetically drawn to Jamie's. But just before they touched, she opened her eyes and pulled back, resting her forehead against the smaller woman's.

"What's wrong?" Jamie asked tentatively, her entire body poised for the kiss that she knew would heal her fractured soul.

"This isn't how I want this to be," Ryan murmured. "I don't want to just fall into this, Jamie. Our friendship is too important to me to have the slightest chance of ruining it."

"It's important to me, too," Jamie said, her need for Ryan causing her to place an arm behind her friend's back and press her close. "But so is touching you right now. I want to always be your friend ... I just want to be your lover, too."

Ryan gave her a smile that melted her heart. "I want that, too," she said. "And if you were anyone else, we wouldn't be talking now — we'd be making love. But you're my very best friend, you've just been through a very traumatic break-up and until today, you've claimed that you were straight. Those are some pretty big issues, Jamie, and we have to resolve them, or at least talk about them, before I'm comfortable doing another thing."

"I've been talking to Anna about this," she said. "I have been for weeks now, Ryan."

The dark woman looked at her, her intense eyes penetrating all of her defenses. "Were you sure you wanted to be my lover yesterday? How about last week? Last month?"

"I've been attracted to you since the day we met," Jamie sighed. "I'm just having trouble making myself take the leap. I feel ready tonight, Ryan. I swear." She nuzzled her head against Ryan's breast, letting the slightly elevated heartbeat soothe her.

"Jamie," Ryan said softly, "I love you. I love you as my friend, and I'd love the chance to love you as my lover. But I'd rather give up that chance than lose you as a friend. If we made love before you were absolutely certain this was right for you, I'm afraid that's exactly what would happen — and I just can't risk it. I have to protect my heart, Jamie. If we made love, and you decided you couldn't commit to me ... I ... I don't know how I'd ever get over the pain. I won't recreate what happened with Sara," she whispered.

Holding her close, Jamie's head nodded slowly. "I understand. I really do." She looked up into Ryan's eyes and asked, "What do we do now?"

"We go on like we have been," Ryan decided. "You continue to talk to Anna about how you feel, and we continue to be best friends. At some point, you'll feel ready to make a decision — I just hope and pray that you choose me," she whispered, placing a feather-light kiss on Jamie's cheek.

"I do choose you," the smaller woman sighed. "I do."

Ryan tightened her hold, squeezing Jamie soundly, the emotion palpable. Dropping another kiss onto her forehead, she pressed the blonde head to her chest and murmured, "Go to sleep now. We'll talk more tomorrow if you need to."

"Okay." She cuddled against Ryan as tightly as she dared and felt herself relax into the warm, comforting embrace. "Ryan?" she asked softly.

"Yes?"

"Promise me that you'll always be my friend."

"I promise," she sighed. "I promise."

⌘

They woke early, lying in each other's arms. Ryan placed a tender kiss on the blonde hair and asked, "You've been up for a while, haven't you?"

"Yeah," she admitted, her voice raspy. "I'm worried."

"About?"

"I'm worried about what will happen if I can't make a commitment to be with you," Jamie said softly.

Ryan pulled her close and said, "I meant what I said last night. If you want me, I'll be waiting for you. But if you don't, I want you to feel that you can tell me. I want what's best for you, Jamie. If you're a lesbian and are willing to commit to following that path, I'd love to build a relationship with you. But if you're not, I want to be your best friend for as long as you can stand me."

"You'd really be okay if I told you that I'd decided I was straight?" she asked tentatively.

Ryan chuckled a little at the question. "I thought you were straight last night, Jamie. I think I've been getting by all right."

She blushed furiously as she realized how her question had sounded. "No, that's not what I mean. I mean, could we go back to how we've been? Wouldn't it change things too much now that we've told each other how we feel?"

Ryan gazed at her for a minute, obviously deep in thought. "I'm making this sound like it would be easy," she admitted. "It wouldn't be. You're opening up a possibility that I want very, very much. If you decide that you don't want to be lovers, I'm going to be disappointed, and it's going to take a while for that disappointment to fade. But it will, in time, Jamie. I only want to go forward if this is right for you. If you're straight, I want you to find a man who will love you like you deserve to be loved."

"I love you, too, Ryan. Very, very much," she said, as she closed her eyes and sank into the tender embrace. Within seconds, she was sound asleep again, with Ryan gazing at her lovely face, hoping to one day be able to express all of her love.

⌘

On Monday afternoon Jamie sat in her therapist's office, wishing that she could stay for the entire evening. It took her almost fifteen minutes to relate every detail of what had happened on Friday night, and when she was finished, she looked at the woman with great anticipation, waiting for Anna to react.

The older woman gazed at her for a moment to determine if Jamie was finished speaking, then she said, "How have you felt since you and Ryan spoke? Are you sleeping well, having any dreams?"

"No, I'm not sleeping well!" she said, alarmed. "All I can think about is how I can convince her that I'm ready to move on. This is all on my shoulders, Anna, and I don't have any idea how I can show her that I've made up my mind."

"Have you made up your mind?"

"Yes, I'm sure I have," Jamie said, nodding enthusiastically.

"When did you decide? You weren't sure on Friday afternoon."

Exasperated, she narrowed her eyes and said, "I decided when I was touching her. I already told you that."

"Did you plead your case with Ryan?" Anna asked. "You stated that she said you both had some things to talk about before she was willing to move on. Did you do that?"

The blonde head shook, Jamie's expression decidedly unhappy.

"Why not?" the therapist asked.

Sighing heavily, Jamie said, "Because I don't know why I'm ready. I just am!"

"And you thought that your declaration wouldn't be enough for Ryan, correct?"

Rolling her eyes, Jamie said, "Yes! She's more persistent than *you* are."

Smiling gently, Anna said, "Now *that's* persistent."

Embarrassed by the tone she had used, Jamie said, "You know what I mean. She'll want to know how I arrived at my decision, and whether I'm ready to tell my family, and how I want to handle things with Mia and Cassie…" She shook her head and grumbled, "There are a thousand things that I just don't want to get into right now. Right now I just want it to be me and Ryan. I want to hold her in my arms and kiss her and touch her." She dropped her head onto the sofa and said, "I want to make love to her, Anna. I want that so badly."

"But there's more to it than that, Jamie, and Ryan knows that. Claiming a bisexual or lesbian identity is a complicated proposition, and focusing only on the sexual aspect is asking for trouble."

She dropped her head into her hands and moaned, "Why couldn't I have fallen for one of her old girlfriends? All they wanted was sex!"

⌘

On a Saturday afternoon in April, Jamie stood in her room, trying to decide which of three dresses she should choose. "Hey, Mia?"

"Yeah?"

"Can you come here and help me with something?"

Her friend came into the room, looking curious. "What do you need?"

"I've got to go to a wedding, and I can't decide which dress to wear."

"Is it an afternoon or an evening ceremony?"

"Evening. The ceremony is at 6:00, and the reception is right afterward." She gave her a tiny frown and said, "I told you about this when I got the invitation. This is that couple that Jack and I used to be friends with, remember?"

"Oh, right," she nodded. With a puzzled frown she commented, "Didn't they move to New Jersey last year after the guy graduated? "

"Yep. They were the only couple we ever did anything with. I was bummed when they left."

"But isn't Jack gonna be there?"

"Yeah," she sighed. "He's not only gonna be there, he's in the wedding party. I spoke with Judith about it, and she really wants me to come, Mia. I finally decided that I had to do what I thought was right — and I think it's right to go."

"I understand your reasoning, but I can't imagine that it's gonna be fun to have to see Jack. He'll undoubtedly bring a date — even if he has to hire someone," she joked.

"I know that's likely," Jamie said. "But we're broken up, and we're gonna stay that way, so I can't complain if he's moving on. I'll just have to try to appear gracious." She shrugged her shoulders and added with a smile, "I don't have to *be* gracious — just appear so."

⌘

Driving down to Palo Alto, Jamie thought of Ryan, and her teasing offer to accompany her to the wedding if Jamie was uncomfortable going alone. *She's so sweet to me,* she sighed. *I don't have a doubt in the world that she would have come with me if I'd asked her to.* Her fond musings were halted abruptly when she considered taking Ryan to an event such as this. *I could never do something like that!* she thought with true alarm. *Those people know me — they know me as a straight woman! There's no way I could ever face all of them with Ryan on my arm.* Her mind started to turn the issue over and over, and with each turn she grew more anxious.

Having never been to a Jewish wedding, she was mildly puzzled when Robert was escorted down the aisle by seven people. She guessed that the middle-aged people were his parents, but two elderly couples were in the group as well — obviously his grandparents. A young woman who looked quite a lot like his mother was included, as well as Jack and the other groomsmen, and she spent a moment considering how nice it was to have your whole family included in the ceremony. She laughed silently as she considered, *Wouldn't have made a difference for me. Poppa would conduct the service, and it's just the three of us — any way you slice it.*

Judith was accompanied by her mother, her two sisters, her older sister's husband and their two small children. Jamie felt tears spring to her eyes seeing the look of pure joy on Judith's face. Her entire family was showing their support for her union with Robert — joining together as a group to bless the pairing.

Her anxiety faded as she grew more and more engrossed in the celebration, delighting in the mix of traditions that her friends had chosen. Finally, she was able to put her own concerns aside and just let herself feel happy for them — pleased that she had allowed herself to come and share in their joy.

At the reception she was seated with a group of people she had never met, but she was well able to converse with strangers, and after a while, they were all chatting companionably. One of the women at the table leaned over and commented for the second time, "I'm sure we've met before. Maybe at some Stanford function?"

"Maybe …" Jamie began, but before she could finish, she felt a warm hand on her bare shoulder.

"Hi, Jamie."

Knowing who the voice belonged to without even turning around, Jamie smiled as the woman she was speaking with said, "That's where I met you! You're Jack's fiancée."

"Was," she said quietly, deciding to get it out of the way so Jack didn't have to. "We're not together any longer."

The hand on her shoulder tightened, and she heard Jack say, "I might not be the world's dumbest man, but I'm probably in the top three, Becky. I let one of the best women in town slip away."

Looking up at Jack with gratitude, Jamie stood and asked, "How about a dance?"

"Love to," he smiled, taking her hand.

When they were on the dance floor, she said, "Sorry if I put you on the spot by asking you to dance, but I couldn't bear to go into the details with old Becky. She'd already spent ten minutes giving me the 'What's an attractive woman like you doing at a wedding alone' speech."

"Not at all. I was on my way over to ask you to dance. I thought it was really nice of you to come tonight, and I wanted to thank you." He cleared his throat and offered, "I'm sure it wasn't easy for you."

"No, no, it wasn't," she said. "But Judith called me and said it would mean a lot to her."

"That's one of the things I always loved about you," he said. "You try to consider other people's needs — not just your own."

"Thanks," she said, touched by his words. "So, how are things? Are you here with someone?"

"Ahh ... no, I'm not. I guess I could have roped someone into coming with me, but I can't imagine a woman would have fun sitting at a table alone while I was at the head table."

"No," she chuckled, "I can guarantee she wouldn't."

"Oh! I didn't mean to imply that you weren't having fun just because you're alone ..."

"That's okay, Jack," she said, smiling up at him. "You know, that's one of the things I always loved about you. You thought about whether a date would enjoy herself — rather than just what you wanted." Giving him a curious look, she asked, "I would have thought you'd want me to see you with someone else."

"How about you?" he asked guardedly. "Didn't you want me to see you with someone else?"

"Yeah," she chuckled, "I did. I just didn't know which escort services were the top quality ones."

He laughed heartily at her joke, saying, "You've never had a hard time getting a date, so don't even try to pull that one on me."

She shrugged her shoulders and said, "I'm not seeing anyone right now, Jack." Blinking up at him she asked, "Are you?"

"No," he said quietly. "I haven't started to date yet. I'm still ... I'm still a little shaky, to be honest."

"Me, too," she sighed. She felt like she was about to cry, but she wasn't sure why. He sensed the change in her mood and tightened his arms around her, pressing her body against his.

"I miss you, Jamie," he said softly.

"I think about you all the time," she acknowledged honestly. "I don't think I can start dating until I figure out what went wrong between us."

"I'm not sure what happened, either," he agreed. He took in a breath and held it for a second, then asked, "Why don't we talk about it together?"

"I, uhm ... I have a therapist ..."

"I don't," he said quietly. "It would help me, Jamie. Really."

"Uhm ... okay," she nodded, unable to refuse the longing look in his eyes. "When do you want to talk?"

"How about tonight?" he asked. "We can find a quiet corner after a while."

"O ... okay," she agreed.

The newly married couple came out to dance just as they were speaking. Jack said, "I have to go do my thing. Don't go away now."

"I won't."

She watched him walk away, looking tremendously handsome in his perfectly tailored tuxedo. As the music began to play, the bride and groom sat down and their chairs were grasped and hoisted into the air by the members of the wedding party, family and friends. The music was joyous, as were Robert and Judith's smiles. Jamie felt her breath catch when she saw the nearly giddy look on Jack's face as he participated in the celebration.

The gathering included all of the newly married couple's family and close friends, and Jamie felt herself transported by the vibrant joy that was flowing through the room. She had always assumed that she and her husband would have this same type of celebration when she married, and she found that she was deeply reticent to give up the dream. Yes, she was enormously attracted to Ryan, but was her attraction enough to overcome the loss of her hopes, of her plans and dreams? She wasn't at all sure of the answer to that question, and as she watched her former fiancé being so playful and boyish and felt her attraction for him once again flicker to life, she began to doubt all of her feelings.

All of this therapy, and I'm more confused now than I was when I started! she moaned to herself. When the dancing ended, the wedding party went back to the head table and a round of toasts was offered up. With each one, the guests all took a sip of wine. Not knowing how many were to come, she took a normal sip, not noticing that her glass was emptied rather quickly. Her tablemates were drinking right along with her, and by the time the numerous toasts were finished, she had consumed three glasses. Nonetheless, she didn't feel too intoxicated, having had a substantial dinner.

After a while Jack came to get her, and they took a seat at a table far in the corner. The table was set, but no one had occupied it, and a full bottle of wine sat in the center. Jack poured a glass for each of them, and they began to talk.

Touching the rim of her glass with his own, he toasted, "To self-awareness." He took a deep sip of the wine and said, "I've given more thought to our relationship and the problems that we had than I can ever remember devoting to any topic. And do you know what I've decided?"

She shook her head rather dully, her eyes never leaving his lips.

He leaned over slightly and said, "A lot of the problems we had were my fault. In some very basic ways, we got off on the wrong foot, and things just got worse and worse. I spent a lot of time talking to Robert this week, and he reminded me of how things were when we were first together." He looked at her, and a small smile settled onto his face. "We went out to dinner and did things with Robert and Judith. We played golf on the weekends and used to spend hours at a time talking about our plans and our dreams." He shook his head slowly, "What happened, Jamie? Did I take all of the joy out of our relationship? Am I just too selfish to be with a woman?"

The wine served to thoroughly loosen her tongue, and she found herself being honest — completely honest — with him. "I, uhm … I don't want you to think that what happened between us was all your fault, Jack," she said softly. "It wasn't."

He tilted his head in question, but didn't speak, waiting for her to continue.

"I … I had … I have … feelings for Ryan." It felt so terribly odd to say those words to him after all of her months of denial. But there was no point in talking to him in this way if she didn't trust him enough to be completely candid. "I wasn't able to give you my full attention, because I was spending so much of my time wishing I could be with her."

He nodded, then peered at her quizzically and asked, "Are you in love with her?"

"I … I don't know," she said honestly. "I don't know if it's love or just attraction or a schoolgirl crush … but I have very strong feelings for her."

"Have you … have you, uhm … been with her?"

"No." She shook her head quickly. "It's not like that, Jack. I'm too confused to even think about that."

"How does she feel about you?"

She swallowed, trying to get her bearings. Their discussion was so calm, so rational, that she had a hard time believing that she was speaking to Jack. "She cares for me too," she said quietly. "She says she'd like to try to have a relationship with me, if I'm sure I'm a le — if I'm sure it's right for me."

"Is she involved with anyone right now?" he asked.

She blinked at him, wondering why he cared. "No, no, she's been single since February."

He nodded thoughtfully and asked, "Don't you think that's kind of odd?"

"What is?"

"Well, you just admitted that part of the reason we had problems was because you were attracted to her. Then you and I broke up. She's not with anyone, either. She's interested in you." He gave her a penetrating stare and said, "If this was right for you, why wouldn't you do something about it? You have the perfect opportunity, Jamie, but it's been two months now, and you're still unsure." He cocked his head and again asked, "Doesn't that seem odd to you?"

She found her head nodding slowly, then heard her voice say, "Yes, it does seem odd. I keep telling my therapist that as a matter of fact. If I know this is what I want, why don't I just make the decision?"

"Have you ever … uhm … made out with her or anything?"

"No." She shook her head and said, "I've kissed her, but just once."

"Did you like it?" he asked, his voice tremulous.

"Yes." Her eyes fluttered closed as she recalled the wondrous sensation. "I liked it very much."

"And you could have done it again, right?"

"Well, sure, I guess I could have."

"But you didn't. Even when you had the opportunity, you didn't kiss her again." He gave her a puzzled look and asked, "Do you touch her? Hug her?"

"Yeah, we hug. But it's not sexual," she admitted. "It's just warm and soothing and it makes me feel cared for."

"Kinda like a sister?" he asked.

"Yeah, I guess so," she admitted. She nodded slowly as she thought about his query. "I suppose that is mostly how I feel right now. I want to be close to her, to have her hug me and comfort me when things are tough. I guess that's mostly it."

He looked at her for a few moments and said, "You don't have to answer this if it's too personal, but do you fantasize about her? Do you dream about her?"

Her head nodded briefly. "I did … I did more often when you and I were together. But since then … it's much less frequent."

Staring into her eyes he asked, "Want my opinion?"

"Uhm … sure."

"It sounds to me like you're most attracted to her when you know you can't have her. That seems more like a fantasy than anything else. If you wanted her, you'd have her by now."

She nodded, having been thinking along the same lines for weeks. "I just wish my stupid therapist would help me more," she moaned. "I know she knows what I'm really feeling — but she won't tell me!"

He chuckled mildly and commented, "If she told you the answers, you'd stop seeing her. It's in her best interests to keep you as confused as possible."

Blinking at him in amazement, she felt her head begin to nod. "That's exactly true! I'm paying someone to help me find answers, but as soon as I find them, I'll fire her! That's a disincentive to help me!"

Jack shrugged and said, "Who ever leaves therapy? Once they hook you, you're theirs for life."

Her mind was swimming, and she felt as if she didn't know up from down. "I … I honestly feel worse than I did before I started seeing her," she admitted. "I keep telling her that, but she says that if I keep coming, I'll feel better soon."

"She'll probably be saying that next year and the year after …"

Dropping her head to the table, Jamie moaned, "Who can I trust?"

"Yourself," Jack said softly. "No one else can know you as well as you know yourself. Just trust yourself, Jamie."

She gave him a look that spoke of her deep confusion. "I'm the last person that I can trust right now, Jack."

He reached over and gently touched her hand. "You'll get there. I'm sure of it. Just be patient, Jamie. You'll figure this out."

⌘

It was nearly one o'clock when the party finally broke up. She hadn't had anything to drink for two hours, but the damage had been done, and she was admittedly in no shape to drive.

"So, what will it be?" Jack asked as he walked her to her car. "I can take you to Berkeley, or I can take you to your parents house."

She sighed and shrugged her shoulders. "I don't like either option. You'll be up for another hour and a half if you take me to Berkeley, and I'll have to wake my parents if I go home. I either inconvenience you or them."

"Berkeley it is then," he smiled.

"No." She placed her hand on his arm and said, "I'll worry about you if you're out that late. Besides, then I'll have to come all the way down here tomorrow to pick up my car."

"I could drive you home and sleep on your couch," he offered. "Then I could take BART over to the city and hop CALTRAIN back down here tomorrow."

"And you have to do all of this just because I drank too much? I think I should be the one who suffers the consequences. I'm the one who got drunk."

"Okay," he said slowly. "What's your plan?"

"Can I sleep on your couch?"

"No," he smiled, "but you can sleep in my bed and I can sleep on my couch."

"No deal," she insisted. "I either sleep on your couch, or I sleep in my car. The only way I'll learn not to do this is to pay the price."

He shrugged his shoulders amiably and nodded. "Okay. I'll drive you to my apartment and then bring you back tomorrow to get your car."

"Now you've got a deal," she decided.

⌘

Jack stuck to the agreement and allowed Jamie to sleep on his couch. He provided a T-shirt, but didn't have anything appropriate to offer in the way of pants. She felt a little uncomfortable in a T-shirt and her lacy black thong, and she ruefully reminded herself to never get drunk when she had to drive home or when she was wearing sexy underwear.

She was actually fairly sober, she acknowledged with regret. Her mind would not slow down the way it would have if she were drunk, and she was consigned to lying on the couch, worrying about Jack, about Ryan and about herself for what seemed like half the night.

Unsure of what time it was, she fumbled blindly to find her phone when the familiar chirp woke her. "H'lo?" she croaked out.

"Uh-oh. Someone forgot about our bike ride this morning, didn't she?"

"Oh, damn," Jamie grumbled. "I'm sorry, Ryan. I … I can't make it. I was out too late …"

"And had too much to drink," she helpfully supplied. "I recognize your hangover voice by now, you know." Her tone sharpened and she asked, "You didn't drive when you were drunk, did you?"

"No, I didn't," she assured her. "You'll give me a rain check, right?"

"Sure. Hey, do you want me to come over in a while and bring you breakfast? I know you get a little grouchy when you're hung over. Besides, I could use a change of pace. I haven't ridden around the Berkeley hills lately."

"Uhm … no, that's okay. I, uhm … I'm not in the mood for breakfast."

"Are you sure? I really don't mind ..."

"No, food isn't in my immediate future."

"You sound pretty bad," Ryan murmured. "Are Cassie or Mia home?"

"Uhm ... I'm not sure," she said, hating herself for lying to her friend.

"Well, if they're not, I'm going to come bring you something to make you feel better. Go check and see if they're there."

"Jamie?" Jack's deep voice called out from the hall. "Are you awake?"

There was dead silence on the other end of the line. It seemed to go on forever, but it was probably just a few seconds. "You're obviously busy," Ryan said crisply. "I'll let you go."

"Ryan, no! Hang on a second."

"I'll see you," she said, then hung up.

"Bad time?" Jack asked tentatively, sticking his head into the room.

"Decidedly," she grumbled, falling back onto the couch.

⌘

After a shower and a cup of coffee, Jamie looked merely horrid. Regarding herself in the mirror, she had to admit that few things looked worse than a hung-over woman in a tight, black, cocktail dress, first thing in the morning. She had little to say to Jack, but when he dropped her off, he looked at her and said, "I'd like to talk to you again, Jamie. You sound as confused as I do about what happened. Maybe we can help each other work things through."

"Okay," she nodded. "I'll call you." She got out of the car and walked over to the driver's side. Giving him a kiss on the cheek, she said, "Thanks for taking care of me last night. I owe you one."

"Nah. Just feel better, okay?"

"I'll try, but I have a feeling it's going to take awhile."

She got into her car and headed straight for Noe Valley, knowing that she looked more like a call girl than herself, but feeling that it was vital to speak to Ryan in person.

To her complete dismay, Martin and Rory were home, but Ryan was on her ride. Martin wasn't sure where she had gone, commenting, "She was in a foul mood when she left, Jamie. Barely said a word."

"I, uhm ... she's ... she's angry with me, Martin. We had a little fight on the phone earlier. Uhm ... could I possibly wait for her?"

"Certainly, Jamie. We'd love to have you. Care to watch the television with us? The Warriors are playing."

"Sounds appealing," she smiled, "but if you don't mind, I'd love to go

361

to her room and catch a nap." She indicated her dress and said, "I was out late and haven't had a chance to change. I think I'll just put on some of her sweats and wait for her downstairs."

"Suit yourself, love. If you change you mind, we'd love the company."

"Thanks," she said gratefully. "You're a lifesaver."

She took off her dress and slipped into one of Ryan's T-shirts, smiling wanly when she smelled the distinctive aroma on the fabric. *Don't be mad at me*, she sighed, hugging herself tightly while she rocked her body back and forth, trying to lull herself to sleep.

⌘

After a long nap, Jamie went upstairs to hang out with the O'Flaherty men. Ryan didn't get home until four o'clock, nearly seven hours after Jamie had arrived. Neither Martin nor Rory were worried about her, but Jamie was nearly beside herself with anxiety. When Ryan walked in the door, she poked her head into her father's room, blinking in surprise when she saw Jamie sitting cross-legged on the bed, watching a basketball game with Rory. "Uhm ... did I know you were coming over?"

"No." Jamie stood, hitching Ryan's sweatpants up so they didn't fall off. "I, uhm ..." she cast a quick look at Rory, who was trying to disappear.

"Come on down to my room," Ryan said. "Who's winning?" she asked Rory.

"The Knicks," he said. "Da said to tell you dinner will be at 6:00."

"Thanks," Ryan nodded. "See you in a bit."

When they reached her room, she went to her built-in drawers and took out some dry clothes. "Be right back." She walked into the bath, and Jamie wandered around the room, not feeling welcome in the least.

Ryan emerged in dry clothes, her face washed and her hair pulled back into a ponytail. "When did you come over?"

"Just after we spoke. I had to explain, Ryan, and you wouldn't let me."

Ryan sat on her loveseat and gave Jamie a very cool look. "Not much to explain. You slept at some guy's house, or you had some guy in your room this morning. Seems pretty clear to me."

"It wasn't a guy!" Jamie insisted. "It was Jack."

Nodding briefly, Ryan commented, "I don't think he'd like to hear that you don't think he's a guy. I certainly consider him one."

"He was just taking care of me, Ryan. I had too much to drink, and I wasn't in any shape to drive. Rather than have him have to take me to

Berkeley and then drive all the way home, I slept on his couch. That's all that happened. I kissed him on the cheek when he dropped me off at my car, and that's it!"

"No, that's not it," Ryan said, enunciating each syllable. "You intentionally deceived me. Why would you do that if you had nothing to hide?"

The headache she'd been struggling with all day began to pound in her head with a vengeance. Her stomach was roiling, and she knew she was on the verge of throwing up the light lunch that Martin had forced on her. "I had nothing to hide, Ryan. I just … I don't know why I didn't want you to know where I was. I just didn't."

"Well, I just don't like to be lied to." She stood and cocked her head. "Anything else?"

Jamie got up and approached her hesitantly. A few tears started to roll down her cheeks, and she whispered, "Please don't be mad at me. I know I was wrong to mislead you. I just …" She dropped her head and sighed heavily. "I guess I am trying to hide something."

Ryan didn't say a word. She just continued to look at her with that cool, impassive stare, making Jamie feel profoundly guilty.

"I felt confused last night," she murmured, shifting her weight from foot to foot, feeling like a miscreant in front of the judge. "I started thinking about Jack again, and I found that I was a little attracted to him. I didn't want you to know that."

"Because?"

"Because I'm so confused!" she cried, now starting to cry harder. To her shock and dismay, Ryan didn't move a muscle, didn't in any way try to soothe or comfort her. "I was going along just fine, making a little progress, and then this happens! It's not what I want, Ryan! I want to make up my mind and be with you!"

The pitiful look on her face started to melt some of Ryan's reserve, and she sat down and patted the cushion next to her. Pathetically grateful, Jamie fell into the seat and curled up against Ryan's body. "I'm sorry," the blonde whispered. "I don't want to be confused this way. I just don't know what I want or how to get it."

"I understand that," Ryan murmured. "It's a very common thing, Jamie."

"I spent the whole night thinking about something Jack said," the smaller woman commented. "I told him how attracted I was to you, and he asked me if we kissed." She looked up at Ryan and asked, "Why don't we kiss? I want to so much."

"We don't kiss because I'm not going to let you experiment with my heart."

The harshness of her words shocked Jamie, and she stared at her with a stunned expression. "I don't want to …"

"Yes, you do," Ryan insisted. "You want to kiss me and have me show you how I feel about you. You want to be intimate to help you make up your mind. But I'm not going to do that, Jamie. You have to make up your mind on your own. Either you want me or you don't — but you're not going to make me fall even further in love with you and then go back to Jack or some other guy. It's not going to happen."

She buried her head against Ryan's chest and sobbed, "I don't want to hurt you — I swear I don't want to."

"I know you don't," Ryan sighed, leaning forward to kiss the blonde head. "But you're very confused right now, and I have to protect myself."

"We're still friends, right?" Jamie asked shakily.

"Of course we are," Ryan said, giving her a squeeze. "But I think I need a little break, Jamie. I know that you're struggling, but I'm not the right person to help you through this. I think you need to rely on Anna."

"She's no help at all," she grumbled. "I feel more confused than I did when I started with her. Jack told me last night that I just have to trust myself." She nodded confidently, "I think that's what I'm going to do."

Ryan nodded, then disentangled from the smaller woman. "Whatever you think is right," she said, her expression flat.

Jamie got up and started to gather her clothing. "I guess I'll get dressed and go on home." She was waiting for the dinner invitation that did not come. Sparing another look at Ryan, she saw that her expression had not changed. She looked completely emotionally disconnected, and Jamie had a very bad feeling in the pit of her stomach.

She went into the bath and got dressed, still looking a little like yesterday's trash. When she emerged, Ryan was sitting down again, giving her a neutral look. "I, uhm … guess I'll see you tomorrow at the gym," Jamie said quietly.

Ryan's head shook almost imperceptibly. "No, I don't think that's a good idea. I meant it when I said I needed a break."

Jamie managed to hit the edge of the bed as her legs gave out. "What? You mean … you don't want to see me at all?"

Again the dark head shook. "No, not at all. I'm getting into that dangerous area, Jamie. That place that I'm not sure I can come back from." She got up and walked over to the bed, then squatted down in front of the smaller woman. "I can't watch you struggle with this, never knowing where I stand. I'm too invested already," she insisted, shaking her head. "If I want to be able to be your friend in the future, I have to pull back now. I'm sorry, Jamie. I really am." She went to her knees and wrapped the shaking woman in a warm hug, holding on for a very long time. "I'm sorry," she whispered. "I just can't let you hurt me." She kissed the soft, blonde hair repeatedly, trying to express the love she felt in the tender caresses.

She got up then, gazing sorrowfully at her friend. The tears were flowing down Jamie's face, and she gasped, "I need you, Ryan."

"I know that," she said softly. "But I made you a promise, and I'm sticking to it. This is the only way I can be your friend if you decide to go back to men. The only way, Jamie."

"No bike rides?" she whimpered.

"No, not with me. There are dozens of practice rides in the Bay Area. The schedule shows which ones I lead. Please honor my wishes and don't come on my rides. I swear I wouldn't ask this of you if it weren't important."

"No training?"

"No. You know your routine now. At this point I just work with you because it's fun."

She looked at her as she felt her heart breaking. "What will I do without you?"

Ryan shrugged mildly, asking herself the same question. "We'll get through it. If it's meant to be, we'll be together. If not, we'll still be friends. That's all that I can do, Jamie. I wish I were stronger, but I'm not."

Feeling like she was walking away from the most vital, life-sustaining part of her existence, Jamie went up to her friend and stood on her tiptoes to kiss her cheek. Tears were rolling down the soft cheeks, and Jamie lingered to kiss them away. Then she dashed up the stairs, knowing that she was on the verge of hysteria. Ryan followed her and stood on the deck, watching her stumble down the quiet street, hearing her heart-rending sobs. It was all that she could do to not run after her and tell her that everything would be all right. But she couldn't. She held onto the deck railing until she felt splinters under her nails from her death-grip. Jamie got into her car, but she didn't pull away. Unable to watch for another moment, Ryan went back into the house and called out to her brother, "I'm not feeling well, Ror. Tell Da I'm gonna skip dinner."

She heard him hop to his feet and make for the door. But by the time he got there she was already heading downstairs. "Are you okay, sis?"

"I guess so," she muttered. "I'm just ... I'm just tired." She closed her door so that no one would disturb her, then lay down on her bed and cried until she had no more tears to shed.

⌘

Jamie wasn't able to get up for school the next day. She lay in bed, unable to sleep — unable to do anything but obsess about Ryan. She had spent the previous evening in a deep depression, but as the dawn broke, she began to allow some of her anger to have a voice. She knew that Ryan was trying to protect herself, but she had been able to come up with dozens of scenarios that would allow them to maintain contact while still allowing her to keep some distance. After twelve hours of going over the situation, she felt drained, more than a little angry and somewhat betrayed. Ryan was really the only person whom she trusted to help her through her confusion, and the thought of not seeing her for the foreseeable future was both heartbreaking and infuriating.

Finally making herself get out of bed, she stood in the shower for a very long time, trying to allow the warm water to revive her. When she emerged, she spent a little time making herself look presentable, then picked up her cell phone and dialed Anna's office. "Hi, this is Jamie Evans. I'm not going to able to keep my appointment ... for a while. Actually, I might not be back at all. This isn't working, Anna, and I'm going to try to work things out on my own. Feel free to charge me for as many of the appointments as you wish. I know I haven't given you adequate notice. Uhm ... thanks for your help. It was nice knowing you."

Picking up her bag, she took a novel that had nothing whatsoever to do with her class work and went to her favorite coffee bar to occupy her mind for the rest of the day.

⌘

At noon her cell phone rang, and she blinked in surprise when she noticed how late it was. "Hello?"

"Hi, Jamie, it's Jack."

"You know, I guessed that," she said. "I haven't forgotten the sound of your voice."

"That's nice to know," he said. "Uhm ... I really called to check to see if you were all right. I tried to reach you yesterday, but your cell was turned off."

"I wasn't in the mood to talk to anyone," she said quietly, deciding not to tell him about what happened between her and Ryan. "I'm not a whole lot better today, but it's nice to hear your voice."

"How would you like to see my face?" he asked. "If you're not busy, I thought we could have dinner."

"Dinner?" She started to say that she couldn't since she worked out with Ryan on Monday, and when the realization hit that she wasn't able to see her, she found herself needing to see Jack. "Dinner would be great. I'm having a tough day, and I'd really rather not be alone."

"What time?"

"Come any time," she said, sighing with regret. "I have no plans at all."

⌘

He came early, leaving Palo Alto just after his last class. They met at her house and then walked to a restaurant not far away. Nothing earth-shaking occurred during their meal, and that was just how she wanted it. The evening was just comfortable — no expectations — no pressure. Walking home, he reached down and took her hand in his, and she allowed the contact, feeling that it was more friendly than romantic.

Both Cassie and Mia's cars were parked on the street, alerting her to their presence, and she was loath to go into the house, unwilling to let either of them know she was reestablishing contact with Jack. He sensed her reluctance and suggested that they sit on the porch and talk for a while. Pleased with both his suggestion and the fact that he seemed to sense she needed to be outdoors, she sat in one of the comfortable wooden chairs and he took the other.

For a long time, they didn't speak, each of them enjoying the quiet sounds of the night. He moved his chair close and took her hand again. For almost an hour they sat in silence, both somehow feeling very connected to one another. Finally, at around 9:00, he stood and said, "I should get going." He gave her a quizzical look and asked, "Can we do this again? This was one of the nicest evenings I've had since February."

"Sure." She smiled up and him, and her eyes widened when he drew near. She was sure he was going to kiss her, and she wasn't at all sure that she wanted him to. But he veered away at the last moment and kissed her head, lingering to breathe in the scent of her shampoo.

"I'll call you." He gave her a wide smile and walked down the sidewalk, headed to his car. At that moment she regretted that he hadn't kissed her, and she almost ran after him, chickening out at the last minute.

⌘

There was a message on the machine from Anna. "Hi, Jamie, it's Anna Fleming. I got your message, and I'd really like to speak to you. I don't want to try to convince you to change you mind, but I have a few things to say, and I don't feel comfortable leaving a personal message on your machine. Call me when you can, all right?"

No way, she said, shaking her head as she thought the words. *I'm not coming back, so there's nothing left to say. Just bill me!*

⌘

It didn't take Mia long to notice Ryan's conspicuous absence. "Hey, why haven't I seen you at the gym?" she asked on Wednesday. "You weren't there on Monday, and you missed again today."

"I don't have time," she lied. "What with going over there, working out, taking a shower when I get home, that's two hours wasted. Those extra six hours of studying might be the difference between an A and a C."

"I noticed that Ryan's bike's not in the garage," Mia commented. "Isn't she leaving her motorcycle here in the morning anymore?"

"Oh, she must have needed it at home," Jamie said, not having noticed that Ryan had removed it. She walked up the stairs to her room, unreasonably jealous that Mia was still able to spend time with her friend. She wanted to ask how she seemed, to find out if Mia had detected that anything was wrong, but she couldn't. She didn't want Mia, or anyone else to know how much she missed Ryan, and she had no reasonable explanation for why they weren't seeing each other, so she swallowed her discomfort and went to her room to spend another night cursing the dark-haired woman for putting her through this torture.

⌘

She saw Jack again on Friday night, with him once again suggesting that they have dinner in Berkeley. The evening went as well as the previous one had, but this time, when he announced he was leaving, she put her hand behind his head and drew him down for a kiss. It wasn't a spectacularly sensual kiss, but it was more than friendly. He obviously noticed the heat, because when he picked up his head his face bore a very pleased smile. "How about tomorrow?" he asked quietly.

"I'm going down to Hillsborough," she informed him. "My parents are out of town for a couple of weeks, but I thought I'd go down and crank up the heat on the pool so I can jump in when my studying gets too boring. Want to join me?"

"I'd love to," he smiled.

They studied and they swam, enjoying the warm day and the even warmer pool. She frequently caught him checking her out and finally teased, "Looks to me like your mind is less on your books and more on my butt."

"Ow! Don't you know that guys hate to get caught?"

"Then don't be so obvious," she laughed. "You really haven't had many dates lately, have you."

"No, I haven't," he said quietly, now gravely serious. "I was just sitting here wondering what in the hell was wrong with me to complain about the way you looked. You look absolutely fantastic," he said, his appreciation obvious.

"Thanks. I've worked hard." She ran a hand over her toned stomach and said, "I've been slacking off, though. I haven't been to the gym all week."

"Too much work?"

Deciding to be honest, she said, "No. Ryan's decided that she can't see me until I make up my mind about what I want."

"What you want?" he asked slowly.

"Men or women," she informed him, staring at the ground.

"Oh." A full minute passed before he said, "What's her hurry? I'd think she would know that you can't force a decision like that."

"Thank you," she said pointedly. "This is hard enough to get through without losing my best friend." She was on the verge of tears, but she struggled and composed herself.

"I'm really sorry to hear that, Jamie. I know how much she means to you."

"Do you?" she asked. "I'm not sure I do any more. I'm just so angry with her that I can hardly remember what attracted me."

Fixing her with an intense gaze, he asked, "Do you remember what about me attracted you?"

She smiled, unable to resist the half-sexy, half-boyish look on his face. "I do. I was attracted by a lot of things, actually. Your confidence, your maturity, your kindness, the fact that we shared some of the same life goals. I liked how well you got along with my family, especially my father." She looked at him carefully and said, "I liked your smile and your eyes. You have just the kind of body I like, too. Broad shoulders and narrow hips." Giving him her most playful smile she added, "You have a great butt, too."

369

Shifting onto his side, he tried to get a look, teasing, "Hey, I do!"

Getting up to share his chaise, she placed her hands on the armrests and leaned over. "I loved the way you kiss," she said softly. "You could do more to me with a kiss than any other guy had ever managed."

"Wanna see if the magic still works?" he asked, looking deeply into her eyes.

"Yes." Her voice was confident, and her actions matched her tone. She leaned over him and started to kiss him, letting her body sink into the familiar embrace. She had missed this contact so much — the gentle, intimate touch of a lover's kiss — that she let the caress continue long past what she had planned.

The kisses grew hotter and deeper, and soon she was lying on top of him, writhing against him while her tongue explored his mouth. Eventually, she slowed her attack and finally stopped, resting her head upon his chest, panting softly. "Wow," she muttered. "Where did that come from?"

"I don't know, but I'm not gonna complain if it comes back," he chuckled. He twitched around a bit and said, "I envy women."

"Huh?"

"It must be nice to be able to hide your arousal."

She giggled softly and said, "You know, it really is. I can't imagine how embarrassing that must be."

"Oh, it's not as bad now," he said, grimacing while he shifted. "You should have seen me in junior high. I had a gorgeous home room teacher." He sighed in memory. "Ms. Hooker. Nice name for a horny bunch of ninth graders to fixate on, huh?"

Jamie rolled off the chaise and tossed him a towel. "I don't mind, but I know you don't want Marta to see that."

He looked up at her and said, "How was that for you? I mean, I don't want to overanalyze this, but you seemed to really enjoy yourself."

"I did," she assured him. She produced an imaginary checklist and made a tick mark on it. "One thing's off the list. I must not be a full-blown lesbian, because I don't think I'd be throbbing like I am if I were. That just leaves two more categories."

"You'll get there, Jamie," he said encouragingly, and for the first time in a while, she privately thought that she might.

⌘

She surprised herself later that evening when she offered, "Why don't you stay over? We could study again tomorrow. I thought it worked well, didn't you?"

"Yeah, I did. I'd like that."

"I'll go get the guest room ready," she said, making it obvious what her boundaries were.

⌘

The next morning she woke early and got up to go downstairs and read the paper. It was so early that the *Chronicle* hadn't yet arrived, so she looked around the room for something to entertain her. The plethora of neatly labeled photo albums that chronicled her childhood caught her attention, and she idly thought that she hadn't looked at them in years. *Mother sure wasn't very good at being involved in my life, but she was great at memorializing it,* she thought wryly as she perused the books.

The first book was labeled "1978" and showed several photos of her mother and father looking very happy together as they anticipated the birth of their child. Catherine was a very small woman, and she obviously had not gained much weight during her pregnancy. Her belly was very protuberant, but she actually looked like she was wearing a balloon under her clothing, since the rest of her body looked exactly like it had before she was pregnant.

There were a number of shots of the shower that her mother's sorority sisters had thrown for her, the happy-looking young women joining in the traditional rite of passage into motherhood. Jamie thought ahead to the future, picturing herself in a few years, surrounded by friends from high school and college, preparing to welcome her child into the world. *It would be a far different experience if I were with Ryan*, she thought wryly. *For one thing, I'd have to get a whole new set of friends. Different parents wouldn't hurt, either*, she added with a grimace.

Jesus! she thought grumpily. *It's easy for her with that fabulous family! They'd think it was great that she was going to have a baby with a woman! No matter how society treats her, she always has her family to remind her of how special she is. But most of us don't get that. And I don't want to have to lose my family if I don't have to!* she thought defiantly. *And if my attraction for Jack stays as strong as it is now, I don't have to!*

⌘

Going back upstairs, she opened the door to the guest room slightly and observed Jack, sprawled out across the bed, consuming nearly all of the king-sized mattress. She slipped in next to him in the scant space left, and snuggled against him, taking in his slightly musky scent and the smooth, lightly tanned skin that her cheek rested against. *God, I missed this*, she mused as sleep claimed her almost immediately.

⌘

As her eyes blinked open, a deep voice whispered, "Good morning."

"Oh, hi," she said with a shy grin. "I hope you don't mind that I snuck in here this morning." He was lying on his back, and she was curled up against his chest with her head resting on his muscular shoulder. His arm was securely wrapped around her shoulders, and his large hand rested on her hip.

"Best surprise I've had in weeks," he replied as he placed a tiny kiss on her head. "But I need my arm back for a minute." She released him and watched his cute butt twitch as he padded into the bath. A few minutes later he emerged with his face washed and a toothbrush sticking out of his mouth. "What do you want to do?" he asked through a mouth full of toothpaste. "Ready to get up or would you like a little cuddling?"

She was a bit surprised by that offer since cuddling was never his forte. "I'd love to cuddle if you really don't mind."

He gave her an adorable grin that lit up his whole face. He dashed back into the bath, spitting noisily, then ran a few steps towards the bed and launched himself at her with a wild look in his eyes. She laughed heartily at his antics, trying to remember the last time he was so playful. He grabbed her roughly and plastered his toothpaste-smeared mouth against hers, making her giggle uncontrollably. She calmed down after a minute, and he braced himself on one arm, leaning over her and saying in a very serious voice, "I missed cuddling with you, Jamie. After we broke up, I would lie in bed in the morning and just ache to feel your body next to mine."

She gazed up at him in amazement, both at the sentiment and his very successful attempts at emotional openness. Her face curled into a welcoming smile, and he lowered his head to place a few delicate kisses on her lips. But true to his word, he immediately flopped down next to her and wrapped her in a warm embrace. She turned onto her side and scooted up against his lap, relieved to find him flaccid. *I don't think we've ever cuddled in the morning without his getting an erection*, she mused. *Maybe he really is serious about just being close.* They were both still tired, and after a few

372

minutes of the tender embrace, she slipped back into a contented slumber. They cycled through sleep and hugs for another half-hour or so, turning from one side to the other several times.

⌘

To her extreme pleasure, when they woke, they kissed and held each other tenderly for a long while, just reconnecting with each other's touch. "This is exactly — and I do mean exactly — what I needed," Jamie mumbled into his chest. "I love touching you and kissing and hugging in the morning."

"I love it, too," he sighed. "I didn't realize how much I loved it until I didn't have it any longer."

This is what I thought marriage would be like, she mused as his hand ran slowly up and down her leg. *Nice long cuddles, lots of kissing and hugging and when problems happen, you just talk about them.*

CHAPTER SIXTEEN

THE NEXT WEEK WAS A CLOSE APPROXIMATION OF THE PREVIOUS ONE.
Jack drove up to Berkeley on Wednesday, and on Friday they went down to
Hillsborough together to spend the weekend. They slept together on both
Friday and Saturday nights, but she was careful to make clear that all she
was ready for was a few kisses and some cuddling. Whatever his inner
feelings, Jack was completely supportive, indicating that he wasn't ready to
be intimate either, a claim she privately doubted but appreciated his making.

She still missed Ryan desperately, and on the nights that she slept
alone, she spent hours tossing and turning, feeling so abandoned, so
totally bereft that she didn't understand how she was still able to function.
Any solitude found her obsessing about Ryan. But being around Jack
seemed to occupy her thoughts and ground her — however temporarily.
His easy, familiar, undemanding style made her feel that everything would
eventually be all right. That always proved true until she was alone again,
and her thoughts returned to Ryan.

She was cutting across campus on her way home on Monday afternoon
when she saw her. Jamie had to grab a small tree to remain upright, and as
she tried to catch her breath, she allowed herself to take her in.

Ryan was sitting on the long, low concrete wall in front of one of the
newer classroom buildings. Her back was propped up against the building
and one long leg was drawn up, supporting a heavy textbook. The
afternoon sun was angled low in the sky, and the warm, golden glow made
her look as beautiful as Jamie had ever seen her.

She was wearing stylized sunglasses — the frames a close-fitting silver,
the lenses, iridescent blue. Jamie could just imagine the blue of her eyes,
hidden behind the snug glasses. Her hair was loose, and it tumbled across
her shoulders in a fantastically attractive fashion. The light wind pushed
her bangs off her forehead, highlighting all of the subtle and sharp planes
of her strong face.

Wearing khaki-colored cargo shorts and a long-sleeved, sky blue knit
shirt, she looked casual, confident and perfectly at home in her own skin,
an attribute that Jamie had always found incredibly sexy.

The dark head tilted up when someone called her name, and Jamie turned to see the woman that Ryan had been making out with at the lesbian bookstore. Jamie couldn't recall her name, but Ryan had certainly not forgotten her. She stood and gave the woman a friendly kiss, and Jamie had to restrain herself from running across the lawn to take the woman's place.

They chatted for a while, and as Ryan's face became more animated, Jamie had to sit on the ground, since her legs no longer wanted to hold her up. The remarkably beautiful smile, the way her head tilted when the other woman was speaking, even the casual way she brushed her hair back against the breeze. All of Ryan's attributes and habits converged to make Jamie's entire body thrum with unquenched desire. She could occasionally hear Ryan's gentle laugh, brought to her on the wind. *I miss that laugh*, she moaned to herself. *I miss that smile and I miss hugging her and I miss the way she drapes her arm around my shoulders when we walk together.*

Unsure of where she got the strength, she finally stood and forced herself to turn and walk in the other direction, unable to spend another moment watching her lovely friend, since she knew she would soon run across the lawn and make a complete fool of herself. *Is that such a bad idea?* she wondered as she headed home.

When she reached her room, Jamie lay down on her bed and let her mind wander, an activity that had begun to take up larger and larger portions of her day. She was trying hard — putting more energy into figuring out her sexual identity than she had ever devoted to another endeavor. But no matter how hard she tried, she was unable to make any progress. She'd never felt more attracted to Ryan than she had just a few minutes ago — her need to run to her and bury herself in her arms was as real to her as the bed she lay on. But something — something she did not understand — held her back. It was the indecision that was driving her mad. Her overwhelming desire for Ryan was tempered by her feelings for Jack — for the safety and security and normalcy that she experienced when he held her. She knew she couldn't go on like this. Her schoolwork was suffering horribly, she barely spoke to Mia and Cassie, she even avoided talking to her grandfather. All she wanted to do was lie on her bed and dream of Ryan; dream of a world where sexual orientation was an unknown concept.

⌘

On Saturday afternoon, Ryan was lying on her father's bed, watching the Giants play the Dodgers. Conor came in from running a few errands and offered to make her a sandwich. As expected, she accepted his offer, and he came into the room a few minutes later, carrying the forbidden food. "Don't you dare drop one crumb on the bed," he warned. "You know Da will tan your hide."

"Yeah, I know," she smiled. "I'll be careful."

They ate in silence, both watching the game with some interest. After finishing his food he came over to stretch out next to her. "You've been home a lot lately," he commented.

She shrugged, not answering verbally.

"You've been in a pissy mood, too. Everybody's noticed."

"Everybody?" she asked, raising a brow.

"Well, Da, Rory, Brendan, Aunt Maeve."

"Nobody said anything to me," she groused, her eyes still focused on the game.

"You're too grouchy for anybody to get up the nerve," he advised. "I've never seen you like this."

"Well, you're seeing it now." She got up to leave, but he reached out and grabbed the back pocket of her jeans.

"Come on, Ryan, don't shut us all out. Something's obviously wrong. You haven't been out on a date for weeks, and ever since that fight you and Jamie had, she hasn't been around. Is that what you're pissed about?"

"Who said we had a fight?" she asked, eyes narrowing.

"Rory. He was here you know. He said Jamie told him you'd had a fight, and then she ran out of here just before dinner."

"Big mouth," she grumbled.

"Come on, sis. Tell me."

"I don't want to," she insisted, clearly irritated. "This is between Jamie and me. I don't want to talk about her life."

"Well, then tell me about yours," he urged. "Are you upset with her?"

She sighed and said, "It won't make any sense unless I talk about her private life."

"Look, I know you don't like to talk about your friends, but you're obviously not doing very well at resolving whatever it is that's bothering you. Let me have a crack at it."

Scowling at him for a long moment, she finally relented. "I shouldn't, but I'm about to go mad, so I'll make an exception." She faced him and said, "Thanks to you, I tried to break my no friends into lovers rule."

"Excellent!"

"Yeah. I'm feeling like this because things are going so well," she growled. "We each told each other how we felt, and even though she wasn't ready to commit to being with me, she was working towards that."

Her scowl grew deeper as she said, "She got cold feet. Her former fiancé's back in the picture, and I told her that I couldn't see her until she'd made a decision — either him or me." She crossed her arms over her chest and gave him a challenging look. "Make me feel better."

"Is she currently seeing the guy?"

"I assume so," Ryan said, nodding briefly.

"And you're just gonna stand on the sidelines and take what's left? Are you nuts?"

"No, I'm not nuts," she huffed. "I can't make this decision for her, Conor, and it hurts too much to watch her struggle with it. Seeing the indecision in her eyes is just awful!"

"Ryan, have you learned nothing from living with a house full of men? You can't let him have full access to her. He'll run the table before you take your cue out of the rack!"

"She's not a billiard ball," Ryan sniffed. "She's a person. A very confused person whom I refuse to have undue influence over."

"Believe me, Ryan, you're the only one who's playing the game that way. Her boyfriend's working on her 24/7 to convince her that he's Mr. Wonderful. If you let him do that, you might as well throw in the towel and not even bother."

"What are you suggesting?"

"You've got to let Jamie know that you want her as much as this guy does! Letting her go off and contemplate is gonna backfire on you, sis, I swear!"

She collapsed against the mattress, moaning pitifully. "I don't want to lose her, Con, but I promised I'd stay away until she's decided. I can't go back on my word!"

"Did she ask you to stay away, or was that your idea?" he asked.

"Mine."

"Then you're only going back on your word to yourself. You'll get over it."

She stared up at the ceiling, her thoughts unfocused, knowing that Conor had a point, but also recognizing that her self-protection was paramount.

⌘

Ryan mulled over Conor's advice for days, but she was unable to act on it. Even though she desperately wanted to remind Jamie of exactly how much she cared for her, how much she missed her, she felt so fragile and vulnerable that she didn't want to expose herself any more than was absolutely necessary.

Her mood was so foul that her brothers cut her a wide path, having learned that she turned inward when she was upset — and only she could pull herself out of her funk.

It had been just over three weeks since she'd seen Jamie, and she was beginning to lose hope that she'd ever get the chance to be her lover. Lost in her musings, she found herself by Strawberry Creek, the narrow channel of water that cut a path through the Cal campus. The creek ran through a dense stand of trees and shrubs, and the air was always cool and moist near the banks, reminding her vaguely of a small stream near her grandparents' home. She was often drawn to the place when she was feeling discomfited, finding herself stopping by the stream more and more lately. Something caught her eye, and she stopped abruptly when she recognized Jamie, sitting by the running water, idly tossing pebbles into the stream. Unable to resist, Ryan quietly approached and said, "Hi."

The blonde head swiveled, and Ryan felt her heart nearly stop when she saw the red-rimmed eyes and tears dotting Jamie's pale cheeks. She dropped to the ground next to her and gently placed a hand on her thigh. "Why are you crying?"

Wiping at her eyes, she asked, "Do you have any tissues? Mine are long gone."

Ryan dug in her backpack and found a bandana that she kept in case she needed to tie her hair back. She handed it to her friend and said, "You can have this. I've got a dozen of them."

Blotting her eyes, Jamie smiled wanly and said, "It smells like your hair." Seeing the concern in Ryan's eyes, she once again lost her composure and started to cry. The larger woman slipped an arm around her and tugged her against her chest, holding her tightly while Jamie let some of her sorrow out. Ryan ran her hand through the short, blonde strands that had fallen into her friend's eyes. "Tell me, Jamie. Tell me why you're crying."

"The usual," she sighed deeply.

"I cry, too," Ryan revealed. "But my usual is to bark and snap at the boys. They'll barely be in the same room with me." She kissed the head that was nestled just under her chin. "Will you tell me how you're doing? I think about you constantly, but I just haven't had the nerve to call you."

"I guess things are about the same," she said, not wanting to hurt Ryan by telling her too much.

Her embrace tightened, and the larger woman said, "I really want to know, Jamie. Be honest with me, okay?"

Jamie looked up and met her eyes, seeing the resolve. Sitting up, she nodded and said, "I'm more confused than I was before. I've been seeing Jack a couple of times a week, but I'm not really sure why." Shaking her head in dismay she said, "I shouldn't say it like that. It's been wonderful to have him to talk to, and when we're together, I feel pretty good." She blinked up at Ryan, looking more confused than the taller woman had ever seen her. "I'm just so damned unsure of myself. Nothing makes sense anymore."

"Are you still seeing Anna?" Ryan asked softly.

"No, I stopped when I realized I was just feeling worse and worse. It just seemed stupid to pay someone to torture me."

Ryan nodded, saying nothing, but hearing Conor's words come back to her with a vengeance. Looking around at the lovely setting, she commented, "I haven't been down here in a while. Not since fall I guess."

"Do you remember coming down here for our juice break one day?"

"Yeah, I do," Ryan smiled. "That was just after you agreed to do the AIDS Ride."

Jamie tilted her head and met Ryan's eyes. "That was the first day that I ever consciously wanted to kiss you. You were sitting by the bank, and there was just a tiny bit of water in the creek. You took off your shoes and socks and put your feet in, and you had this totally blissful look on your face. You lay down with your feet still in the water and started to hum a little tune. God," she sighed. "You just looked so peaceful and seemed so content. I wanted to lean over and kiss you to get some of whatever it was that made you so happy."

Looking down at her, not speaking for a moment, Ryan finally said, "It was you. Being with you made me happy. The cool creek, the nice warm day and being with you made me blissfully happy." She stared into her eyes and said, "It still does. Even more so now. You make me happy."

"Oh, Ryan," Jamie sighed, leaning into her again. "You make me happy, too. I never feel better than when I'm with you."

Ryan reached down and placed her fingers under Jamie's chin. Lifting it slightly, she looked into her eyes and asked, "Do you still want to kiss me? Like you did the first day we came here?"

"More," she whispered, eyes fluttering closed. "So much more."

One powerful arm slipped around her shoulders, and Ryan leaned forward, gently lowering her to the ground . The larger woman lay alongside her friend, much of her weight braced against an arm. Her hand rose and began to trace the contours of the lovely face, fingers memorizing the shape of her brow, her cheekbones, the full, warm lips.

Jamie just lay beneath her, nearly holding her breath, her entire body thrumming with anticipation.

Finally, Ryan leaned over her and paused just above, whispering, "I love you, Jamie." Then her warm mouth covered the coral-tinted lips, and she let herself go.

Removing all boundaries, the dark woman allowed every long-controlled emotion to escape from her body — forcing those fierce feelings to flow directly into Jamie. Her mouth moved slowly, nuzzling and nipping against the smaller woman's lips, until Jamie's mouth began to open tentatively. Ryan's tongue slipped inside, drawing a deep, sensual moan from both women.

They were right in the middle of campus, the path and bridges that crossed the creek a popular shortcut for hundreds of students. But for once in her life, Jamie didn't care who saw her; she didn't care if they were surrounded by every person she'd ever known. All that mattered was that she was in Ryan's arms, and that their mouths were merged like molten iron.

Their tongues slid against one another's, and a shiver worked its way up Jamie's spine. Ryan continued to let out tiny, sexy moans, now holding Jamie so tightly that the smaller woman could feel her heart thudding dramatically against her breast.

Her hands slid to Ryan's back, exploring the firm muscles, each one coiled tight. Her arms tightened with each beat of her heart, the solid, warm body feeling like her safe harbor in the storm. It seemed as if the kiss lasted several lifetimes, and as Ryan started to pull away, she once again nibbled and sucked at Jamie's desire-swollen lips, unwilling to relinquish her claim on the woman she loved.

She lay on her side, pressed tight against Jamie. Her lips were just inches from the smaller woman's ear, and her breath was warm and moist as her words caressed her. "I know you're confused, and I'm sorry if this adds to your confusion. I'm confused, too, and I'm frightened. But I'm not going to let my fears stop me from letting you know exactly how I feel. I love you with all my heart, and I want you to be mine. I'll wait for you, Jamie," she whispered. "For as long as it takes." Once again, she pulled the smaller woman to her and placed a heartbreakingly tender kiss upon her golden hair. "Don't ever doubt that I love you," she murmured, unable to stop the tears. She got to her feet and looked down at Jamie, then gave her a tender smile and strode away. Leaving the smaller woman lying on the ground, confused, distraught and devastatingly aroused.

⌘

Nearly an hour later, still lying exactly where Ryan had left her, Jamie fought through the intense fog that had settled in her brain following their kiss. She fumbled in her bag and found her cell phone, speed-dialed the number she had not removed from memory and said, "I'll pay you $10,000 to see me today. Make that $20,000," she added as an afterthought. She hung up and lay back down, vaguely noting that she hadn't identified herself. *She'll know*, she reasoned. *I'm probably the richest crazy client she has.*

Anna made time for her, agreeing to see Jamie at eight o'clock that night, chuckling mildly when she assured her that she'd charge the usual amount.

Jamie wasn't sure what she'd done for the long afternoon and evening, and she wasn't certain why Anna gave her such a puzzled look when she opened the door to the waiting room at seven o'clock. The therapist showed her seven o'clock client into her office, then came back out to say, "I'm seeing you at 8:00, Jamie. Did you mix up the times?"

"No," she said blankly. "I just wanted to be close to you." She started to cry once again, and Anna came over and patted her gently on the shoulder. "Why don't you lie down here on the couch. No one else should come into the office. I'll come get you in forty-five minutes, okay?"

"Okay," she mumbled, walking over to the couch to sprawl along it in a complete daze.

As promised, Anna opened the door in exactly forty-five minutes. It was all Jamie could do not to crawl into the older woman's lap, but she had enough mental acuity to recognize that would not be appropriate. Taking a seat, she started to apologize, stumbling over her words. "I'm so sorry I quit like I did and then refused to return your phone calls. That was so rude and insensitive …"

"Jamie," she said quietly, "is that what's troubling you now?"

"No, no, but —"

"I'm not angry or disappointed in you for terminating therapy. We can talk about that if you want, but it seems like there's something pretty critical going on, and you might want to spend the time talking about that."

She nodded, then dove in. Telling Anna about the wedding and how it led to her spending time with Jack. About how nice it felt to be with him and have his unflagging support. Then she told her about Ryan's ultimatum and that afternoon's kiss. "I never, ever thought she'd do this," Jamie mumbled for the fourth time.

Anna gazed at her sympathetically. "She's a human being, Jamie."

"I know," she sighed. "I just didn't think she'd make this so much harder for me. That's just not like her."

"How has she made it harder?" Anna asked quietly. "If one of your roommates kissed you and told you she loved you, would that make you doubt your feelings for Jack?"

"Of course not," she scoffed. "I don't feel about them like I do about Ryan."

"I honestly think that Ryan's made this easier for you, Jamie. She's made it clear that she's serious about her feelings and that she loves you very much. I think it makes your choice obvious. It sounds like you were trying to shut off your feelings for her," she added. "She's not going to let you do that. Now you have to decide, based on two people who love you — two people whom you love as well. At least it's above board now. Jack knows how you feel about Ryan, and Ryan knows how you feel about Jack."

"Then why don't I know how I feel about either one of them?" she moaned.

"Do you really not know?" Anna asked softly.

Jamie looked at her and gave her a wry smirk. "You know, this is exactly why I hate to come here. You make me admit to stuff I don't want to face."

"This is difficult for you and very painful, Jamie. No one would *want* to face these choices. You're being very brave to do so."

"I don't feel brave," she muttered. "I feel like I've been jerking two perfectly decent people around."

"It sounds to me like you've been as honest as you can be with both of them," Anna offered.

"Up until today."

"Pardon?"

"After what happened today, I can't deny my feelings any longer, Anna. Ryan didn't just kiss my lips." She leaned her head back against her chair and sighed, "She touched my soul. I can't walk away from her, no matter the cost."

"Will you tell her that, Jamie?"

"Yes, I will, but I still have all of the same issues that I had when you and I first started talking about this. All I've managed to do is waste three weeks and get Jack involved in the mess."

"I can see that you feel that way, but isn't it better to resolve your doubts now, rather than after being with Ryan for a while?"

"For Ryan and for me, it is," she agreed. "I don't know that Jack will feel the same."

⌘

She spent the next day considering every permutation of her plan. Should she have him come to Berkeley? Should she go to his apartment? Should she do it over the phone? Or in a letter? But none of the options seemed quite right. She had never broken up with anyone special before, and she truly hated that Jack had to be the one. Finally, deciding that she had to get it over with, she called his apartment at seven o'clock on Tuesday night.

"Jamie, hi," he said warmly. "Do you want to make plans to see each other tomorrow?"

"I need to talk to you, Jack. Can I come down?"

"Tonight?" he asked in surprise. "What is it? Is something wrong?"

"Yes, Jack, something is wrong, but I need to tell you in person."

"No," he said firmly. "I don't want to wait an hour. Don't keep me in suspense, please," he begged.

She drew in a breath and let it out slowly, trying to steel her nerves. "It's about us, Jack," she said with a tremulous voice.

"I assumed that, Jamie," he said calmly. "What about us exactly?"

"We ... we can't be together," she whispered as the tears began.

"Why?" he asked so softly that she could barely hear him. "I thought that I had ..."

"You did nothing wrong, Jack. You were absolutely perfect," she said as the sobs shook her body. "It's not you ... it's me."

"What is you?" he asked, again in a barely perceptible voice.

"It's not right, Jack. I need things that you can't give me, and you want things that I'm unable to give you."

"Is this about Ryan?" he asked softly.

"Only partially," she said honestly. "She's shown me things that I need, Jack. Things that I'll never be able to get if you and I stay together."

"Jamie, I said I'll do anything!" he said, his voice rising in alarm. "I mean that!"

"I know you do. I truly believe you, Jack. But you have to be who you are. You can't change just to please me."

"I will! I'll change to please you, Jamie. Please, let me try!"

"No, Jack," she said, feeling as cruel as she had ever felt. "It won't work. We need to move on — to find other people who are more suited to us. I hate to hurt you ... God, I hate to hurt you," she whispered, her tears falling freely. "But I can't be with you. I'm so sorry, Jack. I'm so very sorry."

A long silence developed since she had nothing more to add. Finally he

383

asked, "Are you absolutely certain?"

"Yes," she said quietly. "I'm certain."

He blew out a long breath and whispered, "I love you, Jamie." Then the phone went dead.

⌘

After hanging up with Jack, she called Anna's emergency number. The therapist returned the call promptly and spent a long while trying to soothe her near-hysterical patient. Finally, Jamie was calm enough to catch her breath, and they agreed to see each other for two hours on Wednesday. Jamie clutched to the prospect of the session like a lifeline.

She went downstairs to get something to drink and was just heading back to her room when the doorbell rang. Peering out through the glass, she saw Jack, and her heart leapt to her throat. She didn't want to see him, but she didn't have many options at that point — especially if she wanted to avoid a scene.

As she opened the door, he strode in and took her hand, decisively leading her back upstairs. As soon as he closed the door to her bedroom, he faced her and asked, "Why?"

"Jack," she sighed, "This is the right thing. I know it's not the outcome you wanted. Hell, it's not the outcome that I want most of the time, but it's the right outcome."

"Not for me, it isn't," he said, tears springing to his eyes. "I love you, and I think you love me! You just have some crazy obsession with Ryan that's confusing you."

"That's not it," she said softly. "It's not an obsession, Jack. She's the right person for me, and as soon as I can get through some of my paralyzing fears, I'm going to tell her so."

"Two days ago you were holding me and kissing me, Jamie. What changed?"

"I don't really want to talk about this, Jack. It's not going to be helpful to you, I swear."

"I want to know," he decided. "I want to know what makes you so sure all of a sudden."

"She kissed me," she said, wishing she didn't have to see the look on his face as her words sunk in. "I ran into her on campus, and she told me that she loved me, and then she kissed me."

"One kiss? You're going to make a life-changing decision based on one kiss?"

"Yes," she murmured. "It was … it was …" She shook her head, unwilling to reveal how that one kiss had changed her life. "It's right for me."

"But you just admitted that you haven't even told her! What if she doesn't feel the same?"

"She does," she said, her eyes closing at the memory of Ryan's pledge. "But even if she didn't, I couldn't be with you, Jack. There's a passion between Ryan and me that I can't be without. If I can't get it from her, I'll have to get it from someone else. All I know is that I have to have it."

He swallowed, trying to stop the tears. "You never felt passion for me?"

"Of course I did," she said, stretching the truth just a bit. "But this is different. This is life-giving, Jack. I've got to have it."

His shoulders slumped as he saw the unwavering determination in her eyes. He started to speak, but finally just shook his head and headed for the door. When his hand was on the knob he stood, facing the door, then said, "I love you, Jamie. I just wish … I wish I'd known sooner that you didn't feel the same way."

"I did and I do love you, Jack," she sighed. "But I didn't love you the way you love me. I wish I'd known *that* sooner."

Without another word he left the room, and she heard his heavy tread descend her stairs for the last time. She didn't even take her shoes off, just switched off the light and fell face first onto her bed, falling into an exhausted slumber, fully clothed.

⌘

When she returned home from her marathon therapy session the next day, she took Anna's advice and sat down to write in her journal. At the end of the evening, her hand was completely fatigued, but her mind felt much clearer. Summoning her courage, she sat down at her computer and composed an e-mail to Ryan, smiling as she typed in her rather odd address. *I have no idea what a googolplex is, but I love that little math nerd, and I'm not going to have her worrying about this any more than she has to.*

She kept it relatively brief, simply telling Ryan that she had decided to stop seeing Jack and that she was going back into therapy. Promising to work hard and keep her apprised, she closed by saying, "The kiss we shared changed my life, Ryan. No matter what happens between us, I know I'll never be the same. For that, I thank you with all my heart."

⌘

385

The rest of the week seemed like an endless therapy session. She talked to Anna every afternoon, then went home to pour out her heart onto the tear-stained pages of her journal.

Her desire to see Ryan was so strong that she didn't understand how she was able to resist it. But she did resist it — knowing it was the best thing for both of them. Only she could find her way through her fears, and seeing Ryan caused her to lose focus. It was so apparent how much she loved her and wanted to be with her when they were together. But her desire wasn't really the issue at this point. The bigger issue was whether she had the courage to face all of the repercussions that would accompany being in a same-sex relationship. They actually hadn't spent any time at all discussing the topic, but she knew Ryan well, and she knew that she lived openly in every area of her life — and that she'd need Jamie to be just as open.

The fact that she couldn't interact with Ryan didn't stop her pressing need to see her, and after some wrestling with her conscience, she decided that she had to at least be able to catch a glimpse of the woman. She knew Ryan's class schedule as well as she knew her own, and for the next two weeks, she made it a point to see her each and every day.

It wasn't always easy to accomplish her goal. Their class schedules were roughly similar, though Jamie's classroom buildings weren't close to Ryan's. But she figured out a way to manage it so long as she took her bike and rode like hell. No matter how much work it was, she found that it was entirely satisfying. Just a quick glimpse and Jamie felt immeasurably cheered, able to focus on her school work and work on her journal for hours at a time.

The work with Anna was going well now that Jamie wasn't as afraid to face the truth. She was certain that she'd be able to tell her friends and her family about her relationship — even though she was certain she wasn't ready to do it yet. But she didn't think that would be an impediment to forming a relationship with Ryan. She knew her friend was the very soul of patience — she just had to know that her patience would be rewarded.

Jamie continued to send short e-mails to Ryan, just letting her know that she was all right and still managing to get some bike rides in. Ryan replied to every one — her tone consistently light and friendly, never asking any prying questions.

Sitting in class on a Thursday afternoon, she heard her professor mention that the following week was the last full week of class for the term. Her eyes nearly popped from her head at this bit of news, and she realized that she had totally lost track of time. She'd been keeping up with her class work, but had been putting off doing two major papers that she knew would be difficult to complete.

She left class in a daze, remembering at the last minute that she had to rush across campus to have a chance of seeing Ryan. Pedaling as quickly as she was able, she reached her usual spot and waited. After twenty minutes she realized that she'd been too late, and she went home in a deep funk. Seeing Ryan, however briefly, was keeping her grounded, and she spent the next two hours moodily glancing at a book. Finally, deciding that it was doing her no good at all to sit and stare at the same page, she drove to Noe Valley — just to be close to Ryan. The dim light in the doorway next to the garage showed that she was home, but Jamie didn't have the nerve to call or to knock. Instead, she dropped the top on her car and just sat there, staring at the house — feeling strangely cheered by knowing that Ryan was near.

After about an hour the light switched off, and a few minutes later, she saw Ryan descend the stairs with Duffy scampering alongside her. She smiled warmly when she spied the pair — so very much wanting to get out and call to her. But she didn't. She sat in her car and watched them walk down the street, feeling her heart swell with such love that she felt faint. *My God, just seeing her walk her dog gives me a bigger thrill than I can handle,* she sighed. *I'd risk anything to be with that woman,* she thought. With a start, she repeated her words aloud, just to hear herself express them. "I'd risk anything to be with Ryan," she said, her confidence building as she spoke. *That's it!* she cried to herself. *That's the truth! It doesn't matter what anyone else thinks! All that matters is that we're together. That's all that matters!* She almost leapt from her car and ran after her to tell her, but she stopped herself. Heart beating wildly, she recalled that her resolve had wavered before, and she was not going to toy with Ryan ever again. *I can't even consider telling her before I'm absolutely sure.* And though Jamie was still reticent to tell her, she knew the time for second thoughts was gone. With a smile brightening her whole face, she started her car and headed for home, her mind fixated on memories of the last kiss they'd shared and dreaming of the ones to come.

⌘

"After seeing her last night, it hit me, Anna. It was just as clear as day. I'm certain that I'm willing to risk everything to be with Ryan. I know it will be hard, and I know there's a possibility that I could seriously harm or even lose my relationship with my parents, but I have to do this. It doesn't even feel like it's my choice, Anna. It feels like my destiny."

387

Anna gave Jamie her usual enigmatic smile and asked, "When will you talk to Ryan?"

"Well, that presents a small problem. I refuse to tell her until I've had a little while to let this sink in and to get comfortable with it. I know Ryan, and if I tell her this became clear to me just yesterday — after watching her walk her dog ..." She gave Anna a smile and said, "In some ways, she's very impetuous, but she's very careful with her heart. I think she'll worry that I'm moving too quickly."

"Why don't we spend a few days talking about how it feels to have made the decision?"

"Well, if I do that, I've got to wait until finals are over to tell her. Next week is our last week of class, then two weeks of finals. Don't you think it would be irresponsible to stir this up during finals week?"

"Well," Anna said thoughtfully, "let's look at it from a practical perspective. Are you in good shape for finals?"

"Uhm ... no. I've never been so ill-prepared," she admitted. "I have a couple of papers to write that will take me a good two weeks to do properly. Luckily, I only have one class with a final, but I'm way behind in that one. It'll take a week to get ready for the test." She gave Anna an unhappy look and said, "This isn't great timing, is it?"

"No, it's not the best," she agreed. "If you decide not to talk to Ryan yet, I think we should concentrate on helping you focus on your schoolwork for a few weeks. You could try to limit the amount of time you spend thinking about her and your future, and dedicate yourself to your studies."

"It's not what I want," Jamie decided. "But I don't see any options."

⌘

Anna suggested some techniques to help Jamie concentrate, one of which was to only allow herself to think about Ryan twice a day. She got up extra early and spent an hour writing in her journal, allowing herself the luxury of giving voice to some of the sexual fantasies she'd tried for so long to repress. Strangely, she found that she had more energy than normal during her day, and she decided that starting the day massively turned on was an odd, but effective study tool.

For her second daily Ryan moment, she allowed herself the pleasure of sending her a quick e-mail at the end of each day. She'd been unable to get her daily fix of seeing Ryan, since their exam schedules were so different, but the e-mail was equally calming for her.

Ryan certainly didn't seem to mind the increased contact, and she replied to each one almost immediately. During the last week of finals, the dark woman made it clear that she not only didn't mind receiving the notes, she had come to rely on them. On Wednesday, Jamie had let the time get away from her, since her final was the next day, and she was trying to cram weeks of study into just a few days. Her mail program chirped, and she looked up from her daze to see a message from Ryan. Clicking on it, she read, "Hey, it's eleven o'clock, and I'm ready for bed. Where's my message?"

Jamie giggled when she noted the signature, "Googolperplexed."

She dashed off a reply.

> "One day I'm going to take the time to ask you what a googolplex is, and I'm going to make you explain it until it penetrates my thick, math-challenged brain. Actually my brain is just plain challenged tonight. I have my final tomorrow, and things are looking grim. Wish me luck — I need it. Jamie"

In moments her computer chimed again, and this message was even briefer, but just as welcome.

> "I have confidence in you, Jamie. Here's a big virtual hug for good luck tomorrow. (((((hug))))) Ryan"

Even though she felt silly doing it, she printed out the short message and placed it under her pillow, willing herself to feel the hug all night long.

⌘

As soon as she got home on Thursday, she sent a message to Ryan.

> "I'm finished, and I believe you are, too. Why don't we get together in person to celebrate the end of the school year? I have a few things to talk to you about, Ryan, and now that finals are over, I'd really like to start sorting things out. Are you, by any chance, free tomorrow night for dinner? I'll cook — you choose the menu."

She didn't get a reply until ten o'clock, but the message was worth the wait.

> "I have to work until 6:30, so I'll be there at 7:00. For the menu, I chose to have whatever it gives you the most pleasure to cook. I love to be surprised. I'm really looking forward to seeing you, Jamie. It's been far, far too long."

⌘

The bell rang at 7:00 on the dot, and Jamie took a few deep breaths on her way to answer it. Her heart was racing when she opened the door, and it kicked up a few notches when she saw Ryan. "D … Didn't you have to work?" she asked.

"Yeah, I did." Ryan cast a quick look down at herself. "I brought a change of clothes. I didn't want to wear my warm-ups to dinner." She looked at her friend and asked, "Can I come in?"

"Oh! Yes! Come in!" She backed up and let the tall woman enter, catching a whiff of some cologne that made her mouth water.

Ryan just stood there, looking fantastically beautiful. She wore a bright blue and white, horizontal-striped, knit shirt that was so snug that Jamie could see skin peeking through the gaps between the buttons. Keeping with the form-revealing theme, she also wore a pair of stretch khakis that were stretched to their limit. A look of indecision came over her, and she started to lean towards Jamie. The smaller woman saw her lean in, and she did the same, but they were both so nervous that all they managed to do was bump into each other rather roughly.

Giving it another try, Ryan slipped an arm around her friend's waist and gave her a surprisingly awkward one-armed hug. She pulled back almost immediately, looking completely flustered. "Uhm … I'm sure I've been more nervous," she said. "But I sure as hell can't remember when."

That self-effacing comment broke the ice, and Jamie felt some of her normal confidence return. She smiled up at her friend and gave her a proper hug, wrapping both arms around her and holding on tight. Ryan's heart was beating quickly under her cheek, but the longer they held on to each other, the slower the cadence grew. "I've missed you so much," Jamie sighed.

"Me, too," Ryan agreed. "Especially these last two weeks. It was so hard not to see you every day."

Her body grew still, and Jamie's head tilted up to look into twinkling eyes. "You knew!"

Ryan released her, but not until she gave her another squeeze. "Yeah, I knew. The first time was a fluke," she admitted, "but from then on, I couldn't leave campus until I'd caught a glimpse of you. A couple of times, I had to sit on that wall outside of my last class for twenty minutes. Least you could do is hurry when I'm sitting on cold concrete, ya know."

"You must have thought I was insane!" she gasped, clearly mortified.

Ryan placed her hands on her shoulders and looked into her eyes. "I thought no such thing. I knew how much you were struggling, Jamie. It made perfect sense to me that you'd need to keep a little bit of contact. I swear, it was important to me, too. During that first finals week, I almost walked Duffy's legs off, going outside every hour to see if you were parked near my house."

"You saw me?"

"Of course I saw you. I'm very aware of my surroundings, Jamie. I never go outside without checking out the street. Heck, I could tell you what cars are parked in front of your house right now. Besides, I'm remarkably attuned to yellow Boxsters. I don't think I ever miss one."

"You didn't mind?" she asked tentatively.

"No, of course I didn't mind. It let me know you care. Actually, knowing that you care is the only thing that let me get through these last weeks. It was vital, Jamie."

Suddenly shy, the smaller woman said, "I think dinner's ready. I know having your evening meal is vital, too."

Ryan nodded, willing to let the intimate moment pass. "You'll be pleased to know I'm starving. I worked all day and only had time for a couple of protein bars for lunch. I haven't been working much because of finals, so I had to squeeze in a lot of clients today."

"I can fix you up," the blonde predicted. She surprised herself by taking Ryan by the hand to lead her into the kitchen, but it felt like the most natural thing in the world. Ryan just smiled at her, and she felt her confidence begin to build once again.

Over dinner, Ryan tilted her head and asked, "Are you alone tonight? I haven't seen my favorite person around for a while. I miss her desperately."

"Oh, sorry to say Cassie's down at her parents for the weekend. She's going to New York for the summer. I think she leaves right before the AIDS Ride."

"Darn it!" Ryan said, snapping her fingers. "I so miss our little interactions. Mia said she was going home, too," she commented. "Are you the only Hillsborough girl who didn't head home as soon as finals were over?"

"I guess so. I might go down for a day or two, but I have pressing business here. I couldn't think of leaving before I got my affairs in order." Her choice of words made her color a bit in embarrassment, but Ryan thoughtfully didn't comment on the implication.

"So, what's on your agenda? I hope you're planning on riding every possible moment. The ride's in three weeks."

"Don't worry about me," Jamie assured her. "I'll be in shape for the ride. I had a good coach." She summoned her courage and reached across the table to take Ryan's hand. "I miss my coach. I'd really like to have her back."

Ryan shifted uncomfortably and purposely avoided Jamie's eyes. "I, uhm … I don't know if that's wise. We had a deal, Jamie, and I think I need to stick with it. I just came tonight because I thought maybe you'd … uhm … made up your mind."

This wasn't how she'd planned on telling her, but Ryan looked so profoundly sad that Jamie tightened her hold on her hand and said, "I have."

Blinking slowly, Ryan pushed her half-eaten dinner away and placed her hands on the table, looking like she was waiting for bad news. "Tell me," she said quietly.

"Are you finished with your dinner?" Jamie asked.

"Yeah. My appetite's not really up to par."

"Let's go outside," Jamie offered. "It's a really nice night."

Rotating her broad shoulders to work some of the tension from them, Ryan stood and waited for Jamie to lead the way. The smaller woman walked down the stairs and showed Ryan to a weathered teak bench. It sat under a nice arbor which was filled with tiny, white roses. Failing to comment on the setting, or the fact that she'd never seen the back yard, Ryan sat stiffly, waiting for Jamie to give her the news.

She didn't have long to wait. The smaller woman took her clammy hand and chafed it between both of her own. She gazed at Ryan with a depth of affection that made the brunette's heart start to race in anticipation. "I've spent a lot of time on this. More time and more tears and more periods of gut-churning fear than I've ever been through. But I'd do it all over again — a hundred times — to come to the conclusion that I have."

Ryan's eyes grew wide, and she looked like she was going to speak, but she didn't. She just ran her thumb across the back of Jamie's hand and waited for her to continue.

"I'm in love with you, Ryan. And I very much want to build a life with you." She leaned forward and placed a soft kiss upon her forehead. "Do you want that, too?"

"I do," she whispered, and Jamie could see tears forming in her eyes. "But I have to be sure you mean that, Jamie. I won't have an affair with you. I won't just have sex with you. I won't even consider this, unless this means to you what it does to me."

"Tell me what you need, Ryan," she urged. "Tell me how you feel."

She closed her eyes for a moment and took in a deep breath. "I've treated my body and my sexuality pretty casually," she admitted. "But that's not how I view relationships. I'll only risk this if you feel like I do. If I pledge my love, I'll dedicate myself to you, Jamie. Forever." She blinked back her tears and said, "I want the kind of relationship that my parents had. I want to love you and only you until the day I die."

"I want that, too," Jamie whispered, fighting her own tears.

"I understand that you might want that," Ryan sighed, "but can you commit to it? Can you make our relationship the most important one in your life? Is it something you can be proud of?"

"Yes," she said firmly. "I can."

She said this with such determination that Ryan felt her heart start to believe. "How long have you felt this way? This isn't something you just decided, is it?"

Jamie chuckled mildly. "I told my therapist you'd ask me that." She brought Ryan's hand to her lips and kissed it. "It makes me happy to be able to guess how you'll react to something."

"Did that answer my question?" Ryan asked pointedly.

"I knew you'd say that, too!" the blonde said excitedly. Beaming at the slow smile that formed on Ryan's face she said, "I've known since the day you kissed me. Since then I've been testing myself, fantasizing about how it will be, making plans for how to tell my parents, deciding how I'll live if they cut me off financially, wondering if you'll move in with me, and lastly, praying that you love me half as much as I love you."

Ryan cupped Jamie's cheek and inclined her head. "What if I love you twice as much as you love me?"

"Then I'm a very, very lucky woman," she said softly. "Actually, I'm a very lucky woman just to know you. To have you love me is so much more than I deserve."

Head shaking slowly, Ryan said, "As you know, I don't give my love away easily. I'd certainly never give it to someone who didn't deserve it." She slid her arms around the smaller woman's shoulders and held her in a loose embrace. "I think you're deserving of the very best of my love."

Cocking her head in question, Jamie asked, "Is there any chance we can stop talking and start kissing? My lips have been aching for you ever since that day at Strawberry Creek."

Not wasting the time to answer verbally, Ryan tightened her hold and pulled the smaller woman to her, tilting her head to brush her lips against the soft, pink flesh. That first, light touch made Jamie's heart start to race, and she let her senses have free rein, taking in Ryan's alluring scent, the feel of her arms tightening around her body, the softness of her breasts as they pressed against her own, and the fantastically arousing feel of the solid warmth of the larger body moving against her.

The next kiss was more deliberate, as Ryan shifted gracefully to pin the smaller woman against the arm of the bench. Ryan's body felt so strong, so powerful as it pressed against her that the blonde wanted nothing more than to surrender to her completely — to let the beautiful woman own her very soul.

Kisses continued to rain down on her, Ryan smoothly moving from her lips to her ears, nibbling on a sensitive lobe, then traveling down her jaw line and along her neck, pausing to trail a moist path along her collar bones.

Jamie would've been perfectly happy to let Ryan kiss her until they had to leave for the AIDS Ride, but something inside told her that she couldn't be passive. She had to show Ryan that she wasn't just a willing follower; she was confident and sure enough to lead.

Pushing gently, she felt Ryan begin to yield to her. When she was sitting up, she maneuvered the larger woman into the opposite corner of the bench and started to kiss her with the same ferocity that Ryan had shown. "Are you sure you love me?" she murmured between kisses.

"Yes, yes, I love you, Jamie," the dark woman panted.

"Do you know what people do when they're in love?" she asked, after nipping gently at Ryan's tender neck.

Head shaking, Ryan waited for the answer, unable to process such difficult questions at the moment.

"They make love." Jamie gripped her head firmly and planted an incendiary kiss upon her lips, then began to probe her warm mouth with her tongue. After a long while, she lifted her head and tried to focus. "Do you want to make love with me?"

"Yes!" Ryan gasped. "More than I've ever wanted anything!"

Jamie leaned into her again, celebrating her answer with a flurry of kisses. She eased her hand between them and brushed her fingertips across Ryan's breast, feeling the pulse between her legs when the nipple popped up with astounding speed. Continuing to kiss her ravenously, her fingers went to Ryan's shirt and started to unbutton it. She dipped her head and started to kiss each inch of skin as it was revealed.

Ryan leaned back against the bench, her breathing ragged. She held Jamie's head in her hands, her skin burning from the kisses that blazed a path down her chest. Suddenly, determined hands were working her belt open, then her zipper was being lowered, and Jamie's lips were on her belly.

Her body thrummed with so much energy, such rabid desire, that she was afraid she'd throw Jamie to the ground and ravish the smaller woman. Framing the question with the only word she could get out, Ryan gasped, "Bed?"

Looking up at her, glassy-eyed, Jamie found herself nodding. She pulled away and took Ryan's hand, smiling at the state of her dishabille. Ryan didn't bother fixing her clothing; she just zipped up enough to be able to walk and followed the blonde into the house.

They entered the bedroom hand in hand, and by the time Ryan was across the threshold, she'd wrapped Jamie in her arms and was kissing her hungrily. Without missing a beat, Jamie's hands went to the taller woman's shirt and eased it from her shoulders, groaning when her hands encountered smooth, soft skin and a bit of sky blue lace that one day might grow up to be a bra.

As Ryan's tongue slipped into her mouth, Jamie's trembling fingers eased the zipper of her fly down, the combination of both acts making her heart hammer in her chest. Her hands cupped Ryan's ass, pushing the khakis down as she did so. Her helpful partner kicked off her sandals and stepped out of the slacks, her mouth never leaving Jamie's.

Now she was able to give her hands the gift they'd been craving — access to what seemed like acres of soft, smooth skin. She'd been expecting a sturdy sports bra and Ryan's usual knit boxers — and that had been her fantasy in every one of her racy daydreams over the past weeks. But this reality was exponentially more appealing than her fantasy had ever been. As her hands slipped across cheeks as smooth as silk, she thanked the genius that had created the first thong, knowing that he or she would crow with delight to see it covering the body that was obviously created expressly for the glorification of the garment.

She was shaking so hard that Ryan held her tighter and cooed to her, "It's okay, Jamie. Just hold on to me and let me undress you. You don't have to do a thing."

"I can't do a thing," she murmured. "We're not standing on a live wire, are we?"

Chuckling softly, Ryan said, "You know, I think we might be. I sure keep getting jolted." She was staring right into Jamie's eyes, and the blonde found herself mesmerized by the warm gaze. Only vaguely aware of her surroundings and the gentle movement of Ryan's hands against her, she felt a sudden chill, then realized that she was bare to the waist.

Ryan began kissing down her body, pausing to brush her lips against the hardening nipples. Moments later, Jamie was completely nude, standing before Ryan fully exposed. "My God, what a gorgeous woman you are," the dark woman sighed, her hands already beginning to explore. As her fingers traveled over each swell and dip of flesh, her head shook slightly while she continued to murmur, "So beautiful. So very beautiful."

Jamie squirmed under the attention, never having felt so completely revealed. But Ryan's gaze and her touch were so tender and worshipful that she couldn't even think of moving. For the first time in her life, she believed the words being spoken, allowing the praise Ryan heaped on her to penetrate the defenses she'd always maintained.

The tall woman moved around her, examining her in minute detail, exclaiming softly at each discovery. When she stood behind Jamie, lavishing compliments on the perfection she found, Ryan suddenly couldn't stand to have even the thin layer of lace between them, so she tossed her remaining clothing to the floor. She pressed her body against Jamie's, and the smaller woman groaned from the feel of the heated skin and round, full breasts rubbing gently against her. Firm nipples trailed across her back, moving teasingly, driving her mad.

Ryan's hands roamed everywhere, cupping her breasts, hefting their weight, then squeezing them firmly, while her mouth latched onto the tender skin of Jamie's neck, sucking lustily. Jamie's hands covered Ryan's, moving with her as she fondled her body thoroughly.

She had never felt so desired, had never felt the rush of feeling that pounded through her body, making her moan and writhe against Ryan without any ability to control or censor her movements.

Finally, needing to see the body that was driving her to distraction, she turned in Ryan's fevered embrace, moved back just a bit, then gasped in astonishment.

Times too numerous to count, she had dreamed of how Ryan's body would look, always focusing on the elements that most appealed to her — the full breasts, narrow waist and concave belly. But her dreams had left her ill-prepared for the reality of the woman. Of course every attribute that appealed to her when Ryan was clothed was there, and each was fantastic. But it was the things she hadn't considered that made her knees weak. She knew how powerful Ryan's body was, but she was unprepared for how that dynamism evinced itself. Muscles lurked under every inch of skin, but they didn't make her appear course or hard. They seemed to highlight her womanhood, defining the smooth swell of her hip, the resplendent curve of her breast.

Every element was firm and full and lush and incredibly sexy, and Jamie had to explore every inch of her beauty with appreciative hands.

The experience was more wondrous than she could have imagined, and even though her hands were shaking, she kept on, unable to tear herself away from the delights before her. Ryan sensed that she needed this time to grow comfortable, so she waited patiently, eyes locked upon her partner, gauging her reaction.

Jamie gazed up at her, her expression a little dazed. "I'm … I'm … I'm so incredibly aroused that I don't know how I can stand," she finally said, her face breaking into a helpless smile.

Ryan smiled warmly in return and stooped slightly to sweep her into her arms. She placed her on the bed, then slid in next to her, gently turning Jamie's head to kiss her again. The kiss was slow and long and probing and made her entire body sing with sensation.

When Ryan finally pulled away, the smaller woman reached out and touched her cheek, gazing into the depths of her eyes. "My God, what you do to me," she murmured.

Smiling gently, Ryan continued to look into her eyes while her hand began to trail over her body. As her questing fingers touched and caressed, Jamie's eyes closed, and her body shook with each new sensation. "Just relax and feel," Ryan soothed. She knew what Jamie was experiencing — knew perfectly well how overwhelming it was to finally be able to give voice to feelings that had been repressed for so long. "Lie still and take a few deep breaths. Your heart's racing like it's going to burst from your chest."

"I *feel* so much," she moaned. "My body's on fire."

"I know, I know," Ryan gently assured her. "It's hard to focus on so many things happening at once."

"My head's spinning," Jamie said, her voice shaking with pent-up desire.

"Lie back and let me love you. Feel my touch, Jamie. Breathe deeply and feel me."

Her eyes closed, and she took a breath, nearly gasping when she felt Ryan's warm mouth close around a nipple. "Oh, God," she moaned throatily.

"Breathe," Ryan urged again. "Breathe and feel me loving you. Just let yourself feel the sensations, Jamie. Let it flow."

She fought her conscious mind for several minutes, intruding thoughts claiming her attention time and again. But Ryan was patient and gentle and so very calming. She kept touching her lightly all over her body, letting only the tips of her fingers play along her skin. Ryan had tucked an arm around her shoulders, and her warm hand occasionally squeezed her gently, giving her something to focus on to ground herself when the sensations grew to be too powerful. Eventually, she reached out and covered Ryan's hand with her own, feeling as if it were the rock that she was anchored to.

Slowly, she opened herself more and more to the wonder of Ryan's gentle caress, letting the soft stroking carry her away on a cloud of pure pleasure. She didn't know how long they'd been there; she didn't know how she'd managed to wind up nestled between Ryan's legs with her cheek resting upon an incredibly soft thigh. She didn't understand how her entire body could orgasm, even though she had experienced the marvel of that very sensation. All she did know was that the strong yet gentle hand still lay upon her, now softly gripping her shoulder and calming her. Grasping the hand and bringing it to her lips, she kissed each knuckle, rubbing it against her cheek like an object of adoration. "I love you so much," she sighed. "I've never felt so alive."

"I've been born again," Ryan murmured. "I'm a new woman."

Fighting the languor that tugged at her, Jamie climbed up the long body and curled into Ryan's embrace, breathing in the beguilingly sexy aroma of her own scent. "How are you a new woman?"

"I belong to you," Ryan vowed. "I'm yours, Jamie, body and soul."

Overcome with emotion, Jamie held her lover's face in her hands and pressed a kiss to her lips. As the kiss deepened, she realized that Ryan's distinctive taste had merged with her own. Blinking back tears, she whispered, "We're one. We're part of each other now."

"We are," Ryan rasped, tears streaking down her cheeks. "We're one until death parts us, Jamie."

With a smile breaking through her tears, the blonde touched her lover's trembling lips with the tips of her fingers. "We're one as long as we're able to share the joy and wonder that each day will bring."

"What a lovely wish," Ryan sighed, closing her eyes as a serene smile lit up her face.

"It's not a wish," Jamie whispered into her ear. "It's a promise."

The Masked Author at Age 4

Every time S. X. Meagher read a lesbian-themed romance novel, she found that she was left with a host of questions that continued to dart through her head long after the story came to an end. She decided to write her own series of stories, so that she could create a group of people, joined together by familial and social bonds, to investigate some of the issues that draw women together and sometimes conspire to keep them apart.

S. X. is interested in exploring how a relationship develops—the bumps and turns that make the road both fascinating and treacherous. She's a firm believer that there is no such thing as love at first sight. Interest, attraction, desire and lust come easily, but love is something you have to work for.

Being the creator of a small universe has proven to be addictive for S. X. She is frequently found roaming the streets of Los Angeles, advising strangers on how to conduct their lives to create compelling drama or to move the plot along more quickly.

THE AVERAGE OF DEVIANCE
BY K. SIMPSON

After *Several Devils*, Devlin Kerry and Cassandra Wolfe aren't just friends anymore, but they'd rather not advertise. Trouble is, they're already in advertising, where secrets are practically illegal. Word is out ... so to speak.

Worse, Dev has a demon. Cassie says it's her own fault for being celibate for years ("You can't go around not sleeping with people and *not* expect to get into trouble"). They thought they'd exorcised the demon, but Monica is back. And this time, she plans to stick around.

This sequel picks up where *Several Devils* left off, as the staff of J/J/G Advertising tries to get back to normal the morning after a wild Halloween night. But every day is Halloween at J/J/G, the way these people behave, and everyone there is a devil of some kind. The last thing Dev and Cassie need is an actual demon — a chance for mischief that Monica can't resist. Thanks to her, they have trouble coming from all directions: co-workers, clients, TV reporters, the family-values crowd and even a possum.

Worst of all, a new co-worker may not be what she seems. Dev and Cassie are about to learn the true meaning of "hell to pay."

ISBN: 0971815011

Also by K. Simpson

SEVERAL DEVILS
Published: August 2001
ISBN: 0967768799

Even though she's in advertising, Devlin Kerry doesn't believe in Hell; she thinks that would be redundant. But a demon named Monica believes in her. Between her demon and her best friend, Dev's in for a devil of a time.

Now Available from Fortitude Press

THE BLUEST EYES IN TEXAS
BY LINDA CRIST

Kennedy Nocona is an out, liberal, driven attorney, living in Austin, the heart of the Texas hill country. Once a player in the legal community, she now finds herself in the position of re-evaluating her life - a position brought on by a personal tragedy for which she blames herself. Seeking redemption for her tormented past, she loses herself in her work, strict discipline of mind and body, and the teachings of Native American roots she once shunned.

Dallasite Carson Garret is a young paralegal overcoming the loss of her parents and coming to terms with her own sexual orientation. After settling her parents' estate and examining her failed past relationships, she is desperately ready to move forward. Bored with her state of affairs, she longs for excitement and romance to make her feel alive again.

A chance encounter finds them inexplicably drawn to one another, and after a weekend together, they quickly find themselves in a long distance romance that leaves them both wanting more. Circumstances at Carson's job develop into a series of mysteries and blackmail attempts that leaves her with more excitement than she ever bargained for. Confused, afraid, and alone, she turns to Kennedy, the one person she knows can help her. As they work together to solve a puzzle, they confront growing feelings that neither woman can deny, complicated by outside forces that threaten to crush them both.

ISBN: 0971815003

THE LIFE IN HER EYES
BY DEBORAH BARRY

Real love is not for the faint of heart, and the courage it takes to survive its loss, and love again, is more than the average soul can bear.

Rae Crenshaw does not lack for companionship. The tall beauty radiates charm and confidence, but this attractive combination conceals a vulnerable heart that has known far too much pain. She finds solace for her emptiness in casual trysts, maintaining a severe emotional distance, all the while seeking that which she feels can never be found again.

Evon Lagace's young life has been one of extremes - a failed dance career, a precious, beautiful relationship, and a traumatic, crippling loss. Once so full of exuberance and happiness, she must now struggle to find peace amidst the despair and loneliness.

Share the tears and the triumphs of these two remarkable women as you celebrate their journey to the realization that perhaps, for a lucky few, second chances can exist.

ISBN: 0971815046

Now Distributed by Fortitude Press

AT FIRST BLUSH
A JANE DOE PRESS ANTHOLOGY

Twenty-two stories of first glances, first blushes, first loves and first times – of all kinds. Representing a variety of voices, the stories reflect a diversity of experiences. All profits from this anthology will be donated to charity.

The table of contents from this wonderful collection of stories:

ISBN: 0971154996

Now Distributed by Fortitude Press

Conspiracy of Swords
by R.S. Corliss

FBI Agent Alexia Reis is an out-lesbian determined to make it in the bureau. As a junior agent she spent time in the research department, as well as the serial crimes unit where she and her partner, David Wu, were recognized for their work. After breaking several major cases, the two are moved to the hate crimes unit, which is Alex's true area of expertise.

Following the murders of several prominent activists and politicians, Alex and David become part of a task force charged with solving the killings. Together, they are sent to protect a newly declared candidate for the U.S. Senate. For the first time in her career, Alex is named the agent-in-charge, and when the candidate is assassinated, she can't help but take it personally.

During the investigation the agents run into ex-CIA assassin Teren Mylos, who is convinced her partner's death is somehow connected to the FBI case. While wary of each other, Alex and Teren agree to share information in an attempt to find answers to the deepening mystery.

The case takes them to Europe and back, searching for pieces to the unfolding puzzle. As they dodge killers and turncoats, they come face to face with Nazis old and new, stumble upon a hoard of looted gold, and uncover a conspiracy that stretches over forty years and two continents.

And, somewhere along the line, they discover each other as well.

ISBN: 0971154902

Now Distributed by Fortitude Press

EXCHANGES
BY JOHN-DAVID SCHRAMM

Can God change gays? This question tumbles around inside the minds of both lead characters in *exChanges*.

Marcus and CJ both give up a great deal to join Crossroads, a year-long, residential program dedicated to helping gay men and lesbians find "freedom" from homosexuality through the power of Christ.

"Camping out" with five other men and a house leader, CJ and Marcus begin to confront themselves while being strangely drawn to one another.

Follow these two men as they dive into the rules and policies of this ministry program led by former drag queens and pornography kings. As each man confronts his own issues, he begins to see a path that could never have been covered in the Crossroads recruiting brochure.

ISBN: 0971154937

To Order:

Title	Quantity	Cost per Unit	Total Cost
At First Blush		$21.99	$
The Average of Deviance		$12.99	$
The Bluest Eyes in Texas		$15.99	$
Conspiracy of Swords		$19.99	$
exChanges		$13.75	$
I Found My Heart in San Francisco		$18.99	$
The Life in Her Eyes		$13.99	$
Warlord Metal		$13.99	$
Shipping and Handling	First Book	$4.50	$
	Each Add'l Book	$2.00	$
	Texas Residents Add 8.25% Sales Tax		$
	Total		$

To order by credit card, please visit our Web site at: www.fortitudepress.com.

To order by check or money order, please mail the above form to:

Fortitude Press, Inc.
Post Office Box 41
Melbourne, FL 32902